OUTSTANDING PRAISE FOR *NEANDERTHAL*

NEANDERTHAL

JOHN DARNTON

St. Martin's Paperbacks

Grateful acknowledgment is made to ABKCO Music, Inc., for permission
to reprint five lines from "You Can't Always Get What You Want" by
Mick Jagger and Keith Richards. Copyright © 1969 by ABKCO Music,
Inc. All rights reserved. Used by permission.

Published by arrangement with Random House

NEANDERTHAL

Library of Congress Catalog Card Number: 96-11045

ISBN: 0-312-96300-9

Printed in the United States of America

Random House hardcover edition/June 1996
St. Martin's Paperbacks edition/June 1997

St. Martin's Paperbacks are published by St. Martin's Press, 175 Fifth
Avenue, New York, NY 10010.

10   9   8   7   6   5   4   3   2   1

FOR NINA, OF COURSE

And the Lord said unto her,

Two nations are in thy womb,
and two manner of people shall be separated from thy
     bowels:
And the one people shall be stronger than the
     other people.
                    —GENESIS 25:23

BEIJING, June 9—Chinese scientists are hot on the trail of
a mysterious hairy wild man and have found indirect evidence that might prove the reclusive human-like creature is
no myth, Xinhua news agency said on Friday.

                    —REUTERS, 1995

ACKNOWLEDGMENTS

A senior editor at Random House championed the manuscript of this book and helped form it in its early stages. This man is legendary in literary circles; he edited a long list of famous writers during his thirty-five years at the publishing house. He was respected by writers because he knew how to improve their work and yet keep it theirs, and he was also beloved by many of them. But his name never appeared in their acknowledgments. He would strike it out each time, being a member of the old school, which held that editors must at all costs remain invisible. In November, he died suddenly in his office. Had he been less modest, his name would have been stamped upon hundreds of books. Had all gone well, it would not have appeared here. So this is to render gratitude and homage—words that are clearly inadequate—to Joe Fox.

I would also like to thank Arthur Kopit, friend, author, and co-conspirator. It was he who first suggested telling the story in the form of a novel and who helped with major contributions of plot turns and twists late into many a night.

I am indebted to Nicholas Delbanco, for his critical reading and comments; to Michael Koskoff for his assistance and advice; to Christopher Stringer of the Natural History Museum of Britain for his reading of key scientific passages; to Myra Shackley for invaluable material in two comprehensively researched books on the Neanderthal; to Walter Parkes for helpful suggestions; and to Peter and Susan Osnos for their support and the use of their home during several summers in which much of the book was written.

Thanks, too, to Joseph Lelyveld and Bill Keller, executive editor and foreign editor of *The New York Times*, for graciously giving me time off to meet a deadline; to Marion

Underhill, Sue Nestor, and Tony Beard in the London office of *The New York Times* for their uncomplaining logistic support; to Jon Karp, my new editor at Random House, who jumped in to shape and shepherd the manuscript through its final stages; and to Kathy Robbins, my agent and friend, who is simply the best in the business.

And then of course there are my children, Kyra, Liza, and Jamie Darnton, whose excitement and suggestions were invaluable, and the person who did more than anyone else in encouraging, listening, brainstorming, rewriting, editing, hand-holding, brow wiping, negotiating, and in general being there always, Nina Darnton.

NEANDERTHAL

PROLOGUE

In 1910, Geoffrey Bakersfield-Smyth, a scholar-adventurer from Leeds who was pursuing his passion of collecting and classifying alpine flowers, chanced to enter the National Museum of Antiquities and Artifacts in Dushanbe in the Khanate of Bukhara. There in the basement, amid crates of crockery, rain-soaked files, and other debris, he came upon a unique stone. It was a tablet, shaped into a rectangle the size of a small coffee table and painstakingly carved. Part of it was missing—a serpentine crack formed the outer right edge—and some of the carving was eroded. But other lines stood out in relief as sharply as boot prints in mud; they depicted human figures of some kind.

Bakersfield-Smyth found a brief notation in a shaky hand in the museum's dusty records room. The tablet had been found in 1874 by a peasant plowing his field in a mountain village clear across the Tajik lands. (Bakersfield-Smyth noted that the East had undergone an earthquake in 1873 and surmised that the tablet had been tossed up from one of the underground limestone caves that honeycomb the area.) The peasant brought it in a wooden oxcart to the provincial town of Khodzant, where he left it on the doorstep of a dry goods store. There was no record of how or when the stone was transported to the museum in Dushanbe.

Bakersfield-Smyth sketched the tablet. He picked out the grit in the cracks and indentations with a penknife and made rubbings of the carvings. He fetched his stand-up box camera and photographed it. He searched the entire museum for the missing piece but could not locate it.

In London, Bakersfield-Smyth showed his notes and photographs to P. T. Baylord, later Lord Uckston, a practitioner of the relatively new field of physical anthropology. In 1913, Baylord produced a monograph and an article in the *Journal of the Royal Society for Archaeology,* "The Pictograph of Khodzant." By duplicating the photographs, cutting them into separate pictures, and rearranging them in a linear sequence, Baylord was able to reconstruct a historical narrative. He asserted that the tablet told the story of an ancient battle, one so significant, he theorized, that its survivors felt compelled to record it for later generations.

> Note the attempts to situate the action in time and place [he wrote]. Specifically, we see symbols that could represent moons and others that seem to represent seasonal foliage. In one frame, there is what appears to be a mountain and a peculiar outcropping of stone with ridges that make it appear to resemble the back of a clenched fist. Exactly where this mount is located is unknown, but it should be noted that the largely unexplored region of the higher Pamirs of Afghanistan, Tajikistan, Jammu, and Kashmir contain numerous rock formations unusual in both gigantesque size and odd shape attributable to glacial sculpting.

Baylord's narrative of the battle was arresting but ultimately unsatisfying because of the missing portion; the ending, if there was one, was unknown. His story disappeared in midair, so to speak. But he was able to discern two separate lines of warriors and to delineate three distinct clashes. He even detected what he theorized was a body count up in one corner, though the corpses were curiously represented by what looked to be human eyes placed in trees. Peering for weeks on end through a magnifying glass and sculpting clay painstakingly with a surgeon's scalpel to reconstruct the obliterated lines, he was able to re-create his tiny soldiers' weapons, which, he wrote, "were notably primitive in nature."

But the work was scientifically flawed. Without the original, the tablet could never be dated. So Baylord was left in the final analysis with a hypothesis that was largely guesswork: that the combatants most likely comprised small clans of Mongols that clashed sometime in 100 or 200 B.C. And he never really took note of an intriguing detail on the tablet—the fact that one group of warriors was unlike the other, marked as they were by strangely sloping foreheads that ended in distinctive bulging ridges across the brow. Baylord made only a passing reference to "a band across the forehead."

His work created a slight stir in academic circles. It soon died down. Some thought it was a hoax. His slim little monograph survived into the second half of the century only among a handful of archaeologists who regarded it as a curio. "The Khodzant Enigma" became a favorite lecture among graduate students. The stone itself was left in the museum basement. Then came the Russian Revolution, which spread to Tajikistan, and it was lost.

I

THE
KHODZANT
ENIGMA

1

Akbar Atilla rested his AK-47 against a tree trunk and moved away from the campfire in search of a place to relieve himself. There was barely enough moon to see by; bands of clouds spread across the night sky in layers and from time to time blotted it out altogether.

The Mujahadeen guerrillas had ascended higher and higher into the Tajik mountains in search of a secure base. Here they were safe. No government forces could reach them short of mounting a major expedition, and if they tried, the guerrillas could lie in wait in any one of thousands of crevices and pick them off. The mountain was an unassailable fortress.

He felt along the path with his feet as he climbed the rocky slope, then stopped and listened. There was the wind whirring through the fir trees and the voices of his comrades below talking quietly. Someone was telling a story.

He loosened his tunic and reached inside for his belt. Then he heard something: a sound, unmistakable, a step behind him. He straightened and started to turn.

The attack came quickly. He had no time to react. He felt a crashing blow on his head and stared up in panic as the clouds parted. There in the moonlight he saw a vague form, grotesque and savage, then a snarling face, an elongated visage with a protruding bonelike brow. He didn't have time to scream as he felt a second blow and then encircling arms that crushed his ribs. He was carried off into the night.

Early the next morning, the others found his rifle still resting against the tree. There was nothing else. They wondered if he had run off into the valley, maybe to join his family, maybe to work the crops. But why would he leave his weapon behind?

The story of the disappearance was like other recent stories and so eventually made its way to a village and then to a town in the foothills. By then, imaginary details embellished the tale and there was barely a resemblance to what had actually happened. Only the central mystery remained: A man was there one minute and the next had vanished into the ether.

The report was picked up by an American traveling through the Pamirs, who, for convenience' sake and to avoid too many questions, was called a consul. He transcribed it onto a disk and also appended a brief clipping from that week's local paper, which had been translated by his secretary:

HISKADETH, Nov. 8—A 24-year-old woman from Surrey, England, who was part of an Upward and Outward group climbing Mount Askasi was found dead last week. After being missing for four days, her body was located on a ledge about two miles from the summit.

The instructor, Robert Brody, from London, said the group had been worried about the woman, Katrina Bryan, after she apparently walked away from the campsite. He said the party launched a wide search but she was not found until they gave up and started their descent.

The group had been hiking and climbing for three weeks in the region, which is rarely visited by outsiders. Locals tell stories of "mountain men" that prey on people who venture there. Mr. Brody said the group had been frightened by several mysterious apparitions, but he refused to go into detail.

An autopsy performed by Dr. Askan Katari showed multiple abrasions and extensive damage to the cranium. There were "inconsistencies," Dr. Katari said, without elaboration. The body is being flown to England for burial.

The consul coded the disk, placed it in an envelope, and addressed it to the college in Bethesda, Maryland, that he had been advised to use for such occasions. He sent it through the diplomatic pouch of the American embassy in Dushanbe, the capital of Tajikistan.

Matt decided to take a break. He heaved himself out of the gravelike hole, walked over to the water jug, and was hoisting it on one shoulder when he spotted a small speck out of the corner of his eye. He lowered the jug and stared into the valley at a dust cloud swirling in the far distance. A car.

It was the first car he had seen in four months. What was it doing in the middle of nowhere? He took off his broad-brimmed hat with its ring of sweat stains and looked up. Instantly he felt the East African sun shoot into his brain. He rolled his shoulders and felt a pleasing ache across his back muscles.

On the barren slope below, five figures were working: his students. He liked looking down on them like this, each of them busily engaged on the dig. One pushed a wheelbarrow of rocks; another lay prone inside a trench and scrubbed a stone surface with a toothbrush. It looked exotic, in all the heat and dust, like a lunar landscape.

He looked at his watch. Time for lunch. He loped down the hill with long strides, sliding down sideways, until he reached his tent. It was stiflingly hot inside. He tied the flaps open and flicked on a fan with a four-inch rubber blade, which did little to move the torpid air.

Flies buzzed thickly. In a mirror hung from the tent pole, Matt caught a glimpse of his face. He studied the sweat lines running like rivulets across his brow and cheeks, disappearing into stubble. A thicket of brown hair hung across his forehead, topped his ears, and curled up around his collar. The dirt engraved the crow's-feet around his dark brown eyes and the down-turning wrinkles on either side of his mouth.

He kicked off his boots, lay on the cot, folded his arms under his head, and looked up at the luminous canvas of the tent. A shadow shifted above as the tarp overhead waved lethargically in the breeze.

"Sleeping?"

Nicole's voice had a light, solicitous tone with a hint of mockery.

"Not really. Just a catnap."

"It's only one o'clock."

He sat up. "Well, you know, these old bones. . . ."

She smiled and shook her head in exasperation. She hated it when he made references to his age. It was one more way he had of driving a wedge between them. She removed her bandanna and let her hair fall down her back. It was walnut-colored and streaked with dirt and moved across her shoulders in the fan's breeze.

"You saw the car," she said. It was more of a statement than a question.

"Yeah."

"Who could it be?"

"I don't know. We're not expecting a mail drop for two weeks."

"Could be something important. Maybe a part for your computer."

"Like an instruction booklet." Matt's computer sat in a corner, unused as always. He had not been able to master it—he was a man of the past, not the future, he liked to say—and his incompetence made him the butt of jokes from his students.

"It could be a message from the university. Maybe the dig's being funded for another six months."

"When they hand out money they don't send someone halfway around the world to do it. They announce it at night—in an empty room."

She laughed. He stood up and stretched.

"Anyway," he said, "whoever they are, they're too late for lunch." He moved toward the opening.

"I just hope it's not bad news," she said. "I love it here. I've found my life's work."

He smiled. "It's got its moments," he said, then bowed and gestured past the tent flap, an invitation to leave. She shot him a glowering look, and as she passed she ran her forefinger slowly across his lower abdomen, mussing his shirt and brushing his skin below the navel. Despite himself, he felt himself stir.

Why didn't he sleep with her? It was not that he didn't feel desire—that, thank God, had not abandoned him. He thought back to the evening when Nicole had made her move. She simply slipped unnoticed into his tent, and he found her waiting in his cot. She was naked under the canopy of the mosquito netting, which hung around her like a transparent gown. Matt had felt a tangled rush of desire and dread. He reached into his box of gear and pulled out a fifth of whiskey and sat on a crate near the bed. They passed the bottle back and forth. She sat up, holding a blanket across her chest, and once or twice as she reached over to take the bottle she let it sag and he caught a full view of her breasts, small and firm. How long had it been since he had made love, ten weeks? Three months?

They drank in a spirit of camaraderie until they had killed the bottle. He staggered out for a walk under the stars, and when he returned an hour later she was gone. For days afterward she was furious. Then, strangely, her anger melted and she began acting as if she had a special claim on him. At meals she sat next to him, and she looked up to him and smiled in a wifely way at his jokes.

Once or twice she engineered situations to be alone with him to talk. He spied the moments coming and, feigning blindness, he diverted the conversation with a banter so unartful it was almost cruel. He felt base, but it struck him as so predictable and wearying—the campfire romance between the graduate student and the safari-hardened professor—as much the lore of digs as the serendipitous bones in the earth. He didn't want to go through all the declarations, the revelations, the recriminations. Perhaps I'm getting old, he mused, but I feel like embracing abstinence the way I used to revel in self-indulgence.

Suddenly, at thirty-eight, Matt had become conscious of time. He chided himself for hypocrisy in romance; all the games, the stabs at mystery, the flirtatious routines he had perfected over the years like a politician's hollow patter now struck him as vapid. Only once had he been able to strip away all that pretense, years ago. And that he had messed up.

He felt restless and dissatisfied, his edges worn away like stones awash on a beach. He told himself that he treasured his solitude, which was true, but something else also was true, and he was honest enough to recognize it during the odd sleepless night: He was lonely.

Still, the situation with Nicole was unstable. He had to do something to acknowledge her feelings or they would explode, and that could wreck the expedition. It always amazed him how the cohesive sense of the group was essential to a successful dig.

Outside, Matt looked into the bowl of the valley. The car on the plain below was closer. The dust seemed to shoot straight up like an explosion and then rain down behind in a plume.

"Thing I like about this site," he said. "No one can sneak up on you."

"Gives you time to rig the defenses." Nicole turned and

looked meaningfully at him to emphasize the double enten-
dre. As she walked ahead on the path, he stared at the back
of her frayed shorts. The bits of thread hung like whitened
bangs upon the exposed flesh of her upper thigh, and as
she led him along slowly he could see the outline of her
panties and watch the rolling sway of her buttocks.

Dr. Susan Arnot felt the customary excitement of speaking
to an audience, even if it was only to the undergraduates
of Anthro 101. It was something about being at the hub of
things, the focus of all those uplifted eyes. And the sense
of control—she had to admit she liked that too. Is that what
demagoguery is all about?

Susan Arnot's class on prehistoric man was one of the
most popular at the University of Wisconsin, even though
she was known as a tough grader. There was always an
extra thrill in taking a course from someone who was well
known in the field, especially someone controversial, whose
theories had shaken up the establishment. And of course
she was something of a campus sex symbol. She cut a striking figure, long-limbed, sometimes wearing blue jeans and
black leather and riding a motorcycle on her days off, her
long raven hair tucked into a cherry-red crash helmet. When
she walked into a room, it stirred as if molecules were
heating up.

Susan's lectures were fabled on campus, so the auditorium was crowded. Standing on a creaking wooden stage,
with a beam of light projected above her from the back of
the hall like a spotlight, she could see only featureless
heads. One or two bits of jewelry gleamed in the semidarkness, and a pair of eyeglasses reflected back like tiny
headlights.

She had softened them up with jokes: the usual fare
about rare archaeological finds, comparisons between Java
man and a certain eminent campus personality, and the Piltdown hoax and a professor's research. It was cheap but it

worked, and she felt gratified when they had laughed at the appropriate lines.

Abruptly she raised her right fist, flexed her thumb, and triggered a distant whirring sound. Behind her appeared a huge map, starkly drawn in thick black ink, with meandering cracks for rivers and eyelashes for hills. The students focused on it and some raised their pens, ready to scribble notes. German place-names from the Rhine valley: Oberhausen, Solingen, the Düssel River. She raised a pointer and walked over to the map, all business.

"And so we come to the main event. The year is 1856: August. It's three years before Darwin will publish *On the Origin of Species.* He's been laboring away on it some twenty years now, and he's in no particular hurry. But soon he will hear that a rival is working on a manuscript proposing something called 'natural selection,' and this will send him into a frenzy of competitive production."

She looked out at the students to make sure they were with her, and for some reason she began to feel slightly on edge, a vague, disorienting feeling that came upon her out of nowhere these days.

She raised the pointer. The red rubber tip touched the map, and she caressed the center in a slow, circular motion.

"Here in this little valley east of the Rhine, something is about to happen that's going to turn the scientific establishment of the nineteenth century on its ear. A discovery. And like many important discoveries, chance will play an important part."

She raised her fist. Another click, and a color photograph of meadows and glades flashed on the screen.

"It's a tranquil little valley, filled with edelweiss and daffodils. The gorge you see was named in the seventeenth century after a headmaster from Düsseldorf, Joachim Neumann. He roamed the valley for inspiration for his poems and music—both rather dreadful, by the way. But he was a beloved figure, and after he died the village elders decided to bestow his name on the fields he adored. Joachim was a bit of a pedant. He preferred to be called by the Greek translation of his name, which meant New Man: in Greek, *Neander*.

"Two centuries later—in 1856—on a quiet August day, quarry workers discovered a cave, which had scores and scores of bones in it, piled up around the edges and scattered about, but mostly heaped in a mound near the center. The workers threw them away, all but a handful. For some reason the owner of the land, one Felix Beckershoff, took an interest in these old bones and managed to salvage a few: arms and thighs, part of a pelvis, a fragment of skull."

Another slide came on the screen: bits of bone, shiny like polished gems and as dark brown as wet cardboard. Parts were identifiable—the roof of a brainpan, a familiar-looking femur, a slender tibia. The tip of the pointer danced among them and drew a figure eight.

"Luckily, Beckershoff was acquainted with a J. C. Fuhlrott, the founder of the local Natural Science Society. When Fuhlrott saw those fragments, he couldn't believe his eyes. What manner of bones were these? The low-vaulted skull with its awesome protruding ridge: how to explain that? The bowed limbs. The injured ulna of the lower arm. Whose were they? Surely from no animal, and yet from no man—or species of man—still living."

Susan returned to the lectern. The students were writing feverishly now. She didn't have to consult her notes; she had given the lecture a dozen times. But still she couldn't shake the feeling of being off stride, vulnerable. Who are all those people out there listening to me? she wondered. What are they really thinking? She forced her voice into an easy, conversational tone.

"Fuhlrott brought in an anatomist from Bonn, one Professor Schaaffhausen. He became the first to theorize that the specimen was something truly unimaginable—not an ape, not a man, but some type of pre-man, perhaps an ancient being who roamed Europe long before the Romans and Celts. Try to conceive for one second what a bold leap that singular induction was.

"Then the professionals got involved. The theory of evolution was in its infancy. Its threatening cries were already echoing up and down the staid corridors of science. The establishment was split: Evolutionists seized upon this handful of bones and held them up—presto!—vindication of their revolutionary theory. The antievolutionists went on the attack. They insisted the bones were an insignificant fluke. Sides were drawn. Famous thinkers came up with explanations. Plausibility was not a prime consideration. Rudolf Virchow, the best-known German anatomist of his time, concluded that the owner of the bones was an ordinary human suffering from rickets. The unspeakable pain, he reasoned, caused him to knot his brow, which then became ossified into those bizarre heavy ridges.

"Most preeminent scientists sidestepped the controversy. Certainly Darwin did." Susan shook her head slightly. "But we shouldn't be too judgmental. Remember, it was an age of dark superstition, pseudo-religion, straitjacket conservatism. It was anathema to imagine a human with an apelike ancestor, not to mention a flat-headed cousin who looked as if he had been run over by a truck.

"But then providence intervened. The evidence kept piling up until it became incontrovertible."

She raised her fist again and another map popped onto the screen, showing Europe, North Africa, and the Indian subcontinent, with black crosses scattered across it. They clustered around southern France.

"There were more fossil finds. And there were bones of huge mammals—some of them extinct, like the mammoth and the giant deer. Pretty hard to argue with that." The tip of the pointer tapped the screen. "Bones began turning up like mushrooms after a rain: Gibraltar, Italy, Belgium, Russia, Iraq, Israel."

She smiled. Her anxiety had lifted a bit. She backed up to the lectern, still watching the screen, as if waiting for something magical to happen, and her voice took on the clip of a narrative climax.

"And so . . . the evidence carried the day. Science won out. William King, an Irish anatomist, identified the fossil as a new species of humanity. Paleoanthropology was founded as a field of study. Our creature was recognized, baptized, analyzed. He was given a name. It came from the valley of the mountain flowers and our beloved headmaster with the insufferable rhymes, Joachim Neumann.

"And now, folks, here he is"—there was a touch of the carnival barker in her pitch, as she raised her fist high over her head and punched the button with her thumb—"the star of our show . . . *Homo sapiens neanderthalensis,* colloquially known to you all as Neanderthal Man!"

The hall darkened as the giant figure usurped it. It was immense, hirsute, and ran from one end of the screen to the other. There was the too-large visage, so oddly familiar from hundreds of sketches and half-remembered dreams: the crooked sloping brow; the bulging cage of the forehead, horribly ribbed; the prominent, slightly hooked nose and weak, rounded chin. It was unspeakably misshapen, ugly, close enough to a human head to be recognizable and thus render the differences even more grotesque. It was as if a giant hand had taken a waxen head and pulled it forward brutally, elongating it.

The Neanderthal dwarfed Susan, and as she walked across the stage in front of its hairy chest, oblivious to the gigantic form looming behind her, the contrast gave it an aspect of menace: King Kong peering in the window at Fay Wray.

The sketch, by the Czech illustrator Zdenek Burian, was her favorite. She liked the way it caught a distinctly human aura. Something about the lines in the mouth made them look like smile lines, and the fiercely intelligent eyes seemed to be looking off into the distance as if they were gazing at something momentous—the creature's own extinction, perhaps. They were so sagacious, so wistfully hopeless. There was a hint of inexpressible weariness in the stoop of the shoulders. This was no beast. This was every bit man's equal.

2

Matt didn't put credence in portents—he was too skeptical to believe the universe could be organized, even by a malevolent force—but he was unable to shake the conviction that this plume of dust augured ill. The sensation heightened now that the car was approaching, but he swallowed it in front of the students. "Maybe it's that pizza we ordered," he joked, as they finished off a lunch of goat meat, warmed over from the night before and washed down with tepid Tusker beer.

He picked up his drink and walked off by himself far along the ridge, where he could sit on a boulder and survey the lower portion of the dig: the pit cut in layered trenches, the wheelbarrows topped with screens, the old trailer that served as their lab, the toolboxes lying flat on the ground like small wooden coffins. Amazing how no other place counted to him now.

He thought about all the finds over the decades: bits of bone and teeth, flint scrapers and arrowheads—all those pieces of the puzzle. Knowledge of Lower Paleolithic man had grown exponentially over the last few decades, but what was really known of his universe, his mentality and soul, the way he tried to make sense of the world before falling asleep at night or responded when he saw a sunset or a galloping fallow deer?

As Matt sat there, he imagined prehistoric man standing on this very spot. It would have been the shore of a great lake, perhaps, judging from the sedimentation deposits. Deep caves honeycombed the hills behind and opened almost at the water's edge. Perfect for safety; that would matter above all else. Matt knew something of this creature's habitat and beliefs, and he tried to conjure up even the dimmest glimmer of his psyche: one part warrior, another part fearful shadow quaking in the recesses of a cave. He tried, as he had many times before, to empty himself and to take on those fears, the smells of blood and lard and hair, the brain tripping over itself with a capacity for understanding that outstripped the few puny grunts given to it. It was all so unknowable. Was it possible even for a split second to feel a connection with something so primitive and so much greater, that had passed this way eons before?

With a clamor, the Land Rover rounded a bend, plunged into the center of the campsite, and stopped abruptly. The dust caught up with it and enveloped it in a cloud that drifted away as the motor was cut.

A man bounded out of the back and headed for them with a quick step. He was peculiar-looking. His hair seemed to hang in clumps. He was plump but surprisingly agile, a white man in his early forties. He wore new hiking boots, a Banana Republic safari jacket, and wraparound sunglasses.

"Dr. Mattison?" He walked directly over to Matt and amiably offered a fleshy hand.

Matt took it. The man's grasp was stronger than he expected.

"Or should I say, 'Dr. Mattison, I presume'? We are in Africa after all. At least I think we are. Can't be sure— might have taken a wrong turn back there in the dust bowl."

"And you are . . ."

"Van Steeds. Frederick." A pause. "People call me Van."

The name was familiar but Matt couldn't quite place it. The visitor took off his dark glasses and wiped them on a shirttail. The skin around his cheeks was puffed with fat and his gray eyes darted around once his glasses were off, giving him an inquisitive but furtive air. He bent over and swatted his pants legs. A billow of dust came out. "Look at this. Don't know how you get used to it."

Matt saw Van looking at the table. "Want something to eat?"

"Don't mind if I do."

The students made room while one of them foraged in the larder and returned with some cut slices of meat, bread, and another beer.

The chauffeur sat under an acacia tree and promptly fell asleep, his hands lying on the ground palms up. Van looked over at him. "Don't know what it is with these guys. Soon as they get out of the car they fall asleep. You'd think it was in their contract or something."

"Khat," said one student. "He's chewing khat."

"No! How do you know?"

"The eyes. Dilated pupils. Everyone around here chews it."

"Son of a gun."

Matt tired of the small talk. "Look, Van. I appreciate your driving four hours from Djibouti in the noonday sun, but—"

"Ten, to be exact. I landed in Hargeisa, drove to Djibouti, and picked this car up there. He got lost twice. Said he knew the way."

"Yes, but now you're here, so perhaps you can tell us why."

"Certainly," said Van, and smiled inscrutably. Matt realized he was enjoying his little mystery. "Only thing is"—he looked around at the others—"I've got to talk to you alone."

"Okay."

Van finished his lunch slowly in silence and then stood up, licking the grease off his fingers. Matt led the way to his tent. As soon as they were inside, Van held out a long brown envelope without a word. As Matt tore it open, the man peered out the tent flap, lit a cigarette, and said, "I can't answer any questions. You're bound to have them. I wish I could, but frankly I don't have a lot of answers."

The letterhead was discreet and important-looking: The Institute for Prehistoric Research, 1290 Brandywine Lane, Bethesda, MD 09763.

Dear Dr. Mattison:

I have every reason to believe that this letter will reach you at the most inopportune of times, and I apologize in advance for that unfortunate coincidence. It is, I assure you, only a matter of extreme importance, indeed urgency, that would drive me to seek you out at a time like this and to place a demand upon you that, I am confident, your magnanimity will not permit you to deny.

As you may or may not realize, we have contracted the services of Dr. Jerome Kellicut, whom I believe you know well and who has often spoken favorably of you. For that reason we feel we may confide in you. Dr. Kellicut has been abroad in Tajikistan on an exciting project that we are sponsoring. The project is of utmost importance to the scientific community and to the field of paleontology and prehistoric research in particular. He has not been heard from in several months, aside from a message that he sent to you through us and which we are holding for you. The message is in the nature of a summons, which we are convinced you will want to respond to favorably once you know the facts. I am afraid I must add that we have grounds to believe that Dr. Kellicut's life is in danger.

For this reason I urge you to immediately depart upon receipt of this letter and to present yourself in our headquarters in Bethesda, Maryland, at the above address. In anticipation of your positive reply, flight reservations and accommodations have been made for you, as have arrangements for others to take in hand your current project.

In closing I would like to emphasize the compelling nature of the request being placed upon you. I am sure you will understand the paramount need for speed and for secrecy.

There was a boldly scrawled signature and underneath the typed name and title: *Harold Eagleton, Director.*

Matt was dumbfounded. He had thought often of Kellicut, his mentor at Harvard, but he hadn't seen him for at least five years and hadn't heard anything about him for . . . what? At least two. Kellicut. No one had influenced Matt's life the way that man had. He ruled the powerful archaeology department like a prince, and the students were his subjects; they lived in the hope of being chosen for his digs, joining the elite. Kellicut would prowl the bars of Cambridge with them late into the night and then they would return to his apartment, where he would put on Fats Waller or Maria Callas and cook up a mound of spiced scrambled eggs in a black iron pan that he never washed.

Matt was impressionable—he had never known his father, who died when he was two—and Kellicut bombarded him with revelations, subversive thoughts, the poetry of Blake, composers he had never heard of. Why me? Matt had always wondered, feeling pleased but unworthy. It had only been a matter of time until he succumbed to Kellicut's fascination with "the ancients"—not the Greeks and Romans, who left behind writings and so were knowable, but the true ancients, prelapsarian beings in the process of becoming human.

On Matt's second dig, years ago, at Combe Grenal in a

tiny valley carved by the Dordogne in southern France, they unearthed over 2,000 Neanderthal bone fragments and even a partial skeleton. The whole bed of rock was lifted out by a crane, to dangle precariously while Kellicut jumped up and down, cursing and shouting in broken French. The French crane operator had tilted it so that it was about to slip out of its sling and smash against the ground when finally Kellicut himself jumped into the cab and managed to stop the rock from swaying and settle it onto a flatbed truck. Matt remembered the image still: Kellicut slapping the gears, still cursing, then laughing. Later that evening, he produced four bottles of chilled champagne from God knows where and they all got drunk. And then, always one to break the rules, Kellicut gave them each a little Neanderthal skull fragment, drilled and mounted on a silver chain. Matt had dutifully worn it around his neck for years before he took it off and carried it in his pocket. Even now, he kept it near as a talisman.

To be honest, Matt had been a little hurt that Kellicut hadn't been in touch. Now he was in some kind of trouble—that much was clear. But what danger? What was the project and what was his message? Matt had heard of the Institute for Prehistoric Research, a new but well-endowed outfit on the cutting edge of research in related fields, but he didn't know much about it. What project was Kellicut on? How did this Eagleton know where Matt was, and how could he assume that he would come just like that?

He glanced up at Van, now smoking and taking pains to exhale the smoke through the screened flap.

"Van, what's all this about?"

"Sorry. Like I said, I can't tell you."

"Can't or won't?"

"Believe me, if I could add anything to what's in that letter, I would. Kellicut is missing on a dig in Tajikistan and we need you to help us find him."

"You hand me this letter and expect me to just drop everything and come?"

"Yep."

"Why?"

"Because his life may be in danger." Van unzipped the tent flap and spat out a large globule of saliva.

"Why do you say that?"

"It's a dangerous place. He's supposed to keep in touch. And like the letter says, we haven't heard from him in months."

They were silent a moment. Then Van spoke up.

"So you'll come."

Matt felt a thickening in his throat. "How soon are we talking about?"

"I'm leaving today. You can come in two days."

Matt protested. "But how about the dig? I can't just walk off and leave it. These kids are depending on me."

"It's been taken care of. We have somebody to run it. A guy from Columbia. He'll be out here tomorrow, Thursday at the latest."

"You seem to have thought of everything," Matt said.

"We can't be sure of that. That's why we need you."

"Why me?"

"You know Kellicut. You know the field. You're the only one—practically the only one—who does."

Along with alarm, Matt noticed something else, a feeling he recognized. It was a little buzz of excitement in the ear, a tingling of the extremities, that old sensation he got when an adventure was in the offing.

They made the arrangements. Van stayed only half an hour more. When Matt walked him over to the Land Rover, Van roused the dozing driver, who shook his head, jumped up, and got into the car.

Matt looked into Van's dark glasses again. "One more thing. Your name is familiar but I can't place your work. What's your area?"

"Me? I began in psychology, then paleoanthropology. Now I'm involved in psycholingualism."

"Of course. Van Steeds. I've read some of your stuff—

it's fascinating, all that new research about communication without language. Forgive me.''

"Quite all right. I'm impressed that someone of your stature bothers to read the obscure publications that feature my work." Van smiled toothily and slid into the back seat without another word, and the car pulled away, trailing another cloud of dust.

Later on when Matt went back into his tent he looked out the flap. There on the ground was Van's globule of spit. He couldn't believe it. It was green. Son of a bitch, he thought. The bastard was chewing khat.

Susan raised the pointer to tickle the Neanderthal's chin.

"Here he is. You know what people say about him: 'Nature's practical joke'; 'Evolution's dead end.' Our poor ape-like cousin, a shuffling moronic figure who frittered away his hour upon the stage.

"Well, nothing could be further from the truth. We have learned a lot in the past ten or fifteen years, and everything we know now contradicts that slanderous stereotype."

An old photograph flashed onto the screen, of an eminent-looking man with a bow tie, a trim white goatee, narrow eyes, and a mouth slightly parted in a self-satisfied smile. He looked a bit like Sigmund Freud.

"Here's the villain, Marcellin Boule, renowned French paleontologist. More than anyone else he is responsible for the gross misconception of the Neanderthal that perseveres to this day, in everything from literature to cartoons."

Susan sketched in Boule's background, his desire for fame, his obsession to keep human lineage pure by rejecting primitive ancestors; and the fateful day in 1908 when a skeleton from a small cave near La Chapelle-aux-Saints fell into his hands. She clicked on a slide of his reconstruction of the skeleton—a faulty job intended to make it look as apelike as possible with neck vertebrae sticking up like a gorilla's and the bone of the big toe splitting off to form an opposable thumb.

"No wonder generations looked down on him as a dumb oaf. Well, look what happens when you correct Monsieur Boule's distortions." The screen changed and the skeleton stood up erect. "Look at that. A bit more majestic. He's not quite as tall as we are, but he's not really that different. Certainly he doesn't look simian. Today people are fond of saying that if you gave him a shave and dressed him in a suit and tie, you could lose him on Madison Avenue. Perhaps. But the moment you were introduced, you would know. When he shook your hand he would probably break every bone in it."

Susan saw a square of light in the back of the hall, and against it a darkened figure slipped inside the auditorium. She thought she saw it stoop to sit down in a back row as the door closed and the light dimmed. Again she felt that free-floating anxiety.

She forced herself to concentrate on the lecture and crossed the stage, grasping the pointer tightly. "We know that the Neanderthal had fire. Fire had been used for tens of thousands of years, and without it he could not have survived the last glaciation. He was a fire producer, not just a fire conserver. He used iron pyrites and flint to ignite it and perhaps dried fungus as tinder. In fact, he was downright homey in keeping his hearth."

Susan was sure there was an interloper sitting in the back row, a man. Who could it be? Who would enter in the middle of a lecture like that?

"He buried his dead. Interestingly, many of the burial sites we've discovered have been children's. One particularly well-preserved site is at Teshik-Tash, a cave in the Gissar range south of Samarkand. It's a whole chamber and it contains six pairs of horns of the Siberian mountain goat. One pair is slightly charred. Everything points to an elaborate ritual, perhaps to bring the child back to life in the future. Death was very special to the Neanderthal. In fact, I believe he built a cult around it.

"At the very least we can hypothesize that he practiced

religion, although of course we haven't an inkling about what kind of religion it was. Fire was almost certainly part of his worship. Some caves have what appear to be fire chambers, either for practical reasons—to keep the fire going at all times—or for ritualistic purposes. Perhaps in borrowing fire from lightning storms, when the skies opened up and pelted his poor universe, the Neanderthal, like Sisyphus, was reaching beyond his station. Perhaps he was usurping the power of his gods, and perhaps they, like the Greek gods and even Jehovah, demanded expiation through some form of sacrifice. Do these bones of children speak to us of Abraham and Isaac? We don't know and we may never know.'' She paused a moment.

"So let's stick with what we do know. We know the Neanderthal lived in groups and cared for the aged and infirm. We have discovered skeletons with recovered fractures and incapacitating illnesses that prove this beyond a doubt." On the screen appeared a withered skeleton. "Here we have the find by Ralph Solecki in the great Shanidar cave in Iraq. Our prehistoric man here was killed by a rock fall. He was old, perhaps forty, which in Neanderthal years makes him ancient. See that damage to the skull? It probably comes from the cave-in. But look at his right arm. It was amputated some years before—see?—just above the elbow. He had arthritis. Now look at the left side of the face. See that bone scar tissue? He was blind in the left eye. There's no way someone like this could have survived on his own. Others kept him alive. The tribe supported its weaker members, those who could not hunt or work. In this sense, Neanderthals were *human*—maybe even more human than we are. Those of you who have been inside a nursing home lately will know what I mean.

"Here's something else for those of you who think of Neanderthals as submoronic cartoon characters. Monsieur Boule took an endocranial cast of the La Chapelle skull and thought its owner simpleminded. Today, of course, we know that brain size is not an indicator of intelligence. Anatole France, the French philosopher, had a brain only two thirds as large as the average adult Neanderthal.

"But we also know more about Neanderthal skulls, and from measurements of craniums it is indisputable that their brains were *not* smaller than ours. Quite the opposite: They were nearly ten percent larger. What's more, some say the ratio of brain size to body size—the so-called cephalization, which is a more accurate measurement of intelligence than mere brain size when projected across an entire species— is also more optimal by a factor of point twelve." A table showing the cephalization for twenty species was displayed. The highest was Neanderthal, the lowest was labeled MODERN COW. "There is no way to reconcile these data without admitting the likelihood that the Neanderthal was our equal in brainpower—or perhaps even our superior."

Susan walked across the stage, paused for dramatic effect, and raised her fist. "Consider modern man."

On the screen popped a grainy picture of a handsome man in his sixties. He was resting in a khaki safari suit against a tomb of some sort. Balding, with a peppery beard, a roguish glint, and a slight smile, he had a jaunty air, and though he was relaxed, leaning back against an ancient crumbling wall with a piece of straw between his teeth, he seemed ready to pounce at the camera. His eyes were dark and penetrating. It was hard not to look at them.

"Here's the paradox. If Neanderthal is so intelligent, what happened? How did this guy behind me get to be top dog? What happened to our man of the valley of the alpine flowers? Why are we here and why is he gone? To quote Jack Nicholson in *Prizzi's Honor,* 'If he's so fucking smart, how come he's so fucking dead?' " There was tittering at the profanity.

"Why did Neanderthals appear some two hundred thirty thousand years ago, flourish for millennia after millennia, ranging from western Europe to central Asia and the Middle East, extending their reach into different flora and fauna, only to drop from sight all at once?" Susan tapped the pointer against the screen so hard it began to shudder. "You see here one of the most eminent thinkers and paleoanthropologists of our time"—there was a reverential pause—"Dr. Jerome Kellicut. Simply put, his work has revolutionized the field we study."

She looked up at him. She had always liked the photo. She took it herself, on Crete, years ago. Perhaps I'm laying it on a bit thick, she thought. Recently she had caught herself questioning some of Kellicut's achievements, demythologizing the man. It was bound to happen. He had been such a glamorous character, the sort of professor who changed the lives of his graduate students. Who wouldn't worship a man who thought in terms of eons?

"Through a unique method of dating stones called thermoluminescence—I won't bore you with the details of how it works—Dr. Kellicut has examined flint from Neanderthal caves in southern France and has been able to fix their age more accurately by far than anyone before him. His astounding conclusion is that the Neanderthals lived much later than we had thought—up until thirty thousand years ago. Previously their extinction had been placed at forty thousand years. The difference is only ten thousand years, but these aren't just any ten thousand years, for it was precisely at this time that modern man appeared on the scene, rising up in Africa and migrating through the Middle East to Europe. In other words, Kellicut was able to prove conclusively that modern human beings—*Homo sapiens sapiens*—and *Homo sapiens neanderthalensis* coexisted. Coexisted!

"Think of the possibilities." Susan's voice was rising now. "Was there commerce between these two members of the same species, so close in so many ways? Did they exchange ideas? Did they trade tools? Hunt together? Breed together? Did they wage war?

"Now maybe at last we have at least the beginnings of a solution to the great enigma: What happened to *Homo sapiens neanderthalensis*? For now we know that his exit more or less corresponded in time with the entrance of *Homo sapiens sapiens,* a subspecies that is uncannily similar to Neanderthal but different in some critical way that allowed us to survive and become Earth's chosen child.

"We need to find the key to unlock the riddle. If it wasn't a matter of straightforward intelligence—and we have no reason to think it was, given our best estimates of cranial capacity—what was it? If we could find the answer to that single question, we would know everything. We would know exactly what it is that makes us different from other animals. What it is that makes us, of all creatures, special: set apart, aware, endowed with history, conscious of mortality. What it is that makes us *sapiens.* We would finally reach the hidden chambers that have concealed the secret of our existence."

The lights went on quickly. There was a loud round of applause, a blur of voices, and the sound of seat bottoms snapping up and books slapped together as the room began to empty.

Susan gathered up her papers, walked down a few steps, paused and talked with a circle of students, and then started to the back of the auditorium. She was halfway up the aisle when she noticed the figure sitting in the last row.

Her heart raced. He was a peculiar-looking man, round and muscular, with an ill-fitting jacket and black wraparound sunglasses dangling from a cord around his neck. He remained hunched down in his seat until she stood before him.

"Dr. Arnot?" A half smile. "My name is Van Steeds."

Susan smiled back and bowed her head almost imperceptibly. Her hands felt cold. He was holding something toward her, a long brown envelope.

3

Susan's plane descended toward the Washington Monument, then the Ellipse and the Lincoln Memorial. Tiny cars rolled with precise, miniaturized movements.

She detested Washington. She had lived there for a year on a Smithsonian grant after graduate school at Harvard. She still shuddered at the memory of those hot afternoons, cataloguing bones in a basement and daydreaming about faraway countries. Also, of course, "nursing a broken heart," as her friends unkindly said behind her back.

She retrieved her battered suitcase and was met at the curb by a limousine driver with a DR. ARNOT sign. They drove to a residential neighborhood of two- and three-story frame houses and squat brick ranchers. Children played outside.

It reminded her of the small logging town in Oregon where she grew up, unforgiving country she could not wait to leave. Her childhood had been miserable. She was the daughter of an alcoholic father who deserted his frail, thin-blooded wife and ran off to captain a ferryboat. Religion had been a comfort; Susan's only warm memory was of the white clapboard church on a hilltop.

She drew her strength from her grandmother, a great Hungarian beauty from whom she had inherited her dark skin, high cheekbones, and long legs. It was her grandmother who had left Budapest at the age of twenty-three to make a long trek across Canada and down to Oregon. Susan inherited that independent streak from her—it had skipped over her poor mother. When she was starting out on a dig or an adventure like this one, she liked to think that she was a pioneer too.

She had received Van's message only two days ago, but she was feeling guilty that it had taken her that long to get her affairs in order. Visconti, the department chairman, had not been gracious. Still, he had let her go. He did manage to prick her curiosity about the Institute for Prehistoric Research by raising an eyebrow and insisting that most scientists would kill for the honor of speaking there. She found many references to it in the library—all since 1987—and wondered how it was she didn't know more about the place.

Van had not been a communicative messenger. He volunteered little about himself or Kellicut or what kind of research expedition he had been on, and he hadn't told her what to expect here other than "a second-rate academic grilling." He also seemed to know a great deal about her—not so much from what he said but from what he didn't say, questions he didn't ask and assumptions he made.

Soon a college campus cropped up on the right and a sign pointed to the Institute for Prehistoric Research. Inside, busy at their desks, were two secretaries. Susan was nodded through to another, smaller room, where Van was waiting. He rose slowly from an easy chair and bowed slightly. "Welcome," he said.

"Thank you." She looked around. The room was furnished with comfortable and understated antiques. "What kind of place is this, a college?"

"Part of it. We find it makes for helpful synergy." He led the way through another room and yet another corridor. When they came to a set of double oak doors, he opened them and stepped to one side to let her pass.

Disoriented, feeling almost dizzy, Susan stepped into a small conference room with plush carpeting and thickly cushioned seats in which a dozen or so dim figures sat. They turned to look at her with interest but no surprise. But sitting right in the center, she saw someone who took her breath away. There, big as life, was Matt.

Eagleton spun his wheelchair around to face the bank of video screens and checked to make sure the tape was recording. This moment was important. He wanted to be sure to capture his expression and hers, their eyes at the precise moment when surprise lifts the curtain to reveal truth. He could analyze them later at his leisure. He always prided himself on his ability to spot telltale clues, "the heart's clumsy spies" as he called them, which were missed by less-observant analysts.

Mattison knew she was coming, which meant of course that he had prepared himself. Old Schwartzbaum had seen to that, the idiot, by blurting it out earlier this morning. Eagleton could have killed him. Still, what could he have done differently? He had wanted the senior staffers and consultants to meet the two of them and question them in person. Interrogation by experts was best for extracting scientific information that could turn out to be valuable, he had discovered. Even if the experts themselves had no idea what the information was to be used for. He knew the virtue of compartmentalizing subordinates and keeping them in the dark. It was second nature by now—first nature, to be exact.

Eagleton was keenly aware how much this little venture meant. He felt the pressure. But he felt something else, too, that rising bubble of excitement, the sweaty palms. God, how he detested sweat! But how he lived for the excitement. Just like the old days. He knew the nicknames they called him, "Captain Queeg," "the Metal Cobra." That was the trouble with internal surveillance; you found out more than you wanted to know. Still, it was impossible to know too much. Information is power, as they say. A healthy dose of paranoia never hurt anyone. He recalled that droll joke about defining the opposite of paranoia: "The outrageous belief that one is *not* being persecuted."

For silver-haired Harold Eagleton, now sixty-two and counting, surrounded by enemies and hemmed in by a vindictive bacteria-filled world, this expedition represented his comeback. But everything had to go exactly right. This business with Kellicut was worrisome. He didn't trust Van. He needed Mattison and Arnot, and he had to make sure they functioned just the way he required them to.

He lit a cigarette and fiddled with the remote control. Good closeup of her. Him, too. She wasn't bad-looking, even he had to admit—he who usually thought of a woman in terms of her street value. But he could see the attraction here, something about the turn of the lips, the flowing hair, and the way she brushed it back with one hand when she was nervous—and she was clearly nervous now, taken aback when she saw Mattison. But she recovered quickly, Eagleton was glad to see, and entered the room with poise.

She made the rounds, shaking hands. The men stood up with an ostentatious show of politeness and the women remained seated and grasped her hand tightly, smiling in that complicity of sisterhood that women scientists affected these days. It was a varied collection of talent: a morphologist, a neurologist, a physicist, a mathematician, and an astrophysicist; two geneticists; a geologist, an anthropologist, a psychologist, and a parapsychologist; an archaeologist, an ecologist, an evolutionary sociobiologist, a paleontologist, an anatomist, and an archaeohistorian. Susan recognized most of the names and even knew some of them. When she was introduced to Dr. Ugo Brizzard, a man who published studies on telepathic communication that most scientists regarded as crackpot, she barely registered a flicker of surprise.

Eagleton watched closely as she approached Mattison. His hand was out and she took it.

"We already know each other," she said.

"That we do," he replied.

They smiled at each other and she moved on.

Very cool, thought Eagleton. He was beginning to allow himself to be optimistic. They can handle this, he thought, as he filed away their dossiers in a drawer marked DIRECTOR ONLY.

"We are lucky to have both Dr. Arnot and Dr. Mattison together in the same room." Dr. C. B. Simpson, a white-haired anthropologist, was acting as a moderator. "That way we can get two different answers to every question." They laughed. Then, with tea and coffee, the group tossed out questions. Easy ones at first, then more and more specialized. Eventually they got to the topic that the discussion was leading to inexorably: the extinction of the Neanderthal.

"Can you provide us with the current best thinking on when and why this occurred?" inquired a mathematics professor named Eugene Pringle, a benign-looking man with thick glasses that magnified his eyes into bulging orbs of blue and white.

"The when is easier than the why," said Susan. "Current evidence is that the Neanderthal disappeared about thirty thousand years ago. The richest new finds are in parts of the former Soviet Union. Radiocarbon dating puts them about then."

"On the other hand," said Matt, "we also have signs pointing to a transition, not an extinction, within the Upper Paleolithic. There are indications of a regional industry, the Châtelperronian, in southwest France and Spain—"

"Excuse me," came an interruption from the back. "What is a regional industry?"

"Production of tools over a large area. If it is Neanderthal—and the well-struck blades tend to make me think it is—the date could go somewhat later. There are even signs of an association between the Neanderthal and the Aurignacian. On that basis we can't rule out population-mixing."

"Some of us do rule it out," put in Susan.

"Because?"

"Because the remains in question, the Vindija remains, are too inconclusive. They were found on a level with only a single Aurignacian bone point. That's not enough to hang an entire theoretical framework on, especially one with such a significant claim. There are just too many questions."

Matt grimaced. She had always been meticulous when it came to science, he thought. He gave her a long look for the first time. She still could knock his wind out. The years haven't been bad to her, he thought, though her skin now was lined by scores of little wrinkles, the result of all that tanning. Her body had thickened a bit but it was not unbecoming. It filled out her face and rounded the curves of her hips. As always, her black hair was her most striking feature, though now it was not long and straight but rose up in all directions like a thundercloud. Something had deepened her looks. Was it the markings of a lonely life or new mystery endowed by their separation? How long had it been, fifteen years? In all that time they had never spoken. They attacked each other obliquely, through gossip and in footnotes. He had caught sight of her several times, once at the far end of a conference room, but when he made his way there, pushing and shoving through the crowd, she had gone.

"Face it," said Matt. "There's a lot we don't know. We don't even know when most of them lived. The spread of fossils is simply too thin. Maybe they were dying like flies eighty or ninety years ago and we just blundered across more recent skeletons."

"Eighty or ninety years ago!" interjected the mathematician, Pringle.

"Sorry, I slipped into shorthand. I mean of course eighty or ninety thousand years."

"So much for the when," said Pringle. "How about the why?"

"Well," said Susan. "That's even more debatable. As

you'd expect, theories abound. They all have one obvious fault in common—they come from the survivors. As the saying goes, history is written by the victors.''

''No one else is around to do it,'' said Pringle.

''Right. Anyway, in general terms everyone agrees that the Neanderthal's physiognomy made him able to endure a cold climate, much colder than anything we could survive. During the last glaciation, Würm One, he would have felt pretty much at home once he had a cave to crawl into and a fire to toast his feet. Then something happened.''

''Surely it was something traumatic,'' put in a short squat man whose name Susan had missed. ''The Neanderthal would have stopped at nothing to pass on his genes.''

Oh no, thought Susan, I hope he's not one of those creepy ultra-Darwinist sociobiologists, one of those guys who likes to monopolize cocktail parties by hurling out factoids—such as, rabies lives in spit, so mad dogs bite and can't swallow.

Matt interjected. ''There are those who hold with a theory of catastrophe, some Big Bang that caused a mass extinction. An upheaval in the environment, a volcanic eruption. Some change in the ecosystem that he was particularly ill-equipped to surmount. The problem is that the catastrophists can't come up with the catastrophe. It would have to be something powerful enough to wipe out the Neanderthal but localized enough to spare *Homo sapiens.* That's a hard line to walk. And ice bores in Greenland and ash dusting in the Sahara don't indicate any singular event thirty thousand years ago.''

''Maybe the earth's warming gradually shrank his zone of habitation,'' put in Pringle. ''Maybe it forced him into a smaller and smaller area—say, high up into the mountains until eventually his food supply gave out.''

''Unlikely,'' said Susan. ''The time scale is off. And he would have adjusted.''

''Maybe he tried and failed.''

''Maybe. But bear in mind that everything we know

about Neanderthal paints a portrait of a creative, adaptable being. He uses fire. He lives in caves. He wears animal skins. He's someone who manipulates his environment rather than becoming a victim of it.''

''What are you saying?''

''I'm saying that for hundreds of thousands of years prehistoric man is stuck in this swamp of immutable brutal subsistence. Then along comes a variant that claws its way out of the muck. He applies his intellect. He lives in a social grouping. He's a problem-solver. And this is the creature that nature selects for her cruel joke? It doesn't make sense—scientifically, that is. If science teaches us anything, it is that nature is consistent and logical.''

''That's true,'' said the squat man. ''It's like cholera.''

''I beg your pardon?'' said Susan.

''Cholera spreads through excreting, so cholera makes us excrete,'' he said.

I knew he was an ultra-Darwinist, thought Susan.

''So what's the answer?'' asked the eminent paleontologist, Dr. Victor Schwartzbaum.

''With apologies to Gertrude Stein, what's the question?''

''The question that has brought us all here: What killed off *Homo sapiens neanderthalensis*?''

''You're looking at it.''

''Huh?''

''Us. All of us.''

''How?''

''Simple,'' said Susan. ''We wiped them out.''

''Not so fast,'' said Matt.

''You see,'' said Susan. ''Those of us who follow in Dr. Kellicut's footsteps fall into two opposing camps, and we do not take kindly to each other.''

''That's an understatement,'' said Schwartzbaum.

''My camp is called 'Noah's Ark' or 'Out of Africa Two,' '' continued Susan. ''We believe that long after *Homo erectus* migrated from Africa, a second migration occurred, about one hundred thousand years ago. It was us—anatomically modern humans. We conquered the Neanderthal somehow with a new invention or a new form of social organization. A Darwinian struggle on a massive scale, intraspecies war. It must have been, quite literally, a fight to the very end.

"Then there is what I call the make-love-not-war school of thinking, which is led by Dr. Mattison here. They believe that there was no second migration out of Africa, and that various forms evolved more or less independently in different regions and then mixed together. Modern man's gene pool simply swamped that of the Neanderthal."

"Swamped is hardly the word I would use," said Matt. "Assimilated, engulfed. For whatever reason, *Homo sapiens* is the most sexually minded creature the world has ever produced."

"Warlike, too," added Susan.

"Yes, and war leads to further interbreeding. The separate subspecies in effect became one. We won by our wiliness in bed, not our wizardry on the battlefield."

The alliteration threw Susan off stride and she paused. "Anyone can trivialize another's theory," she said.

"True. But the point is, if you follow your theory you have to be willing to accept the idea of the bloodiest massacre in history—a Pleistocene holocaust, some have called it. Where are the mass graves? Where are all the skulls with smashed braincases? I find it less taxing on the imagination to believe that the Neanderthal continue, inside each of us."

"I know it's hard to believe—when you look at Dr. Mattison's smooth brow," Susan said sarcastically.

"It took forty thousand years to get it that way. Each of us has a trace of that genetic heritage."

Their eyes met for a moment, and then Susan cut in. "Lately we've come up with some finds that I feel are significant. I'm especially interested in one in Uzbekistan near the Caspian Sea. Two years ago I found a cache of Neanderthal bones. I found them, literally, under my lunch one afternoon; I spilled my coffee on them. I'm still cataloguing them. And although we haven't yet examined them all, it appears that many Neanderthals died together. It could be the remnants of an ancient killing field.

"What makes the site so intriguing is that Neanderthal caves are all around and contain thousands of animal bones. Some are undeniably humanoid. Many of the bones have been split open—painstakingly, as if by a tool. We have reached a conclusion that we feel is inescapable: They were opened for the extraction of the marrow."

Susan paused a beat, to let the significance of what she was saying sink in.

"There are also skulls with a telltale mark of Neanderthal handling: a slight but unmistakable mutilation at the base where the spinal cord enters, at the foramen magnum. Similar mutilations have been found in skulls in Neanderthal caves since at least 1931. No one knew what to make of them. We think we do." She looked around at the group. "Ladies and gentlemen, the evidence appears incontestable: Neanderthal man was a brain eater."

As Van led them out of the room, Matt turned to Susan and said, "A long time."

"Oh, did it seem that long? I thought I was being brief."

He shook his head at her misunderstanding—intentional, an old trick. "Where did you drum up that make-love-not-war line?" he asked.

"I thought you'd like it," she replied. "Old times and all that."

"Do you really believe that stuff about brain eating?"

"Maybe they got carried away with kinky sex."

Matt turned serious. "Susan, what's going on? Do you have any idea what the hell we're doing here?"

Van cut in unceremoniously. "Hold on for another minute and all will become clear." He rolled ahead down an antiseptic corridor.

Susan leaned close to Matt and whispered, "I don't

know any more than you. I simply got a message to come, that it's something to do with Kellicut, and that he's in some kind of danger."

Van stopped before a heavy oak door, knocked, waited for a reply, and entered. The room was unexpectedly dim; it took a few seconds to focus and find the angular figure seated behind a desk along the wall, away from the window, which was blocked by closed blinds. The man was smoking. A cloud hung over his head.

"Ah, come in . . . welcome." The voice was nasal but seductive, authoritative.

They stepped closer. The man behind the desk did not rise but offered a bent hand across the spotless blotter.

"Dr. Arnot, Dr. Mattison. I am Harold Eagleton. Welcome to the Institute for Prehistoric Research."

His tone suggested that he was accustomed to having his name recognized. He held his cigarette in the Eastern European manner, between the thumb and forefinger of his left hand, the other fingers splayed like a fan.

As Matt shook his hand, towering over him, Susan studied Eagleton. He was an extraordinary sight, hunched over, all askew: pale skin, cocked head, tilted steel-rimmed glasses. There was a glint of metal under the desk, the rounded steel and black rubber of a wheelchair. So that was why he seemed sprawled out, caved in like a soufflé. She smelled a peculiar odor she couldn't place. Disinfectant, perhaps.

Eagleton turned to face her. "We're grateful, my dear, that you could come so quickly. Kellicut needs your help, as do we."

"There didn't seem to be a lot of choice," said Matt. "What's it all about?"

Eagleton looked him over. "Well, let's not stand on ceremony, shall we?" He puffed another cloud. "The Institute . . . you've heard of us, yes? Good." It was hard to tell if he was genuinely pleased. "We're involved in many aspects of prehistoric research—many areas. Areas that other institutions might not look into. We have ample funding and we place a strong value on good fieldwork. We have projects around the world and we want nothing but the best. People like Dr. Kellicut. We need them.''

Matt was struck by the wording: need? ''Why do you need them? What do you need them for?''

''Whatever,'' said Eagleton, waving him off.

Matt looked at Susan, who was staring at Eagleton, fascinated. Van sat wordlessly on a sofa. The walls were covered with maps and what appeared to be satellite reconnaissance photographs. A small Degas was in one corner. Matt spotted some framed degrees and plotted the ascent they represented: University of Tennessee, Columbia, Harvard, Edinburgh, St. John's Oxford.

Eagleton followed his gaze. He didn't miss much. ''Ah, the old paper trail,'' he said. ''So meaningless, isn't it?'' He paused reflectively.

''Where was I?'' A cloud of smoke went up. ''Well, we've sponsored quite a few expeditions recently and some have been more . . . orthodox than others. Lately, we've decided to specialize on the Neanderthal—or rather, we've had the decision thrust upon us. We're very keen on it. Interesting stuff. Not all of us had that kind of background, you understand, though we've managed to assemble a neat little stable of experts, as I'm sure you'll—''

''I'm afraid I don't understand,'' Matt cut in. ''Why did you get involved in Neanderthal research? What exactly do you hope to gain?''

Eagleton's tone changed. Now there was a hard edge to it.

''Why . . . why, it could change everything. It could change the whole field, don't you see? Actually, it was your friend Dr. Kellicut who got us involved. He was quite enthusiastic, so we sponsored him. To the Caucasus. It sounded a bit crackpot, really, but one never knows, does one?'' He stubbed out the cigarette, reached under his desk, and flipped a switch. The smoke disappeared through a vent in the ceiling and a slight mist fell. "Antibacteriological agent," he explained. "Hope you don't mind."

"Go on, please," said Susan. "Tell us, where is Dr. Kellicut now?"

"Well, that's just it. We don't know. We know generally, of course, but we don't know specifically. That's where you come in. That's why we need you, to help us find him. It takes a paleoanthropologist to find a paleoanthropologist and all that, you know."

Eagleton appeared agitated. His right hand made an arc through the air and came to rest on his forehead, fingers pointing down. He raked it backward through his hair and rocked slightly. Matt began to wonder if this ditzy professorial air wasn't all just an act.

"I mean, he is where we sent him—or rather, where he wanted to go—with our blessing. The thing is, we had not heard from him for a long time—until recently, that is. Until he sent for you."

"For us!"

"Yes."

"Both of us?"

"Yes. Here is how it came." Eagleton opened his desk drawer and pulled out a flattened piece of brown wrapping paper which had Kellicut's familiar scrawl:

Dr. S. Arnot / Dr. M. Mattison
care of: Institute for Prehistoric Research
1290 Brandywine Lane
Bethesda, MD 09763
USA

"Where's the message?" asked Susan. "Where's the note?"

"It's not a note," said Eagleton, "but I guess you could say it *is* a message. It's what was inside the package." He nodded toward Van, who went to a closet and came back with a square, battered, wooden box about a foot high. He set it in the center of Eagleton's desk, lifted off the top, reached in, and pulled out an object covered with a dirty white cloth.

"This is just the way it came," said Eagleton. He reached over and snapped the cloth away.

Underneath, gleaming and surprisingly white, was a skull. It seemed to grin at them from the center of Eagleton's desk. Van held it up, Hamlet-like. A rush of recognition: that long sloping forehead, the clipped chin, and of course the thick impenetrable band of beetle-shaped bone above the eyes.

"It's perfect!" exclaimed Susan, reaching for it excitedly. She held it in both hands, like a Christmas present. "A perfect specimen. I've never seen one so complete, so well preserved. It's the find of the century!"

Eagleton grunted. "That it is," he said.

"It's almost too perfect," put in Matt. "It looks unreal. Did you date it?"

"Of course," replied Eagleton. He lit another cigarette.

"And?"

"That's the strange part."

"What? How old is it?"

Eagleton puffed. "Twenty-five."

"Twenty-five?" said Matt, incredulous.

"That's impossible," said Susan. Matt shot her a look. "Neanderthal was not alive twenty-five thousand years ago."

"Not twenty-five thousand years," said Eagleton. He was caught up in a sudden fit of coughing so that he could barely wheeze out the words. "Twenty-five years."

He waved at the air, and the smoke cloud over his head undulated.

4

Susan was sleeping lightly next to him. Her head was cocked back slightly, her throat exposed. Her breasts rose and fell with her breathing. He looked at her eyelashes, which trembled from time to time. Maybe she was dreaming.

The other passengers were quiet. Matt could hear the faint whine of the music through her headphones, an insect sound. Blues of some sort, maybe Otis Redding or Coltrane. She used to live by them. An image from the past appeared of a stereo blaring in their funky apartment in Cambridge.

He turned and looked out the window, as the plane's wing tipped, and saw for the first time the snow-covered tops of the Pamirs. The peaks, sharp and jagged sheets of rock, showed through the whiteness like metal piercing through flesh. His heart leaped. Unforgiving terrain, he thought—godless, uninhabitable, and irresistible.

Matt still had not recovered from the shock of seeing the skull. He couldn't bring himself to believe it was twenty-five years old; that was simply too incredible. The idea that a Neanderthal could survive into the twentieth century was something that crackpots had been peddling for years and scientists such as himself had scoffed at them without a second thought. Still, there it was. The thing looked authentic; he had handled enough Neanderthal skulls in his time to know that in an instant. Could it have been doctored, washed clean by an acid bath? Even so, it was too well preserved. It must have been made from scratch with a new type of bone-simulating plaster. But if it was counterfeit, it was perfect. Who would have the knowledge to create it—and why?

Susan was more open to accepting it on face value. On the way to the airport they had disagreed. He had cited famous historical frauds from the Loch Ness monster to the Piltdown Man. "They were convincing in their day, too," he said. But Susan seemed to want to believe it; her eyes were already burning with the possibilities. "What if it's true?" she had said. "Imagine—there may be a whole group of them somewhere, and if we find them we could study them as living beings. We'll no longer be reduced to our pathetic little guesses based upon a chipped stone or a bone fragment. A whole other species and we could make contact with it. Imagine what that would mean."

He had to admit he had felt a thrill when she'd said that. It seemed a fantasy and for a moment he indulged in it. It was farfetched but if he didn't seize this opportunity he might always wonder: Could it have been true? Just to disprove it was reason enough to make the trip. And he had a more immediate purpose—to find Kellicut. For there seemed little doubt that he was missing. And if somebody had gone to all the trouble of perpetrating a hoax, he might well be in danger.

He looked again at Susan. They had not been able to talk about their past. An hour out of Kennedy they ordered stiff drinks: scotch for him, vodka for her. As they touched the rims of their glasses in a wordless toast, leaning closer like conspirators, there had been a moment of something close to intimacy. But the moment passed. Once he tried to steer the conversation back to them, but she resisted firmly, so they had talked of their careers and the more recent past.

"And after Harvard, what?" Matt asked.

"I bounced around, the peripatetic young PhD. I was at Berkeley for three years."

"I heard."

"It was pleasant enough, but I don't know—all that sun, the health food, those people on the right side of all the issues. . . . I began to miss cloudy skies."

Matt smiled.

"I didn't publish much. But Kellicut was a dream. He was really attached to us, you know, and he was upset about us afterward, so he pulled strings for me. I heard about a dig in Iraq and I went. God, it was wonderful: the work, the dust, the hassles, all the little unlooked-for adventures, even the flies.

"At night when the desert got cool, I'd swing myself to sleep in my hammock. I'd look up at this huge dark sky and all the stars and think, *This is it. I want nothing more than this.* But of course I guess I did. Still, the dig was a success. We got the bones. I found my first skull. It was a fragment this big." She held up her thumb and forefinger, four inches apart.

"And then?"

"I went to Madison. I got tenure. More digs, more bones, more papers. Dust to dust. The story of my life." She was leaving out the important parts—on purpose. Amazing how bare-boned a life can sound, she thought.

"And all that time, you never thought of getting married?"

She stiffened. "No, not really."

"Ever come close?"

"Look, Matt"—it was, he realized, the first time she had used his name, and it felt both strange and familiar—"we really don't have to get into all that. There are a lot of other things I'd rather talk about." Her voice lowered. "I haven't asked you about Anne."

"Anne. I haven't seen her for—" he paused to calculate; it was important to be accurate now that they were venturing onto thin ice "—must be thirteen years."

They were silent again. She ordered another drink. Had she conquered her fears about becoming an alcoholic? He asked for another scotch. The stewardess flirted with him, ignoring Susan and looking playfully into his eyes.

And so there it was—no soul-baring confessions, no emotional catharsis. Maybe it was just as well, thought Matt; on one level he wanted it, but on another he feared it. How could he explain what had happened and how he had felt back then? It was so long ago. He was never good with words when it counted. He was, he had to admit, relieved.

Susan preferred it that way, too. She had been thrown by the shock of seeing Matt and by not being able to prepare herself. It was so different from the hundreds of chance encounters she had played out in her daydreams. He was still handsome, she thought sadly. But how strange to see flecks of gray on those familiar temples. At least he had not gotten fat; some of her vindictive fantasies had turned him obese, and the thought had made her feel triumphant. But reality was different; she was glad his midriff was still cowboy lean. But mostly she felt distressed to find that he was still such a presence, that her mind's eye was always watching him when he was around.

It had taken years to get over his betrayal. The feelings had not so much disappeared as become covered by the accumulated flotsam of daily life. Her friends had tired of listening, so she eventually stopped talking about him. She pushed the feelings inside until finally she began to confine them to one corner. She went on to other places and had other lovers, but every so often the feelings would rise up, and in those moments she would feel the pain all over again, though not as strongly as before. Now she knew that for the sake of some core part of her, she had to keep a distance.

Susan had put on her headphones and settled into her seat. Her skirt rose up on her thighs as she slumped down. Matt sat, sipping his drink and looking out the window.

        *   *   *

Van was plowing through a stack of papers. Manila folders piled on the seat next to him slid from side to side as the plane rocked. He always worked this way, compulsively. Maybe that's why he was such a good scientist and so good on missions. He always overdid it, reading, studying, figuring all the angles. He was proud of his record—it was one of the few things he *could* be proud of. His work was his life, and there was little room for anything else.

Van had felt superior for as long as he could remember, even as a boy. There were always kids who were bigger, better-looking, faster. They grew into men who were the same, guys like Matt, who made everything look easy, who just sopped it all up without even trying. With Van it was different. He had to struggle for every little crumb. Nothing came to him easily. But he had one advantage: He was smart—smarter than all of them—and he could figure the angles.

His mother had died under strange circumstances when he was four, something about a gas-stove explosion. It was never fully explained to him, certainly not by his father, a distant and bitter man who was an army officer. Van never remembered sitting on his lap or touching him, not once. Mostly he remembered his pockmarked face, the haircut with the band of skin above the ears, the hot smell of his breath. Van and his younger brother were military brats. They moved around a lot. Their father would go ahead and after a month or two send for them. They would take the train. Once on the train from Fort Dix to Fort Bragg they were so nervous about missing the stop they took turns staying awake at night to read the station signs. When they arrived, their father barely spoke to them.

Then Van discovered science. He began with mathematics, where he found the order cleansing to his spirit, and moved on to chemistry and physics. In college he discovered the social sciences—less certain than the natural sciences but more attractive because they presupposed the manipulation of human behavior. He fell under the spell of experimental psychology and, at Chicago, the behaviorists. He ran rats through mazes and operated on them and ran them again. He climbed up the evolutionary scale, reaching monkeys and then people, working with brain-damaged patients at VA hospitals. The techniques were all the same, he joked, "a bit of cheese at one end, electric shock at the other." A taste for the cutting edge led him to the emerging field of psycholingualism.

Van didn't go in for the domestic life. He wasn't cut out for it. He didn't have many relationships. He was always on the go and he liked his work, which kept him hopping and appealed to his loner streak. He enjoyed being on the inside, knowing things other people didn't. And he was good at it, even if he didn't get enough credit from Eagleton, a difficult man to work for.

This was a strange one, this Neanderthal expedition. He didn't know enough, didn't feel comfortable with it, but it could be the one he was waiting for, the one that was— what? His destiny, he thought, if that's not too corny a word.

"Mind?" said Matt, pointing to the seat next to Van.

Van grunted, but he closed the file before him, and looked out the window at the mountains. Below were sheer rock faces and pristine snow bridges.

"Probably the most unexplored land in the entire world," said Matt. "Look at it. You wonder how anything could survive there."

"It couldn't—not if it's human."

Matt looked past Van at the peaks and recalled information on the Pamirs he had lifted from a gazetteer last week: seven or eight separate ranges in the uncharted terrain of Kashmir, Afghanistan, and the remote Central Asian republics of what once was the Soviet Union. Known through the ages as the "roof of the world"—not so much for the height of its mountains, which were indeed high, but for the hidden uplands of its valleys, plains, and lakes. The first to use the word Pamir was the Chinese Buddhist monk Hsüan Tsang, who crossed from Badakhshan to Tashkurghan in the seventh century. But it was Marco Polo who best described it as a forbidding labyrinth of mountains and glaciers, moraines heaped with scree, and hidden valleys filled with deposits of lapis lazuli.

"On the other hand," said Matt, "if something did survive there, it would be hidden from the outside world for years."

"Decades. Centuries." Van turned back abruptly from the window. "You know, there was a hidden village somewhere lower down there. Leztinecia. It was totally cut off. It existed for who knows how long—seventy, a hundred years. No contact with the outside world. It was discovered in 1926 by a Russian expedition. The villagers had reverted to barbarism. They had almost lost the use of fire. The scientists who found them were treated like gods and were given everything the villagers had. They went to sleep one night, and do you know what happened?"

"What?" Matt asked.

"In the morning, when they opened the doors of their hut, they found two dead children on their doorstep. They had been slaughtered."

"Why?"

"The whole village had done it. It wasn't clear whose children they were. You could hardly try them for breaking laws they had never heard of." He chuckled. "Sacrifice to the gods is one of the oldest instincts in human history."

"And the village?"

"The usual story. Wiped out by disease. Some of them wandered off or intermarried with outsiders. The rest perished. They were probably doomed anyway. Face it, any culture that puts its children to death isn't taking the long view."

They fell silent. Then Van said awkwardly, "You know, I've read your work."

"You have?"

"Uh-huh. *The New England Journal of Archaeology, The Fossil Review,* the lot. I even read *Neanderthals: Killers or Kissing Cousins?*"

Matt didn't often encounter people who read the esoteric journals and obscure publications that carried his articles, and he had always been slightly embarrassed at his title for that book, a concession to a sales-struck and ultimately disappointed editor. He noticed that Van had not complimented him on any of it.

Van asked him what he was currently working on, and Matt said he was examining the morphology of the Neanderthal vocal tract, specifically the pharynx.

"Why?" asked Van.

"It might turn out to be primitive. From this we could deduce that his speech was limited. He probably couldn't say certain consonants—a *g,* for instance, or a *k.* His vocalic range was stunted."

"And where does all this lead?"

"Too early to tell, but here's the theory in a nutshell: Language is the essence of thinking. It's both the cradle and the gate of intelligence. The Neanderthal didn't have full linguistic ability, so his capacity for abstract thought never developed. As social interaction became more and more important for survival, he lost out. In activities like a group hunt, where communication and anticipatory thinking are crucial, he was unable to cope. He fell by the wayside."

"Doomed to extinction for want of a proper epiglottis?" sneered Van.

"Something like that," replied Matt defensively.

"You've got problems, professor."

"Like what?"

"You're overreaching," said Van. "For one thing, communication can occur with very limited vocalization. We know of tribes in New Guinea and the Amazon that survive very nicely with languages based on no more than twelve distinct sounds."

''For another?''

''For another, why should abstract thinking correlate with a multiplicity of sounds? Or why should the complexity of language, for that matter? We intuit this to be true, but we might be mistaken. And then of course there's a third possibility, and that's the most interesting of all.''

''What?''

''Communication beyond sound.''

''You mean ESP?''

''Or something like it. I don't like the term. It presupposes that perception not conducted through our senses is extraordinary.''

''Well, isn't it?'' asked Matt.

''Obviously I don't think so, or I wouldn't have devoted my life to it.''

''So that's your field?''

''Yes. I may not be a hotshot professor at the University of Chicago like you, but I do have a doctorate. I don't need to be lectured to like an undergraduate.''

''Sorry. I didn't mean to do that.''

Matt was intrigued by what Van had said and tried to draw him out, but Van refused to discuss his latest research. ''It's not publishable,'' was all he said.

There was an awkward silence; then Van said, ''Let me ask something.''

''Go on.''

''Why haven't you ever postulated that Neanderthals may still exist?''

''Because the possibility is so remote it's absurd.''

''Oh, yeah? How can you be so sure?''

Van was almost snarling as he said this. What an odd piece of work, thought Matt. So maladroit. For someone who so clearly was intelligent, the man exploded in bursts of irrationality.

Now Van was lecturing and he was enjoying it. There were, he said, an estimated fourteen million species on the earth of which only one point seven million—less than fifteen percent—had been identified and classified. New species turned up all the time. Over the last hundred years, an average of five hundred were discovered every decade up until the 1920s; now it was about one hundred a decade.

"And I'm not talking about two-bit mammals," he said. "I'm talking about big game. The snub-nosed langur, the African pygmy chimpanzee. Ever heard of *Meganuntiacus vuquangensis*? Of course not. It's a rather large deer. *Pseudoryx nghetinhensis*? An oxlike thing. They were both discovered in Laos—in 1994. A French expedition in Tibet came across a four-foot-high ancient breed of horse in 1995. It looked like it leaped right out of a cave painting.

"New species turn up all the time. The meat is found in a local market; a new hide with strange stripes is spotted on some native's chest. Last century nobody believed in the mountain gorilla even though there were a lot of tales about it, because no one had seen it. Only about three thousand Africans had."

He recalled the giant panda in western Szechwan, which was hunted seventy years before one was captured. "It always happens the same way. Myth and rumor come first. People don't believe it until they see it with their own eyes. Then suddenly there it is, and afterward nobody even remembers we disbelieved. It seems ridiculous to have discounted it. It's all hubris. We think of ourselves as the chosen ones, the supreme beings on the whole planet. We think we own the place, but we don't know the first thing about it.

"Take the earth's surface, subtract the oceans, then the deserts, mountains, and arctic regions. You know what you're left with? About twenty percent. We inhabit one fifth of the globe and we think we're everywhere, that there's no room left for anyone else. We can't even imagine competitors. But it's just as preposterous to think we're the only hominid on earth as it is to think that earth is the only planet in the universe with life on it."

Now Matt felt like an undergraduate and he didn't like

it, either. "Wait a minute," he protested. "We may not
live everywhere, but we sure as hell *travel* everywhere. If
we have competitors, why don't we ever encounter them?"

"For the same reason that most Americans don't encounter Indians."

"Meaning?"

"It's a natural law. The victors expel the vanquished and
make them invisible. They push them into the least desir-
able areas: the desert where nothing can grow, the scrub-
lands, the arctic. The same reason the Eskimos—you
probably call them Inuit—keep moving farther and farther
north."

"But we do see the native Americans and the Inuit."

"Yes, but now imagine if your vanquished group is not
just another tribe or race but actually a whole different subspecies. Practically wiped out. Think of this poor, pathetic
dispossessed minority, down to a handful. And what if they
were scared and, God knows, had a reason to be scared,
wouldn't they make damn sure to stay out of sight?
Wouldn't they turn and run at the first sign of the dominant
species, the dreaded enemy?

"Take it a step further. What if this particular minority
had some special adaptive feature? For instance, like the
Neanderthal, able to survive in climates where we would
freeze to death in minutes. Wouldn't that further reduce the
likelihood of contact—at least, contact on any significant
scale?"

Matt listened in silence.

"Look," continued Van. "I don't know who's right, you
or Arnot. Maybe there was a genocidal war or maybe we
bred them out of existence. Either way, it's easy to imagine
some of them living on. Like those Japanese soldiers surviving in the jungle. If there was a war and some kind of
apocalyptic victory, what's to prevent a small band from
retreating? Even if it's a question of living in caves and
sitting around a fire recounting the dark days of their defeat
over and over, generation after generation.

"Or how about a group that resists assimilation, that simply moves away. It preserves the purity of the subspecies by turning its back on the mainstream of evolution. Hermits. A relic band living high up in the mountains where almost no one goes. From time to time they spot one of us coming around a bend. The word goes out—an interloper!—and they retreat higher, their world shrinking even more. But at least they're undiscovered, still safe. You know, even today we're uncovering new tribes in the Amazon—and people go there. People don't go into the high Pamirs.''

Matt saw Susan stirring five rows ahead. "Okay," he said. "Say there is this relic band, this . . . parallel species. Why do they always spot us? Why don't we ever spot them? I mean, one Neanderthal wandering down a path . . . somewhere. . . . Even the law of averages—''

"Oh, c'mon, pro-fessor!'' Van drew the title out sarcastically, like an insult. "What do you think got us here? What do you think is in all these folders?'' He picked up a handful and opened one. "People *have* spotted them. They've just misidentified them.''

Matt glanced down and saw printed pages, italicized descriptions, dates, maps. He flipped through one and came to a compilation of news stories, dozens of pages of them. He picked one at random from *The Hong Kong Record*, 1948:

CHINOZCHIA, Dec. 12—Dr. Peter Armstrong and his crew of three assistants returned from an inland excursion with news of a startling discovery, a six-foot-tall wild man completely covered with long red hair. Dr. Armstrong said he encountered the beast on a path near a stream. . . .

He flipped the pages. There were scores of others, in English, French, German, Chinese.

"These reports aren't new, professor. They go way back

in history. Medieval manuscripts are riddled with references to strange wild men living outside civilization. How are you on Roman authors? Lucretius, *De Rerum Natura:* He described them perfectly, a primitive race, built upon larger and more solid bones within.' Check out Pliny and you'll find the Blemmyes, who lived in the Libyan desert. He carried a club and his head was actually on the top of his chest, which is pretty much the way a Neanderthal would look if you stumbled on one dead ahead of you while out for an evening walk.

"If you want a historical record, it's all there," said Van. "Sightings galore. Hundreds of them, all over the place, by all kinds of people. You just have to be aware of them, all these little two-inch stories in little newspapers every few years. You have to spot the relationships. The dots are there; you just have to connect them."

He selected a folder and spun its pages through the air so closely that Matt felt the breeze. "I don't care what you call it. Bigfoot. Sasquatch in America. Yeti in Tibet. Alma in the Tarbagati. Chuchunaa in the Verkhoyansk—"

"Wait a minute," Matt cut in. "You mean to tell me these are all Neanderthals? Yesterday it was hard enough to believe they're in Outer Mongolia. Now you expect me to believe they're in Washington State?"

"Of course not." Van shifted his tone, as if he were reasoning with a recalcitrant child. "Look. I'm not saying these are all Neanderthals, far from it. I *am* saying there's a notable similarity between all these sightings and descriptions of large hairy primates living above the snow line. It goes beyond the laws of probability or coincidence. Almost every country has stories that are told around campfires late at night about strange creatures, and for some odd reason these creatures are almost always the same. What does that tell you?"

"Maybe they're just legends."

"Maybe—in fact undoubtedly. That's my point. C'mon, remember your Taylor? Your Rosenthal? *The Significance of Folklore. The Realm of the Unreal and the Collective Psyche.* We both know that legends have meaning. They don't simply leap into existence spontaneously. They are a means of communication across generations and for coming to terms with something. And these are universal legends, legends that appear all over the world—with local variations, of course. So they are likely to incorporate an objective reality that actually happened. Origin myths. The flood. Why does the flood appear in dozens of cultures? Because it is historical fact. It just occurred before history was written.

"The sightings of these creatures are everywhere. That means that the myth is everywhere, and that should tell you it's based on a reality."

"All right," Matt said. "Let me grant you that for a minute. Maybe the reality happened, but maybe it was a long time ago—thousands of years, tens of thousands— kept alive in our collective unconscious."

"Ah, that's where we move from legend to evidence. Scientific evidence."

"Okay, give me the evidence."

Van smiled an oily smile. "On the simplest level, there are footprints. Not one, not five, not a dozen. Scores and scores. One hundred and seventy-one authenticated, to be exact. Many more questionable." He opened a folder and flipped the pages sideways so that Matt could see them. There was page after page of photographs, drawings, maps, and diagrams—a book of nothing but footprints. Most were large and flat, with a curiously distended big toe. Many had wooden rulers placed alongside. There were also photographs of the discoverers, holding up giant white casts or pointing to the ground. Most seemed to be strange-looking men and women with pinched features, mismatched clothes, triumphant, fanatical smiles.

Matt stopped at one page. It was the genuine article: an imprint from a known Neanderthal cave in Tuscany. He compared it to the others. They were virtually identical. For comparison there was the footprint of a modern human, three quarters the size.

"There are a lot of other things. Clumps of hair. Many of them are reddish, at least those found in China. A lot of it is found on the trunks of trees about four or five feet high."

"Scratching their backs, no doubt," said Matt. He was being ironic, but Van missed his tone.

"Then there's feces—all kinds of feces."

"Spare me the photos."

"But most compelling are the sightings. There were one hundred sixty in the Caucasus alone between 1923 and 1951. Most have been by illiterate villagers, so they're not taken seriously. There are not so many recently—in fact, damned few. It's possible that they are beginning to disappear there."

"Why, if there are so many of these things wandering around, hasn't anyone captured one? Or found a dead one someplace?"

"Funny you should ask." Van handed over another folder. Inside were photostats from a book by Myra Shackley, a British academic, describing numerous encounters, including several in which the manlike beast was killed.

Matt looked at Van. Physically this strange man with his broad square forehead, hair that stuck out burrlike on the sides, and hooded eyes did not make a pleasing impression, but something about him was formidable.

"I'm not trying to proselytize," Van continued. "Like I said, I don't care if you believe it or not. All I'm saying is you should be open to it, because if the major argument against their existence is that there's no evidence, the argument is incorrect. There's a great deal of evidence."

"If it's all there, as you say, how come no one but you and a few other nuts have heard of it?"

Van gripped the armrest. "You really want to know?" he asked after a moment.

"Of course."

"Because it's disreputable. It's crackpot. It goes against the grain. Do you have any idea how vicious the scientific establishment—guys like you—can be when something threatening comes along? It's like any bureaucracy with a vested interest in the status quo, only worse. If a new theory surfaces that contradicts accepted wisdom, it's shot down—*bang!*—as soon as it's picked up on the radar. God forbid it should penetrate and get through to the masses!

"If it's only mildly threatening, it's subjected to ridicule. Journals weigh in, academics scoff, the popular press writes funny stories. But if it's something truly revolutionary like this, they play hardball and it gets the full treatment. Careers are ruined, people are run out of town, nothing appears in print. No one wants to look foolish."

"Okay," said Matt. "I'll grant you there's resistance to something new. That's true in any field. But if evidence accumulates and becomes convincing, then the new theory or whatever it is gets a hearing."

"Let me tell you a story. In 1906 a Russian explorer named Badzare Baradiyan was leading an expedition across the desert of the Alachan. One night when the caravan stopped at dusk they saw a hairy creature standing on a hill of sand. They pursued it. It got away. But they had all seen it, close up, for certain. The observation created a stir back home, but when Baradiyan wrote up his official report of the expedition, the president of the Imperial Russian Geographical Society made him suppress the incident. The president, no less! And he did. Why? I'm sure if he were here today he could give you any number of reasons. But that sighting was by far the most significant event of the expedition.

"The point of the story is the way the establishment reacted—the way it always reacts. It prefers to blot out something for which it has no ready explanation. It's an old story, older than Galileo. Science will turn to superstition and torture to defend its right to be wrong."

"But ultimately," said Matt, "the theories that don't

hold up are junked. It all comes back to evidence.''

"And I say the evidence is there but is disregarded."
Van gestured to the mound of files. "And of course you've
seen some of the evidence firsthand, even handled it. The
skull."

Matt took in the last point. He let the fantasy play out a
moment. What if there really was another species as yet
undiscovered, a relic band living in a region uninhabitable
to humans? Suddenly anything seemed possible. He imagined the three of them working together, him, Kellicut and
Susan. They would see things no other human had seen,
answer questions deemed unanswerable, publish works that
would astound the world. It would not just change what we
know about the Neanderthal, Matt thought; it would change
what we know about ourselves. Van had mentioned Galileo. This would be greater than his view through the telescope.

Reality intruded. The larger part of him, the scientific
part, still could not conceive of their existence, but he had
to admit his resistance was beginning to crumble.

The stewardess came by with an unasked-for free scotch
and smiled as she placed it on Matt's tray. He handed her
the empty glass. "Tell me something," he said. "Why did
Kellicut send that package to us?"

"We can only assume he knew you would know what
to do."

"Why didn't he tell us? Why all these games?"

Van was silent.

"And why no note?"

"Can't help you there."

Van was quiet for a spell and then spoke slowly. "I think
you got the message he wanted you to get. After all, here
you are." He turned to look out the window again. "And
we're looking for the goddamned thing."

"I thought we were looking for Kellicut."

"For him too. We're looking for both."

Matt finished his drink. He saw the top of Susan's head

move, and with a grunt he rose and moved up the aisle. She was stretching her arms ahead, looking tousled, sleepy, and momentarily perplexed. As she saw him, she smiled openly for the first time.

Her shoes were off. Matt looked at her feet, bound in black stockings. They seemed so dainty, so perfectly formed with smooth curves and sculpted arches, compared to the photographs of the footprints he had just seen.

5

Matt and Susan's suspicions grew as they entered Tajikistan. The trip had been rigorous; the jet made a bumpy landing in Dushanbe on its second try. The country was newly independent and embroiled in civil war. Adolescent olive-skinned soldiers with Mongol cheekbones dozed on metal chairs in camouflage uniforms, their AK-47s pointing listlessly to the ground.

The customs officials, who wore sparkling new insignias on old uniforms, examined everything in their luggage, more out of curiosity than anything else, and handled Matt's small tape recorder and Susan's cassette player with reverence. Then they hauled Van into a back room, where he got into an argument. The shouting could be heard through the closed door.

"He's got a gun," said Susan.

"What? How do you know?"

"I recognize the case, all the markings on it. I don't like it."

"Neither do I," answered Matt.

"I never heard of a scientist who carried a gun."

Matt tried to calm her fears. "Then again, I've never heard of an expedition like this."

"What is he, some kind of big-game hunter? Is he going to blast his way out?"

"He's a cowboy. You know the type."

"A cowboy with Ray-Bans. But there's something peculiar about him—I can't put my finger on it."

"I know what you mean," replied Matt. "He's definitely unorthodox. I've read some of his articles and I listened to him on the plane. He's a real believer in the paranormal and he doesn't entertain any doubts."

"I still wonder why Kellicut didn't write to us directly if he wanted us to come."

"Maybe he didn't know where to reach us," replied Matt. "I know he didn't have my address. We've been out of touch for some time."

"Maybe. But what was he doing with these guys? You know what a snob he is. You saw the people in that room. None of them were first rate except for Schwartzbaum and he's been off the scope lately. Most of the others are pretty far out."

"I wonder about the whole Institute. Why is it affiliated with some junior college no one's ever heard of?"

Susan pondered his question. "I've even considered the possibility that we've fallen in with some kind of a cult—that I've gone and left my research and risked my reputation for a chimera. But the truth is, it doesn't matter who they are. If they're on to something, the prize is too great to let slip away because of the risk of being wrong."

"I think if we keep our eyes open and are careful, we can follow our own agenda and do what we have to do," said Matt.

Van emerged, carrying the case under his arm. It had some new stamps and red labels on it. "Amazing what a little baksheesh can do." He grinned.

"What kind of gun is it?" asked Matt.

"Three-forty-five magnum."

"What's it for?"

"Insurance."

"Goddamned big insurance."

From Dushanbe they caught a small prop plane that carried them high into the foothills. Goats stood in the aisle tethered to the armrests. A stewardess in a veil passed out hard candy. The plane circled the airstrip, which was an asphalt runway in the middle of a meadow, and landed with a series of bounces like a skipping stone.

When they stepped outside, the altitude seemed to suck the breath from their lungs. They were met by Rudy, their guide and factotum, a Russian whose services had been contracted for in advance. He waited at the gate, waving as soon as he saw them, then rushed over, pumping their hands and scooping up their backpacks so that from behind, staggering toward the Land Cruiser, he looked Chaplinesque.

"Please, this way, miss. This way," he shouted over one shoulder.

Rudy was a big man with an open face and a boxer's nose. His blond hair hung down over his ears and his hands were immense. Susan liked him on sight. She sat next to him as he drove wildly, clutching the wheel with both hands, elbows raised like chicken wings. The car careered from side to side as he shouted observations above the thumping engine, moving his head up and down with violent enthusiasm and peering into the rearview mirror for eye contact with Matt and Van.

Rudy swept a hairy forearm across the windshield, a dismissive gesture that took in the boulders, stubby clumps of brown grass, and barren pockmarked hills. "In my country we have real trees. Not these stupid little things. And grass. You feel it in your toes. Cows that give real milk. Radishes as big as . . ." He was stumped.

"Your fist," said Susan.

". . . your fist. And water. In the rivers all the time. Not this crazy flooding when the snow melts and then nothing. All this yes-and-no."

"So why did you come here?"

He shrugged. "Life is funny." He sketched his background. His father built a dam over the Kzazhastak, married a Tajik, and became a functionary in the diplomatic corps. They went to New York City. Rudy went to a public high school. "On the East Side. Julia Richmond. 1976."

"No!"

"Yes, yes, I promise. I learned so much. I learned English. I learned new books. I learned new music. I learned the meaning of this." Susan laughed. Matt leaned forward to peer over the seat. Rudy was holding his right hand on its back, the middle finger extended straight up.

"Songs. I know every song that year. Top ten. WABC. Give us twenty minutes, we give you the world." He began singing a chorus of "Don't Go Breaking My Heart," thickly accented and badly off-key. Van groaned, but even he seemed to enjoy the zany spontaneity.

Rudy was driving them to a hotel for the night, where they would meet Kellicut's guide, the last person to see him alive.

"Tell us everything you know about the mountain men," Van demanded abruptly.

"The Tajiks around here have a lot of stories about them. They call them Alma or sometimes Czechkai. That means the snow livers—not livers, snow dwellers. No one actually sees them. Or no one I've met. But you know, because I am a Russian, they do not really trust me. They do not like to talk about it. They just open their eyes wide. I can't always get what they say.

"People believe in them, that's for sure. Some claim even to have traded with them. They go up high in the mountains and leave salt and sugar and beads and things in a certain place. Then they go back after a week or two and the salt is gone, but there are animal skins in the same place, bear, rabbit, that kind of thing."

Van interjected. "Who does this? Did you talk to anyone who did this?"

Rudy said he had not, and no one could actually tell him

where the trading spot was. He was not even sure the story was true.

"Sometimes people disappear if they go way above the snow line. They vanish without a trace. When this happens everybody gets upset. They light candles and blame the Czechkai. Some say it is getting worse, that it happens more and more. No one knows why. I talked to one father who had a son who disappeared. The boy went way up in the mountains hunting. He did this all the time, and then one day he did not return. They searched for him and some say they found his body without the head. But who knows? The father will not talk about it.

"There is a lot of superstition among these people. If you say that word, Czechkai, people do not like it. Children run away. It is like that monster in America. What do you call it? The one grown-ups threaten their children with?"

"The bogeyman," replied Susan.

"What?"

"He's the monster who hides under little children's beds."

"Well, it is a lot like that."

The road became rutted with potholes, the sign of an approaching village. Matt turned to Susan, his voice animated. "Do you know where we are? What town we're in?" She shook her head. "I saw it on a signpost. We're in Khodzant!"

It took a while for the name to register. "You mean," she asked, "as in the Khodzant Enigma?"

"The very same."

"I'll be damned!"

"What's the Khodzant Enigma?" asked Rudy.

Van answered. "It's a pictograph of some kind. Thought to be old. But nobody knows how old because the original's disappeared. A portion of it was missing and it's never been deciphered."

"And it comes from here?" Rudy asked.

"Apparently, unless there's more than one Khodzant."

Matt was surprised. A handful of archaeologists knew about the Enigma but not many others. "How do you know all that?" he asked Van.

"I keep up with these things. You never know when they might come in handy."

The car turned through narrow streets past houses of stone and mortar and into a courtyard. The single word HOTEL was written in faded blue paint over an arched door.

Rudy was the first out of the car, already barking orders to a boy who opened the hotel gate. He led them in to register at a narrow wooden counter. The owner, a man with a fez, black eyebrows, and few teeth, wore a DUKE sweatshirt with a blue devil over his heart. He had never seen American passports and fingered the pages slowly before showing them to their rooms.

Dinner, a passable stew, was helped by the flow of vodka that Rudy provided. Whenever a glass was emptied, he leaned over with his long arm to fill it to the brim.

Afterward they adjourned to the bar, a small cavern decorated with a tangle of vines and plants growing out of upended cinder blocks. The owner entered with a tray of china coffee cups and whispered something in Rudy's ear: The boy who had served as Kellicut's guide had arrived.

He stepped into the room. About thirteen or fourteen years old, with pure black hair and watery brown eyes that took them in one by one, he was wearing a loose blouse, a robe, and sneakers.

Van started to talk but Susan cut him off. She walked over to the boy and took his hand in a firm grip, smiling. He squeezed it and shook it solemnly, then bowed.

"This is Sharafidin," said Rudy.

The others shook his hand. After each handshake, he bowed.

Rudy motioned for the boy to sit but he remained standing. They exchanged a few words in Persian, and then the boy began his narrative easily and without hesitation, in a steady stream. Finally Rudy signaled to him to pause while he translated.

"He says the Teacher—that's what he calls your Mr. Kellicut—came here many months ago. That he stayed right here in this hotel. People did not know what he wanted or why he was here. Many people did not talk to him, but they were curious so bit by bit they began to speak. He talked in Persian, not very good Persian."

While Rudy was speaking, the boy was staring at Susan and she looked back at him.

"Gradually people got accustomed to him. He took long walks. Up in the foothills, sometimes into the mountains. He knew medicine and cured some people. Bit by bit, houses opened to him. One evening he came to our house for dinner. We slaughtered a goat. He gave a gift to my father, a beautiful plate. It has a picture of a woman on it, a statue of a huge woman holding up a fire and a book, with water all around. It says New York City. My father liked it so much he hung it over our oven."

Van interrupted. "What did your father tell him about the Alma?" Rudy translated. The boy did not understand. When Rudy tried again, the boy looked away.

"He says he was not there," said Rudy.

"Go on," Matt said gently.

This time the boy talked for a long time. Rudy encouraged him by nodding slowly every so often. He recounted how one day the Teacher revealed his desire to go up into the mountains to see the Alma for himself and how they had tried repeatedly to dissuade him.

"So one night my father said, 'If you must go, you must. But I tell you to take my first son.'" It was, he said, his father's way of ensuring the Teacher's safety. Then the boy described the preparations and the ascent—days and days of climbing. "One day we reached a point where even the trees did not go. There we built our hut. Every day we took walks, higher and higher. Wherever we went the Teacher studied the ground. Then we set up camp. At night it was freezing. I had this little bed that he made for me but I was still cold.

"The Teacher began to go off alone. He would not let me come. He took long walks. Then he was gone overnight, and then for a long time. Days and days. He would come back and write. He was acting strange. He sometimes talked to himself out loud. Then he got sick and trembled. He was very weak. He got better and went away again. Again he stayed away a long time.

"We did not have much food left. I would have to go lower on the mountain and catch rabbits and birds and bring them back. I do not know if the Teacher came back while I was gone. I looked for his tracks. Sometimes I saw them.

"Then the Teacher did come back. He looked bad. He seemed different. He did not pay me much attention. It was as if he did not know me. He talked a lot out loud, but in that other language so I could not understand what he was saying.

"We had almost no food, but he would not leave. I asked him why and he would not tell me. He talked a lot about the Alma. I asked him what he meant. He laughed more. He was gone for longer and longer.

"One day I came back from hunting and he was there. His beard was long now. He was very excited. He said I must go home and take something with me. He gave me a box. It was heavy and had writing on it. He said I was to give it to my father and my father was to mail it right away. So I did."

"Then did you go back?" asked Susan.

Rudy translated and the boy shook his head.

"Did you see him again?"

Again he shook his head.

"Did you see the Alma yourself?" asked Matt.

"No." The boy bit his lip and spoke slowly. "Once I looked for the Teacher's tracks and I did not find them, but I saw other tracks. Bigger ones."

They all exchanged looks. Rudy took a swig of vodka. "Any more questions?"

"Ask him," said Matt, "if he opened the package."

Van looked up darkly. The boy said no, then looked at Susan and said something. Rudy barked back a reply.

"What did he say?" asked Susan.

"Nothing, miss. It is not important."

"I want to know what he said."

"He wants to know if you and the Teacher know each other."

"Know each other?"

"His exact question. . . . I do not get it. It means nothing, I am sure."

Van looked perplexed. "What the hell does he want to know that for?" he asked.

"Tell him yes," said Susan.

"I don't get it," said Rudy.

"He's trying to work out who we are." Susan's tone was brusque.

When Rudy relayed the answer, the boy looked at Susan and then, bowing all around, backed out of the room.

Outside, dusk was falling. Susan sat with her back to the window, her dark skin glistening in the candlelight, her eyes black caverns. Fiddling with the wax, she spoke in a measured tone. "So tell me, Van, what's the plan?"

"At least we know where to start," said Van. "The camp."

"And I gather Sharafidin will take us there?" said Susan.

"All arranged," replied Van.

"Is there anything else that's all arranged? Any other surprises?" Susan asked.

"Not if I can help it."

"So we go to Kellicut's camp," said Matt. "Then what?"

There was a silence. Finally Van answered. "Then we

play it by ear. We see what we can find. We look for a message. We look for tracks.''

"And if we don't find anything?"

"That's where you two come in. You know him and you know what he was looking for. Maybe you try to duplicate his actions, think the way he thought, do what he did, go where he went. Like I said, we play it by ear.''

"How about the gun, Van?" asked Matt. "What are you planning to do with that?"

"Nothing, if I can help it.''

"So why do you have it?" Susan asked.

"In case we need it.''

"Do you have any reason to think we will?" she continued.

"Look, we have no idea what we're going to find up there.''

Matt spoke up. "Are we looking for this thing or are we stalking it?''

"Dammit, you heard the kid. People have been disappearing up there. You want to go try your mumbo-jumbo anthropology bullshit, go right ahead. Pull out your tape recorder and record their innermost thoughts. See how far that gets you. Not me.''

"Just remember, we're scientists, not hunters.''

"Yeah, but I'm coming back in one piece.''

Van was worried: Maybe they're spooked, he thought. Maybe they're going to back out.

They sat in silence in the growing darkness, and suddenly there was little to say. Abruptly Susan pushed her chair back, stood up, murmured some words of good night, and walked off. Matt got up and followed her.

Matt and Susan walked to a teahouse set in a square that was blazing with light. A dozen men were at metal tables scattered across a patio, sipping green tea, smoking dark tobacco, and talking quietly in a singsong drone. Some sat cross-legged next to raised beds covered with Bukharan carpets, playing checkers. Turkish music came out of a lighted doorway. The men looked at Matt and Susan with undisguised curiosity.

They took a table and ordered coffee by pointing.

"Look at that," Susan said, nodding into the distance across the square. There, just above the darkened wall of buildings, was a full moon. It hung in the sky as if it were resting on the roofs, so clear that the gray-pocked craters stood out like spots on a ripe peach.

"Jesus," Matt said. "Nothing like that old moon over . . ."

". . . Khodzant."

"Khodzant. No wonder nothing makes any sense. Ever since we got here I've felt like a riddle wrapped in an enigma, or whatever that expression is."

Susan smiled. "Just think, somewhere up in the mountains our little hominid is probably looking at the moon too."

"Probably howling at it."

"Now, now."

"What?"

"There you go again," said Susan, "assuming they're not civilized."

"What's uncivilized about howling? I do it all the time."

"Which merely proves my point. Anyway, you're the guy who's supposed to believe they're just as good as we are."

"Not as good—equal, compatible."

"And sexy."

"C'mon, I never said that," Matt protested.

"Well, you certainly implied it. Why else would we have fallen for them in a frenzy of . . . what did you call it?"

"Reproductive imperialism?"

"Right, reproductive imperialism. And what's that other term you popularized? All my kids drop it into their exams."

"Gene flow," he said.

"Gene flow, that's it. Good phrase. It sounds like an ad for Calvin Klein."

"Very funny. How about you? Where did you latch on to all this warfare business? Hunting, scouting, running people off cliffs. And this nonsense about brain-eating. I thought that went out with Alberto Blanc in the fifties. Do you really believe that?"

"I don't necessarily believe it," she replied defensively. "I'm open to it."

"Where's the proof?"

"It's not a matter of proof. Just indications. All those skull holes."

"Maybe there's another explanation."

"Yeah, maybe they were machine-gunned."

He looked for the waiter.

"Matt, can I ask you something? In all seriousness."

"Go ahead."

She paused a beat. "While we were together, did you ever have an affair with a Neanderthal girl?"

He laughed. She could still surprise him. "She wouldn't have me. She said my arms were too short and my brow was too flat. Why do you ask?"

"Oh, just curious. I thought maybe your theory about all that sex and cross-breeding was, you know, extrapolation based upon personal experience."

"I see, Susan. As was yours about warfare."

The waiter arrived with two demitasse cups of Turkish coffee and bustled about intrusively, taking his time, turning the cups so that the handles pointed to the right. Susan remained silent until he left, then put on a look of puzzlement. "*Homo sapiens sapiens.* You know, I always wondered how we rated two sapienses."

"The answer's simple."

"What is it?"

"You said it yourself. We're the ones doing the naming."

"The pure arrogance of it."

"Why, what would you call us?"

"How about something like *Homo duplicitous*?" She thought for a second. "Actually, the one that sums up most men I know has already been used: *Homo erectus*. What do you think?"

"What do I think? I don't think single entendres are very funny."

"Neither do I."

She suddenly sounded serious and he glanced at her. She was not smiling. Her skin looked dark inside a white cotton dress cut deep at the neckline. He knew she was not wearing a bra. He looked at her hand resting on the table and felt an impulse to reach for it. But she moved it.

"It's getting late—time to go back," Susan said. They walked in silence to the hotel.

The gate was locked and they had to ring for a long time. The boy came out in a flowing white nightshirt and opened it. Their two room keys, heavy brass ones attached to wooden batons, were hanging side by side. Wordlessly they trudged up the stairs. In the hallway they put their keys in the locks simultaneously and then looked at each other, which made them both smile.

Susan's room was small and desolate. A lamp with holes in the shade cast shadows upon the wall.

She walked over to the closet and opened the door. A full-length mirror was on the inside. She looked at her reflection in surprise; there was sadness on her face, but she still looked good. She lifted the cotton dress over her head. Her figure was taut, her breasts still firm. She slipped her panties down to her ankles and stepped out of them. She straightened and looked into the mirror at her naked body.

She kicked her shoes off, lay down upon the bed, and stared at the ceiling. She felt the room turning and closed her eyes. She opened her legs slightly, slowly, and began caressing her stomach with her fingertips. She could hear

Matt's voice dictating the day's events into his tape recorder. What would he say about her?

She felt everything rushing in all at once. Little things came into focus—a crack in the ceiling, a doorknob, a shoe lying on its side—but they didn't keep the anxiety at bay. They didn't anchor her. She opened her eyes and raised her head until she felt the room settle, then fell back and relaxed again. She moved her hand lower, still circling slowly, and her eyes closed.

Suddenly she heard a sound, a brushing against the door and a slight thump. She leaned over and looked. A white envelope lay under the door.

Jumping up, she put on her dress, rushed over to the door, and opened it. The corridor was empty. She ripped open the envelope. She felt a stab of recognition at the familiar handwriting, bold strokes and slashes, not easy to read.

It was a letter from Kellicut.

6

Van found a good spot, a "secure zone" as Eagleton would have called it. The tarpaper on the hotel roof was already warm from the morning sun. He was behind the chimney, out of sight. He leaned around a corner to check the small closed door across the roof. Above there were only some cirrocumulus off to the east. That wouldn't interfere with the transmission.

He opened his knapsack, took out a black box, pulled the catches on the sides toward him, and flipped the lid up. The keyboard was dirty from the fingers of all those who had used it before him. Leave it to these people to stick him with a secondhand NOMAD, not even the up-to-date model that weighed a good four pounds less. This one was a tank.

He turned it on, tilted the microwave screen upside down at a 45-degree angle, typed in CTERM for the software, and selected IOR for Indian Ocean Region, one of the four satellites encircling the globe. The signal strength bar crossed the screen—14.8, the highest he had seen—so he slipped in the disk and punched in his nine-digit ID code. More letters. There was a slight hum and then a long silence as it searched the sky and he awaited that magic handshake above the stratosphere. Curious how he always felt an undercurrent of tension during this wait. It wasn't like that with a radio or a telephone. It must have something to do with all the space the electronic pulses were traversing, a distance farther than he had traveled in his whole life. He felt the old desire for a cigarette again.

At breakfast Van had detected suspicion in Matt and Susan. It was not in anything they said or did; in fact it was their attempts to be natural, even friendly. He was accomplished at spotting meaning in minor gestures and reading body language. At one point he caught them exchanging a significant look. He wondered idly if the two of them had finally fallen into the sack. They deserved each other: Each was so goddamned perfect.

Suddenly he heard the tiny beeps, the little singsong that indicated a connection, and a second later the screen emptied and the command TRANSMIT appeared. Van typed out the code. It was a routine progress report. There was not much to pass along other than the location. He had already sent a message with the information from the boy. Eagleton loved detailed reports—he was sure to be curious about Matt and Susan—and Van derived a perverse pleasure in withholding as much as he could get away with. He knew that Eagleton would sell him out in a minute, and the only times he felt a modicum of power were when he was out in the field. Then the seesaw tilted. Might as well enjoy it as long as it lasted.

He got a routine acknowledgment: CONF-OK. He shut the NOMAD down and turned the power switch to OFF. He had been warned by a communications officer, an old drinking buddy, that the machines had been retrofitted so that the OFF position activated the automatic SAT-SEARCH system so that he could be tracked down anywhere in the world. Typical of Eagleton to try to pull a fast one. Van made a point of keeping it in the OFF position for the moment—if he didn't, it would alert them to the fact that he knew about it. Then he put the computer back in his knapsack and sneaked downstairs.

* * *

Matt was worried by Kellicut's note: the contents, the fact that Kellicut felt it necessary to send it, and that he had chosen a circuitous route to get it into their hands—into Susan's hands, actually, for it was addressed to her. They surmised that he must have sent it down the mountain with Sharafidin and that it was the boy who had delivered it last night. Which probably accounted for his strange question about Kellicut and Susan knowing each other—no doubt some misunderstanding of a directive from Kellicut to ensure that she alone received it.

When Matt had heard the soft knock on his door last night, he knew at once it was Susan. He dropped the tape recorder and opened the door with his heart in his throat, but as soon as he saw the confusion in her face he knew she had not come for the reason he had hoped. Without a word, she had handed him the letter. He had it still, and now unfolded the soiled paper and read it again.

> Susan,
>   You must come urgently. Only you and Matt will appreciate the enormity of what I have found. Do not delay. And here's an afterthought: Do not speak of this to others. Keep it secret. Only we scientists should make the contact. There are many who are not fit representatives of our species. Hurry, for God's sake! What we are going to experience together surpasses anything in human history.
>   By all the gods, tomorrow will be a day of reckoning.

Kellicut didn't sign it. Typical, thought Matt, looking down at the scrawled hand, egotistical and enigmatic to the end. No date, no place. But the way the paper was creased and wrinkled, it was clearly written in the rough. Its purpose was the warning not to speak about the expedition. But why? Did he want to be the one to break it to the world? That would not be atypical of him. That line about "many who are not fit representatives of our species"—a curious way to put it.

Great. He tells us we're about to make the biggest discovery in history and says we can't talk about it. He delivers a warning when there is nothing we can do about it. Why didn't he bother to look up our addresses if he was setting out on something so momentous? Kellicut the Pied Piper, still leading us into the unknown after all these years. Only now it's not quantum theory and Jung, it's . . . who the hell knows what it is?

Something else was troubling: This note suggested that there had in fact been an earlier letter inside the package. He didn't say it in so many words, but the tone seemed that of a postscript, an "afterthought," as he put it. Which stood to reason. Kellicut loved drama and was not above attention-grabbing antics, but at heart he was a scientist. He would not simply drop a twenty-five-year-old Neanderthal skull into a box with no explanation. Too much was at stake, too much could go wrong. The implications of a missing letter were chilling: Eagleton or Van or both were holding back. Why? What was it Matt and Susan were not to know?

There was no question but that the letter came from Kellicut. It was his style, his blarney. Matt could even visualize him writing that passionate promise of a discovery that "surpasses anything in human history." And the flourish at the end, the Greek quote: "By all the gods, tomorrow will be a day of reckoning." Susan was the one who placed it: Achilles speaking after Patroclus was slain outside the walls of Troy.

Even in a situation like this, where he thinks he's standing on the threshold of a great discovery, where he's leading two of his closest colleagues directly into peril, he still has to be pedantic, Matt thought. The bitterness that he felt surprised him.

*   *   *

In the courtyard Van spread out the equipment, carrying a clipboard and shouting orders to Rudy, who cheerfully packed each item as it was checked off. Matt was exasperated by all the supplies: tents, sleeping bags, boots, polypropylene jackets, a medical kit, lanterns, cooking equipment, axes, knives, canteens, cameras. And all kinds of food: canned goods and strips of meat but mostly unappetizing dehydrated vegetables in vacuum packets.

"My God," Matt said, surveying the small mountain. "Are we looking for the Alma or are we going to open a Wal-Mart?"

Susan came out cradling a cup of steaming coffee, her hair tousled.

Matt pointed to a small canvas bag. "What's in there?" he asked Van.

"Flares."

"What do we need flares for?"

"In case we have to be evacuated."

"And who's going to evacuate us?"

"You never know. Better safe than sorry."

Susan caught Matt's eye, frowned, shook her head, and turned away.

They drove along the Pamir highway, a black ribbon of asphalt that slipped through the mountains all the way to Khorog on the Afghan border and beyond to the ancient town of Osh, once a caravan terminus. Rudy was at the wheel, and he provided a medley of songs from his New York year. Van, sitting next to him, was inexplicably tolerant.

They passed one or two ghost villages, clusters of mud huts on steep hillsides shaded by trees, all shuttered tight with no sign of life. On the outskirts were what had once been cornfields, and even an abandoned collective farm, the huge stone barracks toppled and the roof caved in. Wagons and plows were left in place.

"What happened?" asked Matt. "Disease? Famine?"

"Neither," said Rudy. "This was a government settlement on the River Vaksh. It was forcibly cleared in 1981 after three earthquakes. About twelve thousand people died. This was the epicenter. The whole region is still unstable."

Later, they drove higher into the foothills, where the riverbeds were filled with a torrent from melting snowcaps and the brown grass turned green.

At noon they stopped for lunch. Rudy parked the car near a stream and, after eating, Matt followed it around a bend where it turned into a small pond. On impulse, he threw off his clothes and waded in. He found a sandy bottom, slowly fell backward, and broke his fall with his arms until only his head remained above water.

He felt adrift, like a leaf. All morning he had been having sexual fantasies about Susan, swimming in them. On the path down to the stream he had turned to wait for her, watching only her body. He let her go ahead and stared at the beads of sweat rolling down the backs of her thighs. He imagined pushing those thighs open and burying his head there as he used to do.

His reverie was broken by their shouts that it was time to go. As he emerged from the water and dried off, he felt the air warm against his body and realized that he was aroused.

That afternoon Matt drove. Ordinarily he enjoyed doing so but this was difficult. They had left the highway and were bouncing along on a dirt washboard road, so that if he went too fast a bone-shattering shudder seized the car. With the sun sinking dead ahead, the track was hard to make out amid the glare and glittering stones. He squinted so much he felt his eyebrows aching.

In the evening Susan took over while Van and Rudy slept in the back. The air cooled rapidly. The wind rushed in like a cold underwater stream, but they left the windows open because it felt good. With the headlights bouncing, it was hard to spot obstacles in the road, so Matt served as lookout, shouting whenever he spotted something. He was enjoying himself. So was she.

Every so often they saw a scorpion scuttle through the beam of the headlights with its stinger high in the air, agile and obscene-looking.

"All we need is music, driving music," Matt said.

"Wait a minute." She stopped the car, rummaged in the back, and returned with a leather case, propped it over the dashboard, switched it on, and pulled away. The sounds of Bruce Springsteen filled the night. As she gunned the gas, they were both grinning.

Three hours later they stopped for the night at a grassy knoll surrounded by cliffs and boulders. They built a large fire and dug a trench around the campsite, splashing gasoline in it to keep out the scorpions.

By the fire, Van pored over a map. "We made good time, considering the road. Must have gone two hundred and fifty miles." Matt peered over his shoulder while he traced the route. "I figure we'll be at the base of the mountain around noon." Van was almost sociable.

After dinner they laid out their sleeping bags. Susan unrolled hers next to Matt. Sharafidin put his blanket off to one side and prayed on his knees, touching his forehead to the ground, facing Mecca. With his head down, his cotton blouse billowed over his skinny back. Abruptly, he straightened up and from his bundle extracted something that looked like a tiny box. He held it up to the night sky, brought it slowly to his lips, and kissed it four or five times. Rudy looked at him, then at Matt and Susan, smiled, pointed a forefinger at his temple, and spun crazy circles.

Matt tried to sleep but the road was uncoiling before him and his blood was racing. He listened to Susan's breathing, steady and deep, and fell off to sleep abruptly, like dropping off a cliff.

In the morning they got an early start. Van drove silently and mechanically. They were climbing rapidly and could feel the altitude clog their ears. The topography changed. The scrub brush died away and the road was flanked by scrawny pines. Then the trees thinned out and the road began winding in treacherous and steep hairpin turns. Van slipped into second gear, then into first. Finally the road petered out altogether into a rocky path.

Van came to a dead stop under a tree on the edge of a meadow. "End of the line," he said, killing the engine.

"Can't say I like that expression," said Susan. They unloaded the gear and packed it into their knapsacks, Van directing the operation. He kept his pack, which was larger, separate from the others. Finally he opened the Cruiser's hood and disconnected the battery. "Don't know how long we're going to be up there," he said, as he put the car keys over the visor. "They're up here, just in case."

"In case what?"

"We get separated."

As they crossed the meadow toward the forest, the jagged peaks loomed high and seemingly close, encrusted in glacial ice. Against a sky of moving clouds, veils of mist swirled around them and gave an illusion of movement so that they appeared to totter and lunge.

They hiked for hours up the incline of rocks and thornbushes, following a route set by Sharafidin. He walked steadily, his dark eyes constantly moving to pick up landmarks. There was no path. Once or twice he erred, and they had to backtrack and rest while he went ahead, then called to them when he had found the way. It was hot in the sunlight, and he was stripped to the waist, his lithe body showing his ribs.

The front of Van's shirt was soaked in a triangle of sweat. His backpack was heavier than the others and it slowed him down. Matt and Susan walked easily and deliberately, conserving energy. Rudy was the noisiest. He brushed the scraggly branches of bushes aside as if he were opening doors of a saloon. Under a broad-brimmed straw hat, he looked goofy and talked constantly to anyone within earshot.

They came to a delta, passing the ruins of a *kishlak,* several houses and channels cut for irrigation and fields that had once been tilled. Everything was abandoned. The stone walls had toppled down. The soil appeared dark and fertile, and the land had the look of a place that had been occupied for centuries.

After several hours, they came to an alpine meadow bisected by a raging river. They dropped their packs—Van needed help getting out of his—and drank the cold water deeply. Rudy scooped out hatfuls and poured them over his head, looking so comical that the others had to laugh.

Susan walked off alone into the meadow. On one side she could see great gangling juniper bushes and cypresses, and here and there clusters of briar, honeysuckle, and currants. The lazy hot air gave off the scent of mountain roses.

"Beautiful, no?" said Rudy's voice behind her. He stood gazing at the sight contemplatively before speaking again. "This is one of the reasons I came back to this crazy country." As he looked up at the formidable peaks, his childlike features relaxed. He's downright handsome, Susan thought suddenly.

"You've never been to Tajikistan before?" asked Rudy.

"No, never. Why?"

"I thought you might have come in that earlier group."

"What group?"

"The one that came last year, before Dr. Kellicut. You know, the one with Van."

7

For the rest of the afternoon they continued to climb. The ground became gradually steeper and the going more arduous. Sharafidin was far in front of them.

By evening the green buckhorn and small poplars and birches began to thin out, and soon they left them behind altogether. Now there was small brush, scrub grass, and occasional willow shrubs amid eroded boulders. They pitched camp on a rocky shelf and prepared their bedrolls. Matt and Rudy went off to collect firewood; to find it they had to go a long way down the slope they had just negotiated. They came back with half a dozen logs and armfuls of twigs, just in time to replenish a small fire that Susan had started with meadow grass.

"Here," she said, handing them each a cup. "Life-giving coffee."

After dinner Sharafidin performed his nightly prayers. When he was finished, Susan motioned to Rudy and they went over to him and talked. At one point, Sharafidin reached into his bundle, pulled out the object that had drawn their curiosity the night before, and handed it to Susan. She examined it carefully and, as she handed it back, said something that Rudy translated.

Matt sat down on a rock at the edge of the plateau, his muscles aching pleasantly. By the orange rays of the setting sun, he could see the treeline below zigzagging across the slopes and disappearing in valleys on both sides. Evening mist rose like steam. The land stretched into the infinite distance.

Susan sat down next to him. He was glad of her presence. The view was so sublime he needed company. They were silent until finally Matt turned to her. "I saw you looking at Sharafidin's talisman. What is it?"

"A miniature Koran. He says it was used against Kitchener at the battle of Omdurman. Gained paradise for its owner. It's well worn—from rubbing, I expect."

"Did he tell you what it does?"

"He didn't have to. It protects him. Puts him in touch with Allah and the spirits of the mountain."

"Does he have any extras?"

When Susan spoke again, her tone was serious. She told him what Rudy had blurted out by accident about Van's previous trip. "Who was he with and why was he here?"

"And why has he kept it a secret from us?" put in Matt.

There was little they could do. If they confronted Van directly he would just deny it. Besides, they were committed to finding Kellicut's camp. So they simply resolved to watch Van carefully for some sort of opening to get at the truth—and both felt dissatisfied that they had no better plan.

Now it was almost dark, and as they looked out at the valley, Susan said, "You know something else that bothers me? The longer I'm here the more I believe the Neanderthal still exist. Kellicut believes it, and Van certainly does. As we were walking through the forest I kept thinking about that skull. That was real bone."

"It's beginning to look that way."

"And if it's authentic, maybe all those stories they tell to while away the long winter nights down in the villages are true."

"Maybe," he replied.

"And here we are up here hoping to find one. Or two.

Or twenty. But what if they're dangerous? What are we supposed to do, waltz up to them and shake hands?''

"Maybe we can observe them without being seen," he said.

"Yeah, and maybe not."

"Don't forget," Matt said, "they're the ones who retreated way up here, so they're more scared of us than we are of them."

"Speak for yourself," said Susan. "Another thing. I know it's just my imagination but as we were walking through the forest I kept thinking they were watching us. I began by thinking, What if they're out there? and I ended by believing it. I could practically feel their eyes on me. Did you feel it?''

"No."

"Well, I did. I didn't totally believe it, but I was talking myself into it."

Matt looked out over the hills below, now almost totally black. "Don't forget we're pretty high up, maybe twelve thousand feet by now. Altitude can do strange things to you."

"Like what?" she asked sarcastically. "Hallucinations? Paranoia?"

"No, I'm serious. Hyperventilation. Insomnia. Unaccountable anxiety. A sense of free-floating panic. Water in the lungs."

"Great. Now I feel much better."

"It doesn't mean you're going to crack up. It just makes scary things seem scarier. Don't take it too seriously."

"I'll remember that when I'm in the cooking pot and somebody's about to make my brain into steak tartare."

Matt smiled to himself. Her combination of total self-reliance and unabashed vulnerability—that was part of what had drawn him to her years ago.

"I have to say," he said, with genuine warmth, "you haven't changed much."

"For better or for worse?''

"Better."

She shook her head imperceptibly, annoyed at his presumption. She had spent so many years venting her anger at Matt, an old-fashioned pure-white anger, that by now it was routine, and she wasn't even sure she felt it anymore.

Betrayal—that was the all-encompassing sin that packed all of Matt's misdemeanors and deceptions into a single word. By repeating the word like a mantra years ago, she could reduce their relationship to its essence. There was no question about it: betrayal was what it was, cheating on her with her closest friend. She had no hint that it was going on, she had not known about Anne until the end, which deepened her shame and made his actions unforgivable. Knowing her, he would know how humiliated she would feel in front of everyone. Then she began to see him as contemptible, with all his little lies. That was when she truly fell out of love with him, when her respect for him had vanished.

Actually, she'd had her own secret affair. But there was a difference, she told herself, for on some level she had surely been aware of Matt's deception—it was impossible to be so close to someone and not be aware of it—so in a sense she was protecting herself by matching his transgression. She knew that she was rationalizing her own betrayal, but this did not lessen her certainty that hers was not a dalliance. It had been real and doubly necessary to her because she had not proved to be sufficient for him. It was self-defense.

"Let's go back now," she said.

The next morning they rose early and climbed without talking, their legs aching and their feet throbbing. Each step brought pain. They moved like zombies, and as the sun pounded down, the monotony of their footsteps eradicated all sense of time.

But Sharafidin still climbed effortlessly, gliding like a kite from side to side in search of the best foothold. His thin legs pumped upward and moved unceasingly.

At this altitude the grass had largely disappeared, and they found themselves in a bleak landscape of dirt, pebbles, rock, and scree. By midafternoon they had reached a saddle that ran between two peaks. When it leveled off the going was easier. From here, they could look down into the valley fifty miles below.

They spotted a patch of shade under an outcropping of rock. When they got close they heard a rustling sound, and the ground shivered. Behind a boulder, hidden in the shade, was a hole. Underneath, about an arm's length down, rushed an underground stream.

Matt reached down and felt the ice-cold water. He filled his canteen, brought it up, and passed it around.

"Might as well stop here for lunch," said Susan.

Rudy said something to Sharafidin and he answered. His strained tone and the downward glance of his eye caught Matt's attention. "What was that about?"

"I asked him where we are, and he said . . . to put it exactly, he said, 'We've reached the place where people do not go.' "

"Oh, yeah? Well, tell him they're going to have to change the name of the place," Van snarled. He went off to investigate the stream where it surfaced about forty feet away.

Suddenly they heard him yell. They found him on a bank that was sandy and extended in a semicircle where the water had cut into the rock above. Van's canteen was toppled next to him. Apparently he had been filling it. He gave out short, sharp gasps, then a kind of wheezing. He was kneeling in an erect, unnatural way and his other hand was pointing, moving up and down like a piston.

Matt's first thought was of a heart attack. "Are you all right?" he shouted.

"Look!" Van was pointing at the ground between his legs with that curious piston motion again as they rushed toward him.

Susan got there first. "My God."

There in the sand next to the stream was a single foot-print, deep and abnormally thick. Matt bent down and looked closer. It looked human but it was too wide at the instep.

"Okay, who's crazy now?" Van shouted, looking about them wildly. "I told you, but you wouldn't believe me."

They searched the area and found other footprints and then, strangely, some boot prints with cross-hatching. They seemed to be of different sizes and were better formed, more recent.

They followed the boot prints as far as they could, but they disappeared on hard ground. It looked as if they were made by three people. Three people and, before them, one humanlike creature, a humanoid but not a human. From the way the boot prints clustered around the footprints, it was apparent that the humans were trying to track it.

"Look at this," said Rudy. He held up a cigarette butt between his thumb and forefinger. He smelled it. "It's Russian," he said.

Van was falling behind. His breathing was labored and his backpack felt as if it had been weighted with stones. When he had dressed this morning, he had strapped on the gun holster. A rawhide band held it to his right thigh, and its tightness as it dug into his flesh made him feel the power of the gun. He knew he was beginning to feel the effects of oxygen deprivation. All those years of smoking and all those various substances and chemicals that he had taken were exacting their revenge now: DMT, STP, drugs whose names he could no longer even remember, like the call letters of radio stations in his childhood. He knew the symptoms of altitude sickness: the flights of wooziness, not altogether unpleasant but mingled with little stabs of paranoia, and above all that panicky sensation of gulping to fill his lungs and not getting any air. If it got much worse, it would be unbearable.

He tried to rein his mind in but that just made him feel more anxious, and he let it wander on its own. So the Russians were here after all. He might have known. He had never trusted them himself, and he had been the one to deal with them directly. Glasnost was a load of crap. This was too big for them to ignore. They gave some information, held back some, and in the end went ahead with their own expedition. Maybe the Russians want us to do the scutwork while they sit back and move in for the kill, he thought. Eagleton had had his doubts, too, Van could tell, but he was able to put them aside, basing his argument on what he called "the anarchy factor" in Moscow. Eagleton had always been good at gambling, especially with things that didn't belong to him, like other people's lives.

Late that afternoon Sharafidin suddenly picked up the pace, and as they rounded a bend they saw he was almost running. They shouted but he didn't slow down or look back; he disappeared over the crest of a ridge.

They hurried along after him. Reaching the crest and looking up a long slope, they saw a field and some kind of structure. It took a while for the significance to sink in— Kellicut's camp.

Not a bad location, thought Matt. The spot had a clear view in all directions and commanded an easy route down. For quick escape? Unlikely. Kellicut was not a man to consider flight. More probably he had been attracted by the paramount location so that in the evenings he could gaze out over the mountain he had scaled and the foothills marching off below. The vista would reconfirm his sense of omnipotence.

They reached the edge of the campsite. Inside the jumble of shapes ahead stirred a streak, a blur of movement. Van felt it register in his peripheral vision even before he was fully aware of it. He dropped to a crouch, his right hand slapping at the holster until in one swift arc he came up with the gun, then rose slowly, still aiming. Focusing, his senses suddenly relaxed and he felt relief wash through him. It was only a bird, a large brown hawk perched on the top of a pole, flapping its crooked wings.

He straightened up. "Shit," he said. "Didn't expect that."

The bird was a bad omen, Susan thought. Abruptly she knew with a certainty she could not explain that they would not find Kellicut at the camp. It looked unlived in, disheveled, packed down by rain and snow.

The place looked spartan compared to the vision of a well-stocked base camp that they had conjured up during their ascent. The main structure was a lean-to about four feet high and twelve feet long, extending from the face of a shoulder-high boulder. It ran parallel to a wall of rocks about two feet high, which served as a windbreak.

Fifty feet away was a platform stuck in one of the few stunted trees growing at this altitude. It was a larder of sorts. In the other direction was all that was left of the campfire, and in still another was a makeshift well with a frayed rope attached to a metal cup lying in the dirt. Off on a side path was what looked like a latrine, a pit with two logs over it.

"It's not much," said Van.

Matt was thinking the same thing. "Looks like he hasn't been here for some time."

Susan walked over to the lean-to and bent down to step inside. "Matt, come here!" she shouted.

He hurried over, crouched, and entered. There was barely room for the two of them. It was a mess. A green air mattress was ripped down its length. Pots and pans lay on the floor, one of them bashed in. A coffee mug was shattered and a kerosene lantern broken. A pair of Kellicut's boots, bent and stiff with mud, lay undisturbed on a makeshift wooden shelf.

Distraught, Susan squatted down to pick up some papers and look through them. They were all blank. She raised her eyes to meet Matt's. "What do you think? What could have done this?"

"It's hard to say."

"But was it done deliberately? By some . . . thing? Or could it have happened naturally, a storm or something."

"A storm's unlikely. It couldn't have done this." He pointed to the splintered pieces of a blue plastic cup. "Maybe an animal." His tone was doubtful.

"But it's not totally torn apart. Some of this could have been done by wind or a strong rain pounding down. After all, it's probably been deserted for months."

"Not the air mattress. Look at it. It's in strips." He picked it up. "These don't look like claw marks, but it was done deliberately. This one here"—he touched a hole—"could be a tooth mark. Something ripped it."

"If the hut was vandalized by some large creature, why wasn't it destroyed?" Susan reached up and touched a log overhead, then shook it. "Still solid, pretty much as it was built, I'd say. But it could have been torn apart in two minutes if . . . if something really wanted to."

Matt gave her a searching look. He knew she was grasping at straws. "Let's look outside."

They moved out and stood up. It was a relief to be in the open air. The little lean-to was claustrophobic and had a strange, pungent odor.

They began examining the ground. Without mentioning it, they were both searching for footprints. There were none. The ground was too solid.

Van, who had been searching the edges of the campsite, came over to them. "I don't get it," he said, squatting on his knees to look inside the lean-to. He fit a finger between two of the logs on the roof. "This must have had some kind of cover, a tarp or something to keep out the rain. But there's nothing around anywhere."

The spirit of the hunt seemed to revive Van. He tilted his head and looked at each of them in turn. "Let me ask you, since you knew Kellicut better than I did."

"What?"

"Would you say he was reckless? You know, kind of arrogant?"

"What do you mean by that?" demanded Susan.

"I mean, would you say he would have difficulty imagining anything bad happening to him? You know the type—the kind of guy who never makes out a will."

"I wouldn't say so."

"C'mon, Susan," said Matt, "I'd say he's one hundred percent on target."

"What are you getting at?" asked Susan, annoyed by Van's Scotland Yard airs.

"What he's getting at is, Why didn't Kellicut leave us a message?"

"Maybe he did. Just because we can't find one doesn't mean he didn't. I can't believe he would simply go away and not leave some kind of note behind."

"Maybe he didn't know he was going," Van said.

Susan knew right away what he meant but she played dumb. "Meaning what?"

"What if he was attacked and killed? Or dragged off? Or ambushed?" Van gestured vaguely at the rocky ridges above them.

"There's no sign of a struggle," said Susan. "And I still say he would make some kind of provision for people who came up here looking for him. Don't forget, he asked us to come."

"Maybe he left a note, maybe not," said Van.

"It could have been destroyed. Or taken. Or blown away," said Matt. "Anything could have happened to it."

"Or maybe he hid it," suggested Susan. "That would be more like him."

Van grunted.

"And while we're at it," said Matt, "you said we knew him better than you. How well did you know him? I wasn't aware you knew him at all."

"A little. Our paths crossed while he did some work for us, that's all."

Matt knew Van was holding back again and made a mental note to follow up when the time was right.

They continued looking for footprints and clues, dividing the ground into four sectors like pie pieces and radiating from the center out to the periphery, but the rocky terrain yielded nothing.

Matt joined the others at what had been the campfire, now a broken circle of rocks that held a mound of scattered, sodden ash. Van knelt down and picked up a piece of charcoal and crushed it between his thumb and forefinger. "Six months ago the weather was even colder than now, so he'd have wanted to keep the fire going no matter what." He picked up a half-burnt stick. "Looks like it was doused by water, so unless it was raining at the time, which is possible but not likely, he put it out deliberately."

"Meaning," said Susan, "that it was probably the last thing he did here. A final bit of housekeeping. Doesn't look like he was attacked or scared off. Which means that all this damage we see was done after he left."

Matt sifted through the ashes, which stuck together in wet clumps. "I'd say it's old. It all depends on what the weather's been, but I don't think there's been a fire here for two or three months, maybe longer."

"Yeah," said Van. "He's long gone. Whatever happened to him, he hasn't been back here."

"Probably not since he sent the package down with Sharafidin."

"So what do we do now?" asked Rudy.

"We look for him," replied Susan.

"I'll betcha one thing," said Van, with a depth of feeling that surprised the others. "If we find *him*, we'll find *them*."

At this altitude, the sun set later than in the valley below, but the half-light didn't bring any warmth. Soon the sun was behind low-lying clouds, a chill wind began blowing, and gusts of fog came rolling down the upper slopes like a ghostly avalanche, enveloping them so completely that at times they couldn't see beyond the campsite.

They put their food supplies on the larder platform, built up the fire, and wrapped themselves in sleeping bags while waiting for dinner to cook. Rudy served black coffee all around.

Van was feeling a bit better, though he tired easily and had an off-and-on nosebleed, a little trickle down the side of his face. He ruminated while staring at the sparks flying up into the mist. "You can tell a lot about a man the way he sets up camp," he said. "Even more than his house. The house was there before him, but a camp is something he builds all by himself in the middle of nowhere, and he puts his own stamp on it."

"For instance?" asked Matt.

"For instance look at the latrine. Couple of logs over a pit. Kind of crude, don't you think? And the larder, pretty basic. I'd say the professor is not someone who spends a lot of time worrying about amenities."

"I'd say you're not far off the mark there," Matt said.

"And the lean-to isn't much to write home about. Why couldn't he be bothered to build something more substantial? I mean, it gets colder 'n shit up here. Either he thought he wouldn't be here long or he just didn't care."

"No contest there; I'd say he didn't care," said Matt.

"Then there's the site itself. If he wanted to be secluded, he could have found a cave; there must be dozens of them up here. But he picks the most conspicuous place around. Not very smart."

Susan bristled. "Unless he wanted to be seen."

"Maybe that's it," said Matt. "Announce his presence. Make them come to him."

"Or maybe he figured they'd know where he is anyway," said Susan. Van spun his head and gave her a peculiar searching look. He seemed to be trying to figure something out.

Susan continued. "The person who built this camp certainly wasn't afraid—and knowing Kellicut, I'd say that fits."

"But didn't he see any footprints?" Matt asked. "We did, and we weren't even searching for them. You'd think that would give him pause."

"Probably the opposite," Susan said.

"So you think he wouldn't be afraid."

"No."

"Then why didn't he worry that they might be afraid of him? Why be so open? Why not try to sneak up on them?"

"I don't know," said Susan. "He probably didn't buy into that theory to begin with, all that business about Neanderthals retreating to get away from *Homo sapiens.* Certainly he never emphasized that in his publications. He seemed to romanticize them as some kind of possibly superior beings."

"Or perhaps there's something we don't know," continued Matt. "Maybe he found out something that made him realize they're not fearful after all."

They fell silent around the fire. Rudy was dozing off. Van thought for a minute, then shook his head and looked around again. "Another thing. Look at the way it's laid out. It doesn't make sense. Here's the fire over here, and the well is way over there. Why didn't he put the fire near the water? Surely that's more convenient. And what's the larder doing all the way over there? Think about it. To make a meal you have to walk from there to there to there. It just—"

"Wait a minute," Susan interrupted. She jumped up excitedly. "You're right. Look at that. It's a triangle. A perfect triangle, Matt."

The same thought struck him too. He jumped to his feet. "Could it be?"

"Quick, get some rope."

Rudy opened his eyes. Matt burrowed in his rucksack and came up with a coil of rope. He held one end and tossed the other to Susan, who began measuring the distance between the fire and the well.

"Would you two mind letting me in on your little secret?" said Van. He was trying to sound nonchalant, but there was irritation in his voice.

"It's only a possibility," said Susan. "I don't know if we're right." She measured the rope and marked it by gripping it in her fist; then, still clenching it, she moved over to measure the distance from the well to the larder.

"It's a kind of sign that paleontologists use—or at least Kellicut did. It became a sort of ritual on our digs. Before anything else, we'd go over the whole area and survey it, looking for likely places to dig—you know, judging by glacial development, settlement, erosion, that kind of thing—and wherever we thought we should go down, we'd make an equilateral triangle with rocks. Then we'd come back and dig in the center."

Now she was measuring the third leg, and Matt picked up the explanation.

"Kellicut, clever dog that he is, knew that he had to find a secure hiding place. But where? Rocks are no good; they could be disturbed, or something might come along and disturb them."

"So he used the campsite itself?" Van asked.

"Eureka," said Susan, holding up the rope. "A perfect equilateral triangle."

She cut the baseline in two, marked it with a stone, ran the rope up as an altitude marker and paced off alongside it to the exact center, and dug her heel in at the spot.

Matt got out a portable shovel and started digging. The ground was packed hard and each shovelful yielded only a handful of rocks and bits of flinty earth. Rudy helped by chopping at the hole with a hatchet.

"Can't believe he would do this," said Matt. "Even for him, it's sneaky."

Soon the shovel struck something. He dug around it,

pried it loose with the tip of the shovel, reached down, pulled up a metal box, and brushed dirt off the lid. He had to tug to get it open. Inside was a thick red diary, soiled and dog-eared.

8

Eagleton didn't like the uniformed man sitting across from him, but he knew he was the best in the business and he needed him. So he had agreed to give Colonel Kane a full briefing—relatively full, that is. Eagleton never told anyone everything.

As a gesture of good faith, Eagleton tossed the four-line cable from Van across the desk. It was a useless message in any case. The man leaned out of the shadows to read it and then grunted.

"Where was I?" asked Eagleton.

"Kellicut."

"Yes, Kellicut. Well, as I said, we'd been funding him for years. Little bits here and there, nothing big-time. We never dreamed he would hit pay dirt. It was always low priority."

"Low priority? That surprises me. Especially now."

Eagleton leaned back in his seat and took a drag on his cigarette in his dainty way. "Well, cryptozoology has never been big at the Institute," he explained. "We've had a couple of people working on it from the very beginning, but more as a hobby. Nothing serious, nothing that got the attention of the big boys—at least until now."

"Go on."

"Mostly we just kept files. The odd sighting here and

there. Items in newspapers, that kind of thing.'' He gestured toward a stack of files on the windowsill. ''We really did it because we knew the Russians were doing it. Not to be behind in anything; that was the game then. And they were into it in a big way, God knows why. It was hard, back then, to see any military advantage. Maybe it was just like our intelligence services doing all that work with porpoises—one of those idiotic times when someone somewhere takes an interest in far-out research and the bureaucracy can't shut itself off.''

Eagleton told him of the previous Russian expeditions, beginning with an explorer named Badzare Baradiyan in 1906 and later a Buryat Mongol, a professor known only as Zhamtsarano. They were arrested and exiled for their pains, and their voluminous files disappeared somewhere in the bowels of the Leningrad section of the Institute of Oriental Studies at the Academy of Sciences.

In 1958 an expedition to the Pamirs headed by Boris Porshnev ended in failure and worldwide ridicule, thanks to some mocking stories in British tabloids judiciously placed by MI6. ''Nothing personal. Just the Cold War,'' he chuckled. After the fall of the Berlin Wall, he sent Van to make contact with Rinchen, the expert, who was tracked down in a yurt in Mongolia. Rinchen led Van to the lost archives in the Academy, classified under a Mongolian word that translates roughly as ''the invisible one who exists.''

''A gold mine. Seven hundred and eighty-one separate items. Larger than our whole collection. We got everything we wanted. We entered all the data in the computer, cross-referenced it, and came up with the best spot to look. Presto! A perfect blend of data and analysis—Marxist labor and capitalist technique, if you will.

''Our idea—it was mine, actually—was to forget the big operation, the grid search, infrared, and all that. How can you use an army in that terrain, those conditions, against creatures who know where you are before you do? Better to establish a continual small-scale presence, something that wouldn't attract too much attention. Send over someone who knows what he's looking for. Let him stay months, years if necessary. Get to know the locals, hear all the stories.

"That's how we came up with Kellicut. He was the natural choice, and of course he was interested. He's such an egomaniac. We only had to dangle it in front of his nose."

"Did you tell him about Operation Achilles?"

Eagleton hesitated a split second. He had not been aware that Kane knew about Operation Achilles, the most secret of secrets, the divine intervention that had kicked off the whole damn thing. Christ! If he knew, then others knew. "No. No, we didn't. We didn't see any need to . . . complicate his research."

"I see."

"We weren't even certain he would succeed, not by a long shot. Certainly not so quickly. We didn't give him much in the way of support or supplies. He likes to rough it anyway.

"We got one or two messages at the beginning, nothing of importance. Then silence, months of silence. It was as if he'd fallen into a black hole. We were really getting worried. And then the package came for us."

"For doctors Arnot and Mattison."

"Yes. Well, that's a technicality. We were the ones financing the operation."

"Operation? Or expedition?"

"Expedition."

"I see." The man in the uniform rose. "Thank you for the briefing," Kane said. "I will of course tell no one else. If we have to go in and spring them, I'll have to get a team and start training. Once we're ready we can move within four hours. Is there anything else I should know?"

"No, nothing else."

The man saluted brusquely before leaving. The gesture struck Eagleton as disingenuous. But at least he neglected

to ask me the key question—whether the Russians themselves were mounting an expedition to the Pamirs. He saved
me from having to lie, Eagleton thought with a chuckle.

Feb. 12. Cloudy, cold. Spent all day building the
camp. Totally exhausted. Damned hard to build a
lean-to when there's precious little in the way of material to do the leaning. Chopped down four trees and
lugged them up 40 or 50 feet. Sharafidin's not much
help. He's willing, poor guy, but he has no idea what
to do. I have to tell him everything. Also, I think he
thinks I'm crazy. He could well be right. Anyway, in
keeping with my new domesticity, I am starting this
journal, fulfilling a promise I made to myself weeks
ago—that I would pick up the pen the day I set up
base camp, not a moment before. I have already decided where I will leave the journal. If you're reading
this, Susan and Matt, I congratulate myself and I suggest you should raise a glass to your cleverness and
mine. If you do not find this, no one will, and these
words will never come to light. Perhaps that's just as
well. . . . Too tired to write more now. Tomorrow I'll
pick up the thread of this narrative.

Matt read the journal out loud against a background of
rustling wind. Sitting around the fire as the night pressed
in, the mist reflected back the shadows cast from the fire
and made them dance around like spirits. He had proposed
passing up some of the journal's earlier entries to skip to
the end to see if it shed any light on Kellicut's disappearance, but they would have none of that. Especially Susan;
she wanted to experience it sequentially, the way the author
had lived it.

The entries began in a style both labored and literate.
Kellicut described the early days: his trip up the mountain,
his preparations, and his equipment, which was surprisingly
sparse. He expounded on the flora and fauna, complete with

Latin names for some of the flowers. He wrote about the hawks, who "puff up their chests and circle overhead as if they've been told they're vultures." There were some trenchant asides and a few obscure quotes. Then the style became something more immediate and real, as if fatigue, loneliness, and adventure were stripping away his pretenses.

Somehow Kellicut had obtained a rough map of the upper slopes. Every day he ventured out on a predetermined course that took him to a different sector. The idea was to make himself visible, to call attention to his presence by making noise, discarding objects, or otherwise acting like "a normal obnoxious, despoiling human being," as he put it. Hansel and Gretel in reverse, mused Matt, reeling the ogres in on a trail of litter. The strategy was based on several fundamental premises. One was that the creatures, whatever they might be, wouldn't simply descend on him one night and bash his skull in. Another was that they themselves wouldn't be frightened to death and so wouldn't withdraw to someplace even more inaccessible. What if either of his two premises was wrong?

Matt came to a critical entry dated February 27. By this point, Kellicut was occasionally dropping use of the first-person pronoun, a touch that seemed to correspond with a significant change: His strength was ebbing and his overall sense of purpose was slipping away. Matt read it aloud:

Feb. 27. Had visitors last night. I'm sure it was they, I know it was. Saw something had changed right away in the campsite as soon as I awoke. Hard to say what. Sixth sense, mostly. Also smelled a peculiar odor, difficult to describe—pungent like wet animal skins or a skunk run over on a road. Only thing disturbed was the larder, but it was done in an unusual way. Bits of leftover food were taken, some smoked hare and other meats. They were lifted from the center, for all the world like some shopper in a supermarket. The food around—jam, sugar, condiments, etc.—was untouched. Simply no way an animal could have stood upright and reached over the rest without knocking it over. Saw no footprints anywhere, though searched surrounding area for hours. The good news is that they can't be far away. If they can track me down, I can track them down. Curiosity is a powerful lure. Who knows? Perhaps my nocturnal visitors are picking their teeth and spying on me at this very moment!

Later, same day: Just made it back to camp by dark. Exhausted. No luck. Saw nothing unusual. Don't want to scare Sharafidin.

Feb. 28. Searched all day, dawn to dusk. No success. Shara was glad to see me. Guess he gave me up for a goner. Too beat to write more.

March 1. Nothing.

March 2. Five miles up (quadrant four, sector 5E) began encountering paths. At first I thought I was merely following natural curves along ridges. Then noticed bushes worn away, ground softened, and rocks broken. Could be rams, goats, and even bears. But I have hopes that the paths were made by them. Have new tactic now: I set up a position along a path and simply wait. My strength is flagging—I'm not eating enough, I fear.

March 4. Nothing to report. Sat all day beside what I hoped was a major path and saw nothing except one strange rodentlike animal. Couldn't catch it. Still feeling bad.

March 5. Can't go on like this. Need to make excursions farther and longer, but doubt I have strength to move campsite or rebuild. Will try to take some food with me and make trips of three to four days.

Tried explaining this to Shara but not sure I got it across. Nothing important today in way of sightings.

March 8? (not sure of date, losing track). Spent nights at sites marked on map (quad 4, sector 12F). Covered lots of ground but saw little. Still feeling dizzy. Afraid I'm suffering dehydration. Maybe oxygen depri. Not sure this is best way to go about search.

March 14. Returned after long exploration. Nothing of note. Need time to recuperate. I am afraid.

March 15. Stayed in camp. Fever.

March 19 (approx). Feeling bit better. Able to sit up and drink broth. Sharafidin been wonderful. Owe my life to him. Hope to get strength back.

Days passed without entries. There were scribbled jottings from time to time, odd visions, panic attacks. Then came long rambling passages, sudden illogical leaps, and even bits of nonsense. Every so often the writing rambled off the page and was barely decipherable. At times Matt had the sensation that he was reading the words of a madman. Then Kellicut appeared to make a key discovery, a bridge of some sort, though it was not clear whether it was a natural bridge or a construction made by an intelligent being. He referred to it only as "the link" and provided no coordinates, not even for the nonexistent map. He seemed to have so lost his equilibrium that he forgot he was writing a manuscript for others. It was now only for himself, a record of a declining mind and a still-strong ego spilling onto the pages like blood. He talked again of fever. He raved that he was the greatest explorer in history, Balboa looking at the Pacific Ocean, Galileo peering through the telescope. Greater than any of them.

By now all dates and sense of time had dropped away, and Kellicut referred to himself in the third person. Matt found he was reading out a cryptic stream of consciousness, words tumbling out with tantalizing bits of description. But what did they mean? He flipped through the later pages. His eyes fell upon a passage in the center of a page:

> . . . a rustling in the crevice, the dark and the wind . . . where is Cerebus? . . . He enters the long tunnel, his elbows scraped so the blood spurts out—a signpost for the return trip if there is to be one . . . the dark and more dark and sudden blinding light strikes . . . I know their secret and the power they possess— enough to defeat the reaper, the true afterlife, eternal. . . . They know I know, they know I'm watching. They are watching me without looking . . . extraordinary . . . the valley of life, a whole world, a universe, naked hairy children of God. Wrapped bundles up in the trees, cocoons from giant moths and bones scattered below . . . oh, what a graveyard, and the eyes, *the eyes are upon you.*

There followed a blank page and then the final entry. The tone was calm, rational.

> Base camp. April 7. I am going back to them. I am going to make myself known, to present myself to them.

That was the entire text. The next page was blank, as were all the others.

Matt closed the diary slowly. What he had read confirmed his fears and sent the adrenaline coursing through his body. Was it excitement or fear? He couldn't tell anymore; his feelings were too jumbled. So they were real, after all! Either that or Kellicut was stark raving mad. Matt thought of the outside world, so pervasive, so powerful. So many people, everywhere. All of it—cities, airports, television, cars, computers. That was reality. How could this anachronism, this little backwater of the past, continue to exist? A flood of skepticism flowed in like water breaking through dikes. But when he looked at the fire and the faces of those around it, and when he sensed the barren, isolated landscape of the Pamirs and felt the diary in his hands, a conviction swept through him that held back the flood. Inexplicably from nowhere, a stab of paranoia: Could this whole thing be some sort of elaborate trick, a setup?

Everyone was silent for a moment. Susan held her hand to her forehead. Her chest was heaving, as if she were breathing with difficulty. The display of emotion almost looked theatrical.

Matt opened the book again. There was no map anywhere. He stared at the final blank page as if it held some kind of secret, then flipped the page back and looked at the date of the last entry. Two months ago. And he hadn't come back since. What are the odds that he's still alive? That he wasn't pulled apart limb by limb? Or dead somewhere at the bottom of a ravine? Or collapsed beside a pile of rocks, having succumbed to cold or starvation? It's a long shot for survival, Matt thought.

"Well, *something* happened. He saw something," he said finally.

"Or something saw him," said Susan. "What was all that about eyes?"

"And a graveyard?" asked Rudy.

"He is clearly close to the edge," said Matt. "He went for days without enough to eat, all alone. He has a fever. Maybe it affected his mind. Maybe he's delusional." He was surprised to hear himself using the present tense. It didn't seem suitable.

"He wasn't delusional," said Van, finally speaking up. "He knew what he was writing about."

It's strange how we all seem to be so delicate in our choice of words, thought Susan, tiptoeing around on eggshells. "How do you know?" she challenged.

"It's obvious," replied Van, his condescension so blatant that it was offhand, almost inoffensive. "He found some way across to their world, some link. He looked for them and he found them. It's all there—a passage of some sort, even a graveyard. Where the hell do you think your skull came from?"

"And the eyes—what about that?" asked Susan.

Van shrugged.

"The problem is there's no map," Matt said. "He talks about one—he even gives coordinates—but we don't have it. Without it, how can we follow his trail? We don't have any idea where in the hell he went, just that it was up."

"Even if we did have the map," said Susan, "you notice he didn't give any position for this . . . passageway, crevice, whatever. Why doesn't he describe it?" She shook her head.

"It's exasperating," said Matt. "Why does he persist in being so goddamned enigmatic? Typical—he always did have a perverse streak."

Susan was quiet for a while and then spoke slowly, as if she were reasoning it out. "So it seems he actually saw them, or at least in some way observed them before he found that skull. In which case he had much more concrete proof. He knew they existed; he didn't merely speculate about it. So why be so mysterious? Why just send the skull with no letter? Why not communicate his great discovery? Not to do so poses too big a risk. What if it didn't get through; what if we didn't come? On something like this he's not going to take any chances. It's too important to him. To science. No one, and especially no one with his ego, would willingly keep silent about this."

One by one, they looked at Van. He stared into the fire, then stirred and wiped his face with his sleeve. When he spoke, it was without feeling or remorse.

"There was a note, a brief one." He fell silent again.

"Go on," said Matt. He was seething with rage but kept it hidden.

"Not much to tell, really."

"Go on," Matt repeated firmly.

"It came with the package. One page. Looks like it was torn out of that diary—same kind of paper."

Matt flipped open the book. At the very end was the ragged tear of a missing page.

"And?"

"It was addressed to the two of you. He gave a brief description, or at least seemed to. It was raving like this one. It seemed to say he had encountered them and was going back for another look."

"Go on."

"We couldn't be sure what he was saying. He didn't mention that bit about 'presenting himself,' whatever that means. I don't suppose he would have in a letter. Sounds a bit melodramatic."

"Go on."

"Not much more to say. We had it analyzed, of course, backward and forward: ink, paper, psychiatrists, you name it."

"What was the conclusion?"

"No surprises. It was genuine."

"No surprises!" fumed Matt. "You mean to say you had just been informed about the existence of another hominid on this planet and you say there were no surprises?"

"Well, doctor, I was never quite the skeptic that you were," Van answered, wearing a little boy's sneer. Matt felt like slugging him.

"Did he say anything more?" pressed Susan. "Anything at all that wasn't in the diary?"

"Nothing I can think of."

"A map?"

"Christ, no. If I had a map, I wouldn't need you people along."

"Field notes?"

"Nope."

"Nothing?"

"There was no more information. It's still not possible to say what he saw, or even if he saw anything beyond his fevered rantings—except, of course, we know he blundered into some kind of graveyard. At the end he said we should hurry. *For God's sake, come as quickly as you can;* I think those were the exact words."

Matt and Susan exchanged looks in the fire's glow. It sounded like the note Sharafidin had delivered.

"Okay," Matt said, with menace in his voice, "now tell us exactly why you kept it from us."

Van sighed. "Quite frankly, we didn't think you'd believe it."

"You didn't?"

"You believed it," said Susan.

"Ah, yes, but you see, I've believed it for years." Van gave a short laugh, more of a snort. "And there was another thing. I'm not sure he would have approved of my coming along. He never really trusted us, you know."

"No shit! I wonder why," Matt said.

Van ignored him. "He never really knew what we were about."

"You say he was writing to us," said Susan. "Did he say anything specifically about you?"

"Yes."

"What did he say?"

"He said, *Don't trust them. Come alone if you possibly can.*"

"That's pretty specific," said Matt.

They fell into silence. Matt was still angry, but Van had regained his equilibrium and was even smiling in a peculiar way, like a kid caught cheating.

Susan leaned toward Van. "Tell me; what *are* you up to exactly? Who are you people?"

"We're like you, just like you," Van answered. "We're scientific explorers, more or less."

*   *   *

The mists were deepening now and it was late, but they were too excited to sleep.

"We need Sharafidin," Matt said suddenly.

They looked around. The boy was gone. They spread out from the campsite and found him soon enough off by himself, wrapped in his woolen blanket. Maybe he was disturbed by their altercation, thought Susan.

"Ask him if he ever saw a map," Matt told Rudy.

Rudy translated the question. The boy huddled in his blanket, shivering slightly, and spoke slowly.

Rudy turned toward them. "He says there was one, but the Teacher kept it on him."

"Where did he put it when he went away?"

"He always took it with him."

"Ask him if the Teacher always buried the book before he went away."

"He says he never saw him bury the book."

"Makes sense," said Matt. "He buried it the last time. When he left he had some reason to think that he might not be coming back. And it's obvious he had another fear— that something else might get to the camp before we did."

Van snorted. "Looks like he was right on both counts."

As the fire dimmed, Matt awoke from a light slumber and saw Susan sitting awake, hugging her knees and staring at the tiny flames.

He got up, threw a few gnarled branches on the fire, and sat down next to her. She smiled at him, almost sadly.

"Can't sleep?"

She nodded.

"The diary get to you?"

"The diary, Kellicut, the fact that they could be real, the whole thing." She paused a second. "You."

"In that order?"

Another half smile.

"Matt," she said solemnly, "do you realize we could be on the brink of the world's greatest discovery? Black holes, outer space, the Hubble telescope—they're all great steps in our knowledge outward. This goes inward. It's like DNA—it's about our origin as a species. Who would have imagined? Everything we've ever theorized may be blown up, and I'm glad, because it will be replaced by the truth."

He leaned over and picked up her hand. She let him hold it for a while, then gave his a squeeze and pulled away. "I'm going to turn in," she said. She undressed and slipped into her sleeping bag.

Matt couldn't fall back asleep right away. He heard the others breathing and some sounds way off in the darkness. Finally he fell into a fitful doze, dreaming and then almost waking. He imagined a strange hulking figure walking around the camp. It skulked around the larder, leaning over it to pick out some bits of meat in the center. It rummaged through their backpacks and peered down at them. Once or twice he almost became conscious. Mists streamed across the embers until finally the fire died away altogether, darkness took over, and he fell into a profound sleep.

The next morning the mists were gone and the day was bright. They all awoke at the same time, as if a magic spell had been lifted.

As they prepared breakfast, they noticed that Sharafidin was gone. They looked everywhere, but his blanket and few supplies were missing.

"I could have told you," said Van. He was furious. "He was spooked, all right. I knew it when we talked to him last night. I knew he'd run off."

"I don't know," said Rudy doubtfully, scratching his head.

"I bet it had to do with that goddamn diary," Van continued. "He knew more than he let on. He was hiding something."

Susan was crouching on her haunches where Sharafidin had bedded down. She stared at the ground, then lowered her hand, picked something up, and walked over to Matt, looking as if the wind had been knocked out of her.

"He didn't run off." She opened her right fist; in it was the tiny Koran. Its worn leather surface glistened in the early morning sun.

9

"So what do we do now?" asked Rudy.

No one answered. They had fallen silent after a morning of talk and disagreement over Sharafidin's disappearance. At first each had dealt with it alone. Matt was quiet, Rudy busied himself with cleaning up after breakfast, Van lounged about, ostensibly unruffled, and Susan wrote a long message for Kellicut, which she buried in the "mail drop," as Matt called it, on the off chance that he might return.

They had searched the campsite for signs of a scuffle or what they began euphemistically calling "visitors," but had found nothing. Matt had checked the backpacks. Two were lying askew, on their sides, but it was hard to remember their exact placement the night before. He couldn't say if they had been rifled or not. At the larder everything seemed to be in order. He did not tell anyone about his nightmare.

"Look, I'm not saying he's a coward or anything," Van said. "He got us here. Maybe in his mind he fulfilled the terms of the deal, so there was no reason to stick around."

Susan turned on him angrily. "He wouldn't just pick up and leave without saying a word. You don't know what you're talking about."

Matt tried to defuse the tension. "What we do is we press on. From here on we would have been on our own anyway.

Sharafidin couldn't have helped us anymore. He couldn't lead us any farther than he did.''

"How do we know where to go?" asked Rudy.

"We just keep going up," replied Matt, with a confidence he didn't feel. "We don't have a map, but the diary tells us roughly what we're looking for: first a ravine, then some kind of crossing, then a crevice. Finding the crevice is going to be the hard part."

They began to climb the slope at the far end of the camp. Halfway up to a ledge Susan turned around and looked back. She could see the path they had come on, the spot where Van had crouched with the gun. That was less than twenty-four hours ago, she reflected, but already it seemed like days. Kellicut's diary had changed everything. The existence of a relic band of hominids was beginning to appear more and more likely. From up here his lean-to looked puny, little more than a pile of twigs and pebbles against a limitless expanse of rock and sky.

The sun was out but when the wind stirred, the cold cut to the bone. They moved in single file, laboriously. The effort behind each step was costly, as if the altitude had saddled their feet with weights.

Susan was confused about Sharafidin. What could have happened to him? Van was wrong; he would not just run off. She was sure of that. Of course there was another explanation, but it was too ghastly to dwell on and she tried to push it aside.

They came around the side of the ridge to a spectacular view ahead. There was a gully, then a long sloping incline of rock with patches of crusted snow in the shadows; rising beyond it like a frozen wave was another summit, and in the distance still another. On the top of the farthest one a diamond crest of snow glistened. The world seemed to go on and on as far as they could see.

Matt felt infinitesimal. Oddly enough, the sensation was not oppressive but exhilarating, even liberating in its first rush. But the feeling rapidly dissipated and soon gave way to gloom, born from the pragmatic realization that in all that space and majesty the prospect of finding what they were looking for was impossibly remote.

As they reached the ridge's crown, Susan caught up to him and they walked side by side. Her hair, tucked under a cap, hung down in strands that brushed her cheek.

"There's the haystack. Wonder where the needle is," she said, thrusting her chin at the view ahead. "Let me ask you something."

"Go ahead."

"At this point we could probably turn around and make it back, right? I mean, we could probably find our way down from here."

"Probably."

"But after another three or four days, maybe not."

"Right."

"So?"

"So what's your point?"

"Maybe we should think this over and come to some sort of decision about what we want to do."

"Susan, you already know what you want to do."

"How do you know?"

"Because I know you."

He was right, of course. There was no way she would not keep going, and if anyone else had suggested that they turn around, she would have fought like a tigress. Not for nothing was she the granddaughter of a Hungarian adventurer who had trekked across Canada. But she liked the idea of talking it over and finding strength in a consensus.

"How about the others? Maybe they should have a say."

"Are you kidding? Look at Van. He'd run over his grandmother to keep going. He can barely breathe, but he's not going to stop."

"And Rudy?"

"Harder to tell, but I'd say he's signed on for the duration. And when you come right down to it, he'll do whatever you want to do.''

Susan sighed and smiled weakly.

''Great,'' she said. ''Just the way I always imagined my life would end. Wandering around heaven's door, looking for the absent-minded professor and the Abominable Snowman.''

When they reached the top of the crown, they were stopped in their tracks by the spectacle. A flock of silver-black birds skirted them, fast and low, and left behind a cry that was as thin as a vapor trail. It was dizzying to be thrust up into the sky with clouds churning and dipping all around them.

Matt dropped his backpack. ''Made it, Ma! Top o' the world!'' he yelled, thrusting his two arms out in his best Cagney freeze-frame.

When Susan laughed, a full-throated laugh, Matt spun half around, grabbed her by one arm, and pulled her to him. She tilted her face up and he kissed her, quickly. Her eyes were open. He kissed her cheek. She moved her head slightly, back to his lips, and this time kissed him long and deeply, then moved closer, inside his arms.

Rudy came into view behind them, clapped his arms together, did a little dance, and hurried to catch up to them. ''Aha, I knew it. I was putting down bets. I have a nose for these things.'' He dropped his backpack and bustled around, genuinely happy for them.

''Rudy,'' said Susan fondly, ''here's an expression from the nineties: Chill out.''

''Chill out? Chill out? What's it mean?'' He was delighted.

''Cool it. Remember that one? It's like 'cool it,' only more serious.''

''Chill out. How heavy.''

They sat down and waited for Van. Matt and Susan were silent and suddenly awkward, but Rudy kept up a steady patter. They had to wait a long time, and when Van finally clambered up the slope he was panting heavily. His face was pale and his head was rocking with the effort of catching his breath. He collapsed beside them and cradled his head with his hands.

"I'd think all that smoking would prepare you to do without oxygen," Matt said.

Van glared at him but was too breathless to reply.

They decided to split up the weight of Van's load, and Matt began unloading his backpack. He discovered the NO-MAD. "Well, what have we here?" he said, holding it up.

Susan picked up the device in one hand, examining it. "Fancy," she said. "I've seen one of these before. It's for satellite transmission, isn't it?"

"Have you used this?" Matt was barely able to suppress his anger. Once again Van had been playing them for fools.

Van shook his head, opened his mouth to speak, then dropped his eyes, seeking refuge in frailty.

"It's not a bad idea to have a satellite link," said Matt, "but I don't see why you kept it a secret. And it's too heavy. We can't carry it any farther." He put it down on a ledge, unpacked other gear next to it, formed it all into a mound, and then piled rocks on top of it. "I've always wanted to bury a computer," he said.

Before covering it completely, Matt checked the dial. The switch was turned to the OFF position. He had no way of knowing that this meant the transmitter was sending an automatic tracking signal, and Van did not enlighten him.

Matt pulled out a shovel from the pack and added it to the pile. Finally Van managed to speak. "Figured I'd need that for my grave," he said.

"Bullshit. You'll outlive us all," said Susan.

Van knew he was in a bad way. He felt he was inexorably suffocating. From time to time a wave of panic shuddered through his body; he could feel it coming, then build and course through him like an electric current. He was both sweating and cold. In Barbados he once watched as a group fished a dying man out of the ocean. The diver had the bends and he lay for a while on the beach and then expired, looking directly into the sun with wide eyes. The man, he had learned, was an accomplished scuba diver who had made hundreds of dives, gone down hundreds of feet, and explored countless underwater caves. No one knew what had happened this time, only sixty feet underwater. A fellow diver theorized that he had been seized by an insurmountable panic and suddenly broke for the surface.

Van could understand that now, only there was no surface to rush toward. His defenses were lowered, and so all kinds of crazy thoughts penetrated. He knew this on some level, but the knowledge did not diminish their hold over him. He felt, with a certainty that was hard to explain, that the others were against him. They were intentionally setting a rigorous pace so he would tire and fall behind. The radio computer was a blunder they would regret. Let them take everything. They had no idea, not the smallest inkling, of what was happening. He could see what they were up to. They couldn't fool him. Just give me time, he thought. I know how to even the score.

That night they camped at the bottom of a gully protected on two sides by fallen boulders. There was no wind, but the cold still penetrated like shards of glass.

Van's head was pounding and he felt another wave of panic wash through him. For some reason he began thinking of his father. "Sickness is a weakness and weakness is a sickness," his father used to say.

Later, when he was trying to sleep, he had a bout of Cheyne-Stokes breathing from the altitude. The moment he drifted from consciousness into sleep, his breathing cut off. When the emergency center of the brain took over, his body was racked by shudders as he took in great gulps of air and awoke in a panic, drenched in sweat. It happened three times during the night.

*　　*　　*

They walked all the next morning, and by afternoon Matt's mind began to wander again. It was like having a daydream, only longer and a bit more intense, and the line between fantasy and reality was more fluid.

"Matt, Matt!"

Susan was calling to him from behind. He turned slowly as he walked, still in a fog.

"Look! Look down."

He did. He saw nothing out of the ordinary—rocks and scree scattered about, the tips of his hiking boots moving inexorably ahead, one after the other through dust.

"Look around! Don't you see it?" Susan's voice was more excited than alarmed. It carried sluggishly in the thin air and seemed to come from far away.

Suddenly it struck him: He was on a path! It was rudimentary, and here and there it disappeared in the dusty patches, but there was undeniably the outline of some kind of trail.

He bent down. There were no footprints as such, merely a darkening of the earth. Up ahead where the ground rose slightly, the path remained packed down, curving slightly to avoid a rocky surface.

Susan caught up with him, breathing heavily. "What do you think?" she asked.

"Hard to say. There are no prints at all."

"Could be some kind of animal, like mountain goats. On the other hand, there are no droppings."

"Strange, the way it just seemed to start up out of nowhere."

"Just like Kellicut wrote," Susan said.

Rudy joined them, and then, after a long time, Van. Rudy was exhilarated by the discovery, but Van took it darkly. "Well," he said, with a sigh of resignation and exhaustion, "at least we know we're on its turf now."

That evening they built their campsite in an oval cutout on the rocky slope.

It had been a rough day. The path had widened a bit and grown more distinct. After four hours it had crossed another path, and then another. Matt had stood for long minutes at each juncture, trying to decide which one to take. Finally there had been so many new paths that he had given up and simply tried to keep going more or less in the same direction.

The sky darkened rapidly. Rudy, who appeared less tired than the others, appointed himself in charge of dinner, precooked pasta and dehydrated vegetables. It took him half an hour to collect enough bits of wood for a small fire. ''Best to make a little fire, move close, and get warm,'' he said.

Matt and Susan hadn't touched since their kiss on the ridge the previous morning. Not that Matt hadn't thought of it. Fantasies of sex with her had continued to slip in and out of his head, but exhaustion, hunger, and cold had intervened. Now Van and Rudy were asleep in their bags, their backs to the fire. There were no sounds except for the distant whine of the wind. Even the fire was silent except for the hiss of burning embers.

Quietly, Matt unzipped his sleeping bag. The air felt cold but not freezing on his shoulder. He reached over, felt for the zipper on Susan's bag, and slowly moved it downward. His hand moved inside. He took his time, moving up and down, then deeper, until he felt the wall of her body. When his fingertips touched her T-shirt he pressed down to the flesh beneath, then moved closer.

She was awake, he could tell. Her breathing was coming in short irregular bursts, but she did not move. He caressed her stomach through the shirt in slow circular movements, moved up to her right breast, cupping it, then lowered his hand slowly to her belly. He felt a slight intake of breath, but still she did not move.

He moved his hand up again and felt her nipples harden between his fingers. Slowly he lowered his hand and slipped it down to her mound of pubic hair. As he did so, she shifted and turned toward him. With her arms outstretched, she pulled him to her, and he felt the hard edges of his desire rake through him

Then came the cry, so loud and inhuman that it flooded Matt with adrenaline. He pulled his hand out of Susan's bag and leaped to his feet before he was even aware of its source. A shadow was thrashing about—Van in his sleeping bag, rolling over and over, screaming.

"What is it! What's the matter?" Matt ran over and held him in place by his bended knee. When he unzipped the bag Van rolled out, hugging his stomach, a contorted bundle. Then Matt heard another sound, a low groan, coming from Rudy.

"Poison," gasped Van. "We've been poisoned."

"Quick, drink this!" It was Susan, holding a canteen to Van's lips. He sipped.

"Another," she commanded. "Right now."

She went to Rudy and did the same, then gave Matt some water and took some herself. Slowly Van and Rudy felt the ache in their stomachs receding.

"It's not serious," said Susan. "It's the vegetables. You didn't add enough water. They weren't hydrated enough, so when we ate them and drank tea they began swelling inside."

"Jesus Christ," said Matt. He stood up and walked over to peer down at Rudy, who managed a sheepish smile through his groans.

The next morning, with the sun stuck behind a thick blanket of clouds, there was an even deeper chill to the air. They dressed in layers of polypropylene fiber underneath windbreakers.

They had been under way about three hours when they came to the ravine, hidden from sight down an incline. At first it looked like only a dip in front of the rock face that rose up steeply on the other side, and Matt nearly stumbled into it.

"Looks about thirty feet across," said Matt.

"Too long for the ropes, even if we could hitch them onto something on the other side," said Van.

"Think it's Kellicut's ravine?" asked Susan.

"Impossible to say," Matt answered. "There could be dozens of them up here. Still, he only mentioned one in all his travels, so maybe we've hit it."

The going was harder and slower now that they were off the path. Matt led them up and down rocky ledges and around piles of boulders. Soon, despite the chill, they were sweating and stripped off some of their layers. Several times Van lost his footing and fell, cursing. As they walked they kept the ravine in sight.

After two hours, they rested for lunch—beef jerky, washed down with hot weak tea.

Van sat immobile, as if a single movement was wasted motion. "Have you noticed," he said, "that up here pleasure is simply relief from total deprivation, a slight lessening of pain?"

"Oh, I'm not so sure." Susan laughed, shooting a quick look at Matt.

"Gotta take a piss," said Rudy, and wandered off. A few minutes later they heard him shouting, and he appeared around a corner of rock, his pants unbuttoned, waving both arms as if he were doing jumping jacks. They rushed over, and as they got close he began pointing frantically.

Ahead, just around the corner, so close they could have hit it with a stone, was a strange structure stretching like a thick band across the full breadth of the ravine.

"That's it!" shouted Susan. "What did he call it? 'A link to another world.' "

"A bridge," said Matt.

They ran closer, then instinctively slowed and proceeded cautiously, step by step, looking around for signs of life.

The span was crude, about thirty-five feet long, constructed of tree branches and leaves wrapped together and held in place by thick vines. It was a looping cylinder about two feet wide, sagging precariously in the center and then rising up to a rocky ledge on the other side, where it was attached to poles stuck into the ground.

Matt and Susan stared in awe, but Van was matter of fact. "It ain't the Brooklyn Bridge," he said. "How do you get across that thing?"

"You crawl," replied Matt.

"But will it hold?"

"Only one way to find out."

"Actually there are four ways to find out, because there are four of us."

"Who's going first?" asked Rudy.

"We could draw straws," said Van.

"This isn't ring-a-levio," said Matt.

Susan was busy examining the tangled attachment of vines on the near side, her brow furrowed in concentration. "Matt, look at this. We've never seen anything like this before. It surpasses anything we know about Mousterian culture. Look at the complexity of those knots."

Matt squatted next to her. "I don't know," he said. "If they used ropes or vines like this thousands of years ago the stuff would have decayed long ago. It never would have survived for us to find it."

She stood up abruptly. "I'm going first." Her words had a tone of finality. "First because I'm the lightest and second because I'm the one who wants most to get across."

No one disputed her.

They retrieved their backpacks and sorted through them to lighten their loads. Among the items they decided to leave behind, stored in a small crevice, were tins of food and two tiny pup tents. They covered the crevice over with rocks to keep the cache hidden.

Susan stashed her jacket in her pack and tightened the drawstrings around her legs and arms for flexibility. She threaded a rope around her waist and, leaning over the ravine, looped it around the underside of the span and tied it loosely. She tied another rope to her belt and tossed the end of it to Matt, who secured it around a boulder.

"Here goes nothing," she said and smiled weakly. "Remember, if anything goes wrong, I want coauthorship of the paper."

"You got it," replied Matt.

"When I get halfway across, yell out to me and I'll untie the rope so you can haul it back. It's not long enough to make it."

She began warily, hugging the cylinder of sticks and debris, rising up and crawling a few inches, then leaning her arms down to swing the guard rope ahead a few feet like a logger going up a tree trunk. Progress was slow.

When Susan got ten feet out, the contraption began to sway in a widening arc like a pendulum, and she stopped and clung tightly until it slowed. Then she shifted her movements. It rocked gently front to back, but it held. Once she looked down; quickly she closed her eyes and rested for a while.

Halfway across she picked up speed and fell into a rhythm. Matt kept an eye on the rope and when it became taut he yelled out to her. Without a backward look, she reached down to her belt and untied it. The end sank down quickly into nothingness and Matt felt an unexpectedly heavy tug as he pulled it in.

When Susan made it to the other side, she stood up and gave them a V-sign.

Rudy followed, and then Van. Halfway over Van pulled in the safety rope and tossed it across to Susan. It took him four attempts to get it to her.

Going last, Matt was on his own. There was no rope to hold him.

A quarter of the way across, he felt a wave of vertigo engulf him. He stopped and clung to the branches. It was cold, and the wind whipped his fingers. He could hear the cries of birds—above or below? He rested, then summoned up his strength and went on. As he neared the end, he felt blood coursing through him and a giddiness that took over his whole body.

"Piece of cake, huh?" remarked Van.

They sat for a long time, recovering. Finally Susan spoke. "Whoever made this thing, was it human?"

"How did they get it across the first time?" asked Matt.

"Imagine the effort involved," said Van.

"And why? What pushed them to do it?" asked Susan.

"Something's motivating them," said Matt. "Something is making them leave their precious retreat. But what?"

"Trading? Getting food for animal skins?" suggested Van.

"I doubt it," replied Susan. "That's hardly enough to overcome centuries of hiding and self-imposed exile."

"They're after something."

Matt knelt down by the bridge, peered underneath it, and whistled. He called the others over and pointed to a stake protruding out of a pile of rocks that supported the abutment. "Look at that. It's a lever. If you strike that, the rocks tumble down and the whole damn contraption falls into the ravine."

"Like an eject mechanism," added Van. "Whoever built this wanted to be able to blow it away in an instant."

"So they want the outside world, but they're afraid of it too," said Susan. "That's inconsistent."

"Let's work it out," Matt went on. "Assume for a minute that they're aware of our presence—and I think that's a fair assumption. Why didn't they destroy it to keep *us* away?"

They were quiet for a while. Finally Van said, "Only one explanation. They want us to come."

Looking down at the ground ten feet away, Rudy made his second find of the afternoon. "And we're not the only ones," he said, pointing down at cross-hatched imprints on the ground. "Look, more boot marks."

10

Matt was crossing a small plateau of scree scattered about like chunks of plaster when he noticed the first snowflake. It struck him that it was unusually large as it gently rode the air currents to the ground. It hit a rock at his feet and clung there like a tuft of cotton candy. Then he saw another.

He tried not to succumb to fear, but he had to push it consciously away into a corner of his mind. Maybe the snowflakes were just a random occurrence. It was unlikely, he had to admit, but perhaps it would be a brief, passing flurry; snow dusting must happen often at this altitude. But his common sense and the low leaden sky above told him otherwise.

At first after crossing the bridge they had felt a strange light-headed exhilaration. They were both giddy and frightened and trod warily, as if they had crossed onto an alien planet, staying close together and darting looks around. Who knew what could be lurking behind those boulders? But after an hour passed and then another in the drab and lifeless landscape, eventually the nervousness gave way to a monotonous fatigue.

"Kellicut never told us about this part, did he?" said Susan, when they stopped to rest. "Of course I wouldn't know," she went on, "since I haven't had the opportunity to read his letter.'' She looked at Van playfully.

Then Van did a strange thing: He smiled. ''Hey, hold on,'' he said, almost pleasantly. ''I've already apologized for that.''

Soon enough the good mood was gone. They stopped for lunch but spent a miserable time because of the cold. Rudy's fingers were so chilled he could barely light the wood. The fire was pathetically small, and they huddled together to conserve warmth. Even the beef broth was only lukewarm.

The wind, picking up, whipped through a nearby gorge and whistled eerily, like a pipe organ. They decided to carry on; at least movement would temper the cold somewhat.

More flakes fell. Odd, Matt thought; if you looked straight up they seemed to be concentrating on you. How's that for being egocentric? he mused. They came down individually, like parachutists. He looked into the sky for the hundredth time that day; it was the same as before, a low-hanging gray-whiteness that spread in all directions like a gigantic frozen steam bath.

His mind raced through scenarios. The shovel they had left behind—clearly a mistake. Same for the tents, which were too heavy. So much for shelter. He still had the knife, but it wasn't much good for digging. Van had the gun— no help there. Maybe the sleeping bags could be zipped together, at least two of them and maybe more, to serve as shelter. But they would need to keep them separate for warmth, and in any case the corners wouldn't hold in place if the wind kept up.

Matt stopped and waited for the others to catch up. They were moving sluggishly, and it took some time for them to gather. ''What do you think?'' he asked, when they were all together. He found he was making his voice loud, as if the wind were already roaring.

''Going to be a bad one,'' said Van. ''I don't like the look of it. We're fucked.''

"Look at that sky," said Rudy. "Not a single hole anywhere."

Only Susan understood that Matt was asking what they should do. "I can't think of anything else except what we're doing," she said. "We just have to keep going. There's got to be some refuge someplace."

"Trouble is," Matt answered, "we're on a kind of plateau. We haven't passed anything for hours, not even a hole."

Van said, "Well, we sure as shit can't stop here. Too damn exposed. Nothing to do but go on."

Matt took a quick consensus. "Everyone agree?" They all nodded. "Then we've got to stick together. We also have to make time. That means you, Van. You've got to keep up somehow."

Van started to speak, then looked away.

This time, when they set out, the parachutists had multiplied; a whole swirling airborne invasion was under way. As high and far as Matt could see, flakes were diving down in force. They took up the whole sky. A sense of dread rose from his stomach.

The snow settled first in the recesses of the rock, in furrows and cavities, and began forming little cornices on the undersides of ledges.

The wind was getting stronger too, sometimes driving the snow in circular frenzies that roiled around boulders and cliffs. Matt pulled his hood tighter. He reached into his pocket and put on a pair of goggles, then turned to look at Susan, some twenty feet behind. She was walking with the delicate, constrained motions of someone battling off pain. Around her was a swirling black and white moonscape. The sight touched him on a level he had not known for years. He waved, turned, and walked on, his steps muffled by the snow.

*　　*　　*

Early on in his study of paleontology, Matt had been smitten. On his first trip he loved all of it, but especially the beginning, the digging, the going down layer by layer through all the periods. What were the glacial episodes? He could hear the drone of schooldays returning: Würm, Riss, Mindel, Günz. The pluvials? Gamblian, Kanjeran, Kamasian, Kageran. Digging down through the eons until they were laid bare on the surface of a vertical wall. He had felt like a deep-sea diver descending through the levels so that the earth might yield up her sunken treasure. Was it the going down? Or was it the thrill of the find, a scattering of bones, the brown fragment of a skull? Even the word for it was right, he thought—not "excavation" but "dig." Primitive and basic. He had lost himself in the details, searching with a magnifying glass on his hands and knees like some Sherlock of the desert. He loved lying on his belly on a board and twisting a scalpel to scrape a bit of entombed dirt or using a toothbrush to clean tiny knucklebones. But most of all he had loved the beginning—the first swing of the ax, the digging down. An indescribable, comforting, frightening feeling, like a return to a sanctified place of long-ago childhood.

Now, against the howling of the wind, he barely heard the others call to him. It sounded like cries through sheets of glass. The three were almost invisible in the total whiteness. As he turned and made his way back, he saw that his tracks were already almost covered.

"It's too thick. We can't see each other," said Rudy.

"We're getting separated," said Susan. "Van was going in the wrong direction and we had to search for him."

"Okay. Get your ropes and we'll tie ourselves together."

The snowflakes had grown into small hard pellets, which hit their cheeks like biting insects. The noise alone was overwhelming, and it took forever to get the ropes attached.

Van spoke for the first time.

"Matt"—Matt thought his name sounded unreal in the middle of all this whiteness—"this blizzard isn't going to quit. We're fucked. I mean it. We're really fucked." His voice had a trace of panic.

Susan cut in. "Our only hope is to find someplace fast. We can't keep going much longer."

"I think the plateau ends up ahead," Matt said. "I can't be sure, but I thought I saw the shape of something. Could be a rock face."

"We'd better hurry."

"We've got to get there. It's our only hope."

"I'm going to sing," said Rudy.

As Matt struggled on, he heard Rudy's voice behind him:

> You can't always get what you want.
> You can't always get what you want.
> But if you try sometimes
> You just might find,
> You get what you need.

A few minutes later, Matt came upon a craggy rock rising up out of nowhere. It stood out in the blizzard, a dark and ghostly promontory; he gave the rope a tug to hurry the others and lurched toward it.

He dove at the base, shoveling out snow in heaping armfuls. Soon they were at his side, helping him. The snow was so light that it was like heaving baskets of air.

They hit rock and brushed it. A crack appeared. They followed it, digging out more snow as it widened and deepened. Now it was hard work; Matt was sweating and the snow was suddenly dense and heavy. The crevice widened to a foot and a half across. They pushed away more snow, and then the crack ended.

No one spoke.

Matt tried to lower himself into the crevice, but he struck the bottom after only two feet. He tried dislodging a boulder, which rocked and fell against his arm, bruising it. He rolled up his sleeve and stared; a few drops of blood stood out against the snow, bright red dots in a whirl of white.

Susan held a fistful of snow against the wound and the bleeding stopped. Matt felt no pain. ''Nothing to do but go on,'' she said.

They sat and rested a bit in the little crater they had created, but they began falling asleep. Alarmed, they stood up and went on. The snow was above their knees here, so the going was ponderous, and they staggered more than they walked.

Matt felt a potent thirst deep in the back of his throat but he didn't want to stop to hunt for his canteen, hanging somewhere in the frozen white armor that encased his body. Even on his feet he was beginning to feel sleepy.

Matt didn't realize that he had stopped. So had the others. Susan and Rudy were sitting in the snow up to their waists and Van was crawling about, swaying gently on his hands and knees. They didn't feel cold anymore, not really, just disconnected, vague, and pleasantly sleepy. Somewhere in the recesses of his mind, it came to Matt that they were going to die. But even that certainty seemed muffled, outside him, softened by the whiteness all around. It was not alarming.

But he did feel thirst. He felt for his canteen and raised it to his lips. A swig of water squeezed past a block of ice, and he shuddered, then straightened and began to feel his limbs again. He staggered over to Susan, who was half reclining, dazed. Her pupils were large and she had the trace of a smile on her lips. Van was nodding, almost asleep.

Matt unfastened their ropes and tied them together to make one long rope. One end he wound through their three belts. The other he tied to his own belt. ''Stay here,'' he yelled needlessly, and struck out on his own, straight ahead. Behind him he could hear Rudy's voice, high-pitched and a bit off key.

The voice trailed off, and he couldn't tell whether Rudy had stopped or the wind had obliterated it.

Now the drifts were up to his waist in places. Twice he stumbled, and when he pitched forward, he dove into a cocoon so white and warm and pure he was tempted to rest for a bit, but he got up and went on. The top of his vision was lost to darkness, cut off somehow, like a rip across a photograph.

Abruptly the wind shifted direction so he could see for a moment. Just ahead in the snow was a dark form that looked like Susan, except that as he got closer he could see she wasn't wearing her windbreaker; in fact she was dressed in a summer dress as she had been when he first saw her many years ago. How could she survive up here like that? And her hair was full and flowing in the breeze, just as in those corny old movies. She was beckoning him onward, and when he got there he reached out and touched her and began to draw her to him, except that she didn't yield.

Matt found he was leaning against a wall of rock. The gusts behind him helped to push him along, and he followed the wall until finally he sensed darkness above him, and the wind died down suddenly. Consciousness returned. He realized he was inside the mouth of a cave.

He unfastened the rope but kept it looped through his belt and wound it around a rock and tied it. Then he turned around and followed the rope out of the cave and into the blizzard, pulling it up through the snow like a fishing line until he reached the others.

The light reappeared at the end of a long tunnel. Susan saw it coming closer and closer, almost like a train, except that it was a different kind of light, and she was the one who was moving. She got closer and closer, and just as she burst into the blinding daylight she heard voices around her. "Come on, come on! Get up!" Matt was yelling. He lifted her to her feet and half walked, half carried her to the opening. He was surprised that it seemed so close. Then he went back for Rudy and finally for Van, and they all collapsed deep inside the cave.

When Susan awoke she had no inkling of how long she had been asleep. She felt an agreeable sensation of warmth and sustenance, and when she opened her eyes she saw a fire. Rudy was puttering around it, fixing a meal. The flames flickered off rock walls, throwing shadows. He smiled, brought her a cup of coffee, and stroked her hair.

Next to her, Matt began to stir. "Ah, the hero awakes," Rudy said.

Matt looked uncomprehending for a second, blinking. It was a moment before he could speak. "You're the hero. It was your singing that drove me away."

"That was my plan."

Susan leaned over, put her hand behind Matt's neck, and smiled down at him. "I don't know how you did it but you did," she said.

He thought of his vision of her hair in the breeze; then he looked over at Van.

"He's fine," said Rudy. "He's already been up. You're the only one sleeping late. Now soup's on."

Matt rose and walked to the mouth of the cave. The edges were lined with snow but the blizzard had stopped. Outside the white-rimmed portal, he saw a pristine landscape shimmering white, extending as far as he could see. It was so peaceful and beautiful that it was hard to imagine it had almost been their grave.

The four of them ate heartily—strips of beef with beans and hot coffee. Afterward Van's color revived, and he said he felt much better. He kept patting his left leg. "I thought for sure it was frostbitten," he said.

They were sitting quietly around the fire when Rudy said, "Don't you wonder where I got the wood?" They looked up. "Right here," he replied to his own question, pointing to a corner of the cave.

"Strange," said Matt. "And the smoke goes right up. It must be a natural chimney."

"That's not all," said Rudy. "You ready for this? This fire is not the first one here. When I made it I found ashes."

Matt went to his backpack and took out a flashlight. Van did the same, and they checked the sides of the cave, careful to avoid stalactites and stalagmites.

Something caught Matt's eye and he moved closer. "Holy shit."

Van ran over and shone the beam of his light next to Matt's.

In the center of the beams were crude paintings, smears in ocher, brown, and red. At first it was hard to make them out, but then they took on shape: some seemed to be depictions of humans, others of animals; some of hunts, others of battles.

"My God," said Van finally. "These paintings . . . they're prehistoric. Just like the caves of Lascaux."

"Look," said Matt. "Those figures there. They're hunting. See that one? He's holding a club." He held the torch closer. "Do you see what I see? Look at the forehead." The figure had a massive ridge along the brow. So did all the others.

Van touched the paint, then looked at his finger. It was streaked in red. "It's fresh," he said softly.

Just at that moment they heard a barely suppressed scream behind them, the kind of sound that escapes involuntarily when something unimaginable is happening.

Susan and Rudy were huddled at the mouth of the cave. They looked outside, and there in the snow they saw dark forms, humanoid but not human, rising up out of the whiteness. They were coming toward the cave.

Eagleton shifted his wheelchair over to the window and with a dainty forefinger lifted the blind. It was dusk, always an unsettling time in the suburbs of Washington. Street-lamps were going on with a jolt, the lights in the campus buildings were darkening quickly, and cars pulled out of the parking lot, carrying the tired breadwinners home. These employees are not ones to linger at their desks, he thought. They all had families to go to. He had none.

In fact, he had no one. This was the thought he had been trying to avoid. He knew it was stalking him; it usually did at this time of day. As a young man, still enthusiastic about fighting the Cold War as if it were some gigantic football game, he assumed that everyone was as engaged as he was. They had seemed to be, but somewhere along the line they accumulated wives, children, vacation houses, station wagons, and golden retrievers to lick their hands when they came home. He had not, and he felt duped. No one had told him the rules, that there was more going on than the football game right in front of his eyes that so engrossed him.

How odd that he should have given his whole life over to the Company. He had been legendary, whipping the horses for twenty-five years as assistant deputy director in charge of counterintelligence. But the end of the Cold War had intervened, he had made too many enemies, his career was spent. What did this new crew know about the Berlin airlift, the Bay of Pigs, Vietnam? What did they care about honor? So they had pushed him into this backwater outfit, this odd business of investigating paranormal phenomena. But he would have the last laugh. He had stumbled on to something so big it would knock their teeth out. It would make bugging the Kremlin look like child's play.

He took another drag. Of course a normal life wouldn't have been easy. There was his infirmity; he still dreaded meeting new people, especially women. He felt humiliated whenever he encountered a stairway at the opera or a curb-stone that was too high. Half a lifetime of it, and he had never adjusted. He was not like this new generation, the activists who demanded elevators, special ramps, and equal treatment. They had such confidence. He both hated them and envied them.

Sex was difficult, given his hang-ups. He was not totally inexperienced. He had paid prostitutes, but only when his desperation outweighed his shame. With them he felt a rush of insecurities: the knowledge that they felt nothing for him, that awkward moment heaving himself out of his chair and onto the bed, the sense that he was being pitied, never feared—all of these made an erection problematic. And of course that became a fear in itself, overriding other worries and casting a pall of horror over everything.

Then came Sarah. At first she had appeared like an angel of mercy. She had been his secretary; the day she walked in, her perfume filled his office and he forgot his dread of microbes. The progression of intimacy had seemed so natural. That late-summer afternoon she walked over, put her hand in the crook of his elbow, and then leaned down to kiss him gently on the cheek still burned in his being, still had the capacity to make his pulse quicken. The nights at her apartment, the leering grin of his chauffeur as he dropped him off. Why, she had even cooked meals for him! Then came the doubts, those satanic whispers whistling through his brain, which came, she said, from his own self-loathing. Whatever, the doubts grew, then turned into certainties. She did not care for him after all; it had all been an ugly charade, a career move. He had put a junior officer on her tail to spy on her. He had not turned up much, really—a careless phrase on a wiretap, a letter of questionable interpretation—but it was enough for Eagleton. Pride had always been his downfall.

He dropped the blind and spun the wheelchair around. *That way madness lies.* Had he spoken the words aloud? He almost thought he had. He imagined he heard an echo dimly from one darkened corner.

He returned to his desk and tried to concentrate. Nasty business, this. He opened the top file listlessly. The contents were still slim: some maps, background checks on Matt and Susan, weather reports, Van's few messages, the orders to Kane. Why had Van's computer radio gone on automatic tracking for five days and stayed in the same place? He had run through the possibilities countless times; the most likely, he decided, was that the group had been forced to camp, and for whatever reason Van had been unable to slip away to send a message. Perhaps he had been sick. Perhaps the computer was broken and he had abandoned it.

Eagleton felt a shiver. It wasn't that he had any sympathy for Van; God knows, the two had been at each other too long for that. It was that, without him, the team had no idea what they were up against. How could they? Who could even imagine such a thing? And without any inkling of the extraordinary nature of the creatures they were after, they were bound to fail. The mission would be not his salvation but his ruin.

Eagleton leaned over and opened, for the umpteenth time, the folder marked OPERATION ACHILLES.

11

Susan and Rudy peered out of the cave. The sun glanced off the surface of the snow, and in the blinding whiteness it was difficult to see, but in the near distance dark forms were crossing the snow like shadows.

"Christ!" exclaimed Susan. There was reverence in her voice. Rudy babbled something in Russian. Matt was quiet. Van held his breath.

Outside the dark forms moved slowly, gray hulks converging in the total whiteness. They were slowly approaching the cave from all directions—four of them, six, ten, more than a dozen.

This is what we've come for, thought Susan. At last we've found them. They do exist. Kellicut was right. The scientist in her was exultant. Just imagine, she thought, the first chance for intraspecies contact in—what?—thirty thousand years? Then a darker thought entered: But will it ever be known?

The tableau before her was coldly beautiful and detached, like a Breughel canvas, stark figures against a curtain of white. But the way the creatures spread out and moved toward the cave was also menacing. A stab of fear spread through her limbs, a feeling so overpowering it seemed to come from some deep wellspring of instinctual loathing.

Matt and Van peered over her shoulders. The mouth of the cave was so tight, with its lining of snow, that there was barely room for them to look out. Van let his breath out and gave a short, involuntary gasp. Matt just kept shaking his head. "Goddamn. I don't believe it," he said. "I just don't believe it." No one answered; they were too riveted by the spectacle before them. He was swept away on a flood of excitement. This is worth my life, he thought. To be here and to witness this. No matter what happens, this is worth it.

The creatures drew near stealthily. They seemed to come from all directions, as if they had coordinated their approach. Are they stalking us? Matt wondered. The shimmering sun made it difficult to get a good look at them. There was something unearthly about the whole scene: the snowdrifts, the blinding sun, the dark rock inside the mouth of the cave.

Even as dark silhouettes the figures were recognizably different: more compact, rounded in the shoulders, with fatter, shorter limbs. As they moved closer a cloud crossed over the sun, the glare disappeared, and their features suddenly became fully visible. There was no doubting their otherness. They carried clubs fashioned out of what appeared to be thick branches, wide at the top and tapered down at the handles. They were dressed in animal skins, crudely fashioned into leggings and ponchos. Their arms were uncovered and hairy. On their feet they wore peculiar thongs of leather and sticks that allowed them to walk with a slow dragging movement on the thick crust of snow. They did not sink in despite their obvious bulk. Snow clung to their leggings and to the portion of their upper torsos that faced the wind.

The scientist's voice whispered in Susan's mind: look at how well they have adapted to their inhospitable environment. She picked one out and examined him minutely. His physique was not huge but his body gave off an impression of density. The midsection and chest were large, and the muscles on the forearm twice the size of a normal human's. Long black hair hung down in a stringy mane, curling around a massive neck. But what immediately stood out was the visage, which was outsized, with eyes too far apart, a flattened nose, and features altogether too wide, like an imprint on an inflated balloon. The jaw was thick and the chin shallow and sliced back, as if it had been snipped off. And most of all, bulging out of the forehead was that formidable brow, a bony protuberance like an elongated tumor. It pushed the face down beneath it and made the eyes under the thick eyebrows seem sunken in their huge sockets. The brow was grotesque. In a strange way it was impossible not to stare at it. The creatures were fully erect, but they carried their heads in a peculiar, protruding way, as if dangling on invisible wires. They looked like men peering off into the distance.

To human eyes, the effect was unspeakably ugly. As the four of them stared out of the cave, they were struck by how truly different these creatures were, how freakish and at the same time how natural-looking. The similarities only made the differences appear more exaggerated. They bore no resemblance to any of the sketches and reproductions, those pathetic attempts to extrapolate a likely appearance from fragments of a skull in a laboratory. They were unlike anything any of them had imagined.

Matt was stunned to feel repugnance. He scanned the horizon. Everything else appeared so normal: the snow, the sky. Suddenly everything that had happened from the beginning—the skull in Eagleton's office, the long ascent up the mountain, the blizzard—all struck him as outlandish. How did he come to be here? What were the steps?

"I don't believe it. I never really believed it until now," whispered Susan.

"I know," replied Matt. "I didn't either. I'm not sure I believe it now."

"I feel I'm present at the beginning of time."

Van cut in. His voice had a flat, deadened tone. "They don't look friendly, and they know we're here. They're coming after us."

"They're coming *toward* us," said Susan. "We don't know if they're coming *after* us."

One of the creatures stood out from the others. He was larger and walked steadily ahead as they fanned out behind him. His right hand clutched a large club. Across his sloping crown he wore a distinctive band of black-and-white fur.

"Look, there's the leader," said Matt. "See how they all seem to look to him? They're taking their cues from him."

Van reached down for his gun. He fumbled a bit with the holster flap. It was caked in frozen snow. He tugged it open, then grasped the revolver's handle and raised it to the light, staring at it.

"Shit. Look." He held the barrel out for them to see. It was frozen over, blocked with ice.

Matt felt his heart sink. "Christ," he said.

"Who knows what that would do," said Susan. "Look how many there are. One gun probably wouldn't stop them."

"Unless it scared them off," said Van.

"What do we do now?" asked Rudy.

No one answered.

The creatures were moving closer and more slowly now. They had arranged themselves in a semicircle, as if to block any escape.

Matt spoke first. "The only thing in our favor is that we're as strange to them as they are to us. They haven't even seen us, really. They don't know anything about us—what we are or what we can do."

"It would be making a big mistake to let them know we're scared," said Susan. "We have to act peaceful but unafraid."

"That's some acting," said Rudy.

"She's right," added Matt. "We've got to convince them that we're here with honorable intentions. We came looking for them. We're emissaries, emissaries from the great beyond. There're a lot more like us back where we come from. If they treat us well they can benefit. If they hurt us they're going to pay."

Van looked back into the cave. He seemed to be searching for something. "We need an offering. Or something to trade. What do we have that we can give them?"

"Jacket?" suggested Rudy. "Canteen?"

"No," said Matt. "Not right away. We need to establish some trust first. Anything that looks strange might throw them. It could backfire. We should try food."

Susan went to the fire and returned with strips of beef jerky. "There's this," she said.

Van spoke again. "One of us has to take it outside."

They looked at him. "Why?"

"They know right where we are. So we're not giving away anything. Besides, we have to show that we want to meet them, that we came all this way to meet them. That it's our goal."

The others were silent. They knew he was right.

"Another thing," continued Van. "We can't afford to wait until they come in here."

Matt looked at Susan. She nodded agreement, so he asked the question on all of their minds. "Who goes?"

"No volunteers this time," said Van. "Only one fair way to do it. Draw straws."

They nodded.

"But not Rudy," said Susan. "He shouldn't. He didn't sign up for this. It should just be among the three of us."

"No," protested Rudy. "When I agreed to come, I agreed to the risk. I'm part of the group." He added gamely, "One for all and all for one."

Van shrugged, reached deep into an inside pocket, pulled out a pack of matches, picked four out, and bit the head off one. He covered them with his left hand and spread them out between his thumb and index finger.

They chose solemnly, each holding his match hidden. Matt took a deep breath. Susan's face was tight. They looked at each other. Rudy smiled weakly. He held up the short match.

"Well," he said. "Not my lucky day." He looked stricken. He stood and hugged each of them. He asked Van for a cigarette and puffed it hard. "Always meant to give it up," he said, his voice sounding thin. He handed the matches to Matt, then walked over to the fire and took the strips of jerky in his left hand, clenching them with his thumb.

"It's best to leave your hood down," Van said. "Make sure you show them you've got nothing hidden."

Rudy nodded, then started abruptly talking in Russian. A stream of words came out. After a moment Matt realized he was reciting the Lord's Prayer.

Rudy walked over to the opening and lowered his head to duck through it. Halfway to the outside, he turned around and looked back at each one in turn.

"God protect you," said Susan.

Rudy seemed to want to say something but he only opened and closed his mouth.

The second he stepped outside, the creatures froze in their tracks and stared at him as hard as the four of them had been staring only minutes before. Then several raised their clubs over their heads and two or three stepped back a pace. The leader stood stock-still, thirty feet away. His eyes, recessed under the immense protrusion, seemed to be green, and they were piercing.

Matt thought he could hear sounds, a kind of low throaty muttering, but they were too indistinct for him to be certain. "Damn," he said. They had not taken the snow into account. It was up to Rudy's thigh. He fell through the crust, struggling and twisting to cut through the high drifts, which robbed his appearance of any dignity. It made him seem pathetic, like a wounded animal thrashing about rather than a representative from some higher order.

About ten feet from the cave's mouth, Rudy turned to look back and shrugged, helplessly. His face seemed drained of blood. His look had a plaintive cast that tugged at Susan's heart. Maybe it's to his advantage, she thought, because he doesn't appear threatening. But she didn't really believe it. From the way the creatures were looking at him, she knew that what was required was a show of strength and power, not weakness.

When Rudy stopped to rest, the leader took two large steps forward, plowing the snow easily with his primitive snowshoes. Then he stopped and waited, shifting his weight and turning slightly to one side like an archer. He held the club extending to the ground back behind him. Was he trying to hide it?

Now there was only four feet between them. Rudy pushed ahead gamely to close the gap. Tall as he was, he was sunk so deep in the snow that his head only came up to the creature's waist. He looked like a boy peering up at an adult. Ever so slowly, he raised his left hand. The strips of beef jerky waved slightly in the wind. A strange offering; from the cave it looked like a child handing up a fistful of ribbons. He held his right hand up, too, palm upward in an improvised gesture of peace.

The creature's head moved slowly as he took in Rudy's hands. It moved strangely on the long neck, like a lizard's. He looked at Rudy's face and at his body immersed in the snow. For a moment he appeared unsure, quizzical. Intelligence blazed from his eyes. His teeth were bared, crooked and yellow.

Then, in a movement so quick there was no anticipating it, he suddenly spun at the waist, swung his club into sudden view with a powerful thrust from the hip, and brought it smashing against the side of Rudy's head. It made an incredibly loud cracking sound. Rudy plunged to one side, crumpled up. His head looked like a pumpkin split open.

Instantly a red stain sprouted from his long blond locks and spread in a trail across the white snow.

Van shrieked. Susan grabbed Matt's arm. Matt felt the breath sucked out of him.

All three of them knew with certainty that Rudy was dead.

They watched in horror as the creatures gathered slowly around the body, obscuring the view. One dipped a hand in the blood. Another held up a strip of the jerky high over his head and examined it carefully.

The three stepped back inside the cave.

"I don't . . . I can't . . . believe it," gasped Susan.

"No way he could have survived that," said Van, visibly shaking.

They looked around panic-stricken in the semidarkness.

"C'mon, we've got to try something," shouted Matt. "Grab your packs. Van, try to thaw out the gun. Hold it over the fire."

Van ran over to the fire and held the barrel just above the flame. He was singeing his fingers, but he kept it there until finally a few drops of water began trickling out. "C'mon, c'mon, c'mon," he urged.

"Hurry up!" yelled Matt.

Behind them a shadow flickered across the wall. A creature had slipped inside. Its lips seemed to be curled in a weird half-snarl, half-smile.

"No good," shouted Van. "Too slow. It's still clogged."

"We've had it," said Matt.

Another shadow moved inside, then another. Soon there was a line of them stretching across the mouth of the cave, blocking the exit, close and terrifying.

A vague, sickening smell filled the air.

Kane sat back in his harness in the belly of the C-130 and felt the engines vibrating along his spine. He looked down the line at the men strapped to the pull-down seats along the metal ribs inside the plane. Their training was almost half finished and they weren't nearly ready. As these parachuting exercises had already shown, they weren't functioning as a team. And that was the most important thing for a search-and-apprehend expedition as unbelievably weird as this one.

Lieutenant Sodder leaned over to shout above the engines. It was almost as if he could read his thoughts. "Sir, could I ask you something?"

Kane didn't like the sound of the man's voice. Too much like whining.

"Shoot," he replied.

"Some of the men have been wondering."

"Wondering what?"

"About the mission."

"Like what?"

"Well, sir, it's hard to say exactly. But it seems strange. . . ."

"Yes?"

"The men are wondering, sir, exactly what the nature of the mission is. Are we going to try to capture something?"

Not a bad deduction. Not a hard one to make, either, given all the gear being transported to their base in Turkey—the nets, cages, tranquilizing guns, all stashed away in special unmarked crates. Of course it was impossible to keep anything secret in the military.

For just a second Kane toyed with the idea of taking Lieutenant Sodder into his confidence. He would enjoy watching the man's face, the lines of incomprehension, disbelief, and finally fear tracing their patterns as the true import of the enterprise registered.

"Lieutenant, what makes you say that?"

"Well, sir, we're taking on some unusual equipment, and we're wondering what it's for."

Kane temporized. "I'd say it looks like a hunting expedition, wouldn't you, Lieutenant?"

"Yes, sir. But that's not all."

Kane was getting exasperated. "What else, Lieutenant?"

"Those weird goggles, sir. Those night-vision glasses or whatever they are. When you put them on you can barely see anything."

"Lieutenant, I would think you've been in the army long enough to know that you will know what you need to know when you need to know it."

Sodder's eyes flashed resentment; Kane enjoyed that. He unbuckled his belt, walked into the cockpit, and yelled to the co-pilot, who pulled out the flight plan and a map with a red ring that showed the drop zone.

"Only a few more minutes!" the pilot shouted. Kane went back into the belly of the aircraft and signaled the men. They rose and checked their chutes.

Kane opened the door. Below were the flat dry plains of Turkey. He motioned to Sodder, who approached and braced both arms against the doorway, watching the light above the door. When it went on, he leaped out and was gone. Then another man and another.

In a short while the plane was empty except for Kane. He wondered what would happen if he simply stayed here or waited until the plane circled back to base and then jumped out into the wilds of Turkey. He relished the idea of disappearing forever.

Then the light went on. Reflexively, he sucked air deep into his lungs, braced himself, and pushed off into the void. The wind ballooned his cheeks. He could see the tops of the opened parachutes below, mushrooms in the air. The jump felt the way it always did, a short stab of terror and then the long sinking flight downward.

The creatures blocked the entrance. The light from the fire sent their shadows flickering on the cave wall, making them look even more threatening.

Van lifted the stricken gun. It was still heavy from the ice, and water dripped out the barrel. When he pointed it at the leader, the move made no impression. It was as if Van were holding out a stick of wood.

"Stay together," Matt said softly. "I'm going to douse the fire." He tossed dirt upon it, plunging the cave into darkness except for the daylight streaming in at the mouth.

Matt lifted his flashlight and clicked it on. The beam hit the floor, and the effect was instantaneous. The creatures tumbled away from the narrow shaft of light. Even the leader flinched and shrank away.

Matt played with the beam, moving it slowly across the floor, then inched it toward them, pushing them back toward the mouth of the cave.

Van pulled out his flashlight and turned it on, and a second beam struck the floor, crisscrossing the first. Matt began to shout "Don't—" but before he could say more Van raised the flashlight and fixed the beam directly on the chest of the creature closest to him.

The creature emitted a high-pitched squeal and squinted down at his stomach in panic. His arms whirled as he pitched backward, losing his balance. The others rushed over to him, squealing.

Susan spoke up. "Let's go. Maybe there's another way out. Quick, before he gets up."

In the confusion they ran to the rear of the cave, where they found a narrow passageway. They ran down it as fast as they could, moving rapidly through the dark with the help of the flashlights. Already they could hear the commotion of the chase behind them.

"They're coming," panted Van.

The floor was beaten smooth into a path that sloped downward. The walls slanted in on both sides like a funnel. They had the sensation of running to the core of the earth.

Ahead the tunnel split in two. Quickly Matt flashed the beam each way. The left branch looked less traveled, so they took it. Fifty feet on, the tunnel twisted and split again. This time they chose the passage to the right, which led to a small, narrow chamber with a sloping ceiling. When Matt flashed the beam, it disappeared into a black well on one side. The ceiling was so low they had to stoop. The dirt floor was packed down.

"We've got to stop and figure out what to do," said Susan.

"We can't stop," Van answered. "Got to keep going."

"No," said Matt. "We need to catch our breath."

They found a nook to one side, ducked inside it, clicked off the flashlights, and squatted down, straining to listen in the darkness for their pursuers.

At first they could only hear the sound of their own breathing. Hiding made them feel even more vulnerable, and their own terror caught up with them.

"Listen," whispered Van.

They heard a distant din gradually growing louder and louder. Then, very close, they made out the thud of feet running by and some guttural yells, interspersed with strange high-pitched screeches. The sounds lessened again in the other direction, and for a few minutes there was silence. Matt looked at Susan. Her face was drawn. Van's eyes were closed.

Then they heard the approach of more running feet, along a different passageway behind them. The gait had a peculiar loping quality to it. There was a hole no bigger than a hand, and when Matt looked through it he saw a tunnel and the flickering of lighted torches, diminishing against the wall as the sounds disappeared.

Sounded like three or four of them, he thought. They seemed to be running in all directions. Pandemonium, like a hornet's nest knocked to the ground. He didn't know which was worse, a cold, methodical stalking or this kind of chaos with scores of them chasing around. Sooner or later one of them is bound to run into us, he thought.

Again there was silence for a long time, and their breathing calmed somewhat. Van was holding his eyes tightly closed.

12

Inside their hiding place, Van was livid with fear and anger. Spittle nestled in the corners of his lips. What he had suspected about the creatures for the past three years had just been confirmed. "I was right," he whispered. "They're evil sons of bitches."

"Did you see his eyes as he killed Rudy?" asked Susan. She shuddered. "Not a flicker of hesitation, not a sign of anything human."

"The only saving grace is that it was sudden," Matt said. "Rudy was dead before he hit the ground."

"We should never have let him go," said Susan.

Van snorted. "Maybe he's the lucky one."

"I hate to just leave his body there. What do you think they're going to do to him?" she asked.

"Don't know," said Van. "Doesn't much matter—to him, anyway."

Again, Susan felt a well of repulsion toward Van. In the crisis his worst side was coming forward.

"One thing's certain," said Matt. "If they find us, we're dead too."

They listened again for sounds of pursuit but heard nothing.

Van cleared his throat. "About that business with the flashlight. You're right, of course. As soon as I put the beam on him and it didn't hurt him, it lost its . . . its magic. I wasn't thinking.''

"We have to think about now," said Matt. "How the hell are we going to get out of here?"

"What else do we have?" asked Susan.

"My gun," said Van. "It's the only hope."

"We have to thaw it out somehow," said Matt.

"What we need is a fire. That was beginning to work before."

"But we can't try to build one here," said Susan, "even a little one. They'd spot it in no time."

"No, we have to find theirs. We know they've got one somewhere. They're using lighted torches," said Matt.

"We'd better go," said Van. "This isn't a good spot." They stepped out into the chamber. When Matt flashed the light in all directions they saw a new tunnel, a smaller one that seemed to have crevices and ledges that could serve as hiding places. He led the way, using the flashlight intermittently, while the others came behind, instinctively hugging the walls.

Up ahead was an intersection of two tunnels that looked much the same except that one sloped downward. Matt whispered, "I've no idea where we are. I've lost all sense of direction."

Susan tugged his sleeve and pointed, and they went down the sloping tunnel, groping in the dark because they didn't want the flashlight to give them away. After five minutes they came to another crossroads, and again Susan pointed the way.

"Do you have any idea where you're going?" Matt asked.

"No," she said, "but it feels right."

After a turn to the left and a long level stretch, they spotted a faint gleam of light in the distance. "Could be what we're looking for," she said.

The tunnel curved and rose a bit, then fell again. Matt turned on the flashlight, and its beam caught something along the wall, an indentation. He shone the light ahead and behind. There were niches knocked into the wall, topped by black scorch marks. "I'll be damned," he said. "For torches. We've found some kind of main passageway."

"This goddamned cave is probably their home," said Van. "We've blundered into their fucking home."

The gleam grew brighter, and they heard the crackling of fire and saw the flickering of flames reflected against the brown stone of the walls.

Matt hugged the side and slowly peered around the corner. It was another chamber no bigger than a cellar, open above and ascending into darkness. In the center a large fire crackled and sparked, giving off a furnace blast of heat. A huge jumble of wood was piled along one wall.

The fire chamber was empty, but two other passages leading into it made them feel vulnerable to surprise. Clearly they were in a central area and one of the creatures could appear out of the dark holes at any moment, but there was no choice if they were to make use of the fire.

Matt stepped inside, felt the wall of heat hit him, and waved to the others to follow. "Hurry," he whispered hoarsely. Van ran to the woodpile, broke off a stick, unloaded the gun, slipped one end of the branch through the revolver's trigger, and held it a foot above the flames. His shadow, cast upon the wall behind him, grew and shrank by turns, exaggerating his movements.

Van seemed to be regaining some of his sangfroid. Maybe having something to do revived him. "I can't imagine this place stays empty for long," he said. "Fire's too important to them. Somebody's got to keep feeding it."

Susan stood watch at a juncture where she could observe two tunnel entrances while Matt paced back and forth nervously. "I just don't get it," he said.

"What?" asked Van.

"Killing Rudy like that. You kill because you're frightened, right? Or at least humans do. What did they have to be frightened about?''

''Us,'' said Susan.

''But he wasn't threatening them,'' Matt said. ''They clearly outnumbered him. They had him at their mercy.''

''So?'' asked Van.

''So it doesn't make sense unless their whole motivational makeup is different. They kill for the pleasure of it. Or else it means nothing to them.''

''Maybe they have no concept of death,'' said Susan.

''Or maybe they glorify it, make a cult out of it. Remember your own research—Neanderthals as brain eaters.''

It was the first time any of them had put the name to the creatures.

''I'm not sure they're really that different from us,'' Susan said. ''They killed Rudy because they were scared of him—and of us.''

''But even so it's crazy. If you're scared of something you keep away from it. If you're scared of the outside world, why build a bridge to it?''

''Maybe you need to,'' said Van, ''for trade.''

''For trade? Fair enough, but then why kill the first traders you see?''

''Maybe we're not the first,'' said Susan. ''And maybe something else is motivating them, drawing them off their mountain. Something new, something to do with that savagery we just saw.''

''Maybe,'' said Matt doubtfully. ''But it doesn't seem to jibe with what Kellicut was describing. The creatures he wrote about seemed peaceful, almost friendly. These are homicidal apes. It doesn't fit.''

''Maybe your great doctor wasn't such a hotshot observer after all,'' said Van over his shoulder, still holding the gun to the fire. ''I'll tell you one thing. I'm sure as hell not going to let any of those bastards get close to me.''

Susan glared at him. With his rheumy eyes, his stubble,

his slumped posture, all crumpled up in his anorak as he knelt beside the fire sweating madly, he resembled a beast himself.

Matt cut in. "How much longer is that damn thing going to take?"

"Almost there. It's just about stopped dripping."

"Did you see their snowshoes?" asked Susan.

"Yeah," said Matt. "Pretty primitive. Bunch of sticks bundled together. But they did the job."

"These guys were probably the hunters. They seemed more equipped than . . . than what we used to think. But they're not all that sophisticated. One of them had a spear, I think. I saw it when they were standing there inside the cave. But most of them just had clubs."

"If they were hunters," Matt said, "there are probably lots of others around to cook, tend fires, and cure skins—that kind of thing. Could be they're all down here somewhere, if this is their lair. Unless it's just some kind of outpost."

"It's not an outpost," Susan asserted firmly. "That painting, the tunnels, this," she added, indicating the fire. "It all points to the same thing. This is their home."

Matt started to say something but stopped when he heard a clicking behind him. Van had the gun away from the fire and was spinning the chamber. The handle was hot, so to hold it he had scrunched his arm up inside his sleeve and used his cuff as a potholder.

He tested it by pulling the trigger. *Click.* Then he placed it on the ground, picked up the bullets, spit into the chamber to cool it, and inserted them one by one into the slots, burning his fingers. From his backpack he took a box of spares and slipped them into his pocket. "Back in business," he said, grinning like a madman.

"Not a moment too soon," said Susan. "Something's coming!" Her ear was cocked inside the entrance of a tunnel and she pointed into it as she heard heavy footsteps pounding toward them. They were running and their urgency gave rise to an unsettling idea: Somehow, they know where we are, she thought. They're not just searching—they're tracking us.

Matt glanced at the other tunnels and spoke softly. "Okay, let's choose one. Pretty much a crap shoot."

"This one seems bigger," said Susan. "Maybe we should take it. We don't want to be lost down here forever, and we've got the gun now."

Matt looked at Van. "You ever fire that thing?"

Van snorted by way of an answer.

They ducked into the tunnel Susan selected, which turned out to be broader than the ones that had brought them this far. They could feel a slight breeze and hear a cacophony of noises, indistinct and directionless like the distant rumbling of a city. The vagueness of the sound was unsettling, and instinctively they huddled together, sticking close to one wall. Every few seconds Matt flicked on the flashlight long enough for them to find their footing.

Then, rising up out of the rumbling, they heard sharp new sounds of the creatures approaching—grunts, footsteps, shuffling—but it was impossible to tell where it was coming from. They strained to listen in both directions, but locating it was hopeless. The sounds were getting louder.

They began running, still unsure if they were hurrying away from the sounds or speeding toward them. Then it became clear; the footsteps were ahead.

Matt chanced using the light and for one second flashed it ahead. The expanse of wall showed a darkness to one side, a crevice two feet wide that led to a cul-de-sac no bigger than a closet. It would hide them. They ran to it and squeezed inside, one at a time, Van last, and then waited, their hearts racing.

Van raised the gun and held it pointing at the opening. "Close your eyes," he commanded abruptly.

"Are you crazy?" Matt whispered.

"I mean it. Don't ask questions. Just shut your eyes."

He held his own eyes closed. Matt looked at Susan. She, too, had closed her eyes.

Seconds later the footsteps grew louder, and as the torches approached, the wall opposite their hole took on an orange glow that became brighter and brighter. Matt shut his eyes, and through his closed lids he detected flames and felt heat only a few feet away. Then gradually the light and noise began to fade, and as Matt stood there, he realized for the first time that he could smell them, a pungent odor of animal oil and human secretions that invaded his nostrils and made him feel like retching. Then the blur of movement, colors, and shadows receded, the noise was gone, and all was quiet and dark again. He began to tremble.

Van exhaled noisily and Susan gave a tiny sigh. "Too close," she said.

"What was all that about, closing our eyes?" Matt asked.

"Later," said Van. "First we better find a way out of here before others come." They squeezed out one by one and resumed their flight down the tunnel and their search for an exit.

Fifty feet farther on they came upon an arch that led off to one side. They followed it and entered a gigantic vault that was decorated with drawings. Lines of blue and black designs covered the upper walls, and the lower walls were decorated with graceful shapes and curlicues. A domed roof far above was covered by stalactites that pointed down like daggers and were tipped in blood-red paint. Stalagmites rose up like cones along the edges of the vault and were festooned with strips of leather and beads. There was a heavy smell of animal. In the center, lying on the floor, were flattened skins close to a pile of bones.

"What is this?" asked Susan, her voice shaking.

"Some kind of shrine," said Matt, awed.

The skins were arranged carefully in a semicircle, as if for worshiping or viewing. He turned and shone the flashlight beam on the surface of the wall the skins were facing.

What he saw took his breath away, and he heard Van whistling softly.

The beam illuminated a brilliantly colored tableau that stretched across the entire wall, a huge rectangle with life-like figures elaborately painted in panels. The panels seemed to depict a narrative like Ethiopian scrolls, and the colors were multilayered and deep, as if they had been painted and repainted for generations.

They stared for some time before speaking. The figures were beautifully rendered. They were clearly warriors—they carried clubs and other weapons—and they were divided into two war parties confronting each other. One had the protruding foreheads and squat look of the Neanderthal. The other warriors were taller and gaunt, with jutting chins and narrow skulls: *Homo sapiens*.

Matt circled the spotlight of the beam, engrossed in the craftsmanship, the artistic flair behind the lines and the colors, trying to tease out the narrative: a saga of some sort of battle. Yes, that was it; the two subspecies were at war, a primal conflict of some sort. But why did it seem so oddly familiar?

Suddenly it hit him. "Susan, do you know what this is?"

"Yes," she said, coming to the same realization at almost the same instant. She sounded strangled with surprise. "The Khodzant Enigma!"

"And look, it's complete. It's not missing a fragment. It's probably the original."

"What the hell's it doing here?"

They had not noticed that Van had slipped away, passing through another passage off to one side. While they were marveling at the tableau and trying to decipher the conclusion of its message, his shout interrupted them. "Hey, come here. Quick!"

They tore around the corner. Matt was relieved to see that Van was not in trouble. It had been wonder, not fright, that had prompted his call. He was staring around in amazement at the edge of a vast cavern, the innermost lair of the creatures that were hunting them.

It appeared to be empty, but the signs of habitation were everywhere. Smoke from three small fires curved upward and disappeared into the hazy darkness above. The walls were scorched all around, black marks that reached high up on the rock like chimney smudges. They were hearths, Matt realized, used for cooking and probably curing hides. Instinctively his eyes kept searching for movement. There was none, but he had the eerie sense that the cavern had been teeming with creatures only a short while ago and that they could return at any moment.

With a force of will, Matt calmed himself and then conscientiously began to look for details. Every nook and cranny was filled with animal hides. They lay on mounds and ledges, on the rocky floor, piled up in corners—the brown fur of bear, long-haired buffalo, deer and elk, giant hares, marmots, mountain antelope, and others he could not recognize. They were placed in groupings, he realized.

"Looks like they have divided up into family units maybe," Susan said. Bones were scattered around her feet. "Look at this," she said, pointing to a pile off to one side. It contained hunks of meat and gristle, unrecognizable pieces of animal, half putrid and still dripping blood. "Now we definitely know they're meat-eaters."

Off to another side was a pile of weapons, and Susan bent down to examine them. There were awls, axes, spears, and several chopping and grinding tools. Chips of stone lay around a flattened boulder that had been used as an anvil. Fascinating, she thought, a small tool factory. It was quite advanced for primitive hominids to prepare the core of the stone that way before flaking it, the Levallois technique, she recalled. There were other implements, some one or two feet long, that she had never seen before.

She found a small pen, a natural indentation in the rock that had been closed off with a semicircle of boulders and lined with animal hides. She considered it for a long time before she was able to ascertain its function.

"There are definitely families living here. Look at this."

Admiring how Susan's curiosity overcame her fear, Matt walked over and peered down, noticing instantly the strong, unpleasant stench from the worn-down skins and the tang of urine.

"It's a crib," she said. "More of a pit, really, but it serves the same function. Put the kids in there and you're free to kick off your shoes and cook up some hairy mammoth."

They investigated some more. Some weapons were lined up on a ledge, their tips covered in blood. Matt lifted one and sniffed it. The odor was faint and indistinct. He put it back in the same spot. "If this is their home," he said, "where did they all go? It looks like they were all here a minute ago."

"Maybe we scared them away. Some kind of general alarm to evacuate, protect the women and children."

"Could be they know we're here. They could be watching us. Or setting a trap of some sort."

Van was nervous. He had moved over to the center of the cavern and stood stock-still, motioning for them to join him with one hand and staring up, his eyes wide.

They joined him on either side and looked up. Against the rock face, reaching high into the dome of the cavern, stood a huge icon, built out of the jagged outcropping, a statue of some sort, dripping with tufts of black and white fur. It appeared to be some kind of beast, half-hominid perhaps, half-bear. It had the narrow muzzle of a cave bear with shining fangs; above the muzzle, a pair of tiny eyes stared maliciously at them from recessed sockets. In the dim light above they thought they could detect a protruding forehead and, on top, strands of black hair that hung down and merged into a twenty-foot carpet of bearskins on either side. The apparition looked like a giant voodoo doll, with enough artistry in it and a malevolence of spirit to evoke a mixture of splendor and horror.

"That must be their deity," said Susan. "A zoomorphic godhead. Look how it shimmers with . . . with hatred. Whoever—or whatever—created that is evil, purely and simply evil. It's a pagan god of malice and death."

"This is a shrine, all right," said Matt. He noticed flecks of red embedded in rocks around an upended log directly below the figure. "I wouldn't be surprised if they engaged in sacrifices right here."

It did not take long for them to discover the skulls. They were fixed upon the wall to one side of the icon, in a dark recessed corner. Matt moved the flashlight beam around slowly, illuminating them one by one, like hideous masks on a gallery wall. They were clearly human skulls, with their broad shining white domes and thrusting jawbones. One was turned slightly sideways, so they could spot a telltale hole at the base of the back, just above the spinal cord. The brains had been extracted.

"Matt!" exclaimed Susan. "They *are* brain eaters."

Matt's light moved on and they saw something else that made them gasp. On one side, the freshest trophy, was a new head. It had been crudely severed, and bits of darkened artery and bone hung down from the cheek. It was almost unrecognizable because so much of the flesh had been torn away, but there was no doubt that it was Sharafidin.

Matt felt sick. Susan retched. Van was silent. "Well, now we know," he said after a minute.

"We can't just leave it there," said Susan. "We have to do something."

"Are you crazy?" Van retorted. "This is hardly the time for a funeral—or the place. We better beat it or we'll end up like that." It was not hard to read the depth of his fear because he was shivering.

A noise came from the opposite end of the cavern that sounded like a rock scuttling across the floor. Matt felt Susan squeeze his arm and doused the light, but it was too late.

Suddenly a high-pitched scream filled the cavern, a cry

unlike anything any of them had ever heard before, piercing and plaintive. It sounded as if a set of human vocal cords had been stretched taut and opened wide, like an instrument. It echoed throughout the cavern and up and down side passageways.

Across the cavern, high on a ledge they had not noticed before, a dim figure, small in stature, peered down at them. A child, Susan thought. Then it screamed again.

They fled down the closest passageway, hurtling across the rocky slope as if propelled, not pausing to choose an escape route. They heard the beat of their own footsteps rebounding off the walls. But then came other footsteps, not their own. They thought the sounds came from behind but they could not be certain. They ran faster, feeling winded in the high altitude and dizzy in the stale atmosphere of the caves.

"Can't go on much more," wheezed Van. He had begun to stumble occasionally, and his arms were flailing at his sides like useless flaps.

"Don't stop now, for God's sake!" shouted Matt. But Van's face was sallow, drained of life. He can't last much longer, Matt thought, and he's the one with the gun.

Abruptly the passage ended and they were in a dark canyon. Matt moved the beam ahead. There was a bridge, entirely of rock, across a ravine. It was impossible to tell how sturdy it was. "It's our only hope," he said. "We have to go one at a time."

Van, still badly winded, nodded. "If we get across, they can't rush us. If they try to cross the bridge, we'll set up an ambush." He raised the gun and held it sideways.

Susan crossed first. She did not look down and took her time to find secure footing. Poised halfway across, above the darkened pit, she could hear the footsteps getting louder. She hurried and made it safely. Then Van crossed and finally Matt.

They ducked into the mouth of a passageway on the other side and waited. Soon, with a clamor, the creatures bounded into the canyon. Across the divide they stared at the three humans, and instantly they froze and all sound died away.

This close, they looked truly hideous. Mangy hair fell on sweaty muscles encrusted with dirt. Their look had a leer to it, and they showed their teeth, which had no canines. Most carried clubs. Some had long, thin, stilettolike weapons. They began bobbing up and down and grunting with excitement.

One stepped forward and moved toward the bridge. Without hesitation, he stepped onto it, moving warily but steadily. Another lined up behind him. Halfway across, the first stopped for a moment, puzzled. He looked directly at them. Why were they not running away? What was that object one of them was holding?

Van raised the gun and pointed it at the creature's chest. His hand was shaking. "Now!" shouted Matt. "Go ahead, do it!" His voice rebounded around the canyon. The creatures whipped their heads around and stared at him, and the one on the bridge stopped again and stood, a perfect target. Still Van did not fire.

"What the hell are you waiting for?" Matt yelled. Was Van too paralyzed to shoot? "Give it to me if you can't do it!"

At that moment, he heard the explosion near his ear and saw the kick of Van's wrist as it flew upward. The creature, standing upright in the middle of the bridge, looked surprised at the hole in the middle of its chest. Blood poured out of it. Matt looked across at the others; they shrank back at the sound, so incredibly loud, and appeared astounded and even frightened. The creature touched his chest, still confused, but just at that moment the sound of the explosion came thundering back at them through the canyon and then thundering in from another direction. Now it seemed to be louder, until there was a crack, a rending, another deeper sound, and rocks began to fall. The sound continued until it set up a shaking like an earthquake, and as more rocks fell the canyon filled with dust, obscuring their view.

"Cave-in!" shouted Susan as they fell back.

At that moment the earth above seemed to crumble, and with an earsplitting sound it came crashing down on them, a relentless weight, so fast there was no time to register pain. Matt spun downward in a spiral toward darkness and nothingness.

He awoke, unaware that he had been unconscious. The first thing he felt was a weight on his legs and a kind of deadening sensation. He lay in darkness. He could barely breathe for the dust. He could not remember where he was or what had happened.

Gradually, it all came back: the paintings on the cave wall, the sighting of the creatures in the snow, Rudy's death, the chase, the cavern, the gunshot. He tried to move his legs and found he could not. Had they been crushed in the cave-in? Was this what it would feel like to have no legs? He patted the outside of his pockets. There was the outline of a knife and a pack of matches. The matches, he remembered, had belonged to Rudy who had handed it to him just before he left the cave. When he pulled it out and struck a match, a blinding flash erupted. It dwindled to a halo and he looked around. He saw his legs, disappearing under a wall of rock and dirt that slanted up toward the ceiling. Then blood along his left arm. Through the dust he could make out a form lying next to him. It was Susan, lying crumpled and immobile. He could not tell if she was breathing.

Matt began the long job of extricating himself. It was hard to do on his back in the dark. He pawed at the dirt, leaning forward so hard that his abdominal muscles seized up in a spasm. He pushed the dirt behind him and shaped it into a backrest, using his hands as shovels. His fingers began to bleed. He pulled large rocks down and tossed them to the side. The going was slow because as soon as he dug out a cavity, more dirt and rocks came rolling down the incline to fill it. He felt a metal object. His heart soared; it was the flashlight. He held his breath in prayer while he switched it on. It didn't work. He threw it aside and continued digging. After half an hour he had uncovered all but the tips of his feet. Lying straight back and pushing at the ground with his fists, he was able at last to propel himself free of the rockslide. He found he could move one leg; the other was twisted to one side.

Susan moved and began talking to herself in a low, dull monotone. Matt struck another match, pulled himself to her, and brushed her cheek. She opened her eyes, then closed them and reached down to scratch her arm. He felt a dampness behind her head, rivulets of something sticky mixing with her hair, and knew it was blood. He tried standing and found he could just manage it by putting his weight on his good leg and reaching out to steady himself against the cave wall. He pulled Susan up. She was able to stand, though her eyes were still closed.

Matt struck another match and looked back. The cave-in had blocked the passageway with fresh dark earth, without destroying the walls, as if a bulldozer had pushed tons of rock and debris through the narrow channel. There was no sign of Van or the gun. Not a bad way to go, thought Matt, sudden and final, death and burial at the same time. He moved his arm to touch his knapsack, which he was still wearing, and felt a pain in his shoulder that he had not been aware of before.

They staggered down the passageway, inhaling the dust that was beginning to settle. Susan seemed to be in a coma. She was talking, but he could only catch a word here and there. He tried speaking to her. When he did she fell silent, but he couldn't tell if she heard him or not. She gave no sign.

He felt his way around a bend and struck the last match. Ahead was a straight stretch. Squinting, he saw a shaft of light cutting across the tunnel like a sword blade. Gently he lowered Susan to the ground, hobbled ahead, knelt down—there was that pain in the shoulder again—and put his face to the hole. The cold air struck his face, sank into his lungs, and seemed to spread through his limbs like a shot of whiskey. He drank deeply of it.

He widened the hole, tearing at the dirt, pulling it inside, and pushing it away. It went surprisingly quickly, and soon he could stick his head and then his upper torso through the opening. Outside, where the snow was piled in drifts, it was cold and quiet. The sun was shining, its light so blinding he could barely see.

Returning for Susan, he had to push her through the hole from behind. Her legs fell limply into the snow and she did not awaken. The snow was deep but it had hardened, so that they sank in only partway. He wanted to get as far away from the cave as possible, so he tried to stand and pull her from behind, but he could not manage it, and after a few steps fatigue and pain overcame him. He sank down and his mind began to drift. He felt the wind now, and let it carry him. He wrapped his arms around Susan and placed her head beneath his chin. It was a perfect fit. We are one at last, he thought dimly as the wind gently rocked him.

Sitting there immobile, he felt the cold creep in. It began around the edges, then moved toward the center. He could feel his limbs turning heavy, his senses thickening. He thought of lights going out in the distant rooms of a mansion. He hugged Susan tighter and leaned back into the snow; it felt strangely warm. His eyelids faced the sun. It made the screen before him dazzle with shooting stars and meteors. He found himself being drawn toward the hot vortex, the dawn of creation.

They stayed there, unmoving as statues, until the snow piled up around them. Then, as clouds came to clutch at the sun, lumpy figures approached and long pairs of hairy arms reached down and picked them up, out of the snow.

II

EDEN

13

Kane tilted the urn and held it at the top with a flattened palm to pour the dregs of rotgut coffee into a mug emblazoned with a yellow happy face.

He had arrived the night before on a helicopter that had picked him up from the airport's VIP lounge at Dushanbe, where he had been rushed through formalities by a group of excited Tajik officers who didn't speak a word of English. He had dressed in civilian clothes to keep his arrival low-key.

Then he spent two hours in the helicopter that blazed its way over the barren ground and scrub trees like a flying lighthouse. Finally, they put down in a scruffy clearing outside Murgab, a drab Tajik town at the foot of the Pamirs. The dust raised by the blades coated Kane's forehead and cheeks and circled his eyes, giving him the ringed look of a raccoon.

He was met by the night duty officer, a guy in rumpled fatigues called Grady, who shook his hand perfunctorily and yawned. Kane was not asked to show an ID, which was strange for an operation so highly classified. When they reached the dormitory Grady pointed vaguely to rows of double bunks and said, "Choose any one. They're all the same—uncomfortable." Then he disappeared through a door. Kane set his duffel bag down. From the darkened end of the room came several snores. A TV and a VCR rested on a table in the center, along with a ragged stack of tapes, *Penthouse* and *Hustler* magazines, and empty Coke bottles, some with soggy cigarette butts in them. Two almost empty aspirin bottles stood nearby. The peeling walls exuded boredom.

No doubt about it, the place was a dump. Kane remembered the old photographs he had seen of Los Alamos, the wooden barracks on top of a mesa in the desert where the greatest scientific minds of the century had gathered to create their satanic engine of destruction: the broken-down water tower, the mud-filled streets, the smelly-looking gymnasium, and the tiny ranch house where the bomb itself was assembled. Strange how the most epochal events occurred in the most dilapidated of settings.

He opened the rear door and walked down a hallway toward a faint luminous glow. He found Grady in a side room, his feet up, a paperback propped on his lap. On the wall in front of him, shining down, was a bank of screens. Two were blank but three were functioning. One screen was aimed at a blank wall with a sink; otherwise it was empty. On the other two screens, seen from different angles, was a huddled dark shape lying on a cot. It was hard to make out, and in any case it was immobile, undoubtedly asleep.

"That him?" asked Kane.

"Yep. Sleeping beauty."

Kane looked at digital figures on the lower corner of the screen. "You recording?"

"Yep. Those are the orders. Twenty-four hours a day, seven days a week."

"Sound too?"

"We record it, but we keep it low. Drives you nuts otherwise."

Grady leaned over and turned a dial. Out of a loudspeaker in the ceiling came a strange, slow rasping sound. It took a moment for Kane to realize that it was breathing. He looked at his watch and timed it with the second hand.

Grady watched him, then turned the dial down.

Later, lying in a bottom bunk, Kane pulled out his watch and tried to imitate the breathing. He found it difficult to do, since the pauses between exhalations were abnormally long. He had trouble falling asleep because of the snoring at the other end of the room.

In the morning, over a breakfast of powdered scrambled eggs, Kane met the six other men in the dormitory, all American, taciturn, and buttoned-up military types like himself. They were like jailers anywhere.

He had been well briefed before he left Turkey, but still he didn't feel prepared for what he was about to witness. He had been hearing about Operation Achilles for some time—you didn't get to his level without having developed a scuttlebutt network that might have future strategic value—and he had weaseled and cajoled enough from Eagleton and others to have a pretty good sense of what was going on. But he had still had difficulty actually believing it until a few minutes ago, when he had been given the file.

He had been ushered into a small windowless office and it lay before him in the center of a desk, the only paperwork there. The door closed and he was alone. A large bottle of aspirin was on the windowsill, the third one he had seen. Slowly, as if he were opening a potential letter bomb, he lifted the flap of the thick envelope plastered with labels reading CLASSIFIED LEVEL 5 (the highest) and U.S. MILINTEL. He pulled out an inch-thick raft of papers and plowed through preliminaries written in uncharacteristically non-military prose, probably by a scientist. Then he reached the pertinent summary passages.

Subject was found beside a path in a mountainous zone, exact location unknown. It was lying face down, apparently ill or stricken, when it was discovered by two shepherds. They were immediately struck by subject's appearance and at first left it alone but then returned, placed it in a cart, and brought it to the village of Djibaillot, Tajikistan, where subject was put in an outbuilding for animals. When its condition worsened it was taken to a local clinic, where the doctor refused to provide treatment. It was allowed to remain in the clinic, however, and its existence became known to the American consul, who followed prescribed notification procedures pursuant to DAT-COM 3824. Subject was relocated to new quarters in Murgab under strict security and put in segregated confinement.

Over time subject's condition gradually improved so that it regained consciousness and began eating, although dietary provisions continue to be a problem. Its mental state is at times agitated, and it gives the appearance of objecting to confinement. It has had to be restrained. Experimentation is difficult though not impossible, and becoming harder over time. But already substantial variants have been established in the experimental zone. In fact, nothing like the subject's responses have ever been encountered anywhere before with humans.

"With *humans*," noted Kane, the first indication that "the subject" represented something so totally out of the realm of the ordinary that what was being recorded with such pedestrian nonchalance was nothing less than the world's most startling scientific discovery. He flipped through the rest of the documents. There were medical reports, recorded in a slanted hand with a fountain pen. Blood pressure, EEG, sonographs, DNA testing. There were exclamation points after some of the physical measurements. It appeared that the exam had been done while "the subject" was not conscious. An asterisk explained: It would not "cooperate" and at the sight of a stethoscope or other instrument it flew into a fit of rage or fear or some combination of the two. There followed pages of notes, apparently on perceptual studies: photographs of black-and-white and multicolored blocks, triangles, circles, squares, playing cards, picture postcards, references to frames from videos.

Kane was trying to decode the terms when the door opened and a small balding man walked in, his hand already extended, a bundle of nervous energy in a white coat with the tip of a fountain pen protruding from a pocket.

"I'm Resnick. Welcome to our little hideaway." Kane grunted. He did not feel like being polite. Resnick turned to the matter at hand. He was concerned, he said, because there had been a rapid deterioration in the subject's health. It had stopped eating. This was worrisome and vexing, Resnick said, especially since they had spared no effort to find food that might be appealing. It was not easy to obtain fresh vegetables in this part of the world. They had even taken to flying in shipments of fresh vegetables from the provincial capital, but it was still losing weight precipitously.

Resnick sighed. "It's almost as if it has made a decision to just pack it in. We cannot allow that, of course. We may be compelled to use force feeding. I'd hate to do it, but there may be no other way."

"Tell me about its special ability," said Kane.

"Ah, the gift." Resnick gave a half smile and looked away.

"Does it really exist?"

"I'd have liked for you to witness it yourself, but I'm afraid that's impossible now. It hasn't been cooperating for some time."

"But you saw it? You recorded it?"

"Unclear. At one point, yes, no question. But then replication became difficult. The data are not scientifically— how shall I put it?—unchallengeable. They can't be, without the necessary rigors. No control group, that sort of thing. How can there be a control group with a subject of one?"

"But did you ascertain that it exists to *your* satisfaction?"

Resnick gave his crooked little smile again. "You must

understand, I'm a scientist first and foremost. I demand facts where others are willing to proceed on faith. Suppositions, theories—none of that interests me.''

Kane remembered what he had extracted from Resnick's dossier: a martinet who worked under Van Steeds, that latter-day disciple of B. F. Skinner who did his dissertation on the thalamus and psycholingualism. A note had been scribbled in the margin by Eagleton: *This man Resnick will perform any experiment, no questions asked.* In short, he was the perfect choice to supervise an experiment bound to call up skepticism from the few scientists permitted to learn about it. Hence, true to form, he probably refused to accept the conclusions of his own work even when they stared him in the face. Kane grunted again. ''Let me see him.''

As they went down a basement staircase, part of Kane balked at going on. He knew why: the power of memory. Almost twenty years ago he had gone down a similar staircase in Uganda. Idi Amin had fled Kampala, and as a young military attaché at the U.S. embassy in Nairobi, Kane had hurried to the destroyed capital. He had been among the first to search Amin's deserted house, and in its basement he had followed an underground tunnel to the notorious State Research Bureau. There he had gone down a staircase like this one, with only his flashlight for light, leading to an underground dungeon where a massacre of seventy people had taken place hours before. Some were still alive, cut into pieces, when he walked over the concrete floor, literally wading through blood. It was a memory that came to him in nightmares from time to time.

He followed Resnick. When they came to a thick steel door, Resnick jangled a ring of metal and held up a jagged-edged master key. When the door swung open, what struck Kane was the stench, an odor with the tang of urine, shit, and stale sweat but something even stronger, a pungent smell that overwhelmed all the others. Despite himself and his training, he felt fear closing in on him.

''Mornings are usually better, but you never know,'' said

Resnick. "And that begs the question of how it knows it's morning. There are no windows, no distractions of any sort." He was speaking over his shoulder, as officious as a doctor making the rounds with a new intern. They passed half a dozen empty cells and he stopped before another door.

"Now it's best for you to go on alone. We don't want to upset it. When you come into its field of vision, keep your head down, sort of bowed. We've found that works best. And move extremely slowly. No sudden movements—that's the worst. Keep away from the bars. You may feel strange sensations inside your head. And don't talk. *Above all, don't talk.* Even if it makes a sound, don't reciprocate." He unlocked the door and stepped aside, and Kane walked through. He steeled himself and took a step forward silently, then another.

Even before he crept into full view, Kane was shocked. In one sharp instant, he saw the creature: saw it and smelled it and somehow sensed it with senses he didn't even know he possessed. His eyes searched it up and down, bore in, changed focus, measuring, assessing, judging. The creature was slumped over on a mattress, turned to the wall, its back humped into a mound. It was hairy but with humanoid skin, darkened to a grayish hue. The hairs were long, thin, and dark like a chimpanzee's, but sparse and matted together. Its shoulders were rounded and powerful but hunched in an unnatural way. Kane saw that this was from arm irons that bound the creature into a ball. Thick bands circled its wrists and pulled its arms around its stomach and across its lower shoulders like a straitjacket. The chains had opened sores, which festered with pus and dried blood. It was wearing yellowish pants, split along the thighs to accommodate its bulging muscles and with the bottom cut out so that its buttocks, huge and caked with dried feces, stuck out. Its bare feet were large, with the toes splayed. One sole was showing, bright pink.

The cell was largely bare. There was a sink to one side

but Kane saw that the creature, tethered by a chain, could not reach it. There was no toilet or slop bucket. The concrete floor was slanted toward a drain, and a thick hose attached to a faucet hung in one corner.

Kane felt a strange sensation. Maybe it was the stench or the rush of adrenaline, but his head felt heavy, as if something were growing inside, and he squinted because of an ache deep behind his eyes. He had no time to dwell on it, for at that moment the creature stirred and managed to raise itself to a sitting position. It turned and faced Kane without surprise. They locked eyes. Kane looked deeply into the blue irises and the tiny dark pupils within and knew in an instant that he was peering not into the dull surface reflection of some animal but into the deep pools of an intelligent being. Their stares held each other like two aircraft painting each other in radar and then boring in on the targets. Kane did not like what he saw. He felt an instinctual loathing rising up within him. His eyes moved up to the forehead, sloping forward, perfectly formed and symmetrical but grotesquely out of place, like a node. It repelled him. The creature's eyes looked back, fixing him in a trance, almost challenging. Kane felt not an ounce of compassion. He did not keep his head bowed. Quite the opposite, he tilted it up and stared directly at the helpless creature. He uttered aloud without thinking the words that came into his head from somewhere deep inside: "You would do the same to us, wouldn't you?" Instantly the figure whipped its head back, tilted it upward, and poured out a high-pitched half-human scream of anguish that reverberated in its cell and through the narrow corridor.

Kane found himself being rushed away by Resnick. The man was whining so close to his ear that he could feel his breath. "What did you do? What did you do? I told you, I warned you." As he climbed the stairs toward the light, he could still hear sounds behind him, a moaning now. Then a door slammed and abruptly it was muffled. Upstairs, he sat down, badly shaken, in the tiny office. As he looked at Resnick, fussing around and smoothing his white coat, again Kane's head was racked with that curious ballooning ache.

Matt awakened slowly, rising through levels of consciousness like a diver surfacing. He lay without moving and then opened his eyes and closed them again. Questions took a long time to form in his laggard brain. Where was he? He wanted to retreat into a long sleep. But something was forcing him upward toward the surface and to the light above it. He opened his eyes for good and blinked.

He moved and instantly felt pain. It shot through his right thigh, moved along his back, and encircled his right shoulder. He raised his left hand into the air and held it before his face. Three fingers, from the middle finger down, had practically no feeling. He clenched his hand. At least the fingers could move. When he hoisted himself up, shifting his weight onto his elbows, the pain cut into his right side again and dug deeply. What had happened? With an effort of will, he forced his mind into reverse. Slowly the memories fell into place. He was fully conscious now and with consciousness came a rush of pure fear that seized his gut: Where was Susan? Was she alive? He shifted his legs and sat upright—the pain striking a minisecond later, as reliable as an aftershock—and looked about.

There was green all around him, leaves and plants and vines. He stared; it seemed so long since he had seen trees. Their miraculous bark was a rich deep brown. There was a light breeze, not cold, that set the branches waving slightly, a rhythmic flow that made him a bit queasy. Overhead the branches met and wove into a canopy. He could see patches of sky. In places the green foliage was so dense that the sunlight came through in slanting shafts, like biblical etchings of the forest primeval at the beginning of creation.

Matt had been resting on woven branches and leaves and grass. It was not uncomfortable, but neither was it natural.

Something—someone—had assembled this primitive bed. Who? Again, he tried to push his thoughts backward. He could recall almost nothing after the cave-in. The dust and the rocks and the beam of the flashlight slicing upward: that he remembered. Then pushing the rocks and dirt off, which accounted for the pain along his right side. He saw dried blood on his shirt, and when he tugged at the cloth a pain shot through him. The shirt was stuck to his side. Carefully he peeled it away and looked; a round wound, red with bands of black dried blood, extended from his hip to his lower rib. Ugly-looking but superficial, he decided. He held up his numb fingers and moved them again. They responded slowly and grudgingly. Frostbite. Now he remembered breaking out of the cave, clawing at the rocks with his bare hands, and pulling Susan through the snow. The blinding whiteness and paralyzing fatigue. But how had he gotten here—wherever *here* was? And where was she?

A few yards away, at the base of a tree, he saw his coat, crumpled into a ball. Next to it was his knapsack. The sight filled him with a rush of hope. It was a token that augured well. Clearly something had brought him there, and whatever it was, whatever superior strength had been responsible, it had not killed him—at least not yet. Perhaps Susan was here with him somehow; perhaps she was the one who had put his belongings nearby.

Matt grunted, summoned up his strength, and stood up. He felt dizzy at first and stretched out his arm to lean against a tree. When he felt level-headed he walked over to the knapsack, knelt down, opened it, and pawed through it. Everything seemed to be there, even the flares he had taken from Van. Near the top he found the blue plastic medical kit, snapped it open, and took out the container of antiseptic. The top spun off easily; it had already been opened. He held it to the light. A good quarter of it was gone. Pulling up his shirt, he looked again at the wound. There was no sign of infection, and a scab was already forming at the edges. Somebody had been treating it. He poured more antiseptic over it.

He was in some sort of bower. The foliage stretched away on all sides and large ferns covered the ground, giving off a rich, dank smell. He found a path and followed it, moving cautiously. Every dozen steps or so, he stopped to look in all directions and held his breath, the better to listen. Nothing moved, nothing was in sight anywhere, and there were few sounds.

He was puzzled by the lush flora. It reeked of moss, leaves, and ripening fruit, and the trees were festooned with vines. Clearly he had descended thousands of feet from the cave and treeless plateau where the snowstorm had struck. Even so, the vegetation was too luxuriant and fecund to be in the Pamirs unless he had been transported to some hidden valley with a freak meteorological profile, perhaps a place that was sheltered by high peaks, fed by melting snow, and warmed by volcanic vapors.

The path led through a darkened grove and he walked warily, trying to plant his feet soundlessly. He came to the edge of a tiny meadow and sat down to think of what to do next. Walking into the open didn't appeal to him. He stared over the grass, which was at eye level. Flies buzzed past. He realized with a sudden pang in his stomach just how hungry he was, but he had little energy, hardly enough to go foraging for food. He sank down, raised his left hand, and looked at his fingers; at least they were feeling a little less numb. He recalled the Jack London character, surrounded by wolves beside a campfire, whose last waking gesture was to contemplate the sheer beauty of the human hand, all of creation caught in the rolling movement of fingers clenching.

Then he saw it coming across the meadow with its peculiar loping gait. It moved rapidly. This one was naked and carrying something on one shoulder. Matt slunk lower and stopped breathing. It was coming directly toward him. He had to fight down the instinct to leap up and race away.

Instead, he wiggled around and crawled through the grass back to the woods, then crouched low and ran with his head down. When the trees were behind him, he straightened and ran flat out, leaping over logs and careening into vines. When he came to an upended tree, he dove under it, hidden by the branches.

There he held his breath and watched it on the path some thirty yards away. Suddenly, as if struck by something, it stopped, paused a moment, and then turned into the woods at a sharp angle, coming straight toward him until Matt could see the hideous misshapen skull, the huge hairy chest, the stump of wood held balanced across its shoulder by a drooping hand. He spun around, pushed aside the branches on the other side, squeezed through, and ran for his life.

He ran and ran. Gasping for breath, he recognized the bower, and as he ran toward it he saw through the trees a flash of movement, a shape. It was Susan. Susan! She was standing in the center. But before her, moving toward her, was another shape, large and hairy. Matt summoned his last reserve of strength, ran toward them, and burst into the bower. He felt himself leaping high into the air, leaving the ground with the driving momentum of his full weight, to land square on the creature's back. He felt the impact of his blow, heard the painful grunt of expelled breath, and caught a glimpse of alarm on Susan's face. Then he felt himself sailing on and falling downward toward a tree trunk. He smashed his head on it and heard more sounds, vague and indistinguishable, as he sank down once again toward the dark and peaceful depths of unconsciousness.

"Matt, Matt." Susan called to him softly and brushed his forehead with her hand. He opened his eyes. She was kneeling next to him, looking down. She took his head, cradled it in her arms, and then placed it on her lap and caressed his face with her fingertips. "I have to admit you're brave," she said. "But what was your plan exactly? Were you trying to ride him to death?"

"Susan, for Christ's sake, I was trying to stop him. He was coming at you." He tried to get up.

"Not *at* me, *to* me. He's my friend. Calm down." She pushed him back down. "There's so much to tell you."

Matt sat upright and looked around quickly. The Neanderthal was standing off in the distance near a tree.

She laughed despite herself and said, "You frightened him as much as he frightened you. Don't worry, he's harmless. His name is Longface—at least that's what I call him."

14

"How long was I out?"

"A full day. Of course it seemed longer to me than it did to you."

"No doubt," Matt replied, rubbing a bump on his head.

"Before anything else, eat something."

She busied herself preparing some food. She put some nuts and berries on a tin plate from her rucksack. Out of a bottle—Matt could see it was Rudy's vodka bottle—she poured water into a carved wooden bowl, mixing up a kind of gruel. "This isn't as bad as it looks," she said consolingly. "Think of it as something Swedes would have for breakfast."

"What about that creature?"

"Shush. All in good time."

Finally, having satisfied his hunger for food if not for answers, she patted his knee. "Stay right there," she commanded. "Are you ready for the experience of a lifetime?" She disappeared behind some bushes and returned a few minutes later, proudly walking arm in arm with the same hominid that Matt had jumped.

"Matt meet Longface. Longface meet Matt. Don't worry," she added, smiling. "He doesn't bear a grudge."

Matt gaped incredulously, instinctively shrinking back at the sight of the naked primate. He stared at its stocky physique, short legs, barrel chest, and bulging biceps and then up at its huge projecting face with the flattened skull, disappearing chin, deep-set wide eyes, and the unmistakable bar of bone. He looked so almost human—almost but not quite. Susan chuckled at Matt's confusion.

"You can say whatever you want," she said, warming to her role as the expert. "He can't understand you. They don't have language."

The hominid approached and squatted on its haunches, looking at Matt with interest but not profound curiosity. It seemed neither frightened nor frightening. Matt looked it up and down; its back was long, its legs were short. It had more hair than a human but was not completely hirsute. Everything about it seemed a little bit off, and yet it was humanoid enough to—to what? Matt leaned close and stared at its face. He saw intelligence in the eyes, perhaps even intelligence to rival his own, but he did not see wonder.

Longface touched the sleeve of Matt's shirt, and fingered the material. Matt looked down at the rotund fingers, rough nails, and large knuckles. The line creases across the palm were not at all like a human's. On impulse, he reached across and took the hand in his own, and as soon as he felt the powerful grip, a wave of emotion swept through him, a pulsating thrill so strong it seemed a throwback to some earlier age, as if his genetic core was ignited by that spark of contact. He felt exhilarated.

"Amazing, isn't it?" said Susan. "To think that touch goes back thirty thousand years."

"Listen!" Matt exclaimed. "He's talking." Sounds were gurgling up from the thick chest.

"I'm afraid not. They make noises at certain moments. And from what I can tell, the noises seem to register reactions in a crude sort of way—alarm, surprise, joy. But they definitely don't talk. They do something else."

"What?"

"They think."

"What do you mean?"

"They convey thoughts—or images—something."

"You mean telepathy?"

"Sort of. You'll see what I mean. You can feel it when it's happening. And then they seem to know what you're looking at, almost as if they're looking at it too."

"How do you know this?"

"Try hiding and you'll see what I'm talking about. It's almost as if . . ."

"As if what?"

"As if they're in you."

"Incredible."

"I know. I can't explain it. It's some kind of extrasensory communication."

Abruptly Longface lost interest and walked off. Something about the stately way he carried himself, the tilt of his head as he walked with a rolling sway to his stride, was oddly revealing.

"My God, he's old," Matt blurted out.

"That's right. You tried to mug one of the tribe's elders."

"Tribe. Are there a lot of them?"

"You wouldn't believe how many."

"But how could this be the same species that we ran into before? They look roughly the same, but the others were so ruthless. These seem much more human."

"I don't know which is more human, but you're right—the two are completely different."

"Van is dead—killed in the cave-in," said Matt.

"I guessed as much. There was nothing we could do. Now sit back and rest. That was one helluva bump you got. You've got another surprise ahead. But that's for later."

Susan led Matt along the path toward what she called the village. She was chattering, glad that Matt was all right and happy also for the human companionship, for someone to share observations about the implausible world they had fallen into.

"I'll teach you their names," she said, "beginning with the three who rescued us: Genesis, Exodus, and Leviticus. You can tell I was in a biblical frame of mind. They're still my favorites. You can always recognize Leviticus; he's got a slender build and a scar across his cheek, though God knows what he got it from. Actually, they're all getting easier to tell apart."

Matt looked at her bemused. "You like playing Eve, don't you?—naming all the creatures."

"I guess maybe I do."

"It's a form of control. You always liked that."

She smiled.

"But I don't like it," Matt said. "I need to know some things—like how we got here—before you tell me their names."

Stung, Susan hastened to fill him in. She had regained consciousness coming down the mountain slope, and she told Matt what she remembered. Her first sensation was the iron strength of the arms that cradled her, the hard bulge of the biceps. When she opened her eyes she saw the white fleshy underside of the tiny beardless chin and caught a peek inside the mouth: His teeth were brown. Her first impulse was to panic, since she assumed that these were the same ones who had killed Rudy. But oddly, as the hours wore on and she feigned unconsciousness, she found something indescribably reassuring about them; she didn't know whether it was the gentleness of their demeanor, the arms embracing her, or the glimpses of Matt being carried next to her.

By nightfall they were at the village in the valley. After they put her down near the fire, she continued to try to spy on them unseen, but they appeared to discern the ruse and brought her some food, which they left. She ate it and slept. When she awoke the next morning, she found herself in the bower with Matt and surrounded by scores of them:

males, females, and children. Her fear gradually dissipated, replaced by a sense of marvel. The scientist in her asserted itself.

"Can you imagine," she exclaimed, "we have the opportunity to study another species by actually living among them! No more theories, no more conjecture, no more speculation. Just observation, straight old-fashioned cultural research—except that it's prehistoric."

Matt was amazed at how quickly Susan seemed to feel at home. She was taking everything in, sifting it over, and trying to make sense of it as if she were on some fantastic anthropological field trip. How quickly we humans adapt to the unexpected and to adversity, he thought. Is that quality the secret of our survival?

He himself was still feeling shaky. On some primitive level he had decided that danger was receding; the archaic part of his brain that pumped out chemicals in response to aggression was beginning to quiet. But all his senses were stretched taut, and when they passed a hominid on the path, he thought he would jump out of his skin.

There was something else, beyond fear, that Matt noticed. At first he dismissed it, but now he was certain. Matt stared at them and they looked back. But they didn't always look at him and he experienced a heaviness in his brain, almost an intrusion, as if something else were moving through it. And when the hominid passed, the sensation passed, like the sun appearing from behind the clouds.

The village was built around a river. It was not much to look at, a collection of makeshift shelters that dotted the hillside and multiplied as the land flattened out in the bowl of the valley.

What caught Matt's eye were the hominids themselves, the blur of activity as they went about their everyday lives, carrying logs and baskets, sitting on their haunches, eating, tending a fire that sent a lazy curlicue of smoke into the sky. And children—of course there would be children!—

who looked like miniature versions of the adults, only with brow ridges that seemed more pronounced on their smaller faces.

Everyone was naked. None of them wore animal skins, as the others had—in fact, there seemed to be no animals about at all—and none carried clubs or other weapons. The women were a few inches shorter than the men and their female shapes struck Matt as exaggerated, with extremely wide hips, low-slung buttocks, and pendulous breasts. The penises of the men, hanging freely, did not seem to be particularly large and were unobtrusive in the bushy nests of genital hair.

"I know what you're thinking," Susan said. "And the answer is: I don't know. I haven't been here long enough to see them copulate.

"As far as that goes, there doesn't seem to be a great difference between the sexes. Certainly not in the roles. Both of them tend fires and pound grain with a mortar and pestle—those seem to be the two main activities, as far as I can tell.

"Yes, they have grain. They plant crops but they don't kill animals and they don't eat meat. The fire is used to clear the land, not to cook. So we were certainly wrong about that. Settled agriculture before hunting—fascinating, isn't it?"

Matt was in fact thinking about something else. "Susan, we've been standing here a few minutes but nobody's paying us any attention."

"But they know we're here; you can feel them reading you—that's what I call it. So they know we're not a threat. But their curiosity isn't what you would call well developed. Yesterday when I first came, I created a little stir, especially among the children. But by now they pretty much regard me as old hat."

Matt stepped inside a hut. It was built in a cone shape around the base of a tree; the lower branches had been snapped close to the trunk and hung onto the ground. Dead branches had been piled on top to form a kind of tepee and set into the ground to keep away predators. It looked something like the thorn fence of a Masai kraal in Kenya, he thought. There was not much inside: some gourds filled with water, half a dozen flaked tools, several carved wooden baskets filled with grain.

Susan was keeping up her guide's patter. "I can't figure out the social organization, if there is any. They don't seem to live in families. It looks like people and kids move about a lot from one hut to another. The women seem to shrink into the background. But I haven't been here long enough to tell for sure."

Matt still could not reconcile these hominids with the bloodthirsty monsters that had killed Rudy. The others *looked* cruel—not just because they carried weapons but because of something in their posture, a way of thrusting the head forward on the elongated neck, a cruel glint to the eyes sunken beneath that sheltering flap of bone. These appeared altogether benign. They had an openness and calmness, sitting on their haunches and chewing berries and fruit as if nothing in this earthly domain concerned them.

"I'll tell you what puzzles me," he said. "It's only a first impression, but from everything I've seen so far they're much more primitive than I expected—or than I would have expected if I ever dared to even imagine such a thing."

"Yes."

"Compared to that bunch we ran into on the mountain, they seem eons behind. That group—I hate to say it, but they were organized. They had a leader; they acted together in a coordinated, planned way. They carried weapons. And you saw their cave. They were curing hides, for God's sake!"

"What are you saying?" she asked.

"I'm saying that despite the outward resemblances they're just too different—like two different species."

"C'mon. They look alike. They're separated by a single

day's walk. And you say they're two different species?''

"I know it sounds incredible," Matt said. "I'm just saying they *act* like two different species."

"You've been up some six hours and you're already an expert."

"Now take it easy. You've never appreciated regional variation anyway."

"What does that mean?" she fumed.

"It means you always go for the easy explanation—violent replacement, one group conquering another. Maybe there's another explanation."

"Such as?"

"I don't know."

"Next you'll be telling me that these two groups evolved separately because one's in a valley and the other's on a mountain. There's such a thing as carrying multiregional development too far."

They were silent a moment. Then Susan spoke. "Anyway, you're forgetting something."

"What?"

"The Khodzant Enigma."

"Okay, wise guy, what's it mean?"

"I don't know. But I know it has something to do with war, and it's the key to this whole thing. I intend to figure it out."

"Good luck."

The path dwindled to a narrow walkway. Susan seemed confident of the way and went first. Soon they left the village and penetrated deep into the forest. They could hear birds, the buzzing of insects, a thousand tiny scurrying creatures.

"Where are we going?" Matt asked.

"The surprise. Remember?"

Susan leaped across a stream and took long graceful strides. Her luxuriant black hair looked at home in the forest. Matt's side still ached slightly but it felt better than before. They walked for a good hour until Susan turned and said with a smile, "We're almost there. You okay?"

Matt put on a fake grimace. "Certainly."

They climbed an incline and came to a bluff where most of the valley spread out before them. In the distance sheer walls rose up to the mountains above.

"I'll be damned," said Matt. "We're in a crater. I'll bet it's still active. That must be why it's so temperate."

Susan put her arm through his. "You know, a day is a long time to be unconscious. I was worried. Don't let it go to your head, but you just may be worming your way back into my affections."

"Well, being stranded all alone with several hundred cavemen may have something to do with it."

She laughed and led on. Before long they heard a steady roar through the trees ahead: a waterfall. In another ten minutes they were facing a ten-foot-wide chute of water that plummeted down a cliffside. Matt smelled sulfur and realized it was a huge geyser sending up a hot spray. *That* explains the climate, he thought: geothermal springs giving off heated vapors that collide with a warm air stream from the valley.

Below them, at the foot of the waterfall, was a wide basin in the rock formed by the pounding water. Matt looked down and saw that stone steps descended to the basin near the foot of the waterfall. Then he heard another sound penetrating above the roar intermittently, almost drowned out but occasionally distinct. It seemed to be a voice chanting or singing, impossible as that was, but it was so elusive that he began to doubt his senses.

Then Susan cupped her hands close to his ears and yelled something, again indistinct, and pointed to the foot of the waterfall. Out of the mists came a shape recognizable as human in form and then familiar. It drew closer and ascended the steps, but not until it reached the top could Matt be certain. There, approaching with a solemn air, wrapped in a toga like a classical Greek god but with a full beard that made him look like an Old Testament prophet, was Kellicut.

Eagleton was nothing if not a fanatic. When he took on a subject, he immersed himself in it and for hours on end thought about nothing else. His ruminations started at a central point, then expanded in ever-widening circles, like a dog searching for a passage home.

Which was why his office had been transformed by artifacts and totems in the last two weeks. Along one wall were portraits of the great men in paleoanthropology and related fields, ranging from geology to cognitive psychology. There were even practitioners of the new school of experimental archaeology, strange souls who disappeared naked in the rough for months on end, trying to re-create the lifestyles of their primitive ancestors. Even those who had strayed from what came to be the path of accepted wisdom, the maverick conservatives and fighters of lost causes, were represented.

To the right, staring skeptically into space through tiny circular glasses, was a photograph of Rudolf Virchow, the German founder of modern pathology who had sabotaged his reputation by fighting the preposterous theory of evolution. There was a painting of Alfred Russel Wallace, the soft-spoken, lower-class autodidact with watery brown eyes, the man whose theories anticipated Darwin's. There was Thomas Huxley, long-haired and handsome, sneering confidently at the camera; and Paul Broca, the cornerstone of French physical anthropology; and even Edward Simpson, the notable English forger, sitting on a wooden chair surrounded by the tools of his trade, a hammer in one hand and at his feet some fraudulent stones, destined no doubt for gullible Victorian buyers. Towering over them all, both physically on the wall and mentally in Eagleton's hierarchical pantheon, was Ernst Haeckel, the German naturalist, soulful-looking with long blond tresses and an air of tragic destiny like General George Custer. He had embraced evolution with a dangerous passion, converting the survival of the fittest into a tenet for *Naturphilosophie,* the mystical romantic philosophy that led to the eugenic theories and racial doctrines of Nazism. Eagleton was irresistibly drawn to the man, pictured here in boots and broad-brimmed hat, a stein of beer at his elbow.

On a table by Eagleton's desk lay an odd assortment of molds, mandibles, bits of skull with numbers scrawled on them in dark ink, and a variety of prehistoric tools: hammer stones, unifacial and bifacial choppers, polyhedrons, core scrapers, discoids, flakes, and fragments. When lost in thought, he picked the pieces up, turned them over and over like worry beads, and replaced them in new patterns.

On the opposite wall, stretched tight and held in place against a cork backing, was a reproduction of the Khodzant Enigma with its missing panels, the favorite unsolved riddle of all graduate students. No one but Eagleton knew that it was somehow connected to the Neanderthal—at least no one still living. Eagleton had made the connection thanks to Zhamtsarano, the Mongol who inspired in him the respect and affinity an explorer feels for a colleague who walked the same uncharted path decades earlier and disappeared. The pictograph had been uncovered in Zhamtsarano's files in the Institute of Oriental Studies at the Academy of Sciences. There was a sketch of it, with the final quadrant missing, of course, and a scrawled notation in Cyrillic. Again, Eagleton read the translation on a sheet of paper on his desk:

> Every tribe has its own central myth. It is the origin or survival myth that delineates the tribe and creates its separateness. To penetrate to the heart of the myth is to understand the tribe's moment of creation and the dawn of its history.

Mount Olympus, Gaea and Uranus, the Titans, Cain and Abel, the flood and Noah's Ark, Muhammad on the mountain, Krishna, the lost tribe of Israel—all incorporated this basic truth, Eagleton had realized. He believed that Zham- tsarano had solved the riddle of the pictograph but had left the answer unrecorded, typical for someone who believed that the voyage was as important as the destination. Eag- leton stared at it for hours, trying to decipher its message, and sometimes while engaged in another task he would turn his wheelchair suddenly to look at it, as if the secret could be seized in an ambush.

Time was running out for Eagleton. He had decisions to make but no solid information on which to base them. Van's transponder was still dead. There was a good chance that he and the others were in trouble. Should he send in Kane and the SWAT team? If the paratroopers arrived too early, storming over everything and kicking ass the way they always did, it could abort the whole mission. But if they came too late? The only problem then would be con- tainment: how to stop the word of what they had found from getting out—if indeed there was anything left for them to find.

And what about the Russians? He had been distressed to learn from Van's last transmission that they were already on the spot. In his snide way Van had implied that Eagleton knew about their expedition. Which was true, of course, in a general sense and he had seen no reason to put Van in the loop. But he had not thought Moscow would move so quickly and had no idea what the Russian scientists were up to. They'd had second thoughts about handing over all that research and conceding the field to the Americans, glasnost or no. After all, why give away an advantage in a breakthrough field? Cold War habits died hard.

Eagleton lit another cigarette, and opened the Operation Achilles folder with the updates on top. No good news there. The subject had lost twenty pounds over three weeks, had stopped cooperating with the experimenters, had to be chained with hand and leg irons, and was making strange noises.

He flipped through the pages of experimental data on Achilles: summaries of the raw sheets that were recorded over months and shipped in bulk to Maryland to be checked and rechecked, ever since they had discovered the remarkable powers of the creature. Not telepathy, which was mind reading, but definitely a step toward it—Remote Viewing, or RV, is what the scientists called it, and they were absolutely certain that the creature, whatever other lesser traits it might display, possessed it.

Eagleton came upon a transcript of his first interview with the scientist who explained it to him. He read it.

"Is it mind reading?"

"Hardly, no. Not the same thing at all. First of all, thinking—at least in humans—is inseparable from language and much of it takes place in the cerebral cortex. This subject does not have a developed cerebral cortex, at least not developed in the same way. No, the gift is ocular."

"Meaning that it requires eyes to work."

"Yes, someone else's eyes."

"Does it see that person?"

"No, it only sees what that person sees. It looks through that person's eyes—actually, it occupies the optic centers where the visual information is processed. So it would not see the actual person unless that person happened to be looking into a mirror."

"Can it go anywhere and see anything?"

"You mean, can it travel through space at will and, say, hang out on a treetop to catch a sunset? Not at all. As I said, it's a limited form of telepathy, totally dependent on having a channel to work through— another brain that is the primary receiver and data processor."

"It can really see through another's eyes?"

They had first spotted it accidentally on the video cameras, back in the days when its appetite was hearty. They noticed that moments before feeding the creature flew into a frenzy of anticipation; somehow it knew that food was on the way. A sharp-witted observer at the monitors pointed out that this happened at the precise moment that the keeper walked by the open door toward the food bin, seven rooms away from the basement cell. They varied the feeding hours but still it knew, to the exact second. They widened the tests to include all kinds of things: baths, recreation, and the presentation of toys. Somehow it could detect things happening in another room. There was one constant: Someone else had to be in that room and using his eyes.

They had constructed iron-clad experiments: a man on a different floor would look at one of three signs—a triangle, circle, or square—and down below the creature would pick out the correct object. They changed all the variables: the objects, the distance, the timing, the lighting. They even turned off the television monitors, and still it chose correctly, with a margin of error so minute, 0.306 percent, as to be statistically insignificant.

The field of observation was expanded. The creature could achieve RV with three different viewers scattered miles away. Given a sketch pad and charcoal, it could even draw in a crude way the outlines of a scene someone else was looking at, provided that the landmarks were distinct enough. But someone else had to be looking for the faculty to work.

Those who spent time with the creature, the handlers and scientists, noted that they experienced a sensation of fuzziness, and sometimes a headache, when the creature invaded their visual receptors. One particular handler, an Irish American called Scanlon, was the creature's favorite; it seemed to spend a great deal of time ''seeing'' what Scanlon was observing. At Eagleton's suggestion, relayed through the scientists, they rigged the creature up to an ECG, galvanic skin response recorder, and other instruments to measure bodily emotions. Then Scanlon, unaware of the test, was taken for a car ride down a mountain road at 70 miles an hour. The needles kicked wildly and the creature's measurements went off the chart.

Too bad, thought Eagleton, that the creature was otherwise so uncommunicative. The information was all one-way. It was unable to shed any light on its unique ability, like an idiot savant carrying out a multiplication problem to ten decimal points. It was such a crude-looking animal to possess such a sublime gift. Too bad. Perhaps our understanding will come only with an autopsy, and that might not be far off, given the way its health was deteriorating.

This whole operation was too big for any mistakes. God only knew what possessing that faculty could mean. With the advances in genetics these days, a transfer of the gift to humans was more than feasible; it was practically within reach. The applications were awe-inspiring, militarily, if nothing else. An army with such a capability would be invincible. Imagine the possibilities for espionage, information retrieval, command and control. Imagine the advantages during negotiations, economic conferences, setting quotas with the Japanese, bargaining with the European Union. No wonder the Russians were back in the game.

Eagleton closed the folder and pressed the buzzer underneath his desk, and a secretary entered—a new one, the third since Sarah's quick departure. She was wearing perfume but he couldn't tell the brand; his olfactory sense was his weakest. When he handed her the file she looked at him and asked, "Anything else, sir?"

His tone came out harsh, the tone of a man who has lots of work ahead and can't be interrupted by small talk. "No, nothing. Nothing at all." She left, closing the door softly behind her. He picked up a mandible and bounced it in his hand, then looked over at the Khodzant Enigma. Outside, through the blinds, it was getting dark.

15

"I will not talk about Rousseau. I will not talk about Locke and Schopenhauer. I have purged myself of philosophers. They are all know-nothing philistines. They belong to a part of my brain that I have expunged."

Kellicut was resting against a tree, a perfect place for a discussion of man as noble savage. He showed a new edginess, which surprised Matt, coming after the strange, almost mystical spaciness that he had been displaying until now. Susan, who sat on the ground looking up at Kellicut, didn't seem to share Matt's perception.

Matt leaned against a tree limb. Struck by the sight of some hominids foraging for berries nearby, so peaceful in their natural element, Susan had tried to steer the conversation to the philosophers who used to preoccupy them for hours on end in the bars of Cambridge. It was a way to break the ice, but to Matt it seemed as if she had fallen into the old role of the reverential graduate student.

Matt had noticed the changes in Kellicut the moment he saw him. He was taut and brown from his time in the valley. His arms were muscular and his skin was leathered. His age, if anything, gave him more authority, which was emphasized by the fullness of his salt-and-pepper beard. His face was gaunt and his eyes had a fanatic's gleam, like a biblical avenging angel. He was not wearing a toga, after all, but some kind of loincloth made from what had once been a pair of trousers.

Strangely, Kellicut had registered no surprise at seeing Matt. Undoubtedly he knew of his presence from Susan, of course; still, after so many years and in such peculiar circumstances, Matt had expected more. After all, he had just flown halfway around the world in response to an urgent summons; he had expected to find him grateful, not distant. And there had been that frigid exchange when Matt encountered him a few moments before.

Matt had felt a surge of the old affection, and over the roar of the waterfall, he had yelled: "You sent for us and here we are," moving toward him to hug him. Kellicut stayed where he was and arched an eyebrow. His answer was just audible above the sound of the crashing water: "Well, in any case, you're here." Matt had stifled his hurt, but as he did so, he realized he was replaying an emotion that he had often felt before in this man's presence.

"We thought you were in danger."

"That's what I wanted the Institute to think."

"Why?"

"Because I don't trust them. I don't know who to trust. I'm not even sure I trust you. You'll have to be patient."

Kellicut then lapsed into a long silence. It did not seem that he was in turmoil; on the contrary, his mind appeared calm and vacant. It was as if something had reached down to his very soul and pulled him inside out.

But now, hours later, under Susan's prodding, Kellicut began pouring out words that had been bottled up for so long. He spoke without moving his hands, with no gestures whatsoever—only to her. "Philosophy is bunk. It's a sham. It is not the thoughts or the thinking of the thoughts that is at fault, it's the words themselves. By their very nature they are confining. Words cannot capture the thought or even come close to capturing it, and so they become liars. Language isn't a gift, it's a burden. You realize this once you employ true communication through another channel."

Kellicut backtracked and told of his search through the mountains, his discovery of the crevice leading to the valley, and his first encounters with the hominids. "I knew from the moment I saw them that they possessed some extraordinary puissance. I had already watched them from a distance, and I knew with a certainty that's hard to explain that they were aware of me too, that they were observing me as I was observing them. Or, more precisely, that they were observing my *observation* of them.

"I returned to the camp, left the diary, and came back. This time they were all together in a clearing, as if they were anticipating my arrival. Which of course they were, though I had no way of knowing it at the time. I felt no fear; why should I? I already knew quite a bit about them. They were not hurtful, and my motives were pure. I approached them as kindred beings who exist on a higher plane.

"I stepped out from the bushes and walked among them. They were not in the least surprised. They sniffed me and examined me with curiosity, not at all threateningly. I looked for a leader but there was none—aside from a few elders, I was to discover later, who are respected in a general sort of way. Instead, everyone is truly equal, from the smallest child to the strongest man. They have no gesture of greeting like a handshake, because there is no need to display peaceful intent. Their intent is *always* peaceful. What reason is there to suspect a hand when one lives in a world without weapons?

"They knew I was hungry and they fed me—literally fed me: gathered around me and put food in my mouth. This was my first experience with the power. I noticed that when I looked at the food, they gave me more. When I looked away, even a little, they held back. Yet they weren't watching my eyes. How did they know? They just did."

"How?" asked Matt.

Kellicut turned to him with an edge to his voice. "Don't you feel it? Haven't you experienced it?"

"I'm not sure I have."

"You know when it's happening. You experience the sensation. It's as if your mind is filling up in some way; that's the best way I can describe it—like a vessel filling up with water or a fog that takes hold of your head.

"When it happens with one of them it can be a passing sensation. But when it happens in a group it is intense. The fog thickens and thickens, and when it finally lets loose, a shower washes through you and cleanses you. It's not unlike LSD, that same sense of losing oneself totally, of merging with something powerful and infinite. It's not at all frightening; it's—what's the word?—heartening, *comforting*. It's like belonging, like breaking through solitude, like not being alone in the profoundest sense."

The three were silent for a moment, and then Kellicut resumed. "They have achieved a beatific existence. Think of it. They are herbivorous and pacific. They do not kill animals or each other. Their ethos is communal. There is no individuality, no sense of self, no *I*. Why should there be, how *could* there be, when the psyche can move out of the body, when the mind literally exists in the collective? All that counts is the tribe."

"What happens when one dies?" Susan asked.

Kellicut was startled by the question but not because he had not thought about it. He paused. "That's a whole other matter," he said gently.

"But how does this psychic power work?" asked Matt.

"A rather pedestrian and utilitarian question."

"I suppose I'm that kind of guy," Matt replied.

"It is not used for anything, as such. It just *is*," said Kellicut, annoyed.

"What I mean is, are they reading your mind, or are they simply able to see what you're seeing?"

"Simply?"

"You get my point."

"I do. And not being able to perform the feat myself, I

don't see how I can answer it. I've only been on the receiving end—at least until now.''

"What do you mean, until now?'' asked Matt. "Are you trying to learn it?''

"I wouldn't go that far. But one can always hope.''

"It sounds close to ESP,'' said Susan. "For that matter, what's the difference between reading someone's mind and actually seeing what that person is seeing, especially when the phenomenon leaps over the species barrier? If both species thought in the same way, maybe they could read our thoughts. As it is, they can only see what we see.''

"I think you're right,'' said Kellicut.

"And do you believe that they've failed to develop language because they don't need language?'' Matt asked.

"Failed?''

"Okay, forget failed. That they haven't developed language because they don't need language?''

"Precisely. Why crawl when you can walk?''

"So perhaps the evolutionary paleontologists who believe in the linguistic explanation are correct—that the great divide occurred because we acquired language. In the beginning was the word.''

"With one important difference. Their theory is based upon the assumption that *Homo sapiens* went on toward fuller development, that language was an advantage rather than a hindrance. Whereas here we can see that the opposite is true.''

"The opposite?''

"Don't you get it?'' Kellicut was annoyed again. "Here communication occurs in its purest form. The individual is submerged in the group. The world is complete, so there is little need to push ahead to something else. Why strive for progress when change can only mean regression?''

"That doesn't sound very Darwinian to me,'' said Matt.

"Darwin has nothing to do with it. Survival of the fittest was a brilliant concept, but it doesn't admit any moral or ethical dimension. It's the world as a giant, ever-changing, malevolent obstacle course. It's history written after Genesis.''

''And what we have here is before Genesis?'' asked Matt.

''Absolutely. If you can't understand that, God help you. Don't you see that you are surrounded by innocent, naive, trusting beings? You have found Eden itself, the great garden of paradise, before Adam and Eve's transgression. It's all part of nature's grand design, repeating over and over.''

''Eden?'' Matt questioned.

''Yes, Eden. In every way.''

''Every way? Does that mean we can expect to find God here?''

''Most surely. I have. And not only that.''

''What else?''

''You will find Satan too. And he is prepared to turn into a snake.''

''Who is Satan?''

''It's not for me to say. I may be wrong.'' It occurred to Matt, and he realized that the suspicion had been creeping up on him for some time, that Kellicut might be crazy. He looked over at Susan, who appeared enthralled. Why didn't she see it?

Kellicut had retreated into obfuscation. Matt thought back to the chase through the caves only a few days ago. Suddenly he remembered Van warning them to close their eyes when they were hiding in the cutaway, the urgency in his voice. Of course! Van knew about their powers. He knew they could see through another's eyes. *He had known all along.* The realization made him angry. ''Tell me,'' he said. ''Did you know anything about this before you came here?''

''Not a bit.''

Matt believed him. ''And the killer Neanderthals that we ran into, where do they fit in?''

''I can't say. I've never seen them, though of course I know they come down here from time to time on raids.

Susan told me about your experience. I'm sorry about Sharafidin; he was a great help to me. And I heard about the death of your friend. Much of what I know has been conjecture. I have a theory that I'm working on, but it's premature to divulge it.''

Matt and Susan knew better than to press him. Kellicut was not the type to give way once he dug in his heels.

''What I'd like to know,'' said Matt, ''is why they're so brutal. They killed Rudy without a moment's hesitation.''

''I should think the answer's obvious,'' said Kellicut.

''What is it?''

''They hate us.''

''Hate us? Why?''

''Because we beat them. We nearly exterminated them— nearly but not quite. The worst thing to do to a mortal enemy is *almost* kill him.''

That evening Susan tried an experiment. Just before dusk she slipped off alone and skirted the edge of the village, making her way quietly, brushing past branches that hung low across the path. It was not fear that made her move so stealthily; already she had adapted to the valley and was conscious of being drawn to its tranquil rhythms, especially at the day's end. She moved noiselessly because she didn't want to be deterred.

She heard a rustling in the bushes of some small animal close to her feet. It stopped but when she passed it started up again, scurrying away. She paused at a fork, got her bearings, and took a path to the left where the woods grew thicker. She was headed toward a grove of birch trees near a stream, which she knew was frequented by Leviticus.

She thought for a fleeting moment about the outside world, the bustle and jangle that had been her life. That used to be reality. This was timelessness, weightlessness. Could the mind and body move from one world to another just like that? She realized with a pang how much she missed what she had left behind, while at the same time on a different level how ready she was to jettison it. Was there no center to her at all?

As she came around a bend to the stream, she saw Leviticus on the opposite bank, arms bent at his sides like a cat, drinking deeply from the water. Ripples moved out in gentle concentric circles from his chin. The top of his head, thick and bushy black, was arched upward, and from beneath his eyebrows he was watching her. The scar on his cheek glistened. She sat down on the bank across from him three feet away.

He raised his head and stared at her. She waited. In this position his shoulder muscles were flexed and enormous. He's like a panther, she thought, lithe and powerful. She looked at his forehead. There was the beetle brow, standing out starkly against the other features. It was impossible to ignore this ridge of bone, pale and solid, a huge hump where the skin should be smooth. Combined with the receding chin and flattened skull, it pulled the face forward like some sort of distorted reflection in a bottle, an embryo behind glass. It made her shiver involuntarily, like that quick shudder when falling off to sleep. Is there something in us that despises another species because it is so close, because the minor variances loom as unbearable deformations? she wondered. Is it that we are so afraid of deviations in ourselves? Yet the eyes were perfect and clear and human. She saw that his irises were hazel and his whites were webbed with tiny red blood lines. She had an impulse to reach over and touch his brow; would it be hard or would it yield? Repulsion or attraction—they merged into one.

In the dark water below him, she could make out Leviticus's reflection. The view from below was the same as when he had carried her down the mountain. He stopped drinking and stared back. She held her breath, and then she began to feel what she had come for. It started somewhere on the periphery of her mind like a shadow, then gathered force surprisingly quickly and became dense. She sat unmoving and let it wash through her. It grew and expanded until a warmth like melting wax seemed to fill her skull and move down the top of her spinal column. She was transfixed. Her mind was soaring; it skipped above the tree-tops and fled into the clouds; then, like a feather, it floated down slowly until it came to rest. For a moment they locked eyes and held each other in a stare; then Leviticus turned away and moved off into the bushes behind him without a backward glance.

Susan sat rooted to the spot for a long time, savoring the afterglow. It was getting dark, she realized abruptly. She rose, languidly undid the buttons of her khaki blouse, stepped out of her pants and her panties, and slipped slowly into the darkening water.

Resnick did not like to go into the cell himself, because of both the smell and a sense of anxiety that had unaccountably been getting stronger. By now the odor was truly over-powering. It was hard to tell what caused it. Dried-up feces and flatulation due to an alien diet had been his first guess, sweat glands his second, exema his third. They had tried everything, including dousing the creature with shampoo and hosing it down, back when it could stand, but nothing had helped and finally they gave up. When the smell pen-etrated upstairs, they burned incense. When the keepers went into its cell they wore gauze mouth and nose masks smeared with globs of Vicks VapoRub.

There was another reason that Resnick didn't care to ap-proach the creature, but he didn't admit it to anyone; it seemed too weird, the way he got those headaches. Best to keep something like that to himself. It could even be his own mind playing tricks, some psychosomatic problem.

In his student days decades ago, he had been Van Steed's eager lab assistant. That was back when Van was cutting a wide swath through the behavioral sciences department at Chicago. Even Harry Harlow at nearby Wisconsin was forced to sit up and take notice of the brilliant graduate student and, to a lesser degree, the student's helper. Van was a behaviorist back then, before he took up this far-out psycholingual business. He was ingenious and on top of the latest research, always reading papers in journals no one else had even heard of. Resnick had a memory flash: Van sitting in the basement beer hall and explaining, with more than a hint of condescension, the latest theory on DNA bonding.

Van was a bit strange even back then. Once Resnick opened the lab door and found him sitting at a small white table mounting rat brains on slides. The rats, operated upon and run through experiments to test perception, had been "sacrificed," as the scientific term had it. Their limp white bodies with pink tails and split-open braincases lay in a heap on newspaper on the floor underneath a banana skin. Van was still chewing the banana as he sliced their brains with the ennui of a deli-counter worker cutting ham.

From rats, Van and Resnick moved on to rhesus monkeys. These operations were much more complicated and took hours to perform. Standing there in the miniature operating room where even the anesthetizing mask was doll size, Resnick used to pretend that they were doctors, performing cutting-edge neurosurgery on an accident victim, and handed over the sterilized instruments solemnly. In truth the operations *were* advanced—Van was moving into new regions of the brain that were largely uncharted—except that he wasn't trying to repair brain tissue but to destroy it. The method was crude: Van burned lesions, with a needle connected to a tube of liquid nitrogen, and he removed the septal region. Once recovered, the monkey would fly into an automatic rage response at the slightest stimulus, so that just walking past a row of the caged animals, each with a metal plug sticking out of its head, would set them bouncing around like lunatics. When Van removed the amygdala, the monkey turned placid and would smear its feces on the walls of its cage like a kindergartner fingerpainting. When he removed sections of the hypothalamus, the mysterious floor of the third ventricle that is thought to be the core of inner functioning, the monkey would sit phlegmatically, emptied of all affect and personality. Once Van planted an electrode in the pleasure center and rigged up an apparatus so the monkey was self-stimulating. He left the animal alone until it died of exhaustion. "Sixty-one hours," he remarked as he checked the timer afterward. "Not a bad way to go."

Van had secured this job for Resnick, and Resnick was grateful. But he didn't feel that Van had the right to come in here at all hours, the way he did when the creature was first captured. Van had been frustrated at the lack of results from the experiments and he was almost brutal in the way he handled the creature and attached it to the EEG and other machines that the creature detested. Resnick was glad Van hadn't been around for months.

As he reached over for his coffee mug, Resnick caught a blur of movement on the top left monitor. That would be Grady or Allen moving in close to the bars. It was Allen; his handlebar mustache over the mouth mask could be seen easily on the snowy black-and-white screen.

Allen was wearing dark glasses—like the ones Van used to wear—and that was a mistake; it seemed to upset the creature. He was carrying the extra belts, three of them, each two inches thick. Now Grady came into view and the creature began that awful moaning sound. Keys jangled as they unlocked the cell door. Resnick looked into his mug and decided he needed a refill, so he left the room. He wasn't really supposed to do so—the rules called for round-the-clock observation—but two keepers were down there. The third was activating the force feeder and would join them in a minute. It was not, he had to admit, a pleasant sight, even on a monitor.

Resnick busied himself in the kitchen and took his time making the coffee, humming to himself loudly. When he walked back into the control room, the feeding was over. Was it his imagination, or were there bits of food on the cell wall? The keepers were talking. "Fucker pissed all over me," said Grady. Allen laughed. Resnick saw the cell door swing shut and heard the loud clang interrupt the soft moaning. On the screen a huddled object rocked slowly.

Then suddenly, as before, Resnick felt a massive pain inside his head, beginning far back in his temporal lobes and then moving forward and spreading out like lava. It was far worse than any migraine he had ever experienced. He reached for the giant-sized bottle, pulled out four aspirins, and swilled them down with his coffee.

He sometimes wondered exactly what Van had been after during his visits to the basement cell. It seemed that only since then had the creature been so hard to handle.

16

Matt and Blue-Eyes circled each other in the pit, each looking for an advantage. Blue-Eyes—named after Sinatra because he liked to vocalize—was not much of a wrestler, but he was game.

In fact none of the hominids were good wrestlers, despite their superior strength. It was a martial sport, and concepts such as domination, victory, and loss had no place in their mental universe. They did appreciate a hard fall to the ground, but whether they viewed it as funny or not was difficult to tell, since they did not laugh but seemed instead to become excited. Their humor, such as it was, was unfathomable to Matt and Susan. Nothing based upon trickery, cunning, or deceit—games involving substitution of one object for another—drew any response other than blank incomprehension. But certain activities were clearly enjoyable. The children chased each other a lot, squealing in a strident, loud-pitched way, though they did not end by tackling one another. Susan tried to teach them tag but it was a failure because the notion of being ''it'' was beyond their grasp.

Lines and boundaries were also alien to them. Matt theorized that the concept of an arbitrary end to space must somehow be bound up with egocentrism. If your psychic powers allow your world to grow beyond the horizon and then shrink back within an eye blink, how is it possible to comprehend a limit? But he was soon to discover that in one critical area—death—the delineation was starkly made.

As a practical matter Matt found that it made no sense to try to mark out the boundaries of a wrestling ring. But near the village center he discovered a large depression in the ground, which he dubbed "the pit," and it served the purpose as he tried to teach them the sport. The contestants usually stayed inside, though nothing could stop them from suddenly plopping down in the middle of a match whenever the notion struck them.

Matt enjoyed the physical contact. He recalled the jolt he had received the day he took Longface's hand. But he could not say the promise of this touch had been fulfilled. Though they had been living in the valley for days now, neither he nor Susan had achieved a breakthrough in communication with the hominids.

For their part, the hominids seemed to have lost interest in Matt and Susan. While they did not in any way feel unwelcome, they had become to a certain degree unremarkable—in a sense invisible. "It doesn't bother me," Matt joked to Susan one night. "I can take rejection. I've lived in England." But the sense of solitude was growing oppressive. They had only each other—and to a lesser degree Kellicut, who was often away, inside the cavern by the waterfall receiving what he called "spiritual instruction." When he was with them his presence created problems. Matt felt that Kellicut acted as if part of his mind had evaporated; Susan believed his mind had entered a higher plane. Furthermore, he concentrated all his energy and approval on Susan and seemed increasingly hostile toward Matt.

"You still look up to him, don't you?" Matt had said to her once.

"Of course," was all she said.

Now, as Matt and Blue-Eyes circled around in the dirt like two ends of a compass arrow, Matt began to bob and weave, a prelude to the feints and dodges that had worked so well before. Blue-Eyes moved in a clumsy sidestep with his arms outstretched, looking like a hopeless dancer. Matt lunged to the right toward his opponent's left leg. Blue-Eyes panicked and bolted to his right, off balance, tottering and almost falling without Matt even touching him. Then he righted himself and the circling began once more.

Blue-Eyes was young. At first Matt had found it hard to judge their ages. The brow bones affected their pattern of wrinkles, and unless there were clear signs of old age like white hair or sagging breasts, most men and women looked about the same once they reached full stature. But gradually he was able to pick up clues. Strength and sprightliness of step were among them, and by those two criteria, Blue-Eyes must have been in his early twenties. Looking at his opponent's stout biceps and barrel chest, Matt thought, He could crush me to death if he wanted to.

Suddenly Blue-Eyes lowered his head and charged for Matt's right leg. Matt spun back halfway, shifting his weight abruptly, leaving his left leg exposed, and the next thing he knew, Blue-Eyes darted sideways in mid-course, grabbed his left leg, and spun him on his back. He raised Matt up with both arms above his head, as easily as lifting a branch, and tossed him a good eight feet. Matt landed with a thud. He was so surprised it took him a while to realize he had landed right on his bruise. Blue-Eyes sat on the edge of the pit, not at all winded. Watching from a distance, Susan laughed so hard she had to sit down. Kellicut, sitting some distance away in the lotus position, stared into space.

Later that evening, as they sat close to the fire, Susan chuckled again when they talked about it. "I wish you could have seen the look on your face," she said, and then added in a serious tone, "But you know the significance of it, don't you? It shows they can learn."

"No." Kellicut's voice came out of the darkness; they

had forgotten he was there. "We're the ones who must learn." Kellicut was in a febrile state, caused by a breakthrough that afternoon, which he kept to himself. Sitting near the pit, a split second before Blue-Eyes lunged, a vision of Matt's legs had popped into Kellicut's head out of nowhere, as clear as the picture-postcard scene of Mount Rushmore on the View-Master that used to fascinate him as a child.

Two days later, on a warm afternoon, Susan and Matt made love.

It had rained that morning and their clothes were drenched. They decided to take them off once the rain stopped and spread them on a boulder to dry in the sun. Matt, who undressed first, turned his back. As Susan slipped out of her pants, she looked at the little ripples of muscle on Matt's lower back and the smoothly sculpted dimples on his buttocks. "I don't know about you," she said, "but I'm beginning to feel a little silly wearing clothes when everyone around us is naked."

"I can't say I haven't had the same thought."

"It's almost antisocial, like dressing up at a nudists' convention."

"I'll bet they're all talking about us—rather, thinking about us." As he turned around, he could see the dark mound of her pubic hair through her wet panties.

"Well, I for one am ready to take the plunge, at least for this afternoon," Susan said. She deliberately did not look down at his penis as she took off her panties. As Matt looked at her, she felt an involuntary tightening of her lower abdomen.

"I have to say," he said, genuinely admiring, "you look terrific."

She felt proud. Stripping with grace had always been her specialty.

They walked until they came to a meadow. She had to repress her wryness at the image they conjured up, like an old biblical etching: Adam and Eve strolling through the lush prelapsarian garden. Halfway across the meadow they sat down; now its yellow grass walled them in on all sides and made a secure nest. When Susan lay down, he turned and lay down next to her, his hands behind his head. She propped herself up on one elbow and danced her fingers across his chest and lower along his stomach. She felt moist between her legs, a tickling of heat, then looked down and saw his erection building. She smiled at him and moved on top of him, spread her legs, and kissed him deeply.

Later that night, back in their bower, they made love again. Afterward, she lay in Matt's arms and he traced her chin with his forefinger.

"What are you thinking?" she asked.

"What a lovely mandible you have. What a fine fossil you'll make."

They were quiet for a while. "You know, Matt, I never let on, and I swore I would never tell you this if we ever met again—why give you the satisfaction?—but it took a long time for me to get over you."

He nodded slowly.

"I don't know why I'm telling you this. I suppose I think you should know it for some reason. After we broke up, I went to Poland for a bit—it was 1981, Solidarity years—and I met all these people trying to fill in the past. They called it the 'blank spaces of history' and they had to fill them in before they could move on. The Warsaw uprising, the Katyn massacre, the purge trials, the shooting of workers—it all had to come out. It was an obsession.

"This afternoon, after we made love, I thought, I feel like that—that's me. I've got these blank spaces in my life and I've got to tell you about them so I can go on—so *we* can go on—and you've got to tell me about you and Anne."

Anne. Why had he taken up with her? What was his motive? Matt had asked himself that question over and over, reliving the moment with Anne outside the beach house they had all rented the summer he was engaged to Susan. He had walked out with two gin and tonics. He and Anne were alone that warm evening, side by side on a blanket in the sand. When he reached over to kiss her, she had turned away for a moment and then, almost sadly, with a sigh, turned back, and he knew suddenly that she was his—indeed, had been his for some time. But what made him do it? He had sometimes dwelt on the question but had never dug into it; he was too frightened about what he might discover about himself.

"What you are asking is why I did it," Matt said finally. "I can't honestly say, though I've thought about it more times than I can tell you. I know that afterward I felt like a con artist."

They were quiet for a long time.

"Matt, there's something I never told you."

Matt sucked his breath in. Susan continued. "It's hard to say, so I'll just say it. All that time, or most of it, I was with someone too, a guy I took up with while you were away the summer before. He was important to me and I couldn't give him up. I tried to, when you and I were talking about getting married, but I couldn't."

She paused, then said, "There, that wasn't so hard." Once started, she couldn't stop. "So all that time you were with Anne, all that time you were sneaking around, I was seeing him. And all that time when we had those scenes about you being pathologically unfaithful and such a shit, I couldn't bear to tell you. I told myself I didn't want to hurt you. But it was more than that; I was a coward. I would have lost my . . . my right to anger. But after we split up, that's what made the pain so much worse—the knowledge that I was at fault too and you would never know. I've regretted it a lot since, and I'm still sorry for it now."

She squeezed him tighter. "Matt, whatever happens, we need to be able to trust each other. Nothing is as bad as deceit and betrayal."

Matt didn't know what to say. He held her gently for a

long time. In the rush of emotions, he wasn't even sure what he was feeling. He wanted to ask who the man had been, but then he realized he didn't need to; he already knew. It could only have been one person: Kellicut.

Eagleton toyed with the stone ax, a light-salmon-colored piece of rock shaped like a half-moon. It had been sculpted 1.2 million years ago; some unknown hand, already more human than not, had rounded the edge with a necklace series of nicks, each as perfect as a fingerprint. It was a thing of beauty. He had borrowed it through a trustee at the Smithsonian who didn't press too hard into his vague explanation as to what he needed it for. In truth, he wanted it as a medium's divining rod. Like any good detective, Eagleton knew that in solving a mystery you couldn't go back too far.

He was waiting for Dan Wilkinson, the Defense Intelligence Agency's neuroscientist who specialized in parapsychological phenomena. In 1985, Wilkinson had run a series of experiments on remote viewing that were famous within the tightly controlled circle of initiates who followed such things. In the lead-lined conference hall on the third floor of the Old Executive Office Building in Washington, he set up a psychic as a viewer before a team of scientists. Among other experiments, he gave the man specific degrees of longitude and latitude and asked him to draw what he saw there. On the sketch pad a mansion with pillars gradually took shape—almost identical to the one in a black-and-white photograph locked inside a leather briefcase. It was Mikhail Gorbachev's dacha.

Skepticism persisted over the next decade, though the DIA kept three RV psychics on the payroll. They lay in trances in darkened rooms at Fort Meade, Maryland, trying to locate American hostages in Lebanon, track down Saddam Hussein, and ferret out Soviet submarines. In 1994, Congress handed the program to the CIA, which recommended a cutoff in funding, and in November 1995 an article in *The Washington Post* blew it out of the water. Now Wilkinson was unemployed.

Eagleton kept Wilkinson waiting outside his office. He was wary of him, and not simply because the man had risen through the ranks of a competing intelligence agency. Like Eagleton, he was a bureaucratic empire builder, and his goal was the same: to head the CIA's Directorate of Science and Technology. A rival was one thing, an intelligent rival something else. But Eagleton needed his neurological expertise and his laboratory, so he had brought him into the loop—halfway.

He punched the button and ordered the receptionist to send his rival in. Wilkinson carried what looked like two hatboxes, set them on Eagleton's desk, and motioned toward the disinfectant switch. "I wouldn't set off the bug juice, Eagleton. No telling what it would do to this." Eagleton was beginning to regret that he had sent Wilkinson the Neanderthal skull and allowed him to read some of the reports from Operation Achilles. Thank God the location was still a secret.

"The endocast, I presume," Eagleton said. "How did it come out?"

"Endocranial cast, if you don't mind," said Wilkinson. "See for yourself," he added, raising the lid of one box high in the air like a waiter presenting the chef's specialty. Before Eagleton sat a perfect model of a brain, like a Jell-O concoction but made of silicone rubber. It looked like a human brain, but on closer inspection differences emerged; it was elongated and larger at the back, along the occipital lobes, while the frontal lobes seemed smaller.

"Incredible, isn't it?" said Wilkinson. "We've never made such an ideal replica. The grooves along the inner surface were strong, so we got good reproduction. You can spot the specific neural regions easily."

"I can see that," said Eagleton testily. "But what does it tell us?"

"For openers, it's huge. A little over sixteen hundred

fifty milliliters in volume. Modern brains average about twelve to fifteen hundred. There is cerebral dominance—in other words, he's right-handed. By the way, he *is* a he, isn't he?''

''I have no idea.''

Wilkinson picked up a pencil and poked the brain. ''Notice of course the size of the occipital lobes. You'd expect this from the bulging of the occipital bone, sometimes called a chignon or bun.'' He opened the other box, which contained the skull Kellicut had sent. ''See this crest near the occipital bone? That's the juxtamastoid eminence. It's to anchor the muscles running to the lower jaw. That's what gives him his powerful viselike bite. We think he used his teeth almost like a third hand. That's borne out by the cut marks on the incisors, which are extremely large.''

''You're skipping the main part, aren't you?''

''I'm getting there,'' replied Wilkinson impatiently. He tapped the pencil on the sides of the brain. ''Okay, here it is. Take a gander at these regions. Broca's area, Wernicke's area, the angular gyrus. See anything strange?''

Eagleton waited silently.

''They're the centers for speech—in humans. And they're not there. Virtually nonexistent.

''Now look at all this.'' The pencil caressed the brain's surface. ''The cortex. In humans much of it—more than half—receives visual input. Here it's exaggerated. Almost ninety percent. That's the area for remote viewing.''

''How does it work?''

''We can't know that until we get an actual brain. But I would venture a guess that somehow this creature is able to enter into the receptor field of another. It can read the neural impulses, probably on both the parvicellular and magnicellular pathways. I think the only way it could do that is to go right to the main source for the cortex—the thalamus itself.''

The thalamus, thought Eagleton. From the Greek meaning anteroom or bridal chamber, the innermost secretive center, a tiny football set right above the brain stem.

"If I'm right, then of course there are repercussions."

"Such as?"

"For one thing, the faculty may involve more than viewing. In Operation Achilles we've seen it work, more or less, across species. It may well be more efficient within a single species. On some level it may even be closer to telepathy—actual thought transference. Since humans formulate much of thought through language, you wouldn't expect a Neanderthal to pick it up. But it might be different with each other."

"Can the system be foiled? What if you keep your eyes closed?"

"In theory that should make a difference. If your receptor field isn't working or sees nothing but darkness, how can someone else enter it? But in practice, how much of a difference would it make? We just can't say."

"If a human comes near a Neanderthal, would the Neanderthal automatically know he's there?"

"Again, impossible to say. If I had to conjecture, I'd say probably not. Probably the faculty is not passive, like hearing—that is, always operative, even during sleep. I think that would lead to stimulus overload; it would drive you batty just trying to sort out all the messages you're receiving. More likely, the inner eye has to be consciously directed, the way our external eyes are. It's not an alarm system unless you turn it on."

"If you're right about the thalamus, what are the repercussions?"

Wilkinson shrugged. Now he had entered the realm of pure speculation. "We don't know much about the thalamus. But its position suggests two things: It's delicate and it's extremely important. People who believe in ESP like to look here; it's possible humans have a vestigial or as-yet-undeveloped capacity. So do those who search for some physiological template for the ego, the sense of self. And of course there's a third thing."

"Which is?"

"Which is, it is inextricably bound up with all sensation—including most notably pain. Haven't you ever gotten a headache from eyestrain?"

Matt was concerned that Susan and he were getting too thin. He knew that a diet of nuts, berries, and vegetables would stabilize their weight eventually, but he worried that in the meantime their constitutions would weaken. There did not seem to be much sickness among the hominids, but who knew what antibodies they had built up in their separate existence?

Early one morning he rummaged in his backpack while Susan slept. He came across a variety of odds and ends that might come in handy someday—a Swiss army knife, the medical kit, Van's flares—and at last found what he was looking for, a roll of thin wire. He broke a metal clasp off the backpack and held it up to examine it. Perfect. He pulled open a file from the knife, placed the clasp against a rock, and filed it down to make a hook. On the other end he punched a tiny hole, then cut some black bristles off a brush, added a fragment of yellow cloth, tied the minute bundle securely just above the hook, and attached the wire to the hole. He cut down a sapling, trimmed the branches off, and set out.

He followed the stream upriver until he came to a pool where the water ran deep and dark. A hesitant breeze set ripples skidding across the water. Another perfect day in paradise, Matt thought, as he stood on an outcropping along the bank. Now let's see how gullible the fish are in paradise. He flicked the line out to the center of the pool and trolled it back slowly, jerking the lure slightly from time to time in an easy motion, perfected in countless summer mornings on New England lakes.

He did not have long to wait. On the third pass there was a quick splash, a glint of silver, and the lure dived. The tug was strong and insistent. Matt gave the fish some play, then yanked hard and pulled it in. Its tail smacked the water as he hoisted it in the air: a trout—about seven pounds, he figured. It thrashed on the grass until he struck the head with a rock. A bit of blood appeared in the down-gaping mouth and its tail flapped, so Matt struck it once more.

Walking back, Matt felt pleased by his ingenuity. How should he present it to Susan, wrapped in leaves? Ceremoniously, with an unctuous bow, like the maître d' at the Four Seasons? No one was in the village when he returned, not even the children. That was strange. He walked to the fire, set the fish on a boulder nearby, and carried his gear to the bower. Susan was not there. He was returning to the village when he heard her calling his name. He yelled back, realizing as he did so how unusual it was to hear shouts in the valley.

She looked upset. "Matt, my God, what have you done?"

"What do you mean?"

"The place is in an uproar. Kellicut is on the warpath."

"What in God's name for?"

When they reached the village where a few moments before there had been no one, Matt saw that a crowd had gathered. They must have hidden when I came through before, he thought. The hominids looked stunned. The center of attention, Matt realized with a sinking sensation, was the boulder where he had left his fish. As he approached with Susan at his side, the group parted to give him a wide berth, and the children stared at him with eyes swollen wide with apprehension.

Kellicut was at the center surrounded by elders, uttering all kinds of sounds and waving his arms. When he saw Matt his face darkened. "Get over here," he commanded.

Matt walked over to him. By now he knew his transgression had been monumental.

"Don't say anything," said Kellicut. "Not that they would understand you if you did. The same way they don't understand me. But some of it gets across, somehow. Look contrite even if you don't feel it.''

Matt did feel it and didn't have to masquerade the emotion. He looked down but out of the corner of one eye caught a glimpse of Susan; she seemed ashamed.

"You're unbelievable," continued Kellicut. "You come in here and upset everything. These are people who can't understand killing. The idea of willfully taking life! As a concept it simply doesn't exist. But *eating* it! I can't imagine how they'd react if they knew that's what you had in mind."

"Christ, I'm sorry," said Matt. "I had no idea."

"Clearly."

"What should I do?"

"Well, for openers, get down on the ground on your knees and look down."

Matt did so.

"Now look up at me." Kellicut placed his palm on Matt's head and looked up into the sky silently for a long time.

"Now get up," he said.

"What was that all about?"

"I've seen them do that sometimes—when they have something very important to communicate, I believe. So perhaps they'll think we're doing the same thing. I'm showing my displeasure with you."

For a split second, Matt thought he saw a glint of the old humor flicker across Kellicut's face. "Now what?" Matt asked. It was as if he were the graduate student again and Kellicut the all-knowing professor.

"Now you will go over to the fish and carefully remove its eyes and wrap it in vine leaves very carefully. Then you will go where I tell you to, climb a tree, and leave it there."

"You're joking, right?"

"I've never been more serious. It's called a death cult. Remember reading about such things? Well, now you're going to participate in one.''

"What do I do with the eyes? I certainly hope I don't have to eat them."

"Not funny." As Kellicut moved toward the fish the crowd scattered and dispersed. Their eyes met and for the first time he smiled at Matt.

17

It was time to make a plan. At first Matt and Susan had hoped that Kellicut would work with them, and they had visions of a three-way research partnership on a seminal Neanderthal work that would shake the world. But it was clear that things weren't working out that way. Kellicut was changed; he was lost to science. He was so immersed and enraptured by the mysticism and purity of the hominids and so fixated upon acquiring their special power himself that he had lost all objectivity. He was no longer interested in observing and measuring their community, he wanted to join it. He could still be useful, even essential, in communicating with them, but he was dead set against the idea of anyone publishing anything. Sometimes he insisted the outside world could never understand such beings; at others he declared, with the melodrama of a soapbox preacher, that the outside world would destroy them.

Matt and Susan were worried about their destruction, too, but they feared the renegades who had killed Sharafidin, Rudy, and Van. They felt the pressure of time: What was to prevent an attack from the predators on the mountain—especially if they knew that humans were in the valley? The cave-in had obliterated Van. Perhaps the renegades would think that they had been killed, too. But what if they dug it out and found no bodies? Time was critical: They had to gather as much information as quickly as possible and get out while they still could.

But the research was not easy. The absence of language was beginning to tell; even facial expressions were untranslatable. They tried rudimentary signs, but it did not work. The hominids did make sounds, but these were not words; they registered basic responses but had no meaning per se. Kellicut, who seemed to know more than he let on, was not willing to help out and disparaged the whole idea of using a spoken tongue. The real communication, Matt and Susan knew, was occurring in that mysterious realm from which they were excluded.

Still, they were able to collect a wealth of data. Every night Matt recorded his observations on tape. Susan filled her notebooks. Her camera had been lost in the cave-in but she had a sketch pad crammed with drawings that captured Neanderthal life. They worked feverishly against the clock. They collected artifacts to bring back, mostly flaked stones and other tools, crude bowls and vessels. They compiled a list of areas to be covered before they left: religious practices, social structure, burial rites, gender roles. At times they felt the questions were far bigger than the answers. Susan, especially, was frustrated by her failed attempts to learn about the women. They huddled in groups that broke up and dispersed when she approached. She had seen one of them choosing leaves and then returning to a hut where a sick child was lying supine but the woman would not let her observe.

They determined to leave with whatever material they could gather quickly. Later, they could decide about coming back. To avoid the renegades they needed to find the crevice that had brought Kellicut to the valley. Somehow, they would make it down the mountain on their own.

But Kellicut was still strangely cold. At times it was almost as if he regarded them as nothing more than emissaries from the universe beyond the valley rim. He talked darkly of the Institute, and he still refused to answer the questions they put to him about what he thought it was after or why they had been sent for.

For days Matt had been pestering Kellicut for directions to the crevice but each time he had been rebuffed. For some reason, one morning Kellicut had changed his mind. Squatting on the ground, looking more than ever like an Indian holy man, he drew a rough map in the dirt. The valley was more or less circular. He traced lines for the rivers, drew some peaks as landmarks, and marked their present location with an *x*. The crevice was at the opposite end. Along the route he drew an ellipse and marked it in cross-hatching.

"That's the burial ground. If I were you, I'd go around it."

"Why?" Matt asked.

Kellicut looked at him sharply and pointed out that respect for the dead was important in any culture. He himself had been there only twice: on his first foray into the valley, when he had picked up the skull that he gave Sharafidin— which he now regretted—and on the day that he returned for good. No hominid ever went there, aside from the permanent grave tenders, whose faces and upper torsos were painted a chalky white and who were regarded as pariahs, spending all their lives in the forbidden burial zone.

"Death is the seminal event, the most feared principle around which their life is organized," Kellicut said. "The meaning cannot be captured in words, only in symbols."

Drawing the map had loosened his reserve, and seating himself cross-legged in the shade of a tree, his tone reverted to that of the old days: the authoritative instructor.

"Where the ethos is communal, where there is no individuality or self in our meaning of the word, the tribe is the only reality. It overrides all else, and death, which diminishes the tribe, is the only threat. Insofar as the whole tribe has shrunk, the whole tribe is affected, which is why the cult of death arises. A special caste of untouchables is set aside to wrap the dead, and they tend them in a special land where no one else ever goes. The eyes of the deceased are removed.''

"The eyes!" Susan gasped.

"Yes. Why this should be, I am not yet sure," Kellicut said.

"But what do you think?" asked Matt.

"I don't think. I intuit. To understand what life is like for them you must project yourself onto an entirely different plane of existence. You must acquire an additional dimension. Imagine that you are the center of the world—your world—and yet the periphery of that world consists of others. Your horizon is contiguous to the horizon of others. It is like the solar system. You are the sun but you are also the planets. You see through others as well as for yourself. This happens in some fashion that I can't pretend to understand. I don't know how all this information is taken in and processed, much less rendered intelligible. But it is. And then something happens. One day, one of the tribe dies. One of the planets disintegrates, and you feel it personally, not just out of some sense of empathy but because a little piece of *you* actually dies. Maybe it's like losing an appendage. It's insupportable, and so you act against it. You try to retain those organs that are the tribal consciousness, the web of your communal existence. You take out the eyes.''

"And do what with them?" asked Susan.

"You give them to the shaman."

Susan knew whom he meant, an elderly hominid, the one who wore a string of snail shells around his neck. He frightened her.

"And what does he do with them?"

"Ah, that's matter for a different discussion," said Kellicut. He lapsed back into silence, like a door slowly closing and then clicking shut.

Matt stood up. "We'd better be going." Off to one side stood three figures. They were Blue-Eyes, Leviticus, and a third with large front teeth that Susan had named Long-tooth.

"They'll go with you—until they see where you're headed," Kellicut predicted.

The group set off, Matt and Susan ahead and the three trailing them at a distance, moving in their loping, muscular walk.

The sun was almost directly overhead when they stopped for a rest. The three escorts joined them, and they ate some berries. Matt pulled out his canteen and passed it to Susan, who swigged some water and held it out to Leviticus. He took it in both hands, raised it to his mouth, and tilted it upward the way Susan had. The cool water poured over his mouth and chin, startling him. Matt laughed, but Susan approached him and touched him on the arm. He did not shrink away but touched her in return on the inside of her elbow. It tickled slightly.

They started off again. Half an hour later the ground began to rise steadily. Halfway up the incline Susan realized something was missing. Bird songs had stopped. She turned and looked back; the three hominids were nowhere to be seen. Farther up they came upon trees where the bark had been slashed and the yellow flesh of the trunks showed through. Zone markers, she guessed.

She looked at Matt, who was frowning slightly. "Maybe this isn't such a good idea," she said. "Maybe we should listen to Kellicut."

"Maybe we ought to think for ourselves," replied Matt. "He doesn't know everything."

At the top of the ridge the ground leveled into a plateau. Susan had the intense feeling that they were being watched, and when she shifted her gaze she felt a peculiar sensation, as if her head were heavy. They started across the plateau and soon came upon their first corpse. It was in a tree, wrapped in vines. On one side the dried leaves had given way and they saw the bleached shape of a pelvic bone.

As they walked on, the bundles in the trees multiplied,

propped up on branches like weird nests. Some of the wrappings had deteriorated, and parts of skeletons nestled in the crotches of the trees. Piles of bones littered the ground in some areas like fallen husks, and grinning skulls lay about. A vague rotting smell filled the air. Most of these remains were old, Susan realized. The burial ground was large and it took half an hour to cross it, moving as stealthily as thieves and feeling exposed and vulnerable, as if at any moment they might be struck down for their sacrilege. All around was deadly still. She did not see the grave tenders but knew they were being observed by them.

Once on the other side they soon came to the valley wall, which was almost sheer. They searched in one direction and then the other until they came to a split in the rock. Matt slipped through first, then Susan. They walked deep enough to know that they could continue on to the exterior of the mountain. Susan felt a relief she had not anticipated at the realization that a way out did exist. Retracing their steps, they came back into the valley.

They had not gone far when Susan tugged at Matt's sleeve and pointed to the rock face. There was the gaping mouth of a cave. She was struck by the certainty—where it came from, she couldn't say—that it led to the tunnels from which she and Matt had barely escaped with their lives only a couple of weeks ago.

They returned again across the burial ground. "I feel we shouldn't be doing this," said Susan. "Kellicut's right."

"Matt," said Susan with a tone of self-satisfaction the following afternoon, "on balance, I think I've done pretty well. My theories have held up. Yours are mostly shot down."

"Like hell."

They were lying in a meadow, and Susan had plucked a piece of straw and was tickling Matt under the chin. "I seem to remember you backing the idea that the Neanderthal had an incomplete pharynx and couldn't make certain sounds—a *g*, wasn't that one of them?''

"How many *g*'s have you heard here?" he replied.

"Not many, but since they don't talk at all it's a little beside the point, don't you think?"

"A minor correction. A footnote. Anyway, I never really backed that theory; I was just trying it out."

"I see."

Then it was Matt's turn. "But I seem to remember you going along with a theory that the elongated pelvis bone suggested Neanderthal pregnancies lasted eleven months." Susan reddened slightly. "The implications of that were staggering, as I recall; more time in the womb meant a more sophisticated development. I don't see a great deal of sophistication. Or a lot of women running around with huge stomachs."

"It was only a vague hypothesis. I abandoned it early on. Anyway, there doesn't seem to be a lot of women, period. How do you account for that?"

"Raids," said Matt. "By the others up on the mountain."

"I had the same thought."

They were silent for a moment. Then Susan plunged in again. "How about the burials?"

"What about them?"

"You were always denying that they had funeral rites. You always said that a complete skeleton is just a happy geological accident."

"Not always. You may remember that I accepted the crouch position burial. And I acknowledged that in some cases the Neanderthal stocked graves with stone tools and joints of meat and other goods. I just didn't go overboard like you."

"You mean the flower burial of Shanidar, don't you," said Susan, referring to a site in Iraq where pollen grains in sediments around the bones were interpreted by some as a clue that the corpse had been bedecked with garlands of flowers.

"Yes, I still think that's romantic crap. The grains got there by chance—some burrowing animal or stratigraphic shift. Just like Teshik-Tash. You think those Siberian goat horns were hammered into the ground around that child's body to bring him back to life; I think they were put there to protect the body from scavengers."

"So prosaic. You just can't believe there is such a thing as the importance of ritual."

"Susan, I admit I never anticipated wrapping your loved ones up like cocoons and stuffing them in trees. But we haven't witnessed any burials here and we don't know if they have rituals or not."

"Sometimes I wonder about you. You don't see the epic side of things: great battles, struggles for existence, one species crowding out another. All you see is sex."

"You've got me there."

"If your theory is right—if we intermingled our genes and propagated them out of existence—we should be willing to mate with them, you and I. Right?"

"Maybe not. Maybe we've evolved too far apart by now."

"But we should feel some kind of attraction, something. Do you?"

"Do you?" he asked.

"I asked you first."

"What am I supposed to say, I asked you second?"

"Well, a lot is riding on it. If I say yes, that could mean you're right."

"Susan, just say the truth. What you feel."

"Well, that's hard. In some ways no, not at all. I find the whole idea repulsive. But at other times—yes, I could conceive of it."

"If you can conceive of it, then it's possible: There is no barrier to reproduction, and in fact we and the Neanderthal belong to the same species. That's assuming the biological concept of species."

"You mean that if two different populations interbreed they're the same species?"

"Right. And if not, if you and I can't conceive of it, then James Shreeve is right when he suggests that the Neanderthal face, and the eyes in particular, puts them off limits sexually as far as we're concerned. Then we really are two separate species."

"Boy, this is some field research!"

They noticed that the hominids were not bashful about sex. Males and females coupled when the impulse took them, and there was no concept of monogamy; while some went about in regular pairs others did not. For the most part it was the males who initiated it—but not always.

One evening dozens of adults drifted out of the village and walked through the woods. Matt and Susan joined them. They detected an air of excitement in the group, a quickness in the strides and overflowing energy. Overhead was the moon hanging large and low, a giant magnolia-colored disk producing so much pale light on the ground that they cast shadows as they walked.

After fifteen minutes they came to a huge rock formation that neither had seen before. On the far side was a large triangular hole, big enough to admit them one by one. As soon as they stepped inside they were struck by the heat and smoke. They were in a large, low cavern. A fire was burning, stoked by four hominids dripping with sweat. The flames leaped high and disappeared into a dark funnel above, a chimney to the outside. A reddish gleam reflected off the jagged walls of rock, and the heat was so suffocating that Susan thought she might faint.

They sat down beside each other. Through the smoke they could make out those seated around the fire, and for the first time Susan saw Kellicut there, along with Leviticus and others. The fire tenders tossed more wood on the blaze, which damped down and then rose higher. From the rear of the cave they heard a syncopated hollow sound, and two hominid males and two females came out of the shadows, pounding on bamboolike tubes. The sound of the rhythmic beating echoed back off the walls and engulfed the cave, striking a chord deep inside Susan. She noticed the fire tenders were laying long green weeds upon the flames that sent out billowing waves of smoke, acrid but not unpleasant, which filled the cave like fog.

Susan was drenched in sweat, as was Matt, and they each removed their clothes. Now the beating intensified. In a small dirt area in the center, a woman stood up and danced, gyrating wildly. The noise rose as the others began slapping their thighs in unison. The dancer spun, then stopped in front of a male and pulled him to his feet. In the flickering light of the fire Susan saw that his penis was erect, extending from his genitals like a short fat pole. The dancer pulled him to the entrance and they went outside. The slapping continued and the beating of the instruments again grew louder. The fire tenders threw more weeds on the blaze. As she inhaled deeply, Susan realized that her lungs were burning and the blood was speeding through her veins. She felt light-headed, giddy with the narcotic, and her eyes watered in the smoke.

Another dancer rose, picked a partner and left. Then another. Kellicut was staring at Susan through the smoke. Susan got up. With all eyes upon her, the pounding and slapping rolled over her in waves, pushing her out of control. She spun wildly, barely able to focus, carried away by the noise, which had become an intricate, eerie form of music. Covered in sweat, she felt the heat wrapping her up like a blanket and the noise ripping through it with a strange, icy hand. She felt deeply aroused along the insides of her thighs and the tips of her breasts. Vaguely through the haze she was able to make out Kellicut, rising and moving toward her. Next to him she saw Matt, also pushing toward her, his face wild. She stopped, and Matt stood before her, and they fled together into the night.

It was quiet outside, yet the noise and excitement of the cave continued to reverberate in their heads and their love-making was frenzied. Afterward they rolled away from each other and rested apart, too transported to touch each other. It took minutes to return.

"Jesus Christ!" said Matt finally.

They were quiet for a while until Matt spoke again.

"I'm glad you picked me. I didn't think you were going to."

"I didn't know what I was doing. I didn't even think."

"Susan?"

"What?"

"Tell me—did you want to pick *him*?"

"I didn't, did I?"

"How about one of *them*? Did you consider making love to one of them?"

She leaned over and hugged him. "Matt, you sweet dope. Don't you realize? We just did."

Matt became friendly with a young hominid they called Lancelot. He was drawn to him because Lancelot, who had longer legs and a more slender build than most, appeared to be both unusually intelligent and open to new ways. When Matt looked into his brown eyes he was convinced he was looking into a deep reservoir of animation.

Lancelot was curious and enjoyed looking through their belongings. He would take an object like a knife and hold it up in the air, examining it from all angles. When they went on long hikes and Matt got thoroughly lost, Lancelot was always able to find the way back. If they had to ascend a rock face, he stared at it beforehand, tracing a route of ledges and footholds with his darting eyes.

Once when they were on a path, Lancelot dragged Matt over to a tree, practically pushed him up it, and then as-cended after him. No sooner were they off the ground than a large warthog ran past, tossing his tusks in the air. Matt did not know if Lancelot had heard him coming or had somehow sensed his presence with his special faculty. On another afternoon, Matt fell asleep and was awakened to find Lancelot caressing his smooth brow with his fingers and looking puzzled.

During treks, Lancelot sometimes would wander off for long periods, generally going in the same direction. When this happened Matt would make his own way, but from time to time he would feel a slight fluttering behind the eyes and a heaviness in his frontal lobe, and he would know that Lancelot was reading him.

It was frustrating that the communication was so largely one-way. After weeks of intense experiencing and learning, Matt realized that he was at an impasse. In a strange way he had fallen into a routine. What Dostoevsky had written was true: Man, the beast, accustoms himself to anything. Here he was in a paleontologist's dream, a real-life prehistoric laboratory, and yet he could not honestly say that he had penetrated to the core of the mystery of what these beings were truly like. But despite this he had adjusted to a world he could not have even conjured up two months ago, so much so that his day-to-day life seemed almost ordinary.

Out of desperation he decided to try to teach Lancelot how to talk. He made a conscious effort to recall everything he had ever read about experiments with chimps and language. Of course this would be different because he would not merely be attempting to convey the concept of an object—say, the concept of "treeness" inherent in a tree—which was basically associative learning carried to an abstract level. He would also be trying to teach Lancelot to pronounce and use the word correctly and then string it together with other words to create new meaning. That was the quantum leap of language.

For the first lesson he sat Lancelot across from him, picked up a good-sized rock, walked over to him, turned the hominid's hand open, and put the rock on it, repeating over and over the word "rock." Receiving a blank look, he dropped the *r* to simplify the sound, repeating "ock" over and over as he removed it and replaced it on the hand of a baffled Lancelot. For days Matt tried to hammer home the idea, but without success. Sometimes Lancelot would repeat the sound, but he never seemed to connect it to the rock. Matt tried other words—"leaf," "sky," "water." He tried sign language, mimicking such actions as eating and sleeping. He tried "Matt," or "I" and "you," by pointing, a gesture that did not seem to convey any meaning. Clearly pronouns had no context in a world that did not differentiate between oneself and others. At one point, he brought out his tape recorder and recorded the sounds to play them over and over as he presented the objects, but Lancelot was too fascinated by the recorder itself to concentrate.

"I'm getting nowhere," Matt confided to Susan one afternoon.

"That's not surprising. Language has got to be the single most complicated human activity."

"But they're so similar in so many other ways. You'd think that capacity is there somewhere, even if only in a vestigial form that could be reactivated."

"If it's not used it won't develop. It's like those babies born with cataracts; if they aren't treated for six months they become irrevocably blind. Besides, the hominid brain is already specialized; it has to process all that information from the visual channels of others."

"Yet sometimes they make sounds."

Susan suggested that he try it the other way around, learning as much as he could of *their* spoken vocabulary. Perhaps he could use this as a lever to achieve a breakthrough. So he began by observing them in groups. He concentrated on the young ones, especially when they were playing, because that was when they seemed to voice the most sounds. He recorded them on tape, and over time he was able to link certain sounds to specific responses. He detected one sound for surprise, a sort of open-throated grunt. Then he had the good fortune to record alarm when a group of youngsters playing on a riverbank scattered as a predator, a smallish cat that looked like a mountain lion, walked toward them. When Matt retrieved the tape afterward he heard a series of high-pitched whines that sounded like keening.

He practiced making the sound himself alone in the woods, and that evening told Susan half jokingly to prepare for a historic moment. Standing on the outskirts of the village, he drew a deep breath and let the sound rip so that it echoed through the trees. Before Susan knew what was happening, Matt was lying at her feet, writhing on the ground, his hands pressed against his temples.

"Matt, for God's sake, what's wrong?"

He sat up, looking a bit sheepish. "I raised the alarm, all right. I guess everyone wanted to know what was wrong, and they all read me at the same time."

If Lancelot didn't learn to talk, he did learn something else. One evening as Matt and Susan presided over a wrestling bout, he was in the pit with a young hominid when he was thrown to the ground. Instantly, he was up on his feet and advanced on the youth, who spun so that his elbow caught him on the chin. Lancelot teetered back, stunned, then charged straight at his opponent, rammed him in the chest, and threw him roughly to the ground. As he turned in triumph, Matt caught a full view of his face—flushed red in anger. Matt jumped in to end the match.

He and Susan were stunned and a little unnerved. Later they talked it over. "You know what I thought when I saw that," said Susan. "There was real anger there, aggression. That's not in the emotional vocabulary of the others here."

"Whether we like it or not, anger and aggression are human characteristics," Matt replied. "Maybe some of them have already begun to take the path of the renegades and that path leads right to us."

All this time, Kellicut had been undergoing his own instruction and was spending more and more time with the shaman. The shaman lived in a separate hut, the only one that had a door, which was always closed. It was surrounded by a moat of tiny totems like tufts of hair and teeth, and a foul odor emanated from it.

Matt and Susan called him Dark-Eye, a name that captured him in aspect as well as function, which was to guide the tribe through the netherworld of spirits. He took the weight of the souls of departed ancestors onto his frail frame. His upper body was emaciated, with shoulder bones poking under the skin like bat wings, and his face was pinched and sinister, with unruly hair that fell down like a curtain. When it parted, it showed one clouded eye stuck in place, gazing permanently off into the distance as if he were seeing visions that eluded others, spirits that resided in hidden nests and hollowed trees.

Dark-Eye would go off alone to a rocky pinnacle for days at a time, communing with the spirits there and fasting, to return as gaunt as a hatchet blade. The tribe seemed excited when he reappeared and gave him food and other offerings, but they also feared him, moving away when he approached. He held ceremonies to commune with ancestors, complete with shouts and chants, the beating of logs, and fits of possession. Susan noticed that during these times he seemed to fall into a trance and, when he did, he kept his single good eye closed. This, she imagined, cut him off from the outside world altogether and made it impossible for the other tribal members to read him even if they dared to try.

18

Early one morning, with a sky so blue it covered the valley like a luminous globe, a commotion rent the village. Matt, who was bathing in a cool stream, heard shouts of excitement and what sounded like screams. Susan, who was collecting raspberries for breakfast from a thicket, stood erect so quickly that she scratched herself. She picked her way out carefully and then ran toward the village, arriving just as Matt did.

A knot of hominids were pushing and shoving and kicking up dust. Children circled around with solemn faces. A fight of some sort, Matt thought, then realized with a start how completely he had adjusted to the somnolent tranquillity of the village: The thought of a melee for any reason shocked him. Then he saw Longface's head above the throng and, as the hominid turned to face him, realized that his features were twisted in anguish.

"What's going on?" asked Susan. She too was staggered by the scene.

"I have no idea, but we'd better find out."

As Susan stepped forward, the crowd parted to make a path for her and Matt, and she could make out a litter made of branches and leaves. Upon it was a hominid she had not seen before, a dark-haired youth. As the group set the litter down in the dirt, the body rocked and came to a rest, inert.

The youth was badly wounded. He had a gash across one side of his forehead. The flesh was peeled back from the protruding bone, which was starkly white like some swollen packed growth that had burst through the skin. Dark blood ran down the side of his face toward the back of his neck, matting his hair. He seemed to be slipping into unconsciousness. His right knee was smashed and bleeding; his left arm hung limply over the side, the exposed inner flesh upward. His body was adorned in a way they had never seen, as if with warpaint. His cheeks were marked with lines of red ocher and black charcoal, drawn in a downward *V* from the nose, and his powerful chest was streaked with similar lines emanating from the breastbone. His breathing showed his ribs.

Longface could not stop touching him. He hugged the youth's other arm in a posture of distress, like a Pietà, and emitted strange chilling sounds, tossing his head back and stretching his vocal cords in cries of grief. Something in his stance, and the way he cradled the body to comfort it and held the world at bay to protect it, struck Susan.

"Matt," she said. "It's his son."

"It is," came Kellicut's voice from behind them. "And from the look of him he'll be dead soon if we don't do something."

"What can we do?"

"Probably not much, but it will be more than they can. Medicine is not a highly developed art here."

When Longface heard Kellicut, he dropped the boy's arm, ran over, cupped an outsized hand around the back of Kellicut's neck, and pulled him toward the litter as the crowd fell back to make room. He guided Kellicut down so that he had to genuflect next to the body.

Ashen-faced, Kellicut touched the boy on one temple. The youth opened his eyes briefly, looked at his father and groaned, then turned his head to one side. Kellicut held the back of his fingers to his cheek, touched his ribs, and felt his pulse. Abruptly Longface let out a groan, matching his son's in intensity.

"My God!" said Matt. "He's reading his son. He's taking on his pain. He's literally feeling it."

"That's right," Kellicut said over his shoulder. "And it must be excruciating. We can't have even the vaguest notion of what it's like. The problem is, I don't think it lessens the pain for his son or mitigates it in any way. It's simply a way of experiencing it simultaneously, an empathy that is purely altruistic."

Kellicut was metamorphosing into a medic. "First, we've got to wash some of this blood off. Can't see a damn thing. No idea what we're faced with here." He swung around abruptly. "Matt," he commanded, "get your medical kit on the double. We'll take him over to the big hut by the river. Susan, get whatever clothes you have and meet us there. We've got to cover him. He's in shock." He was the old Kellicut now, barking peremptory orders, rushing in to take charge before others had even sized up the situation. "Let's get going."

He began to lift the litter and five men rushed to help him. As it moved it jostled the youth, who let out a fearsome moan of pain; so did Longface. The strange procession made its way through the village but with a sense of purpose now, a huge animal kicking up dust with ten feet and Kellicut out front leading it like a guide.

At the river he motioned for the litter to be set down under a cluster of poplar trees. Nearby was a hut formed by the interlacing branches from two trees. It was open on both sides and a soft breeze blew through it, and here Kellicut set up shop. He sent Matt to the river three times with his canteen, pouring water over the wounds and gently swabbing them with one of Susan's blouses until he could see where the flesh was torn. Dirt was ingrained around the edges of the gash along the forehead.

"What do you think happened to him?" Susan asked.

"It's hard to say, but this one up here was caused by a

blow of some kind," Kellicut replied, still mopping the brow. "Look at the swelling on the side; and here the bone's chipped, see?" He lifted a tiny flap of skin next to the browbone. "That's the frontal torus. Just think, we're looking at a bone that has never been seen in any medical school in the world." He wrapped the youth in the odds and ends of clothing that Susan had left, a pathetically small pile that included a pair of trousers. "They'll never fit him, you know," said Kellicut. "We'll have to use them as a blanket." He turned back to his patient.

"I'm hardly a doctor, but I'd bet he didn't get this blow from a fall. And it's not likely that he would smash his leg like that in some kind of accident. No," he said, tucking the clothes under the body of the youth, who was beginning to shiver, "he got it from a club. I'd say he was in a fight."

"With whom?"

"With the same gang you ran into."

"How do you know?"

"Who else would do it?" Kellicut paused as if wondering how much to say. "Besides, he ran off to join them."

"What?"

"That's right. Some weeks ago. His father was heartbroken. He couldn't accept it." Kellicut looked over at Longface, who was seated on a stump, staring into the face of his son and rocking slowly back and forth. "It's a bit of a stigma, actually, to have a son or daughter join the renegades, but your guy over there is so respected it didn't seem to damage his prestige. Except that he suffered so."

"That's incredible," said Matt.

"Why incredible? They have depths of feelings you can't even dream about."

"I don't mean that. I mean running off and joining the other group like that, the . . . the renegades, as you call them."

"In a way this wounded kid is responsible for your being found."

"In what way?"

"Those three that came across you were a search party looking for him."

Susan looked at Kellicut. "I think there's a lot of explaining to be done. There's a lot you can tell us."

"Yes." He sighed. "I suppose so. But all in good time. First things first. Before anything else, we've got to save this young man."

Longface looked across his son's body directly at Kellicut. Matt was not an expert at reading emotions on the faces of these beings who were still so alien to him, but he had no doubt about this one: Longface was pleading. Stooped with age, he walked over to Kellicut's side, lifted Kellicut's hand and spread two fingers, and gently placed them on his son's eyelids. Then he touched his own fingers to Kellicut's eyes and held them there for a moment, a look of supplication on his face. He's telling us that his son is dying and is begging Kellicut to save him, Matt thought.

Eagleton punched the intercom, and bellowed out "Schwartzbaum!" Then he hit the button to release the disinfectant from above. If there's anyone who'll contaminate this office, he thought maliciously, it's that windbag Schwartzbaum. It was unfortunate that he was even tangentially connected to the operation.

Schwartzbaum had gone through the Harvard paleoanthropology factory and studied with the best of them. He had begun as a classic "bones and stones" man and then, like his subject matter, had evolved. He was now on the cutting edge in evolutionary genetics. Every two years he turned out papers on skeletal physiognomy and mitochondrial DNA that were so obscure and unreadable that his reputation had become unassailable. Eagleton had needed his expertise so badly for this project that he had appointed him deputy director of the Institute with all the perks: a salary of $150,000, a parking space, and a season pass to the Redskins games.

Now he needed Schwartzbaum there to help him reach

a decision or, more precisely, to talk. Eagleton used the man from time to time as a sounding board. Sometimes the decision had nothing directly to do with the subject they discussed. He found it helpful to explore tributaries with a colleague while his formidable intellect navigated the shoals of the main river alone. He used Schwartzbaum the way an experimenter uses white noise to blot out encroaching diversions. This was one of those occasions.

Schwartzbaum walked in with a distracted air, pulled up a chair, and sat down too close for comfort. Eagleton didn't say anything. He simply rocked his wheelchair back and forth like a runner at the starting line, lit a cigarette, and aimed a projectile of secondhand smoke at the winged tufts of white hair that stuck out over Schwartzbaum's ears, mad-scientist fashion. It worked. Looking like a man caught in a cloud of mustard gas, Schwartzbaum moved his chair back a foot.

"Well," said Eagleton. "Did you complete the report?"

"Report?"

"On the session here. The one with Drs. Arnot and Mattison." Irritation was creeping into Eagleton's voice and he made no effort to restrain it.

"Ah, that report. No, not yet. I've been preoccupied, I'm afraid, with a paper on the nasal aperture in the Neanderthal cranium. I've come to the conclusion that—"

"You were to have that report on my desk yesterday morning. I have to know what you made of their differing interpretations."

"Well, you know what they say: Get two paleontologists in a room and you'll get three different opinions. This is a group that can't even agree on the spelling of their subject. Some side with the Germans, who drop the silent *h*, N-E-A-N-D-E-R-T-A-L, and others—"

"I had hoped to have a discussion more substantive than a spelling bee."

"Ah, sorry. About . . . ?"

"About Dr. Arnot's theory on cannibalism, for one thing."

"Hmmm. Cannibalism." Schwartzbaum tugged at his goatee with the tips of his fingers. The gesture reminded Eagleton of a spider on his back flailing its legs in the air. "That, I'm afraid, is not new. It is the dark underside of Neanderthal research, a shadow that extends back to the work of some of the original fossil hunters."

"Explain."

Schwartzbaum settled back in his chair, inhaled deeply, and fixed his eye on a spot on the wall. "Unless I'm mistaken, the first reference came in the 1860s in the work of Edouard Dupont, a Belgian geologist. He was rooting around in a cave in . . . I believe it was Le Trou de la Naulette . . . when he discovered a good-sized piece of lower jaw. It was undeniably human, but also very apelike in the way it sloped back from the teeth to the chin."

Suddenly Schwartzbaum became aware that he was stroking his own jaw. Flustered, he yanked his hand down.

"Don't forget, *On the Origin of Species* had only been out a few years. Evolution was struggling to find a foothold as a credible theory, and this bit of mandible was the first solid anatomical evidence to back up Darwin. Anyway, a bizarre thing happened. The whispering about cannibalism had already begun, so Dupont took it upon himself to say that his bones were definitely *not* the leftovers of a feast. But when his findings were translated into English, everything got turned upside down so that people thought he was saying that they *were* leftovers and that Neanderthals were cannibals. They thought this because they wanted to think it, and the bad rap stuck."

Schwartzbaum skipped a few decades to early 1899 and one Dragutin Gorjanović-Kramberger, a Croat who was the son of a shoemaker and never accepted by the intellectuals in Berlin and Paris. But he got the last laugh; he discovered the site at Krapina, a treasure trove of hundreds of Neanderthal specimens. What struck him was that the skeletons were scattered all over the place and that the large bones were splintered, some even burned. Also, a surprising number belonged to children. All this Gorjanović took to be irrefutable proof that they were victims of prehistoric banquets.

Eagleton seemed to be looking intently at Schwartzbaum, but the words spilling off the old man's tongue came to him through a fog. His mind was beginning to wrestle with the problem he had set for himself. He was already advancing down the main river and his visitor's little excursion boat was disappearing into the side marshes.

Schwartzbaum pushed on like a performer drunk on the limelight. "All the theories and dark whisperings reached a climax years later, in 1939, right on the eve of the war." He told the story of Alberto Blanc, a young Italian fossil hunter honeymooning at Monte Circeo, south of Rome. Some workmen knocked through the roof of a hidden cave and fumbled around in darkness. Presto, one of them picked up a skull for Alberto. The question was, exactly *where* in the cave did he pick it up?

"The debate over the answer brought everything to a head, if you'll forgive the pun. It lasts to this day and has wrecked more conferences than I care to think about.

"You see, Blanc insisted the skull had come from the center of a group of stones arranged in a circle. He called it the 'crown of stones' for dramatic effect. That crack in the right temple? Proof of an ancient murder. That large hole at the base of the cranium was, Blanc said, for the extraction of the brain. His hypothesis was that the Neanderthal, having vanquished an enemy, probably by creeping up from behind and dealing a death blow, separates the head from the body, eats the brain, then uses the braincase as a holy chalice for his ritual, placing it as delicately upon the 'crown of stones' as a priest today balances the communion cup upon the altar. Interesting, yes?"

Eagleton gave out a noncommittal grumble as Schwartzbaum rattled on, oblivious. "Except that today most paleontologists reject the theory. Too many maybes. Maybe the circle isn't really a circle. Maybe the skull was gnawed by an animal. Maybe Blanc was just being an Italian romantic. It's okay for supermarket tabloids but it doesn't pass muster in the Harvard faculty dining room.''

''And Dr. Arnot?''

The query brought Schwartzbaum up short. He liked sitting on the fence, and Susan Arnot was a person who tended to knock down fences. ''Generally her work has been exemplary, and she's respected in the field. But of course she hasn't published anything yet about her latest . . . contribution to Blanc's theory.''

''What do you think?''

''Me?''

''Yes, you.''

Schwartzbaum became cautious, an expert on the witness stand finally asked to commit himself on a bit of evidence. ''I'm not publicly identified with either side. I haven't taken a firm position yet. But I would say here, in the privacy of this room, that I do not subscribe to the notion that they ate each other.''

''You said earlier that people thought Neanderthals were cannibals because they *wanted* to think it. What did you mean by that?''

''You know, today evolution strikes us as so logical and commonsensical; in retrospect it appears obvious. Thomas Huxley said it best: 'How stupid of me not to have thought of it.' We forget how truly revolutionary it was at the time, how it challenged the basic precept of what mankind was all about. In one quick stroke it meant we were no longer God's creation, set apart from the beasts, endowed with reason and a spark of divinity. We were no longer special; suddenly we were knocked off our pedestal. It turned out we were an animal like any other, a little smarter or even a lot smarter—which explained how we got to the top of the heap—but basically an animal all the same. We prevailed because of our intellect, and that developed largely by chance, thanks to two legs or an opposable thumb or a voice box. Let's face it, the image of a creature dragging itself out of the primordial swamp isn't as ennobling to contemplate as the arc between God's finger and man's outstretched hand in the Sistine Chapel.

"So we are no longer lesser gods; we're simply greater apes. Then, to make things worse, along come these fossils filling in the blank spaces, so that our connection to ape-hood is even more stark. Okay, so Piltdown Man is a hoax, but even without it there are plenty of other 'missing links,' and the most important one of all is the Neanderthal. Hence we need something to separate us from him to put us back up on our pedestal. We need to transform him into a beast. What better way to do so than to accuse him of violating the most pernicious taboo imaginable, committing the most heinous crime, the symbol of everything that places us above others on this horrible continuum of struggling savages—eating your own kind?"

By now Schwartzbaum was so enamored of his own eloquence that he had almost forgotten the figure sitting behind the desk in the growing darkness. He was startled when Eagleton interrupted him. "Congratulations. You've answered every question except the most important one."

"And that is?"

"Why would they be cannibals?"

"That's easy," replied Schwartzbaum, tugging at his goatee again. "From time immemorial, the reason's always been the same—to gain the intelligence of your victim."

Eagleton dismissed him, curtly.

Longface's son was laid out on a slab of packed dirt inside the big hut near the river. His eyes were closed and he looked pale and wasted, but he was still breathing. Susan studied his features. The bun-shaped swelling at the back of his head, the feature of the hominids that served as a counterweight to their big elongated faces, tilted his head downward so that in repose his chin almost touched his chest. This posture made him look solemn and peaceful, as if he were already dead, like the stone statue on a sarcophagus in a medieval European cathedral. His long eyelashes flickered. He's not ugly, she thought. He looks noble in a way, though hardly angelic. But he appeared distinguished, like a young prince. He couldn't be more than fifteen or sixteen, she thought. She was beginning to lose that almost unconscious shudder of revulsion that used to overtake her when she contemplated their distorted visages.

She looked at the paint markings on his face, savage slashes intended to inspire fear. They were universal; primitive peoples around the world used such adornment for hunts or battles and sometimes funerals of great warriors. She touched a line of red; a dried flake came off on her finger and she sniffed it. Hematite, or red oxide, which gave the color to red ocher. It was used in prehistoric burials as a blood symbol, and she had seen it recently on the faces of the savages who killed Rudy and tried to trap them in the cave.

Longface sat nearby, quiet but rocking back and forth slightly as if he were swaying to unseen breezes. He might have been in prayer the way he was collapsed in on himself, walled off from the outside world. Kellicut elbowed Susan aside and once again examined the boy, this time more thoroughly, lifting an arm, thumping the rib cage, checking the pulse. He was overbearing, but Susan knew him well enough to realize it came from nervousness. He was trying to dredge up the slim bits of knowledge he had gleaned from six months in medical school some thirty years ago.

"What are you going to do?" she asked.

"You'll see," he snapped. "That is, if you'll get out of the way and lend a hand instead."

She stifled a reply. Kellicut sent her and Matt scurrying around for all kinds of objects for a purpose not immediately apparent. Matt brought a canteen and the medical kit. Susan provided a tiny container of vodka that she had been husbanding and also handed over her jacket. Like Matt, she

fell into the old pattern, obeying her mentor unquestion-
ingly.

As instructed, Matt and Susan dug a shallow hole, filled
it with twigs and branches, and fetched a burning ember
from the communal fire to ignite the small pile. It caught
quickly, sent up waves of heat that made the trees behind
it dance, and released a thin shaft of smoke.

"Boil the water in the canteen," Kellicut commanded.
"A good ten minutes, but not more. I'll have to pour it in
here," he added, lifting the vodka bottle, "because I need
the canteen for something else." He poured the vodka over
the boy's forehead and then on his inner elbow, swabbing
it with a rag. A thimbleful was left in the bottle; Kellicut
raised it and knocked it back. "One more thing," he said
to Susan, setting the bottle aside and turning his back to
her as he bent over the boy. "Go get the shaman. We're
going to need him. You know where his hut is. Don't worry
about knocking; he'll know you're there."

Susan did indeed know the place, with its foul smell and
ominously closed door. She did not like going there. For a
moment she waited outside Dark-Eye's hut, but there was
no sign of life within. Finally she approached the door tentatively and gave it a push. Made of thick branches tied
together, it swung inward to reveal blackness and a stench
so powerful that she almost gagged. She stood motionless,
breathing through her mouth, while her eyes grew accustomed to the dark. Gradually shapes emerged. In one corner
was a rudimentary shelf made of a chiseled log. On it were
containers made of tortoise shells, filled with a thick liquid
of some kind and small round objects, balls of some sort.
She took a step closer. The smell shot up so strongly that
she could almost feel it through her skin. She looked down.
Bits of string were floating in the liquid, attached to the
objects. With a flush of revulsion, she suddenly realized
they were eyeballs: hundreds of them.

She felt dizzy. An odd sensation crowded her brain, a
clouding, as if it were fogging up on the inside like a bath-

room mirror. She took two steps back to leave and fell directly into the arms of Dark-Eye. He carried a long carved stick like a shepherd's staff whose crook was carved into a wolf's head, and he held his ground, so that she stumbled backward and almost fell. He made no move to help her but uttered guttural noises that sounded hostile. His white eye blazed like an exploding star—glaucoma, she thought, an advanced case. He must be completely blind in that eye. The other one also showed signs of the disease. Does he see only through the eyes of others? she wondered. But if so, why does he cast his head in my direction?

Then Dark-Eye took her by the hand and led her outside.

19

Eagleton still had not reached a decision and time was pressing. He lit a cigarette, inhaled deeply, and stared across his desk at Schwartzbaum. The man's a popinjay, he thought, but he is a fount of information. Almost reluctantly, because he treasured the silence, he formulated another question. "Tell me. Dr. Arnot's theory about warfare between *Homo sapiens* and Neanderthal. Do you buy that?"

Schwartzbaum furrowed his brow and stretched his legs out before him. "Dr. Arnot's theory, I hasten to say, is not original.

"Back in the 1920s there was a fellow called Hermann Klaatsch, an anthropologist at the University of Heidelberg. He thought it was impossible for *Homo sapiens* to be descended from brutish Neanderthal. So he evolved a far-out notion that there had been a primal struggle for survival in which the Neanderthals were all killed and consumed. He called it the Battle of Krapina."

"Is it credible?"

"Well, no one else bought it, and for good reasons. For one thing, Neanderthals were scattered all over Europe. It's a little hard to imagine them all grouping together and losing their entire population in a single decisive battle."

"Armies are defeated in a single battle all the time: Gettysburg. Waterloo. Agincourt. Most wars come down to a pivotal confrontation.''

"And one side loses. But it's not completely wiped out. Some of the defeated retreat and go off to a cave to lick their wounds. They're not totally exterminated.''

"I take your point," Eagleton said with a tiny grin. He paused, crushed his cigarette, and asked, "So you side with Dr. Mattison: We merged our genes with theirs?''

The fence beckoned Schwartzbaum. "There are problems there too. The great dilemma of Neanderthal research is how to explain a single mystery: The fossil that is newer is more Neanderthaloid than the one that is older. It has a more pronounced frontal torus—that's the brow ridge. It has an elongated skull, squatter limbs, all the characteristics we associate with the classic Neanderthal. So it appears that they were evolving *away* from *Homo sapiens,* not *toward* us, which conflicts with our sense of how things should have happened. How to explain it?''

"How do you explain it?''

"Well, as you might expect, theories abound. One is that there were different populations of Neanderthal, separated by impassable glaciers during the ice age, and that they evolved in different directions. The critical factor in evolutionary change is isolation, because it obviously stops interbreeding.''

"How does that apply to the Neanderthal?''

"The Neanderthal specimens that look more *human* come from the earlier warmer period and are found everywhere. The classic Neanderthal comes later, during the last glaciation. They're found in pockets, and their morphology is adapted to a subarctic climate. Their limbs are more robust, their skulls longer, their nasal passages wider, perhaps to warm the air. Interestingly, their brains are also bigger. Why that should be, we don't know. Otherwise, it's a straightforward case of adaptation to a hostile environment. It happened through natural selection, or maybe even genetic drift.''

"Tell me about genetic drift."

"A refined concept. Basically it's statistics applied to genetics. In small isolated populations, random events can have magnified repercussions. When genetic mutations occur, they attain a stage where they're rapidly perpetuated. The accidents have more effect than if they occurred in a larger population, and the changes can be quite dramatic.

"Say for example that one small group develops extraordinarily long legs. Those genes become so numerous that they overwhelm all the other so-called normal genes until long-leggedness becomes the norm. The long-legged ones have greater speed, and this in turn brings about all sorts of other changes—say, a change in diet as new types of animals become prey, or a change in habitat because traditional predators can now be outrun. And the changes keep on happening, a kind of self-perpetuating process that results in a quantum leap. But this is not because the new traits are necessarily more advantageous in some way; it occurs by accidental drift."

"I understand. What if this quantum leap involved an abstract ability—say, telepathic perception or something like that. Could that happen?"

"You mean the ability to project images directly from one brain to another? In theory, at least, it's not impossible."

"And wouldn't the large cortex of the Neanderthal provide the physical equipment for such an ability?"

"Again, speaking theoretically, yes. But there's a problem. We know from humans that much of the cortex is already mortgaged—it's for language."

"What if they didn't have language? Then they would have a large brain, larger than ours, just lying dormant."

"But there's no reason for them *not* to develop language. As a means of communication it's preferable because it endures. You can write it down. It can even outlast the speaker. You and I never met Shakespeare but we can hear him talk, so to speak."

"What if something prevented them from developing language?"

"It's difficult to imagine what could arrest language development. I can only think of one such cause."

"What?"

"High altitude."

Eagleton spun a quarter circle in his chair. "Explain."

"Mountain climbers get their judgments scrambled—that's not a new observation. But new research is tying it to speech. A neuroscientist at Brown, Philip Lieberman, has been looking at the cognitive effects of lack of oxygen. His theory is that it impairs the part of the brain involved in sequencing movements, including the motion made by the tongue, lips, and larynx. The basal ganglia are deprived of oxygen, and the syntax of spoken language goes out the window. Hence the thoughts come out jumbled."

"So over the long term," said Eagleton quietly, "a species in such an environment might turn away from language and develop something like telepathy as a compensation."

"In theory—only in theory—yes, that's not impossible."

"And what if this ability served a vital function for a group that was constantly fearful, constantly in retreat? What if it also allowed each member to act as a lookout—a kind of automatic early warning system for the entire tribe?"

"Well, then it would have an added value that would contribute to the likelihood of its continuing. In that case the process of genetic drift would be reinforced by Darwinian selection, which would tend to accentuate the trait—to solidify it, so to speak. But what are you driving at?"

"Nothing at all. We're simply having a theoretical discussion. I'm interested in what you said about different groups of Neanderthal. How does something like that come about?"

"Well, this is all theory, mind you, but some event intervened to split apart the overall population into subgroups. Probably the Ice Age. We know that those in Western Europe developed into the classic Neanderthal and eventually died out. In short, their brook went dry. Those elsewhere may have become more like us. It's called sapienization. Or they may have survived for a while cut off in their little backwater and developing some peculiar traits through genetic drift. The trail runs cold in that part of the world referred to as 'western Asia.' ''

"Western Asia? Where's that?"

"It's a strange term that to this day people use in writing about Neanderthals. It takes in that whole huge region from the Black Sea through parts of the Soviet Union, Uzbekistan, and Tajikistan. A lot of it is unexplored."

Abruptly, again without so much as a thank-you, Eagleton dismissed Schwartzbaum. He didn't need him anymore. He had reached the decision he was groping for. Van had not been heard from for more than three weeks. It was time to send in Kane.

Susan and Dark-Eye walked to the riverbank, he with his bony hand on top of hers like a hawk clutching its prey. She felt a strange, throbbing sense of power emanating from him, as if he generated some kind of psychic voltage. She could not tell if she was leading him or he was guiding her.

Longface met them and walked backward ahead of them, his head held low. When they entered the clearing of the hut, Matt was there, as were three or four hominids. Kellicut was working on something in a corner, his tools scattered around him: a knife, the canteen, the medical kit with its blue-and-white lid open. When he saw them, he carefully laid his work on a cloth and rose.

"Glad you're here. He's not looking good. We don't have much time."

"What are you planning to do?"

"He's got that gash on his head and a smashed knee, but he's also got a wound in his side. I can't be sure but my guess is that he was injured some days ago and has been traveling, so I think his main problem is loss of blood. We're going to have to give him a transfusion.''

''How are you going to do that?''

''Badly is the answer. We'll be lucky to get a significant amount of blood into him, and with all the germs around here, he'll be lucky if he survives. But it's his only hope.''

''Who's the donor?''

Kellicut looked over at Longface, still rocking slowly.

''And him? What's he for?'' Susan gestured with her head toward Dark-Eye, who had not yet let go of her hand. She hesitated to pry his hand off, as if it were some kind of leech that had to be detached carefully.

''I'm hoping that we can explain what we're doing to him somehow, and maybe he can communicate it to the others. He's the only one who can take it in. Also''—Kellicut turned back to his work—''it might be handy to have him around if this turns out badly.''

Susan joined Matt at the fire and watched as Kellicut huddled with Longface and Dark-Eye, making sounds and gestures. At one point he reached over and opened the boy's eyes; at another he jabbed himself with the knife, drawing a stream of blood out of his forearm. It seemed doubtful that he was getting the idea across. Meanwhile the water was boiling in the canteen. She and Matt used it to sterilize a long rubber tube from the medical kit and some rags, and brought the equipment over to where the boy lay.

Somehow Kellicut had convinced Longface to lie down on a bed of woven branches near his son. Now he took a hypodermic syringe, cleaned it with boiling water, and pushed the plunger down. With a knife he made a small hole at the upper end of the syringe, enlarging it gradually until it was round. He stuck one end of the rubber tube into it, held it up and turned it in the air, admiring his handiwork, then handed the other end of the tube to Susan. ''Hold this too,'' he ordered, giving her the canteen. He knelt beside Longface, dabbed his inner arm with a rag soaked in alcohol, and jabbed the needle into a vein, pulling the plunger back slowly so that the chamber filled with the dark red liquid. Seeing it made Susan feel a kinship with the hominids. *Prick me, do I not bleed?* she thought.

"Ah-ha!" Kellicut exclaimed as the plunger passed by the hole he had carved and Longface's blood began to flow down the tube as neatly as a stream detoured by a makeshift dam. "It works!" he cried, so enthusiastically that she realized he had not been sure it would.

"Keep the other end in the canteen," he cautioned, "and hold it low. We've got to keep it coming." Susan could see the tube darken slowly as the stream advanced. She held the tube in the mouth of the canteen and gripped the bottom with her other hand.

They stayed this way as the canteen filled. Though the flow was steady, it took a long time. Suddenly Susan gave a little cry, as blood spilled over the edge. Kellicut rushed over and grabbed it from her. He extracted the needle from Longface, then produced a Band-Aid from the kit to cover the prick in his arm. "Good as new," he barked. Longface rose up on one elbow to cast a suspicious glance at the Band-Aid and then slowly lay back again, closing his eyes.

Kellicut motioned Matt and Susan to the boy's side. "This part is going to be trickier," he said. "Hold the blood as high as you can"—he raised her arm over her head—"and keep it there." He took out the rubber tubing, used a bit of plastic to improvise a funnel feeding into it, handed it to Matt, and raised his arm too. "When I give the word, pour the blood in," he said. "If there's an air bubble in the tube, we're sunk." He lifted the syringe, pulled the plunger back as far as it would go, stuck the needle into a vein on the boy's arm, and pushed the plunger forward a couple of centimeters, taking care not to move it past the hole. It worked: slowly blood began flowing down the tube like a plunging thermometer.

"I should have been a bush doctor." Kellicut's voice

swelled with pride. "It makes you feel like some sort of god."

Afterward they bandaged the boy's knee and forehead, covered him with the spare clothes again, and left him sleeping next to his father. The other hominids stayed, standing around the hut, uncertain what to do and looking at Dark-Eye as if seeking guidance.

That evening, sitting around the fire, Kellicut was looking so pleased with himself Susan seized the opportunity to draw him out. "Tell us about the other ones," she implored. "What did you call them?"

"Renegades."

"That's it."

"There's not much to tell. I learned about them shortly after I arrived. I haven't seen them, of course—I doubt I'd be here to tell the tale if I had. But I've been able to pick up bits and pieces, enough to come up with some theories. As you might expect, they're greatly feared."

"Where do they come from?" Matt asked.

"Right here—this very same valley. For all we know there may be other tribes scattered throughout these mountains. God only knows what they're like. But the renegades come from this valley. They've increased over time—who knows how long, generations certainly. Maybe even hundreds of years."

"But how?"

"They're rejects, outcasts, pariahs. It's simple, really."

"Well, maybe you could indulge us and explain it."

"Every so often someone comes along who is born different. Antisocial—or worse maybe—a criminal. There's something pathological about him, genetically different. He doesn't fit in, he breaks the rules, he flouts the taboos. It's a phenomenon that occurs in every population. Spontaneous misfits. The Sioux called them 'contraries,' people who do everything backward, even riding their horses facing to the rear. Every society produces them, every tribe.

From the point of view of an evolutionary biologist, you might say the society has to if it is to survive. It's a way of experimenting, of trying out new models if you like.

"And this is especially true of tribes that are close-knit, socially cohesive, as this one is because of their special faculty. The ability to share perceptions makes them into a single unit, so that any behavior that's antisocial or even out of the ordinary assumes an aspect that is threatening to the communal whole. Therefore the tribe draws together to expel the rebel—or the rebel chooses exile on his own. Who knows how the process really works? The group cleanses itself, gets rid of the troublesome element, and he goes off into the sunset and that's that; he's never talked of again. Except there's one fly in the ointment."

"What's that?" Matt asked.

"He disappears but he's not really gone," interjected Susan.

"Exactly. He goes off into the wilds alone and learns to survive. He leaves Eden. Eventually another one joins him. Over time their numbers grow. At first it's a small ragged band, but it builds and builds. Soon you have an entire subcolony of outcasts. When they are joined by women, it becomes reproductive in its own right. Then it turns into a competitive population."

"How many are there?" asked Susan.

"I have no idea. But it's not the numbers that count; it's the spirit. It's the driving force. It's who they are."

"They're brutes!" exclaimed Susan, as the image of Rudy's blood in the snow flooded her brain.

"Susan!" chided Kellicut. He turned to look at her. "You've got it exactly wrong. How can you be so stupid? You've been to their cave; you've seen how they live and what they've accomplished."

"What they've *accomplished*?"

"Think, for God's sake! For openers, they hunt. That means they have to cooperate, have to work together, have to plan attacks. It takes six or seven men to bring down a

large animal, so they have to assign different tasks—one to
set a snare, another to beat the bushes, all of that. They
have to think ahead, to actually project themselves into the
future. They eat meat, so their protein intake is higher. That
makes them stronger. They cook the meat over fire to make
it taste good and to preserve it. They wear skins, they dec-
orate their cave. There's a division of labor, with men out
hunting and women staying home to tend the hearth and
raise the children. They're beginning to live in family
groups. They have a social hierarchy.''

''They kill,'' Susan said bluntly.

''Yes, they kill. Unfortunately, killing seems to be a part
of it. Maybe it's a necessary way station on the road to
civilization. Because that's what we're talking about here:
civilization. Don't kid yourself. They represent a higher
form, superior in every way. Remember what you learned
at Harvard? What are the first signs, the first stirrings of
communal life? Cave art, spiritualism, proto-urbanization,
social stratification. It's all up there with those mountain
dwellers, not down here with these lotus eaters. Don't you
see? The renegades represent a giant leap forward, the kind
of thing *Homo sapiens* went through eons ago. It's evolution working its will. They're catching up. It's one of those
sudden vaults forward that occur maybe once in a hundred
thousand years, and we're right here. We're present at the
creation.''

''Why don't they attack our group if they're killers and
have superior martial skills?'' asked Matt. ''They could
wipe them out in a minute.''

Kellicut fixed an eye on him. ''I'm not really sure. For
one thing, they're separated by the cemetery. There's a taboo in traversing it, as you know, but that's hardly a convincing explanation. Perhaps there's a sort of undeclared
truce, a stasis in the relationship between the two. After all,
the renegades need our friends here to increase their number; this is the mother tribe. Or perhaps it's just a matter

of time until they do attack. Darwin would be instructive now."

"What you describe hardly sounds like paradise," said Matt. "If they're being kept as a breeder population, it's a contrived Eden. There's a darkness at the center."

Kellicut paused a moment, then sounded more somber. "Certainly there are worrying signs. I think they are beginning to pick our Neanderthals off from time to time. They're ruthless, as you witnessed, and are in the thrall of a demagogue. There's a frightened screech associated with him, a sound something like 'Kee-wak.' He's the strongest of the strong, and he has led them to worship a godhead of some sort."

"Ruthless isn't the word. They had human skulls hanging up there," said Matt.

Just then the hominids squatting on their haunches nearby suddenly jumped up, wailing and throwing their heads back to let out long, piercing howls. Their movements were so disjointed that it took a few moments for the three to figure out that it was a display of grief. Then they all had the same thought.

They ran to the hut by the river, where a large group of hominids was milling about with an air of aimlessness that suggested trouble. Kellicut pushed his way through, ran over to the boy, and pulled off the clothes. His eyes were closed but his chest cavity was rising and falling. Kellicut felt his pulse: slow but steady. There was no crisis.

"Look behind you!" said Matt. Kellicut turned around and saw that Longface was still lying on the bed of woven branches, inert and pale, his body stiff and his eyes closed. Kellicut walked over and lifted his hand, large and dirty and with the thumb pushed into a stub from a lifetime of picking fruit and berries. It was already beginning to harden, with the half-clenched fingers forming a claw.

"My God," Kellicut said. "Do you know what happened? He sacrificed himself. He was giving his blood to his son so that his son would live, so logically he thought this meant he would die. And because he thought it, he *did* die.''

At that moment the crowd parted and Dark-Eye appeared, his hair wild and his yellow-white eye staring off to one side luminously. The crowd fell silent and pulled back as he reached into a wooden scabbard that Kellicut and the others had never seen before and pulled out a long sliver of stone flaked to a sharp point. He bent down, cradled Longface's head with one arm, quickly inserted the flint into an eye socket near the bridge of the nose, and with a swift, practiced motion pried out the eyeball. He did the same to the other eye and then held them aloft, white orbs streaming dark strands and blood, and gave out a long, piercing, high-pitched scream that chilled them to the bone.

When one dies, all die a little. The tribe that sees and experiences as one is diminished when a single pair of eyes passes into the night, the way a tightly woven tapestry is harmed when a single string unravels.

Longface's burial started immediately, from the moment Dark-Eye slipped the two eyeballs into a pouch dangling from his neck. A huge bonfire was constructed in the middle of the village and everything was thrown into the flames, not only branches but even makeshift beds and crude beams holding up the huts. In their grief, little was spared, and the flames rose ten feet into the air, scorching the leaves of nearby trees.

The entire village turned out, men, women, and children, and for the first time Susan realized how large the tribe was—several thousand at least. There were hominids she had never seen before, including some older ones, both men and women, who must have been leading hermitic existences in the far reaches of the valley, who gathered in response to an unspoken collective summons. All deaths were critical, but Longface's was not an ordinary death; he was an elder of the tribe.

His naked body was elevated on a four-foot-high bier of

logs strapped together by vines and laced with red poppies, that was placed about twenty feet from the fire. Behind it six young men sat cross-legged with hollow logs on their laps, tapping them with sticks in a syncopated, doleful rhythm. Others moved around them in a dance, raising their hands and legs slowly in contorted postures, almost as if they were under water. The fire was fed by children until Dark-Eye appeared again, this time his good eye blindfolded, carrying a shell. The children pulled burning logs and embers from the fire to form a path and he trod upon it, betraying no sign of pain, until he reached the fire's edge and placed the shell in the flames.

Long, thin leaves were tossed into the fire and the hominids danced past, inhaling the smoke. Matt and Susan inhaled it too, and within seconds a giddiness overtook them, then a numbness. The world began to spin and everything shimmered. An aura surrounded the moving figures and it became hard to see. Dark-Eye retrieved the shell from the fire and was led to the bier, where he poured out a stream of warm oil, which fell glistening upon Longface's body. The beating of the logs quickened, a sharp staccato sound that made everyone dance faster until some collapsed. They fell to the ground and others danced over them. Matt and Susan danced too, at first awkwardly but soon losing all inhibitions and giving themselves over to the smoke and pounding rhythm.

This went on throughout the evening. Finally, long vine leaves were laid out on the ground like a quilt and Longface's body, stiff now and easier to carry, was placed in the center and then wrapped. The leaves stuck to the oil, and the bundle was made secure by tying vines around it until the pale skin was entirely hidden and he was mummified. The drummers sped up their pounding—Matt had not thought it possible that they could go any faster—until there was a single steady earsplitting din. At that moment the dancing stopped, and out of the dark stepped six men, their faces and bodies smeared in white—the grave tenders.

They placed themselves around the bier, lifted it easily, and carried it off, all so quickly that it was as if Longface had simply been swallowed up by the growing darkness.

Later that night, as Susan lay sleeping next to him in the bower, Matt heard a distant crack resounding from somewhere on the mountain. It seemed too sharp for thunder. As a faint echo faded out across the valley, he contemplated it with growing alarm. It almost sounded like a gunshot.

Kellicut followed Dark-Eye up the rocky path. The shaman moved quickly for an old man with a single eye; his bare feet deftly avoided the ruts and stones because he knew the route by heart. Ahead of them, against a background of clouds, Kellicut could already see their destination, a rounded peak strangely shaped like a fist.

The funeral had been five days ago and the village had settled down to normal as if it had never happened. Longface's son was getting better by the day; he was already sitting up and eating. Susan called him Hurt-Knee. Kellicut didn't approve of her naming them and had told her so, but she persisted. She doted on the boy.

Dark-Eye had been spending a lot of time with Hurt-Knee. Kellicut wondered if the shaman wanted to make sure that the young hominid had not been tainted by his time in the caves and was still pure enough to rejoin the village—or perhaps he was eager to learn as much as possible about the powerful renegades. It seemed to Kellicut that this wizened elder now single-handedly shouldered the burden of thinking about the future of the whole tribe.

Luckily the shaman still seemed to trust the humans. Kellicut knew that if he had any hope of penetrating the mysteries of communal telepathic perception and mastering the power himself, he needed instruction from Dark-Eye. Already he had been receiving images from time to time. What he had to do—what the hominids could do—was learn to control the process so he could dictate whose eyes he was looking through. Otherwise all would be chaos, a maddening barrage of images over which he had no control. For his part, the shaman seemed to view Kellicut as a colleague in the realm of spiritual matters.

At the pinnacle the shaman stopped and motioned Kellicut up next to him. Kellicut realized that he was being entreated to look out far beyond the sloping wall of the shelf they were standing on, so he did, gazing across the green treetops, the sunken spaces that were meadows, and the canyon walls, all the way to the white spires of the distant mountains. Kellicut felt that sense of another presence in his mind, like a room flooding with water, and understood why the old hominid wanted him there. He was indeed going blind, and he wanted once more to experience the beauty.

The cave at the top of the pinnacle had its usual pungent, musky smell. There were boulders for them to sit on and piles of bones over in a corner, whether human or animal Kellicut had never bothered to determine. The shaman reached into his pouch and pulled out a package the size of his fist, leaves coated with mud, which he unwrapped to reveal a glowing ember. From a corner he picked up a long pipe, filled it with brown shavings, lit it, took a long drag, and handed the pipe to Kellicut, who did the same. Visions leaped into his brain. His mind filled with shapes and color and movement, compacted by the tiny space inside the cave, and he sat back against the rock and let the parade of sensations pass through him. The shaman began singing, a haunting sound that was calming, like a Gregorian chant. When Kellicut closed his eyes, his mind focused; he saw a whitish blur, the fuzzy outline of rocks, a protuberance of stone on the cave wall. Opening his eyes, he looked at the old hominid, whose one good eye was trained on the rocks behind his head. Kellicut turned and looked behind him; there was the protuberance he had just seen in his mind's eye.

*   *   *

That evening Kellicut found Matt and Susan sitting by the river and joined them on the bank. Susan could always tell when he had been "communing," as she called it, with the shaman because he came back subdued and vague. Like someone returning from electric-shock therapy, she thought. This time he was even quieter than usual, and she knew he had something to tell them.

"Prepare yourself for a shock," he said. "It comes from Longface's son—who incidentally did not run off to join the renegades but was abducted from a path on this side of the mountain. He was in the cave when you raced through it. It caused quite a stir, apparently."

"Go on," Matt said.

"Well, it seems that of the three of you, one was captured. He's still being held there."

"Jesus Christ! Van."

"Yes, and there's something worse. It took quite a while for the image to come through, but I worked it out in the end. The renegades have taken the 'stick that thunders.' Congratulations. You have introduced murderous twentieth-century technology into the Stone Age."

20

When he was a boy, Van had passed one summer on Lake Michigan. He spent hours walking along the beach under the cliffs, looking for tiny funnels in the sand. They were miniature traps; buried out of sight beneath them were ant lions. He relished finding an ant and dropping it in, watching it struggle upward, dislodging grains of sand and tumbling backward, until finally it fell exhausted to the bottom and was sucked under by a pair of pincers.

Now Van, at the bottom of a pit, was like one of those ants. He could scramble three quarters of the way up the sides, only to fall back again. There was one spot where he could almost make it to the top, but when he tried to climb to the edge, his guards lumbered over and pushed him backward. Once he was clubbed. Of course they had an advantage; they could see what he was doing without even looking at him. Escape was impossible, and he soon gave up trying.

He was in a bad way, exhausted, broken, emaciated. He rarely slept for long stretches; he had nightmares, and when he awoke he wished he was back in the nightmare. His body was covered with bruises, sores, and rashes. How much better, he thought, if he had died in the cave-in; instead, he had regained consciousness in this pit, his body racked in agony. His head ached all the time, a ring of pain that seemed to encircle it, continuously squeezing, like the medieval torture bands that were tightened around the temples until the brains squeezed through the eye sockets. He prayed for deliverance.

He knew where the pain came from; it was from that bloodthirsty leader who had killed Rudy and from his followers. Of course there was more to the hominids' power than remote viewing; he knew that from Operation Achilles and the headaches he got there. But then he was dealing with only one hominid; now he was subjected to the probings of dozens of them at once and to the strongest of them, their leader and dictator, the one whose presence elicited high-pitched frightened noises. The Institute should have realized that the hominids' faculty could scramble mental processes and stir atavistic recesses of the human mind.

Sometimes he felt that the pressure building inside his skull was driving him insane. There was relief only when the creatures slept; he assumed this was at night, but he couldn't be certain. And when that big one was around, Van felt the power burning into his brain like a laser. Sometimes he fainted and afterward he awakened as if from an epileptic fit, with the pain lessened; in those moments he felt a crystal clearness enter his boiling brain, like a cool drink of mountain water. But the temporary relief only made the pain that much worse when it resumed.

On the far side of the pit, along the wall, was a ledge. Van could reach it, and by hauling himself up he could stand on it and observe what was going on in the mammoth cavern. But he didn't like to do this because it was frightening to watch these savages going about their lives, stripping skins, drying hides, cooking meat over open fires, and fornicating at will. They looked like beasts in the smoke and the reflected firelight, their thick black hair matted like strands of fur, their bodies glistening with sweat and giving off that repugnant smell.

It had been from the ledge that he witnessed the sacrifice. He had known he was not the first prisoner in the pit because he had found writing etched into a rock. It was in Cyrillic, unfortunately, so he could not read it. The letters seemed to be recent and hurriedly scrawled. There were also bones in the pit, smells of urine, and bits of dried feces in one corner. He assumed the bones were from food that was tossed down, the way the odd bone with bits of meat and gristle was thrown to him. Every so often a bowl filled with stagnant water was lowered. It was made from the inside dome of a skull.

Still, Van had no idea that there was another prisoner alive in the cavern until that horrible day when he heard drums beating, a loud insistent pounding that echoed up and down the tunnels. He climbed to the ledge and watched the creatures assemble, spreading out in concentric semicircles in front of the huge god shaped like a bear's head. The big one, wearing a black bearskin flowing backward from his brow ridge, his upper torso naked and smeared in red and black paint, and with feathers as bands around his wrists, advanced from one side. The others fell back to give him room. As the creature leaned forward to seat himself on a carved wooden stool at the base of the godhead, Van saw a dark object swing out from his chest. It was his own gun, still in the holster, which was belted around the neck. The drums picked up the beat and from the other side of the cavern a human man was dragged in, struggling and screaming. He wore only uniform pants, and he shouted in Russian as he was propelled toward a thick log upended into the ground. Seconds before he was forced to bend, he spotted Van a hundred feet away, hugging the ledge. He had stopped screaming by now, and as their stares locked briefly, Van thought he could read a message in the man's terrified eyes: Avenge me.

Then the big one looked directly at the man, as did all the others, and the Russian fell to the ground, writhing in agony, his fists pressed against his temples like a vise. For a moment, he seemed to pass out; then he was pulled to his knees and tied face down to the log with a thick leather thong holding down his head, exposing the line of vertebrae along his upper spine. Empty bowls were placed around the log. The leader stood and waved his arms as if he were conducting an unseen orchestra, and the drums played and a creature stepped forward with a long chisel-shaped flint in one hand and a rock in the other. As he placed the flint at the base of the man's skull, Van yelled and they all looked at him, and suddenly Van felt unbearable pain enter his own head. But for some reason he kept looking. There was no scream from the Russian as the sharp rock was hammered into the base of his skull. His head fell limply forward and Van watched as the gray matter of his brain was scooped out into the bowls. When the creatures began to eat it, Van fell off the ledge face forward into the pit. He lay there not moving, listening to the loud beating of the drums, which went on for hours.

Later he was able to surmise, based upon how long he himself had been captive, that the sacrifice had been made at a full moon. But this was largely speculation since he had no way of knowing how long he had been unconscious after the cave-in. Now that his mind was so undependable, he could not be certain that he had not lost the ability to measure time. Pain and fear did that.

Resnick found it easier to venture into the underground corridor, and even to stand outside the cell, now that the prisoner was in such bad shape. He knew that it was wrong to think of it as a "prisoner," especially since he was a scientist. But he had to face facts: He was terrified of the creature and was glad it was behind bars. Even then it was frightening to be in its presence, so he usually left most of the direct experimentation to others. Who knew what mental powers it possessed? Or what happened to your mind when it was stirred up? The optic nerve ran perilously close to the pain center, he knew, but Grady and the rest certainly didn't. They had no trepidation because they were not cursed with knowledge and imagination the way he was.

Therefore part of him was gratified when its condition sank so low that it was no longer a threat.

These days it rarely moved, just lay curled up on the mattress, sleeping for long periods. Restraints were no longer necessary but intravenous feeding was. The bottle on its stanchion stood next to the bed, and the drip line ended in a needle taped to the inside of its elbow. Sometimes when it moved the needle pulled out, and then whoever was at the monitor rang a buzzer and Grady or Allen cursed, opened the cell, and stuck it back in. There was no longer any point in even trying the experiments, so Resnick had little to do; it was like the old days back in the psych lab when Van was designing the experiments and Resnick sat around drinking coffee and doing crossword puzzles. This had turned into a death watch, but he could handle that, and when it was all over the pathologists would come in for the autopsy. Then perhaps they would learn something by cutting the brain into tens of thousands of paper-thin slices. Right now they didn't have much of anything, merely rows and rows of numbers, vague theories, and half-baked conclusions.

Once the Irishman, Scanlon, who had grown so close to it and had been transferred as a result, came by for a visit. Resnick had been at the monitors and so saw the reaction when Scanlon walked up to the bars: The creature lifted its head and extended a weak arm, palm up and fingers outstretched. But Scanlon couldn't reach it. When he left he poked his head into the control room and yelled something about Resnick rotting in hell. Strange guy. Too sensitive. He wasn't cut out for science.

As soon as they heard that Van was still alive, Matt knew they had to rescue him. He didn't feel they owed him anything; more than anyone else, Van was responsible for luring them up here and never once had he played straight with them. It was simply that the thought of anyone at the mercy of those hideous beasts was unbearable. The image of Sharafidin's decaying skull kept flashing through his mind.

And there was a second reason: the gun. If somehow they could get it and find Van's stash of ammunition, that could help them in their own escape. And Kellicut was right—left up there, it was a corrupting influence that would upset the natural balance.

But how could they do it without getting caught themselves? No matter how hard he schemed he couldn't come up with anything other than a vague plan to penetrate the tunnels through the back cave and search for him—hardly a sophisticated strategy.

Susan wasn't so sure they should try to save Van. She was reluctant to undertake something that seemed so patently impossible and that could bring such dire consequences.

"We could take Hurt-Knee with us as a guide," Matt suggested as they lay together in the bower.

"You'd need a whole team. Otherwise you wouldn't last five minutes."

"What do you mean *you*?"

"Matt, I'm not certain I agree with you. Assuming for a minute we're right to try, how could we do it? Who could we take?"

"We'd have to train them to fight."

"That means training them to inflict harm, maybe even to kill."

"I know."

"It would change them forever, transform everything. This would no longer be Eden."

"Susan, Eden is ending anyway. You heard what Kellicut said. They're being picked off. It's just a matter of time until the renegades destroy them. And I think some of them want to fight back. Things have changed since Longface died. If they fight back, at least they have a chance."

"And what do you think Kellicut would say about our encouraging that? Everything he drummed into us from our first year was about the responsibility of social scientists to observe without meddling.''

"You're putting Kellicut's professional credo ahead of basic human morality. We can't let Van die.''

"I know. I feel that too, but one of the things Kellicut taught us was that scientists shouldn't just think of one individual.''

"Susan, forget science. Think of religion. If it teaches us anything, it's the sanctity of life—any life, anywhere.''

Susan was quiet, which Matt took as stubborn resistance. He lashed out. ''Kellicut. Sometimes I wonder about him. Why is he trying so hard to learn their ability?''

"It's mystical.''

"Bullshit. It's power. And you would know that if you weren't under his thumb. Is it because you're still his student or still his lover?''

She was too stunned to answer.

Susan walked into the forest, seething with anger. Isn't that typical? she said to herself. I think we're talking about science and morality, and all he can think about is whether or not I'm sleeping with Kellicut. Nothing but stupid male rivalry.

She followed the path to the waterfall and stood before it for a long while, listening to the roar. She looked down into the basin and realized with a jolt that Kellicut was there, sitting on the rocks with a group of hominids. She watched, riveted. He sat above them, rocking slowly and at times closing his eyes and then opening them. The hominids looked so trusting. She knew in an instant why he was there, why he was drawn to the place where the crashing water drowned out all extraneous sound. He was the teacher learning from his students.

There was something terribly private, illicit even, about the gathering. She turned away and walked back to the village. Her anger against Matt had dissipated. For the first time in years, she thought back to the small white-clapboard church she had attended as a child on the hilltop in Oregon.

That evening in the bower she turned to Matt. "You were right—not that part about me still being his lover, but about me not being true to myself. Of course we have to save Van."

They embraced, then kissed. As she undid a button on his shirt and moved her hand in a slow circle across his chest, he turned toward her and she caressed the back of his neck and spine. He slipped his hand down the back of her shorts and inside her panties, feeling her buttocks, soft and slightly cool. When she rolled on top of him and kissed him again, he felt desire roll through him, and yet he was conscious of a center of resistance, the nagging presence of someone else. He was able to push it to one side yet was aware of it dimly throughout their foreplay and then their lovemaking. The sense of an alien consciousness did not leave him until afterward, when she was resting in his arms, her hair straggly with perspiration and her breathing gradually calming. Then it disappeared as stealthily as a ghost.

Matt got up, dressed, and walked quickly along the path to the village. Not far away he encountered Kellicut leaning against a tree, and for a moment something in the man's look, flustered at being discovered and yet oddly challenging, planted the ridiculous notion in Matt's mind that it had been Kellicut who had invaded his brain.

They waited in ambush around a clearing in the thickest part of the forest. Longtooth and Blue-Eyes were on one side, Lancelot and Hurt-Knee on a second, and Matt and another youth, Tallboy, on the third. Susan, Leviticus, and several others were making their way noisily toward them through the woods, trying to flush an animal out of hiding and into their trap.

Matt and Susan had thought carefully about who to select for the band of hunters. They began with Lancelot, remembering the flash of anger he displayed during the wrestling match. Hurt-Knee had already been exposed to the renegades and had taken on some of their aggressive traits. There were a few other younger hominids who seemed to be moving in the same direction now that Longface was gone and the other feeble elders were losing their sway.

Now they all held clubs and spears. Matt had spent hours searching for saplings the proper length and weight, sharpening them, and burnishing the points in flame. Instructing the hominids in how to throw the spears was harder still, since they did not readily grasp the point of the exercise. He used a straw dummy as a target, and eventually the hominids entered into the spirit and were actually able to hit it from time to time. Still, whether they realized that it was a stand-in for a living, breathing animal was doubtful.

At first war games were even more difficult. The pacific hominids had trouble grasping the concept of teams, two groups opposed to each other for no discernible reason. Then Susan had a brainstorm. She vanished into the woods, came back with gobs of mud, and emerged from a hut with a concoction of bright ocher, which she proceeded to smear on the upper torsos of one group. At first Matt objected— it made him feel, he said, as if he were a kid playing cowboys and Indians—but soon he noticed what a remarkable effect the streaks of war paint had. It was as if the whole idea was suddenly made clear and some primitive instinct for combat was awakened. What had happened, they theorized, was that the ocher triggered an association with the feared and hated renegades. In effect the battle lines had already been drawn. The psychological construct of enemy was latent; it simply had to be filled in.

Now the crashing sounds got closer as the beaters approached. Suddenly Matt heard a different sound above the others, the crackling and rustling of an animal in flight as its hooves touched down upon leaves and twigs and sprang up again. He looked at Tallboy and could tell that he was listening to it too. But what was he thinking? Was he feeling the same adrenaline coursing through his veins, the tingling scalp, the mind clearing away anything extraneous and concentrating its energies for the kill?

Twice so far Matt had tried to teach them how to ambush and each time he had failed; the only spear that flew toward the animal had been his. Once it had been a marmot and the weapon flew harmlessly overhead. The second time it was a stag, which deflected Matt's spear with a toss of its antlers and sent it rattling against a tree trunk. On neither occasion did any of the hominids make a move. Matt had no reason to think that this time would be different, but he had to keep trying because they needed the skins.

Suddenly an ibex bolted into the clearing and stood motionless for a moment, testing the wind, as if it sensed danger all around. Matt could see its black nose twitching and the gracefully arched horns curving backward. He fell into a special position—crouching down on one leg in a posture of concentration—and tried to send out messages to the hominids, images of spears and blood, as he had done unsuccessfully before. Then he slowly stood, amazed by how much time he had. He raised his right arm slowly, cocked it back, and hurled the weapon with all his strength, sending the shaft directly at the animal's throat. As soon as the spear flew he knew that its direction was true. It sank its pointed head into the animal's brown chest. The ibex leaped back, stunned, and swung back and forth on its haunches. The spear was not so deeply planted after all; it wiggled, then fell on the ground. But the animal was gravely wounded. It could not take flight and fell to its front knees. Though it tried to stand again and again, it finally collapsed and rolled over on its side. Matt could not repress a thrill within him and a swelling of hunter's pride that reached back across the ages. When he stepped out into the clearing, the others did too, though they hung back a bit.

"Well, well," said Susan, running up, still panting. "You Tarzan."

The ibex was bleeding through its mouth, the eyes turning dull, expiring quickly in front of them. The hominids stared. The carcass was oddly positioned, perched too high off the ground. Matt bent down and wrestled with it, turning it over, and saw another shaft, sunk a foot deep into the rib cage, around a wound that was pouring blood. He looked up in surprise. Only one hominid was without a spear. Lancelot stood there, his shoulders square, a smile playing upon his face. Susan and Matt locked eyes. "He did it!" she exclaimed softly.

The other hominids stood around, uncertain of what to do. Two of them dropped their spears and began the high-pitched bleating that sounded like a cry of distress and mourning, then turned abruptly and ran off into the forest. They did not return, but Lancelot looked at the carcass proudly.

Matt and Susan decided to camp for the night where they were. The hominids collected firewood and ignited it with a transported ember. Matt took out his pocketknife and began cutting off one of the haunches, making the incision low to preserve as much of the hide as possible. With such a tiny blade it was difficult to slice through the flesh and he had to cut it in layers so that soon his hands were blood-red. When he reached the ball-and-socket joint of the femur and pelvis, he couldn't sever it with the knife, so he smashed it with a sharp rock and then lifted the joint to his knee and bent it backward, cracking it. As he stood up and approached the fire, holding the mangled leg bone in both hands with blood running down to his elbows, the hominids drew back in horror. They watched closely as he placed the bone across two burning branches. A hiss filled the air, followed by the smell of singeing meat.

Matt cut off small chunks and ate them, gave some to Susan, who ate them, and passed some to the hominids. They stared at the bits of meat. Two of them refused to touch them, but the others held them up and examined them in the firelight. Longtooth sniffed his piece, then touched it with his tongue. The others watched him as he tentatively bit off a tiny sliver, which he then spit out and held between a thumb and forefinger, raising it up to the light as if it were a precious gem. He looked at Matt, who quickly chewed another piece to encourage him, then placed the sliver between his teeth and bit into it. Seconds later he put the rest in his mouth and chewed tentatively. Susan exhaled, realizing only then that she had been holding her breath. All but two of the others began to eat.

Later that night as Susan lay awake, listening to Matt's steady breathing and staring up at the stars, she heard the rustle of footsteps disappearing into the woods and then the sound of vomiting. Was it more than one of them? How unnatural to swallow the sinews of another animal, to force down meat and feel the bloody juice trickling down your throat, she reflected. She knew the hominids had passed a Rubicon and that, whatever happened, life would never again be the same in the valley.

The next morning Matt skinned the ibex. He laid it on its back and, while Susan and Longtooth held its feet in the air, used his knife to make an incision along the white fur of its underbelly. Then he picked up a large rock, rounded on one end to rest inside his palm and sharp along the outer edge, and pounded it like a cleaver against the underside of the hide as he peeled it away from the viscera. He used sharp rocks to cut out pieces of meat and sever the ligaments attaching muscles to the bone. Every few minutes he stopped to resharpen his tools by knocking them against another rock to remove small flakes from the edges. Something caught his attention and he stopped; there, along a shaft of a bone, were tiny cut marks he had made. He had seen hundreds of bones with such marks and had been excited when he found them at early Stone Age sites.

They prepared to move on to another campsite. Today they would learn how to set a snare, Matt decided, then perhaps a pit trap with pointed stakes at the bottom. Half a dozen skins were all they needed, enough so that a group could enter the cave and not be instantly spotted as outsiders. The hominids pitched in to break camp. Leviticus and Tallboy used the hide to wrap large pieces of meat and hung it from a branch they carried on their shoulders. Just as they were leaving the clearing, Lancelot turned back and knelt beside the gutted ibex. He picked up the cleaver stone and smashed it down upon the upper skull. He repeated the movement three or four times, and Matt and Susan were shocked until they saw him dislodge the beautiful curved horns and sling them over his back, a trophy.

Susan knew whenever Leviticus was viewing through her. The sensation occurred often during the hunting expedition, especially when they were separated, one near the front of the line of march and the other at the back. She even came to depend on that familiar feeling, a filling up inside, sometimes lasting only a minute or two—a way of saying hello, checking in, she thought. She could not be positive that Leviticus was the source, but she was convinced that he was by the way she felt when it happened—not violated or invaded but warm and cared for.

She wondered if the hominids could identify those in the tribe who moved in and out of their perceptual fields. Clearly their special faculty was more complex than she and Matt had at first supposed. Perhaps it entailed two-way communication and perhaps it was more far-reaching than seeing through another's eyes, something closer to ESP. Perhaps it was reduced to crude telepathic images only when it crossed the species barrier.

Which would explain a lot—for one, why the hominids had never developed language. On the face of it, language seemed a better medium of communication because it conveyed abstract concepts and could be written down, allowing a compendium of knowledge to accumulate. But if the hominids could do more than send pictures back and forth, if they could actually feel and think what another one was feeling and thinking, there would be no need for language because their communication would be complete. Language—speaking—was only the pale shadow of a discourse so sublime and perfect that it was tantamount to actually exchanging places. In this case it was not the ability to communicate that turned *Homo sapiens* into nature's overachievers, it was the *inability* to communicate.

Susan was proud to call herself an empiricist, but she was also willing to postulate the unproven, so she did not rule out the possibility that in their primordial state humans might have possessed a similar faculty but lost or abandoned it. Perhaps, she speculated, we still have a vestigial capacity for ESP, which is why so many people are intent on establishing its existence. Further, perhaps being exposed to it will reawaken it the way a child who is exposed to language learns to talk. Unless, she thought, by now too much of our brain is consumed in the service of mere words.

She met Leviticus in a meadow under a hot sun, whether by accident or not she did not know. She approached him and stood two feet away, staring into the eyes set deep in his overly broad face. Putting her hands on his bare shoulders and turning him gently around so that he faced away from her, she closed her eyes. Nothing. She tried pushing her mind outward. A breeze came up and she moved closer, hugging him from behind and smelling a pungent odor from the hair and dried sweat on the back of his neck. She leaned to one side and looked over his shoulder at the waving golden grass of the meadow and the trees beyond, then closed her eyes and concentrated, but the meadow and the trees did not reappear. When she felt herself filling up, she released him. "No," she said out loud, knowing he would not understand but saying it anyway. "No, *I* want to do it." But the familiar warm sensation continued.

Their return to the village did not cause a stir even though they came back with weapons, cutting stones, and skins. Remembering vividly what had happened when he had produced a single dead fish, Matt was surprised until he realized that of course the villagers had been aware of what the hunters were doing every step of the way.

Kellicut was a different matter. He was waiting for them at the fire cave and he was shaking with fury. "Don't you understand anything? Didn't you learn anything from all those years?"

Matt stood up to him. "I know what you're going to say," he said, "but we know what we're doing."

"Like hell you do! Teaching them to hunt! You're supposed to be observers here. Do you understand that? It's the first law of social science. You're observers and *nothing* else. You *don't* enter in. You *don't* teach, you *don't* change, you *don't* convert. Got that?"

"This is different."

"How is it different?"

"A man's life is at stake."

"A man's life! You don't even know who that man really is."

"That's another reason to go. We have to find out."

"And what's a man's life compared to all this?" Kellicut swung his arm around, taking in the village, the trees, the whole valley. "An entire species, a species that's been around longer than we have. Our progenitors, for God's sake!"

"Maybe we can save him and protect them in the process."

"Protect them from the renegades, you mean."

"Yes."

"That's what you don't understand. *You* are not supposed to have anything to do with this. *You* are not even supposed to be here. This is a primitive world and you're like some goddamn time traveler. You interfere and you throw the whole thing off!"

"So did you, Jerry," said Susan. She used her teacher's first name softly. "If you feel so strongly about this, why did you give Hurt-Knee the blood transfusion?"

Kellicut spluttered in anger. "That was different. That

was a discrete act that didn't affect the whole future of the species.''

''Besides,'' interjected Matt, ''it made you feel like God, didn't it?'' He reached into his pocket, brought out the skull fragment on a silver chain that Kellicut had given him nearly two decades ago, and held it up. ''Just like teaching made you feel like God. Or taking us on digs and distributing little rewards. Or sleeping with Susan.''

They never had a chance to hear Kellicut's answer, for at this moment Dark-Eye stepped out of the shadows, walked over to them, took Matt's and Susan's hands, and rested his own hand roughly upon theirs. It was hard to tell whether the gesture was a blessing or a curse.

21

Before their foray to the cave, Matt and Susan checked their preparations. Not that they had so much equipment that there was a danger of forgetting some. What they really needed was to prime themselves psychologically, and planning ahead raised their spirits, feeding the illusion that they had a concrete plan to spring Van and then escape in one piece.

They had blindfolds made of cloth strips, with the knot dampened to hold better, which were tied around their necks so that they could be pulled up quickly over their eyes. This had been Susan's idea, recalling Van's directive in the cave to keep their eyes closed. She thought of it as a defensive maneuver against their adversaries' power—a way to thwart it momentarily if they were caught in a tight spot. At least that was the theory; in practice they had no way of knowing whether it would work.

They had decided to take three hominids from the hunting expedition, beginning with Hurt-Knee, who presumably could guide them through the labyrinth of tunnels. Matt and Susan could only hope that he would comprehend his mission once they got under way, because how they would explain it to him, or look to him for help if things went awry, was beyond thinking about. Lancelot, who was becoming a tribal leader, was an indispensable member of the group. He had brought the ibex horns back to the village, placing them at the entrance to his hut with the points sunk in the dirt, and the trophy appeared to raise his stature, especially among the young males. Leviticus was the third, chosen by Susan, who said he would be valuable because of his cleverness. Our Odysseus, she called him.

These three confederates were outfitted in garments made from the skins they had gathered. It had been a long hard job, first to make them and then to convince the hominids to wear them. Matt used strips of gut to tie the hides together, threading it through holes Susan made with a sharp stone. One hide fit over the head like a poncho, hung loose, and was bound around the waist with more gut, while another was used to make crude leggings. As well as they could recall, this was the way the renegades had dressed. The garments weren't firmly fastened but they didn't have to be; their only purpose was camouflage.

At first the three hominids refused to put on the skins. The hides were stiff with blood in patches and smelled of animal, and the idea of wearing them was repellent. Matt and Susan demonstrated how they were worn but made little impact. Finally Matt took the ibex hide and mimicked a hunt, draping it on a bush, stalking it, and tossing his spear at it. Then he ceremoniously presented it to Lancelot, draping it across his shoulders the way a courtier would adorn a king with a robe. Lancelot gravely donned it, and soon the others accepted the skins, moving awkwardly and staring at their bodies and at each other.

They were also given weapons. Lancelot had the spear that had made him a hunter, and Susan made clubs for Hurt-Knee and Leviticus, choosing heavy branches that were tapered and using a stone ax to fashion a rounded top and a smooth handle. She labored for hours over these, surrounded by a circle of hominids who watched her every move in silence.

In his rucksack, Matt tucked away a coil of rope and some crude stone tools. The flashlight would have been invaluable but it had been left in the cave; instead, they would use torches made from branches and straw. Matt had been awake worrying much of the night before they left. There were so many unknowns. What if the renegades' power to perceive them from afar was more sophisticated than he anticipated? What if it operated like a radar system, registering any new presence the moment it presented itself? What if the renegades spotted them, drew them deeper into their lair, and used their superior communication to close off every avenue of escape?

At the edge of the village Matt and Susan turned to peer back. Their scraggly band, waddling uncomfortably in their skins, would have looked comical under other circumstances. A few villagers watched them depart. In the distance, standing next to a tree, so still that he seemed part of it, was Dark-Eye. Susan waved to him, knowing he wouldn't return or even understand the gesture, and he did not.

When they came to the periphery of the burial ground, the hominids refused to set foot upon it. Susan tried to indicate that their intent was simply to cross it, but the hominids were adamant and would not budge. She looked ahead. A spiral of three vultures circled in the sky and others stared down from bare branches nearby, the black-and-white tuft of bristles spreading under their bills like whiskers. Then Susan was startled; two grave tenders, ghostly figures all in white, squatted not thirty feet away, the whites of their eyes matching the chalk smeared over their bodies. There was an unearthly quiet, save for the distant sound of insects buzzing. Nothing stirred inside that zone of death, as clearly delineated as if the River Styx flowed beside it, except for the carrion-eating birds above them lazily riding the air currents.

"Hopeless," said Matt. "They won't cross it."

"We could go ahead and hope they meet us. Or we could go with them the long way around."

"Best to go around." He took her hand and they set off,

keeping the burial ground to their right. The hominids gave
it a wide berth and eyed it suspiciously, as if the earth itself
might open up at any moment and swallow them. Matt was
kicking himself; he should have foreseen the possibility that
the hominids would balk, especially after that first visit
weeks ago. The detour would add hours to their approach
and wear them out before they even reached the cave entrance.

They stopped three times to rest. The hominids didn't
appear to be tired, and looking at them as objective specimens, Matt was again struck by their superior physiques—
the squat legs as strong as columns, the low-slung torsos,
the huge shoulders and thick hands, the brows that served
as anchors for their massive jaw muscles. They're made for
combat, he thought, and if all those many centuries earlier,
Neanderthal had acquired the lust to spill blood that has
possessed mankind, they would surely have pushed us aside
long ago. All they needed was a little bit of original sin.
He looked at Hurt-Knee, whose cut brow had largely
healed, turning into a twisted, ugly red scar that ran from
his scalp line to one eyebrow. Could it be the mark of Cain?
Matt kicked himself; this was no time to turn into a half-
baked philosopher.

The cave was set vertically in the cliff, a gigantic breach
in the rock facade some twenty feet high. They approached
it from the side with Matt leading the way and Susan bringing up the rear behind the hominids, in case they showed
signs of bolting. If they did, she had no idea what she
would do to stop them, but she felt it was wise to keep an
eye on them. She knew how anxious they were; Leviticus
was reading her often and wildly.

Matt crept up to the mouth of the cave cautiously. Total
blackness. He looked down and saw small piles of rocks
scattered at the entrance; perhaps this was a good sign, for
surely the debris would have been pushed aside if it was a
major thoroughfare. Just their kitchen door, he thought,

used whenever a creature wanted to raid the tribe for a wife or a slave. He felt fear creep up on him from behind; he hated the blackness and felt claustrophobic at the prospect of going underground, a phobia that had been well stoked by the terror of their narrow escape only a few weeks before. Taking a deep breath, he stepped inside.

The others came after him one by one, almost as if they were following a drill. A good start, he thought, as he felt the darkness assault his eyes. They lingered at the mouth for a moment to get their bearings. In the half-light, Matt scrutinized Hurt-Knee; his face seemed expressionless—either that or Matt could not decipher whatever expression was there—but he seemed under control. The impulse to flee harm must be universal, Matt figured; if so, then Hurt-Knee appeared to be a cool customer. But he also guessed that the hominids must be using their faculty to scout the passageway before them, the way as a child in the New England winter he used to test a lake for thin ice by tossing ahead rocks. How would they react if one of their rocks struck danger?

Once their pupils dilated, Matt and Susan realized with relief that they were not in total darkness after all. At first the cave had appeared pitch black, but thirty feet ahead it curved to the left; now they could see that the opposite wall ahead flickered faintly with reflected light, presumably from torches beyond the bend. The tunnel was enormous, like a mammoth borehole penetrating directly into the innards of the mountain. They made sure that Hurt-Knee went first, hoping he would adopt naturally his role as their guide.

"So far, so good," Matt whispered.

"Yeah, so far," she replied, her voice shaky.

When they came to the bend, Hurt-Knee walked around it without a flicker of hesitation. It led into a large cavern lit with torches and rimmed with shimmering icicle-shaped deposits of lime carbonate built up over millennia. The middle ground was open under a roof that stretched upward in the center as if it were a circus tent. The rocks above them stirred with furry life: bats, nestling in the crevices, fluttering around in a frenzy, and sweeping down at the intruders in abortive dive-bomb attacks. Matt and Susan began to shiver and could see their own breath. The unnatural warmth of the crater valley, blanketed by its geothermal air streams, was behind them, and once again their bodies were prey to the coldness of the altitude. They lit the torches they brought from those in the cavern.

Crossing the open space, they came to a wall with three tunnels. The labyrinth was beginning in earnest and they could only hope that Hurt-Knee would negotiate it and lead them to the burrow of the Minotaur. He chose the middle tunnel. It soon narrowed and then rose precipitously, which made sense since the innermost sanctum that they were aiming for was high inside the mountain. But the incline made the going rough; rocks had accumulated at the bottom, and at times it was like climbing up a chute filled with coal. What was even worse for Matt was that the height of the passage began to shrink so that he was forced to bend. He felt claustrophobia clutch his heart with a vengeance, and it took all his strength of will to keep going. At last the passage leveled out and they could stand upright again. Their torches were burning but low; the oxygen was thin.

Suddenly, fifteen minutes later, the hominids froze. They looked ahead uncertainly, then turned to face them, and this time Matt had no trouble reading the emotion of fear written upon their broad features. Clearly something was approaching, but, straining to listen, they could hear only the distant *whoosh* of wind.

"We passed a cutoff a little while back," Matt whispered. "We better go back there and hide."

"How about these guys?"

"It'd be better to split up. If we're all together it's easier for the renegades to read us. They'll be protected by their disguises."

"Okay."

Retreating, they found the tiny cutoff. A little beyond was an out-of-the-way chamber where they left the three hominids with the torches, praying that they would appear inconspicuous enough to avoid arousing suspicion. Matt and Susan pulled up their blindfolds and waited, their bodies fitting together snugly in the tight space. They did not have long to wait; soon they heard the telltale loping shuffle of the creatures.

Susan closed her eyes underneath the blindfold and tried to wash her mind clear. Matt put his arms around her and held her tightly as the sounds grew louder, until the creatures were only a couple of feet away, just around the rock face. Susan could hear the wheeze of their breathing and the plodding of their heavy tread on the cave floor. She squeezed Matt tighter. Finally the sounds subsided as the creatures passed them and kept going, moving toward the hominids. Susan removed her blindfold. Their smell invaded her nostrils. They were so close that we could have reached right out and touched them, she thought. Another sensation crowded into her mind, that familiar filling up; Leviticus, she knew, was making contact in the moment of his terror, just as Matt had. She kept her eyes open and received him fully, standing motionless for long seconds while Matt held her body, until finally she relaxed and said, "It's okay. They're safe." Matt gave her a long searching look.

Reunited, the group continued up the passageway with Hurt-Knee still in the lead. They climbed for half an hour, passing small chambers and alleys leading to cubbyholes that contained hearths and hides spread out for sleeping, but luckily encountered no other creatures. Then the soft whine of breezes gave way to the eerie bustling that they had heard weeks ago, like the hum resounding from a thousand wings inside a beehive.

Hurt-Knee stopped for a moment, frozen to the spot

while he concentrated, then crouched and ducked inside a tunnel so small that he had to crawl. For Matt it was a tomb. It curved upward like a chimney, so that they ascended it by using footholds and handholds, until finally they emerged on a ledge overlooking the central mammoth cavern. Below them was the beehive.

Everywhere, on the open cavern floor and in every nook and cranny, the creatures moved about in a tumult of activity that took their breath away. They were cooking, curing hides, making tools, chopping meat, fornicating, brawling, sleeping, eating—a self-sufficient colony of primordial men, women, and children. Matt saw squealing toddlers chasing each other around a hearth. To one side, a woman squatted before a cured hide, holding it in both hands and tearing at it with powerful jaw muscles. She seemed to be making skin bags for water. Another woman nearby pounded a stone, then tossed it onto a pile of other stones. Susan was right, he thought. There *are* more women here than in the valley; I bet they've been kidnapped in raids.

Sealed in, the noise was formidable; the smoke from a dozen fires brought tears to their eyes, and it was as hot as a pressure cooker. Staring down upon it all, no more than thirty feet above the manes of matted hair, Matt felt that they were witnessing the birth of civilization, the moment in which our ancestors turned from the brutish existence of solitary apes to the splendor and rigors of community and industry. But in another respect the colony was still steeped in savagery. Rising up in the center of the huge cavern was the malevolent god sculpture shaped like a bear's head, and next to it was the wall of human skulls.

There was a new addition on the wall, the head of a Caucasian male. Matt forced himself to examine it, his first thought being that it might be Van, but even from a distance he could tell that the physiognomy was different, the nose too long.

"We don't have much time," he whispered to Susan.

"We've got to find Van before they sense us."

She did not reply, apparently lost in the incredible sight before them. Matt followed her stare and zeroed in on the figure she was looking at. How could he have missed him? Kee-wak was at the heart of the throng, a full head taller than the others, and as he moved through them a path opened up before him; the other creatures fell back like whipped dogs, lowering their heads and adopting unmistakable postures of subordination. There was no doubt about it: He was an extraordinary figure, born to rule. His upper torso was adorned with wavy red and black lines that circled around his muscles in fingerprint patterns, his hair hung in long braids decorated with beads, and his mouth was ringed with red dye that looked like blood. As he walked, his head waved slowly from side to side in that curious lizard motion that was seared into Matt's memory from the confrontation in the snow with Rudy.

"Look," Susan whispered, "he's got Van's gun around his neck!" Sure enough, there was the holster hanging down to the abdomen, gently slapping the ridged muscles.

Kee-wak raised his gaze and began staring at the upper reaches of the cavern. Quickly Matt and Susan slipped on their blindfolds and moved back, lying flat on the ledge.

Susan felt Leviticus fill her and knew some seconds later that the danger had passed. She lifted the blindfold and peeked over the edge; Kee-wak had left the cavern. She watched the hubbub of activity for only a moment before coming to a decision.

"Matt, I've got to find the sacred chamber. I want to see the Khodzant Enigma again."

"Are you crazy?"

"I have to. Don't you see? It's got to mean something. I don't know why, but I feel strongly that there's some clue there, something we need to figure out."

"Susan, there's no time. You'll never make it back." He thought of half a dozen other objections and was about to voice them when Hurt-Knee suddenly crouched behind him, placed his fingers on Matt's temples, and roughly turned his head, forcing him to look over in one corner. At the far end of the cavern was a pit, and in it he saw Van's head appear briefly, disappear, then appear again. He was pacing in a circle like a caged animal. Even from this distance Matt could detect a bizarre, ritualistic jerkiness to the man's movements that made him worry for Van's sanity.

He sized up the situation. Two creatures with clubs squatted not far from the pit; they could be guards, since it looked as if the hole was not so deep that Van couldn't get out if he tried hard. Along the rock face to the left was a huge slab that might be the outer wall of a passageway; at the least it could provide some cover if Matt could find his way to it. He had a six-foot length of rope tied in knots every two feet which he could lower down to Van. But if he were to have any hope at all of succeeding, he would have to take care of the guards. What he needed was some sort of diversion; otherwise he had little prospect of escaping their paranormal powers. He felt lucky to have gotten this far.

Matt moved slowly backward along the ledge and realized, with a gasp that sent his heart into his throat, that Susan had gone. He was so startled that he barely registered the disappearance of Leviticus.

Having traipsed through the snow on their way to the lower reaches of the mountain, the five creatures carrying animal skins came upon a mound of rocks and were immediately attracted by the shine of metal. They approached the rock pile suspiciously, as if it were a trap, stopping every few steps to throw their inner eyes in all directions. They found no sign of life.

Slowly and cautiously, one of them touched a rock. Nothing happened. He pulled it off the pile and took another rock until the mound shrank, revealing Van's NO-MAD. The creatures peered at the black box with metallic edges that glinted in the sunlight. Never before had they seen such a strange object.

They feared it because they knew about bait; long ago the hunters in their tribe had discovered how to lure animals to their destruction. One of the creatures leaned over and smelled the object, then backed away quickly, as if he had been slapped; it gave off the acrid scent of the enemy.

Another creature raised a club high in the air and brought it down in a sweeping arc, smashing the computer on one side and sending it flying off its pedestal and careering across the rocky ridge. A third went over, picked the object up, held it away from his body, and carried it twenty feet to the edge of a ravine. He leaned over and let go and it fell for a long time, until finally they heard a distant crash below.

In the sacred chamber Susan stood transfixed before the pictograph. She was shivering with terror. What was more interesting, and what she did not at first perceive, was the other sensation; it counteracted the fear and poured a strange balm through her system, a kind of ecstasy brought on by the sheer power of the shapes and colors spread before her on the cave wall.

She had seen many cave paintings before, renderings of antelope, boar, and musk oxen, often brilliantly done. She had been among a handful of scholars permitted inside the crumbling caves of Altamira in the Cantabrian mountains of northern Spain, and had even sketched the chamber of painted bison, the so-called Sistine Chapel of Quarternary Art. She had been deeply moved by the drawings, but mixed in with the aesthetic appreciation had always been the kick of anthropological wonderment: to imagine the Paleolithic soul who felt compelled to mix natural pigments with animal fat and then give the vision permanent shape by tracing this bit of curved horn or that arching back. The power came from experiencing contact with that soul across 25,000 years. This was different. This painting was masterful in its own right. She marveled at the unknown hand that had so perfectly used charcoal to outline the figures in black, had seized upon the natural bulges in the rock to give depth to body shapes, and had made movement and lightness out of a material so inert and heavy. This was the product of artistic greatness, a prehistoric Michelangelo. But what was the subject that inspired such genius?

She knew she did not have much time. She fingered the blindfold in a nervous tic to make sure it was still around her neck. Should she put it on? Wouldn't she know if she was being read? But by then would it be too late? Would the creatures know where she was? She stepped back to take in the whole pictograph, which was clearly a narrative of some sort. Figures in separate panels were engaged in actions and in what appeared to be battles, but the panels were not in linear sequence. She would have to rearrange them mentally; certainly there was no time to make a sketch.

She wished she could remember more of what she had heard about the Khodzant Enigma back in her graduate-student days. In fact it had been Kellicut who had delivered a lecture on it—a humorous one, she remembered thinking at the time, about archaeological dead ends. Some dead end! Who would have thought she would be risking her life trying to unravel its riddle? She scanned it, from top to bottom, from left to right, and from right to left. There were warriors in two groups, that much was clear, and there were those strange detached open eyes that seemed to be floating in the trees—symbols of the dead. She walked over and peered closely at one panel. One of the warrior groups was beetle-browed and clearly were Neanderthals; the other group was narrow-boned, with domed heads and thrusting chins: *Homo sapiens.* They were at war over what appeared to be a long period of time because there was not one but two or three battles. Then there was a gathering, or preparations for one—could it be a peace council of some sort?—and the two groups seemed to be walking toward each other with their weapons tossed aside. But then something happened to one group, the Neanderthals.

Susan had no way of knowing that at that precise moment, far away in the cave, Kee-wak felt a cloud form inside his head and a momentary vision intruded: The tableau flashed briefly onto his inner eye. He paused and raised his head, but it was gone.

Susan felt a wave of fear and put the blindfold on while she tried to think; which were the panels that were not known outside this chamber? There were moons in the painting, so perhaps the chronology was classified by the phases of the moon. She tried to recall the image of the Khodzant Enigma from that class so many years ago. Could it have been the lower right-hand segment that was gone? She decided to risk a quick glimpse and walked over to stand in front of that portion of the painting. She raised the blindfold and stared. A panel was directly before her, and what she saw she had never seen before, she was sure: a creature standing alone, looking up as rocks or something fell around him—they had little tails like meteors to suggest downward motion—with his mouth open and his features twisted in rage as if he had just comprehended some underlying bitter truth of nature or been witness to some satanic act. The artist had captured the emotion perfectly. She was enthralled and stared at it for some time.

Kee-wak knew, as soon as the vision returned. This time there was no mistaking. He quickly sent four guards to the sacred chamber.

22

Resnick knew the creature was about to expire. Not that it was hard to tell; the drip feed hadn't revived it, it had virtually stopped moving, and its breathing was irregular. They brought in a heart monitor and EEG and attached them, shaving patches like small white moons on the temples and the hairy chest to attach the electrodes, and now one of the cameras was trained on the tiny green screen in a corner. Over and over, a white line traced the same pattern, not a large peak and then wavy subpeaks, as with humans, but a series of spikes and plateaus that reminded Resnick of the skyscraper outline of a big city. They also reduced the alarm sensitivity drastically because the unusual nature of the creature's heartbeat continually set it off.

Now they didn't bother anymore to close the cell door, and this made Resnick feel a lot better, as if he had been the one locked inside all this time. They had also washed the cell down so that the stench was not so bad, though it still hung in the air near the cot. Now even Resnick himself ventured right up to the creature, puffing himself up with professional pride and pretending in front of the others that he had been doing so all along, even when the creature could have flung him against the wall. He had resolved to be fatalistic about its death. It was true that they wouldn't be able to run any more experiments and perhaps would never be able to piece together something meaningful from all the shreds and bits of observations and numbers they had accumulated. But perhaps this was for the best, maybe the creature wasn't meant to live among humans—it was primitive, after all—and the autopsy would probably tell them much of what they wanted to know.

Grady stepped into the cell next to him, which made him feel better. The creature was completely inert and couldn't possibly awaken, but one could never be sure about something so alien.

"Is he coming?" Resnick asked.

"He'll be here any minute."

It had been Resnick's idea to send for Scanlon. He congratulated himself for it; it was a matter of sentiment more than anything else. Scanlon had made the breakthrough, Scanlon had been closer than anyone else to the creature, so Scanlon deserved to be there at its death. It was like having a priest present, or family. After all, Resnick thought, it's just this kind of considerate gesture that makes us different from animals.

He heard a car door slam, then the front door, then the tread of footsteps above, and a moment later Scanlon appeared, looking upset.

"Don't worry, there's time yet," Resnick counseled in his best medical voice.

Scanlon didn't pay any attention to him but went directly to the creature and lifted up its hairy hand.

"Christ, will you look at that?" said Grady, motioning to the small screen. Resnick glanced over and saw that the skyscraper outline had changed. The line was moving faster and the spikes were larger. He looked back at the creature and couldn't believe what he saw: it opened its eyes, looked directly into Scanlon's eyes, and even seemed to raise its head an inch or so. Resnick stepped back reflexively and edged toward the open cell door. Strange, the look didn't seem friendly. Quite the opposite.

Then the creature's head fell back as if an invisible wire

had been cut, and the monitor alarm sounded loudly. The lines along the screen went wild, flickering up and down irregularly, then slowed precipitously. Scanlon fell to the floor. Resnick thought he was making too much of his show of emotion and was going to reprimand him when he took a second look and realized that Scanlon, now thrashing about, was holding both his temples in agony.

Resnick looked over at the creature. It was dead, and the cityscape on the screen was gone.

Susan knew something was wrong, though how she knew, she could not say. Something stronger than instinct took hold, and with it came the certainty that her presence in the sacred chamber had been detected. Then the dilemma arose: Should she use the blindfold to try to fend off their telepathic power, or should she try to escape? How could she get out if she couldn't see?

In the split second it took to form the question, she saw a blur of movement across the chamber, a glimpse of animal skin in the interstices between stalagmites. Just as panic was about to seize her, she felt a mental contact that was reassuring and told her she had nothing to fear. The figure that stepped out into the open was Leviticus. She felt like running over and hugging him, but her relief did not last long; she saw from his agitation that he, too, was aware that danger was approaching.

Leviticus led the way to a dark side passage. With one hand she felt the rock wall; her other hand was in his grasp as he moved ahead, and though his fingers were short, they were as strong as an eagle's talons. He was moving upward along a path that followed an incline and seemed to be a little-used back passageway. From time to time he stopped briefly, and though she could not see him, she knew he was reading the route ahead, probing it with his psychic radar and trying to assess the risk.

After five minutes Susan heard sounds coming toward them. She turned to flee but Leviticus held her hand so tightly she could not extricate herself. She tried to pull her hand away but his grip was so strong that she thought her bones would crack. She flattened herself against the wall and waited. She could hear them coming but could see nothing. She felt the bulk of Leviticus's body ahead of her and wondered if he was planning an ambush. She closed her eyes and held her breath. Now they were only a few feet away.

"Susan, thank God!"

"Oh, Matt!"

In the darkness she felt his arms around her and smelled his familiar odor. Leviticus still held on to her hand. Hurt-Knee and Lancelot were there too.

"Why the hell did you go off like that?"

"I had to look at it one more time to see the final piece of the puzzle."

This was no time for questions about the Enigma. "Listen," Matt said in a tone of urgency, "something's happened to them. They're all in a frenzy."

"I think I know what happened. Kee-wak sensed that I was in the chamber."

"No, they didn't look like that. It wasn't as if there was an emergency. It was as if they had suddenly learned something bad—all of them at the same time. It reminded me of the way the tribe reacted when Longface died. I think that somewhere one of these creatures died—died or was killed."

"What do we do?"

"What we came here to do," Matt said firmly. "Stick together, and for God's sake don't go wandering off again." With that, the group continued up the incline, following Hurt-Knee, who seemed to know exactly where he was going.

Even before he heard the commotion, Van knew that he was losing it. Maybe knowing that you're losing it means you're not really losing it, he consoled himself. He said it out loud—what difference did it make if he talked to himself out loud? They couldn't understand him anyway, the pricks. But people who are going insane know on some level that they're going insane. It's not as if the knowledge means anything; it's not like it's protection. In a situation like this there is no protection. How could there be any when you're helpless at the bottom of a pit, trapped like an ant?

Van thought back to his graduate-student days and the caged monkeys he experimented on. How touching it was to walk past the wire cages of those half-crazed primates. They would fall back, cringing in terror, sometimes covering their heads with their hands, sometimes rocking and sucking their thumbs. He remembered one in particular that paced around in circles, always in the same direction, always at the same speed, hunching its shoulders as it took the corners each time in exactly the same way. As he watched it Van knew that it was dealing with insanity, that the ritual motions were a way both of keeping madness at bay and giving in to it. Maniacal energy was all that was left. It was the only rational-irrational response. Now he felt like that himself.

He was afraid to sleep. Almost every time he tried, he experienced that strange Cheyne-Stokes breathing business. You begin to fall into unconsciousness and just as you lose your footing and start to sink down, your breathing cuts off and you come up to the surface gulping for air. After a while the panic sets in even before you start to fall off so that it keeps you awake, like a little bell that goes off the moment your head slumps. His head ached all the time now.

That big fellow, whatever his name is, rules over everyone like a god. When he stands below the Bear, he becomes the Bear: huge, strong, indomitable. How wrong I was to come here thinking I'd be stronger than they are. Up here on the mountain all the inconsequentials drop away and real strength shows itself. Humans are weak—nothing. Sickness is a weakness and weakness is a sickness.

A commotion began. Van knew immediately that it was connected with death. A full moon, perhaps, the time for sacrifice, and surely this time it would be his turn. When his pacing took him to the far corner of the pit, he could see the wall where his head would hang. He was thankful he had fallen from the ledge after they'd killed the Russian. Otherwise he would have witnessed the final ceremony. What was it exactly that they did?

He knew he was subject to delusions. They had begun in a minor way during the ascent up the mountain but had gathered force with everything that had happened since: the panicky flight, the cave-in, the captivity, the sacrifice. Now the delusions were full blown, strung together around the constant thread of his terror, and they were the only things that seemed real. He couldn't tell where they began and where they ended, just as he couldn't tell when he was awake and when he was having a nightmare. But this was different; now he was actually hearing voices. "Van!" There, he heard it again, his name urgently whispered. How could the creatures know his name? It had to be his mind turning against him, as always his own worst enemy.

"It's no good," Matt muttered. "He can't hear us. Either that or he's gone totally around the bend."

"What now?" said Susan. She leaned around the edge of the passageway to look into the cavern and was immediately sorry that she did. The creatures were doubly frightening seen from ground level, especially now that they were racing around in such agitation. The beehive was quaking, as if someone had tossed it into the air and stabbed it with a pitchfork. But it can't be our presence, she thought, because then they would simply zero in on us and wipe us out. The cured skins hanging on the rock walls were as thick as medieval tapestries, and she realized with a suppressed shudder what superb hunters they must be in using their telepathic communication. It would be impossible to escape their dragnet once they tuned in to her and read her perceptual field. But now hundreds of them were sharing the same room with her and Matt and in their preoccupation didn't notice them. "Maybe we can use this confusion to our advantage," she said.

Matt got down on all fours and peered around the rock slab. There was a small enclosure, an antechamber to the passageway that was out of view of the main cavern. He looked around for Van's guards. One had left and the other seemed as flummoxed as the rest of the creatures, holding its club but walking distractedly close to the edge of the pit, some eight feet away.

Matt stood again. "Let's go," he whispered. He looked in all directions and slowly slipped out into the cavern, sticking close to the rock face. Like a shadow he glided across until he made it into the antechamber. Susan followed, then the three hominids, who simply walked across as if they had every right to be there.

The enclosure was darker than the cavern. Susan and Matt got their blindfolds ready. Now for the risky part. Matt looked out of the chamber at the back of the guard and pushed Lancelot and Leviticus in the direction of the pit. As they approached, he crouched down on one leg in his hunter's posture. He tried to concentrate as he had done with the animals, staring at the back of the guard's head, concentrating on images of clubs and spears and blood, trying to send the message without words: attack, attack, attack. As the two drew closer, the guard turned and there was a flicker of confusion on his features as the clubs came down neatly and quickly, one in the nook of his shoulder, the other across the top of his skull. He fell instantly and Lancelot lifted one of his legs to roll him into the pit.

Matt slunk out of hiding, ran to the pit, and ducked down behind the legs of his two cohorts. He was not totally hidden but it would have to do. As he leaned over and looked down, Van jumped back, his mouth open, a wild look in his eyes. His face was black with dirt, his clothes in tatters. Hurriedly Matt uncoiled the rope, tied it to a rock, and dropped it to him. "C'mon, Van, quick. Grab it, man, and let's get out of here!" he said as loudly as he dared. Van stared back, uncomprehending. "The rope, the rope! Take the rope!"

Before Matt knew what was happening, Susan was at his side. Matt jumped into the pit, shook Van, brought him over to the rope, and gave him a fireman's boost. Like a sleepwalker, he ascended the first few feet until he was within range of Susan's outstretched arm. Matt flexed his shoulder muscles and boosted him higher. Slowly, by reflex rather than design, Van eased one knee up onto the edge while Susan hauled him upward, and then abruptly he was out and sprawling on the ground. Matt was next. "For God's sake, hurry!" Susan whispered, glancing around fearfully. So far none of the creatures had spotted them. Matt moved up the rope swiftly, using the knots to boost himself. He grabbed the edge with both hands flattened against the dirt and Susan tugged on his collar. He was up. Fighting down the impulse to bolt, they moved slowly back to the passageway on either side of Van, practically carrying him. The hominids moved so quickly behind them that Matt feared they would attract attention.

Inside the passageway, they paused and looked back. The cavern was still in chaos. Matt saw four creatures rushing out of the sacred chamber. Hurt-Knee was already off, moving down the tunnel like a deer in flight, the others right behind him.

Their retreat should have gone quickly. They had Hurt-Knee to show them the way, the tunnels were running downhill, and they had their panic to propel them. But Van hampered them; it was not that he wasn't terror-stricken enough to flee—terror was all he knew—but that he was in no condition to run. His legs moved but they wouldn't support him, buckling uselessly like tires in mud; he needed a hominid on either side to hold him upright and carry him forward. Susan turned to look at his face. It had always been hard to read Van's emotions, but now he displayed only blankness. It's totally empty, she thought; something has happened to him—he's burned out.

They came to a large tunnel that seemed familiar. It appeared to be the large central passageway, lit by torches in niches, that they had run through a few weeks ago. After five minutes, just when they were hoping to slow down, the hominids suddenly put on an extra spurt, as if they had clicked into a higher gear. With a sickening feeling in his gut, Matt realized why. "We're being chased," he said breathlessly to Susan, gesturing with his head to Hurt-Knee and the others. "They've just picked it up"—he gestured to the hominids—"that the renegades are on to us and know where we are." He thought back to the four creatures he had seen running out of the sacred cavern, certain that they were the pursuers.

At that moment, Hurt-Knee turned off into a smaller side tunnel which, after a hundred yards, split into two similar-looking passages. They paused for a moment, then took the one to the left, all but Leviticus, who came to a halt. He stood his ground, purposefully.

"What's he doing?" gasped Susan.

"I don't know, but we can't stop," Matt answered. "Just keep going."

They ran on, Hurt-Knee now taking Leviticus's place on one side of Van and, with Lancelot, dragging him along like a heavy gunnysack. Susan led, and felt a surge of strength in her legs. The adrenal gland kicking in its last resources, she thought, until she realized it was an altogether different sensation, that familiar flooding up again, and she knew where it was coming from—Leviticus. He's the decoy, she thought. He's sacrificing himself for us. As she ran on, she felt as if a powerful underground wind was sweeping her onward, a warm flow of energy that spread from the core of her brain through her muscles and her bones. She was no longer fleeing through a tunnel, she was flying through a meadow. Her feet barely touched the ground; she felt as light as a thistle seed rising in air currents.

Then, abruptly, the sensation departed and she felt a void just as they saw a shimmering wall of light ahead of them and staggered to it, finally emerging into daylight. The sun blinded them. Standing at the cave entrance with the valley before them, Matt took in great gulps of air. Van was in a daze, and Hurt-Knee and Lancelot were distraught.

"Where's Leviticus?" Matt asked.

"Dead," said Susan, surprising even herself by the monotone of her voice. She felt stricken, hollow.

"We'll all be dead soon," said Van, speaking for the first time. "We haven't a chance."

Susan whirled around and gave him a look that silenced him.

The light was tricky. It was already late in the day and the sun was beginning to recede behind the crest of the mountains. It seemed chillier than when they had entered the cave, and deadly quiet. Their pursuers were still coming through the tunnels.

This time the hominids had no choice but to cross the forbidden burial ground. As they set foot over an invisible line, their fear could be read in every reluctant step. Overhead, the vultures still circled. No grave keepers were in sight, but their absence was as forbidding as their presence had been before. Despite the late-afternoon chill, the hominids were sweating and kept their eyes averted from the bundles in the trees and the bones scattered on the ground. Van was wide-eyed; it was impossible to know how much he was taking in.

Halfway across the burial ground, Matt looked back and saw the creatures emerging from the cave, brandishing their weapons. Even from a distance their rage was visible. The rage was a good sign; it meant they would not break the taboo and cross the sacred ground. Somewhere among the barren trees he heard a steady breathing but he could not tell whether it was from the grave tenders or from animals.

In the gathering twilight, the village was uncharacteristically quiet. At first it seemed to be deserted, but then they realized that most of the hominids were in their huts. No one came out to greet them, and Kellicut was nowhere in sight. Van was acting strangely; when he spoke, he often did not make sense. A place to sleep was found for him and he quickly dropped off into a stupor.

As darkness descended, Hurt-Knee and Lancelot fell ill. They collapsed in their bowers, at first listless and then delirious with fever. Matt thought they were reacting in some way to their transgression in trespassing upon the burial ground, but he could not be sure. Others in the tribe also seemed spiritless.

Later that night as he and Susan lay in each other's arms, they talked about Leviticus. She was inconsolable. "I'm sorry about him," said Matt. "I know how you felt about him. What he did was heroic. It has to make us question our ideas about how primitive these hominids are."

"That kind of heroism has to rank higher on the scale of evolution than killing animals and curing hides."

"Maybe. Or maybe altruism is more basic than we realize. Do you remember those studies of wolves hunting caribou? The leader of the wolf pack communicated in some way with the weakest caribou, actually sent a message so that the caribou fell back and accepted its fate, sacrificing himself for the herd."

"Perhaps. But that doesn't take away from individual heroism. It makes the whole species more heroic. Maybe we still have some of that in us too, even without the telepathic power."

They heard the sound of drums from up on the mountain. This had not happened before. As they listened, they imagined the ferocious creatures pounding with bones on tightly drawn skins. The sound throbbed and echoed, which meant that the drums were being played inside the tunnels. Then from somewhere else, deep inside the bowels of the earth, they could detect another rumble, and then a trembling. In an instant they realized it was an earthquake.

Eagleton knew he was needed. It was one of those rare situations where his presence on the scene was required; it was time to take charge. There was simply too much at stake, and too much had gone wrong already. First Van was missing, then the NOMAD transponder blanked out, then the damned creature died in captivity and zapped that worker, whatever his name was—Scanlon; it took him days to recover. Who would have supposed that it had such power? There was more to this remote viewing than met the eye, he mused, pleased with his pun.

The DNA report was in; the creature had twenty-three pairs of chromosomes, just like a human. Ninety-eight percent of his DNA was identical to ours. Of course that's true of chimpanzees too, he thought; it's the remaining two percent that counts. The report came back with a scribbled note from the lab technician: *I give up. What the hell is it?*

So Eagleton decided to go himself to the base camp Kane had set up at the foot of the mountain. The problem was, he hadn't been off the campus in years. In fact, with his small apartment linked by an underground passage and an elevator for his wheelchair, he hadn't even been out of the building, so all sorts of arrangements were required to make the trip with a minimum of psychological stress: a van with darkened windows and a hydraulic lift for his chair, a private jet with the seats cleared and straps to hold his chair in place, diplomatic clearance so the aircraft could set down for refueling and then be on its way again. He had never been to Tajikistan and had to admit he didn't like the sound of the place. Too many foreigners, too many flies, too many germs.

III

THE BATTLE

23

The tremors continued through the night and into the next morning but finally tapered off by noon. A chill wind was blowing through the valley, making the leaves shiver and turning up their green-silver undersides as if a storm was brewing. Matt and Susan walked through the village to survey the destruction. Four or five huts had collapsed when the branches that served as beams had snapped, twisting into a splay of yellow fibers, and rocks and debris littered the paths. But the village survived largely intact. Few hominids ventured outside; only children could be seen here and there, fetching water in gourds from the stream or running from one hut to another.

An earthquake was even more terrifying in the high wilderness of the mountains. It was like some primal turbulence between the peaks and the stars, with trees swaying, rocks shifting, and a sickening sense that there was only you and the earth, and that the earth could open at any moment and send you plummeting into a fiery chasm. No wonder humans invent gods, Matt thought.

They looked in on Hurt-Knee and Lancelot. They were being tended by other hominids, who brought them apples, nuts, and water. They were better than they'd been the night before—their fevers seemed to have broken—but they were still lying down and appeared weak and shaken. Susan did not know what had caused their collapse, whether it was attacking Van's guard, abandoning Leviticus to a cruel death, crossing the burial ground, or a combination of everything. She looked for signs that the hominids regarded her and Matt differently, perhaps blaming them on some level, but saw none.

Kellicut was a different matter. He was not in the village, so they went to look for him, taking the path that led to the sulfurous lake and geyser. They went down the wet steps toward the basin and found themselves on a wide ledge that cut deep into the rock face. In the center, sitting with his legs crossed, was Kellicut.

"We need to talk," said Susan.

"It's a little late for that."

She walked over and sat down next to him, with Matt on her other side, and remained for a moment in an awkward silence. None of us have secrets anymore, Matt thought.

Susan broke the silence. "We got Van out."

"And now what?"

"I don't know."

Kellicut sighed wearily. "That's the whole point. You don't know, do you?" As he turned to look at her, his features seemed more sorrowful than angry. Suddenly he appeared old.

"It seemed like the right thing to do," said Susan. "We couldn't just leave him there."

"I suppose not—not if you felt about it as strongly as you obviously did. I'm sorry you ever came here."

"Don't say that."

"Why not? It's true."

"Are you trying to hurt us?"

"No, though I don't care if I hurt you or not. I'm simply stating a matter of fact. If you hadn't come, none of this would have happened. You wouldn't have disrupted everything."

"Disrupted everything," interjected Matt. "You always

talk as if there were some sort of grand plan.''

Kellicut looked at him for the first time. ''You haven't understood from the beginning.''

''Understood what?''

''The whole design, the historical sweep, the extraordinary privilege of being here and being able to witness it. It was like going back fifty thousand years.''

''I think we understand that,'' said Susan.

''No, because if you had, you wouldn't have interfered. That was the cardinal rule: Don't get involved, don't take sides. But you took the side of the pacific hominids. I can see the temptation, of course. They're wonderful souls—truly innocent, truly good, nobler by far than Rousseau's noble savage—but they weren't meant to prevail. If nature had wanted them to come out on top, she would have given them the wherewithal to do so.''

''How can you be so sure?'' asked Matt. ''Who are you to interpret nature's intentions?''

''I'm not *interpreting*. I'm merely watching. If you open your eyes and look around, you'll see that nature has already made her choice, and, as always, she sided with the strong.''

''Maybe the strong shouldn't always survive,'' Susan argued.

''*Shouldn't* doesn't have anything to do with it. They're strong because they're supposed to be strong. If the renegades pick the others off one at a time, it's because they're destined to. If they attack them and wipe them out all at once, they're meant to. Everything is unfolding according to nature's plan. Don't you see that? You've blundered into this world at a critical moment, a hidden world that has stood suspended for thousands of years, and now in a split second it's about to transform itself. A species is going to reinvent itself, shed its old self like a used skin and become something greater, something more advanced, and you're here to witness it. But you're here at that world's sufferance and the ground rule is simple: *Stay out of it*. It's a precarious equilibrium, so don't mess with it. And you did.''

In their mutual anger they fell silent. Then, calmly, Matt asked, ''What happens now?''

Kellicut shrugged. ''Who knows? If I had to bet, I'd say that you have provoked a war that's going to bring disaster down upon us all. You've gone into their lair and attacked them, so now they will attack you and the ones who have befriended you. Then, of course, you'll try to defend your friends, which will only make everything worse.''

''Let me ask you something,'' said Matt. ''What if *we* are part of the design? What if nature *intended* us to rectify the balance?''

Kellicut stood up, livid with anger. ''That's the most preposterous, arrogant idea I've ever heard.'' As he strode in a circle around Matt he looked as if he were about to take a swing at him. ''Who the hell do you think you are?'' He stood directly over him and glowered down. ''Do you remember our first conversation here? That day you met me, right over there?'' He pointed outside. ''I told you then that you had found Eden, and I warned you to beware of the snake. You asked me what the snake was. Well, now you know, and if you want to see it, I suggest you take a good long look in the lake on your way out.'' He turned on his heel, stalked over the rock, hoisted himself up, and disappeared in the direction of the waterfall.

Kellicut's injunction started Susan thinking, though not in the way he had intended. She *did* stop to see her reflection in the lake, and as she looked she was disturbed by his accusation, because on one level he was right, of course. They *were* interlopers, and they had disturbed the equilibrium of this primordial world, setting off repercussions difficult to foretell, as surely as a rock dropped at this end of the lake would send ripples to the farthest shore. But what else could they have done? Let Van die a grisly death to uphold some abstract scientific principle? And now that they were in it up to their necks, how could they possibly withdraw and leave the hominids here at the mercy of the renegades?

Susan knelt down on one knee and sifted through the sand on the shore of the lake. It's morality that sets us apart from the beasts of the jungle, she reflected, that and the certain knowledge of our own deaths. Morality and mortality, the twin pillars of civilization. Doesn't it all count for anything—language, learning, inventiveness, scientific discoveries, medicine, Ptolemy, Galileo, Newton, Pasteur, Einstein? She thought about the wheel, mankind's first advance, then looked down at the sand; it was strange to find sand here. The Egyptians, she recalled, were the ones who discovered that the unlikely mixture of sand and ash makes glass. The stained-glass windows of Chartres. Paint the back in silver and you have a mirror. Narcissism. And now we are looking into our innermost selves—DNA, our genes. She remembered that she had a pocket mirror in her rucksack. Serpent or no serpent, she thought, the tree of knowledge must be worth something.

The hut where they had left Van was empty, but they found him not far away on the banks of the stream. He was drinking with his head half submerged, and when they approached he started like an animal at a water hole, then lowered his head again the way a whipped dog does. Far from being grateful for being rescued, he seemed resentful, as if it were their fault that he had been captured in the first place.

"Did you run out on me?" he demanded, not looking either of them in the eye.

"Run out? Hell, no," replied Matt. "We were lucky to get away at all."

"You're right about that. A lot luckier than me."

"We thought you were dead."

"Oh, yeah? If you thought I was dead, why did you finally decide to come get me?"

"We learned that you weren't."

"I'll bet."

Upset by Van's truculence, Susan left. Matt took him for a walk in the woods, and as they followed a path—Van with a limp that gave him a loping gait like one of the creatures—Matt realized that Van had not asked any questions about the hominids, Kellicut, or the valley. He was obsessed only by his captivity.

They came to a grove with a fallen tree. Sitting down on it, Matt looked intently at him and put the question that had been on his mind for some time. "Tell me, back before the cave-in, when we were running through the tunnel, do you remember when we were hiding?" Van nodded. "Why did you tell us to close our eyes?"

Van cackled. "There's so much you don't know. You don't have a clue, do you? You think you're so smart, but you don't know a damn thing."

Matt held himself in check. He needed answers more than the ego gratification of lashing out at this pathetic man. "So why don't you enlighten me?"

"Why don't you figure it out for yourself?"

"I have, for the most part."

"And?"

"And it's clear that from the beginning you were lying to us and using us. You knew all about the Neanderthals. You knew they really existed. You and Eagleton were playing a little charade with that skull. You didn't need it as confirmation of their continued survival because you already had some kind of proof. Hell, you were probably already experimenting on them."

Van remained mute.

"Which means you already knew about their special mental powers," Matt said. "Why else close your eyes when you're being pursued? What I don't get is, if you already had some, why did you need more?"

"Simple: We only had *one*, and one's not enough. Operation Achilles, it was called. You can't understand RV unless you have two of them: one to send and one to receive. Otherwise, it's hopeless, the old one-hand-clapping.''

"RV?"

"Remote viewing. That's a scientific term you should become acquainted with.''

"I've seen it in action. I can imagine all kinds of reasons why types like you would want to acquire it.''

"It could be useful. Useful, hell. It would mean no other country could ever challenge us. At the very least we had to be sure no one else got it.''

"The Russians.''

"Right.''

"And they got here ahead of you.''

"I don't know that. They weren't even supposed to mount an expedition.''

"Who is behind the Institute?"

"Who do you think? The government. Not the CIA exactly, more of an offshoot, although there's always a lot of fighting over that.''

"Why?"

"Use your head. Psi research has always been big: extrasensory perception, telekinetic powers, nonverbal communication, UFOs—a lot of that; we practically wrote the book on the Roswell incident—alien sightings, transmogrification of matter. You name it, we've done it.''

"But the name: Institute for Prehistoric Research?"

"We've used a lot of different names over the years—different names, different college campuses. For a long time in the seventies we were the Institute for Investigation into Paranormal Phenomenology. When this cryptozoology broke, it was important enough to surface under a new name.''

"And Eagleton?"

"A spook. An old Cold Warhorse.''

Matt danced around the question that was forming in his mind. "Let me ask you something else.''

"Feel free,'' Van replied sarcastically.

''If you knew where these creatures were, why send Kellicut?''

''The whole point was we didn't know. The one we got was an accident. This is a big place, in case you haven't noticed. We needed Kellicut to lead us to them. He was our point man.''

''Did *he* know about the CIA?''

Van produced a crooked smile. ''No, he's as dumb as he looks. He's. in it for the science, just like you guys.''

Matt exhaled slowly with relief.

''Why did he send the skull?''

''To throw us off the track. He sent a note with it saying that all the Neanderthals were dead, that this was the last one. He knew we'd date it.'' Van sneered. ''He didn't know we had already captured one.''

''So he didn't send the skull to us?''

''No.''

''He didn't ask for us at all?''

''No.''

''But we got a note. Susan got it at the hotel in Khodzant when Sharafidin slipped it under her door.''

''That wasn't Sharafidin. It was me.''

''It was Kellicut's handwriting.''

''Forged.''

''Why?''

Van grinned again. ''To make sure you'd come. One more piece of bait. I thought you might back out.''

Matt was quiet. Everything was falling into place now. As he thought back over the events since they began their ascent, Van cackled again. ''I know what you're thinking,'' he said.

''What?''

''The NOMAD.''

''That's right.''

''You think it's dead. You're wrong. It's been beaming its location all this time.''

Matt felt a quiver of fear. "Beaming it to who?" he asked.

"Whom," Van corrected. "Whom do you think? Eagleton, the Institute, the U.S. Marine Corps, the whole goddamn world."

"So they could be on their way right now?" Matt was aghast.

"They are on their way. I wouldn't be surprised if they showed up in a few days."

Matt cursed. "They'll bring the whole thing down. They'll stop at nothing to get the power. They'll hunt down every last one if they have to."

He looked squarely at Van. He remembered an academic paper of Van's he had once read on nonverbal communication among the !Kung bushmen, the brilliance and scientific promise it revealed. "What about you?" he demanded. "Doesn't science mean anything to you?"

"Yes," Van retorted evenly, "it does. Everything. My whole life. Science is the only thing between us and chaos. It gives us control, protection, power."

Matt walked back toward the village, not caring if Van came along or not, but the man followed close at his heels, again the beaten cur.

"I'll tell you something else," Van said, pointing up to the moon taking shape in the darkening sky. "See that? In another few days it will be a full moon. That's why they were getting ready to sacrifice me. Now they'll have to come down here to get me—or get someone else."

In his small frontline headquarters, as he liked to think of it, Eagleton was ensconced like the proverbial bullfrog on a lily pad. The building was a Quonset hut especially adapted to his requirements. It had a concrete floor so he could spin his chair around, but there was no protective shield of disinfectant. To his horror, he had found a spider lurking in a corner web in the first two hours.

The trip had been rough. With his chair strapped in the

center of the plane, he felt conspicuous, at stage center, while various assistants moved in and out of their seats, pouring drinks, flirting, gossiping. Some of the gossip was about him, he was sure. He didn't sleep for fear that he would look ridiculous slumped there, possibly with his mouth open. As expected, when he was carried off the plane he sensed the darting looks. He had missed most of the scenery, and the two windows in the hut were too high to see out of easily. Even at the base of the mountain he felt the difference in altitude, but then he was especially sensitive to such changes.

And now he was dealing with Kane again, never a pleasant chore. The colonel had given him a rundown on the training. Reading between the lines, and not from anything the man said directly, it didn't sound as if the team was ready for action, at least on this kind of assignment. Now Kane had fallen silent as he looked at Eagleton's footlocker, which was upended and divided into shelves crammed with books. His eye had landed on the thick well-thumbed green volume of *On the Origin of Species*.

"Ever read it?" Eagleton demanded.

Kane shook his head.

"Pity. It's a remarkable book. It took Darwin two decades to produce it. He had all the ideas as soon as he stepped off the *Beagle*—we know that from his notebooks—but he dithered about with his studies on barnacles, falling ill at the drop of a hat, walking up and down the same garden path, becoming a recluse. Do you know what held him back all that time? I have a theory."

Kane shook his head again.

"His wife," said Eagleton. "His upright churchgoing wife. There he was, about to unleash the most subversive and powerful idea upon the world—the idea that man was not created by God or in God's image—and he was afraid of his wife." He exploded in laughter. "And I'll tell you something else I bet you didn't know." Kane looked bored. "Nowhere does he actually use the word 'evolution.' Because, you see, he did not conceive of nature's work as a progressive continuum, an ascent. All those drawings and cartoons that start with a lowly primate and end with *Homo sapiens* striding ahead confidently are misconceived. There are no such things as 'higher animals.' We're really all the same in this churning swamp. Some are on top in one millennium, others in another, but all of us are struggling, striving, and changing and none is inherently superior to another. There is no grand design.''

Eagleton could see that Kane wasn't interested and, in truth, he wasn't either. It was his usual gambit. ''Kane,'' he said with an air of finality, as if they had been talking about something else all along, ''today makes it five weeks since we lost contact. I want you and your men on that mountain tomorrow at first light.''

The same juices that made Eagleton babble on so nervously, that sense of being ready to leap over the edge toward unpredictable adventure, made Kane feel calm and in control. ''Yes, sir,'' he replied coolly.

The attack came at night. In their bower, Matt and Susan were not expecting it. The darkness was crystal clear with stars that stood out against the velvety blackness except in the west, where an almost full moon hovered above the valley's rim. There was no wind. The drums had stopped a few hours earlier, but Matt had scarcely noticed. Most of the hominids were in their huts. They had been acting listless since the drumming started that evening days ago, as if they were waiting for disaster to strike, but whether the atmosphere of resignation came from foreboding or from aftershocks of the earthquake was impossible to tell.

First came the screams. They were blood-lusty yells that struck the heart like arrows, a universal cry from vocal cords that Matt and Susan had never heard before, oddly low in pitch yet loud. They were instantly recognizable as the sounds of warriors charging and were followed by yelps of fear and pain and then the cries of mayhem, as clubs rained down upon bodies.

Susan was running by Matt's side, her hair streaming across her face; he could read the terror in her eyes and in the drawn lines of her pale cheeks. Seconds after fleeing they stopped beneath a tree at the top of a small hill and, looking back in the dim light at the bower a hundred feet away, thought they saw a thrashing, the branches and leaves collapsing, and the shadowy movement of squat bodies with a distinctive rolling lope poking around the debris. They waited a minute to catch their breath, then took a roundabout path that led to the village from behind.

It looked as if a hurricane had struck. Branches and rocks were scattered everywhere and huts were ablaze, sending columns of flame and smoke into the night sky. In the smoke haze, figures dashed around screaming. It was not hard to tell them apart; the attackers wore skins and their faces and upper torsos were smeared with gashes of red, blue, and black. They carried torches and heavy clubs, occasionally raising them to smash the supports of huts, bringing them down and then igniting them. Their bleeding victims were running in panic and frantically seeking escape in all directions.

In the center of the chaos, with the gun holster still around his neck, was Kee-wak, his eyes dark under the shadow of his brow ridges and his body glistening. He raised one hand in triumph, holding a club by the handle and shaking it at the night sky, and let out a ferocious scream of victory. At that moment, Matt and Susan saw a figure emerge from the shadows, moving slowly toward him and carrying a spear in one hand.

"Lancelot," whispered Susan, reaching for Matt's hand.

As the figure approached, Kee-wak broke off his scream and turned slowly toward him. Lancelot drew closer. All movement seemed to stop as the renegades froze and watched. Kee-wak stretched himself to his full stature, the black-and-white skin around his head glowing red in the fire, the feathers around his wrist bristling. He stood immobile except for his right arm, which lowered the club and held it behind him, ready to swivel with his pelvis, just as he had done in killing Rudy. Lancelot raised the spear in his right hand and approached still closer. Matt drew an imaginary trajectory through the air, straight at the jeering savage. He stared at Kee-wak's chest. *The heart,* he thought, *aim for the heart!* He tried to imagine Kee-wak falling backward, a look of surprise gripping his face, with his chest cavity torn open and spilling blood. Suddenly, almost imperceptibly, Kee-wak froze all but his head, turning it slightly to one side and then the other in that odd lizardlike movement, as if he were searching out something. For a moment he looked uncertain.

Then Lancelot let fly. The shaft flew through the air fast and powerfully. It arched gracefully, gathering speed as it went, but a split second before it found its target, Kee-wak, spinning faster than seemed possible, thrust up his club to meet it. He smashed it down and it landed with a rattle upon the ground. Kee-wak drew his lips back to show his yellow teeth and walked over to Lancelot, who stood his ground. As he raised up the club and brought it down, Lancelot lifted up an arm to deflect the blow, but there was a deathly crack as the heavy wood smote bone. Lancelot's arm fell to his side, and he crumpled to one knee from the pain. Kee-wak stood above him for a long moment before raising the club once again and bringing it down with a loud thwack on the back of Lancelot's skull. Lancelot fell face forward, spilling blood that soon formed a perfect circle around his head, like a red halo.

Matt felt Susan's grip tighten. He knew it wasn't safe to remain so near, but he felt they should withdraw slowly and tactically. Probably only the excitement of the raid and the thrill of the showdown between Lancelot and Kee-wak had prevented the creatures from detecting them so far. Even now, Kee-wak, standing over the lifeless body in triumph, and poking it with the tip of his club, had apparent fits of distraction, as if on some level he was already aware of them, and from time to time he raised his head in a way that made Matt's gut tighten, as if he were sniffing out invisible currents.

Matt could see that Susan was fighting panic, and he too tried to impose a calmness at the center of his being, out of fear—a superstition really—that panic would somehow attract attention, like a red flag fluttering in the breeze. Slowly they stepped backward in the underbrush, closing their eyes periodically, careful not to set any branches quivering.

Soon they came to the path again. It was dark now because the smoke from the huts blotted out the moon, so they could see only a few feet ahead and had to move cautiously. The screams and sounds of havoc receded as they followed the path, skirting the edge of the village and then approaching it from the other direction. On this side it appeared deserted. Susan stumbled and looked down; she had tripped over a body. She recoiled in horror and clasped her hands to her face.

"Matt, I don't think I can do this. I don't think I can take much more."

"I know. I feel the same."

"That was the most horrible thing I've ever seen. He's pure evil."

"And to think that Kellicut believes he is a higher specimen."

"Where is Kellicut?"

"I have no idea."

"What if they've got him?"

As if by some unspoken agreement, they turned and moved toward the village again, creeping behind the ruined huts. No one was about and the shouts sounded far away. The smoke hung low and dense, an acrid fog. They stopped to rest behind a hut and, crouching there in the darkness, heard a low moan from inside the hut. Slowly they moved around to the entrance.

Van was lying on the ground, rolling back and forth as if he were wounded. But in the moonlight they could see no blood. He gripped his temples with both hands and looked up at them with a hopeless and strangely vacant expression. They rushed over to him, one on each side, and sat him upright. His body was limp and he was perspiring heavily.

"What is it?" Matt asked. "For God's sake, are you hurt?"

Van nodded but it was hard to tell whether he was trying to say yes or no. He gulped with difficulty, as if preparing to talk, and then holding tightly on to Matt's arm, he said, "I told you they'd come. I knew they would. They're after me."

"Don't be crazy. You have no idea what they're after. If they wanted you, they'd know where to find you."

"They have." Van winced again, rubbed his eyes and steeled himself. He stood up, ran his fingers through his hair, then leaned down and swatted the dust out of his trousers, a gesture that Matt recalled from their first meeting at the dig in Djibouti. "Well," he said with an eerie calmness, "time to go. They're waiting right outside."

Susan and Matt moved to the edge of the hut and peered through the woven branches. The clearing outside that had been empty only moments before was filled. The creatures had arranged themselves in a semicircle facing the entrance. Suddenly the pounding of drums began only a few feet away, setting up a distant echo off the valley walls. Keewak stood directly in front of the hut, gripping the holster in one hand and his club in the other. He was standing on a log, which made him even taller; as he eyed the entrance expectantly, surrounded by the drumming, smoke, and fire, he looked like a demonic force of nature.

"This didn't work out the way it was supposed to," Van said at last. He looked them both in the eye and shook his head. "Remember that note you got back in the hotel?" he said. "That bit about some of us not being fit representatives of our species? I wrote that. And I was thinking of myself. But it's not true, you know." Then he squared his shoulders and stepped outside.

24

The moment they saw Van, the creatures froze. The drummers stopped with their hands in midair, the noise dropped away, and the dust and smoke floated in a night breeze that was soundless except for the distant crackle of flames. Van strode into the semicircle, an actor commanding center stage. Watching through the slats of the hut, Matt and Susan could see only the back of his head, held high, and his erect bearing. They thought they could read expressions of astonishment in the creatures' faces despite their heavy lines of ocher, which turned them into masks of childlike cruelty.

Van stopped directly before Kee-wak, now standing erect on the ground in front of the log, and looked him straight in the eye, not with Rudy's supplication but arrogantly. He turned his back on the huge creature to walk in a circle, and as he did so Matt and Susan saw his eyes were blazing. He completed the circle, stood again before Kee-wak, leaned back, and spat at him. The spittle landed on Kee-wak's cheek and dripped onto his painted chest.

The others sprang into action, as if Van's act of defiance had broken a spell, and surrounded him so that he disappeared under a tangle of flailing arms and clubs. At one point his head rose above the melee, held by a fist that clenched his hair. They pinned him to the ground, then clasped his hands behind his back and tied him to a wooden snare. They bent his legs back, until the knees snapped and he cried out in pain, and tied his feet to the back of his thighs so that he lay on the ground on his belly, trussed like a bird before the oven.

Van's mouth was unobstructed and he made the most of it. He screamed obscenities, half in hysteria and half in anger. Turning his head so he could look up at Kee-wak, he yelled, "You son of a bitch, we'll get you. Sooner than you think, we'll get you!"

Four of the creatures stooped, picked him up almost gently, and placed him upon the log, balancing him so that his head and neck extended into thin air. Then they unfastened the snare, wrapped his arms around the log, reattached it so that he was hugging the stump of wood, and brought a round rock, thin and as large as a flagstone, which they placed under his chin. Its edge was as sharp as a guillotine; merely swallowing made it cut into Van's throat, releasing a tiny trickle of blood that ran down his white flesh into the hair of his chest.

Van recited the Lord's Prayer. It came to him out of nowhere, his distant childhood, and he was not even aware that he knew the words. Then he quoted snatches of verse that flowed out in no particular order, a jumble of nursery rhymes, a bit of Yeats, a Shakespearean couplet. He sang "The Star-Spangled Banner," his voice cracking on the high notes.

The creatures sharpened sticks and propped them against the log to hold it in place while Van rattled on. He sang bits of "Onward, Christian Soldiers" as they pushed dirt against the log to steady it further; the dust rose up in a cloud around Van's face, but he continued singing. As the drummers started up again, Van sang the "Battle Hymn of the Republic" as counterpoint: "Mine eyes have seen the glory of the coming of the Lord . . ."

Out of the darkness stepped a creature carrying another heavy disk-shaped stone. As the drumming increased, he moved to the center of the clearing and stood in front of Van. Slowly, struggling, he raised the stone above his head as if it were a barbell and kept it poised over his head at arm's length, his feet shuffling in tiny steps to maintain his balance. Susan looked away but Matt felt he had to bear witness. "His truth is marching on—"

The stone came down with a force so strong that it turned into a blur. It struck deep into the spinal cord to smash against the rock below, then rested precariously on edge for a second before toppling over. When Susan looked up, Van's body, still strapped to the log, was headless.

The drumming struck a strange, arhythmic cycle. Kee-wak stood stock-still as the log before him rolled to one side and stopped when the body struck sideways upon the ground. Blood poured out of Van's severed jugular into the dust like wine from the neck of a smashed bottle. The executioner stooped, picked up Van's head by the hair, placed it in a large earthen bowl, laid the vessel at Kee-wak's feet, and stepped back as Kee-wak gave the long, deep bellow of the victorious warrior.

Matt had been too traumatized by what he had seen to think of moving, but now escape was the only thing to think about. As he turned his head from the slats to look about the hut, his heart sank; the sole exit was the door through which Van had walked, in full view of the creatures. It would be difficult to slip out through the woven branches at the rear, especially without making noise that would attract the killers. Susan was looking at the ground, trying to collect herself. She had heard the sounds outside and felt as deeply distressed as if she had watched the murder. Matt wondered if they could risk remaining where they were, hoping that the revelry outside would continue to occupy the creatures. And maybe Van had been right in thinking that the creatures had come for him alone.

But as soon as this thought crossed his mind, Matt knew it was not true. Already Kee-wak appeared restless, like someone about to scan the horizon who has been momentarily distracted. He lifted his protruding head, glanced around, and then, like a bloodhound homing in on the scent, fixed his eyes on the hut. Matt's legs went lifeless and his insides seized up. He felt the beginnings of a powerful flow of energy in his cerebral cortex and somewhere deep inside his brain stem. When he looked at Susan, the alarm in her eyes told him that she felt it too.

At this moment the executioner standing next to Kee-wak picked up the bowl with Van's head in it and held it aloft with one hand. With the other he reached in and raised up the bloody prize, tossing the bowl to the ground and reaching for a long thin sliver of flint as sharp as a stiletto. Turning the head upside down, he rested the point of the flint at the base of the cranium and was about to thrust it downward when suddenly, out of nowhere, a human voice rang out in song. It sounded like an echo of Van's singing and the executioner actually looked down, perplexed, at Van's face and lifeless dark lips. He was still looking a fraction of a second later when a whizzing sound rent the air, his chest exploded, and out of it sprang a slender wooden stalk, causing him to sink to his knees, making tiny gulps for air. There was still a look of incomprehension upon his face as he dropped Van's head and the flint, pitching forward into the dust and falling on the shaft so that it poked through his back.

The death of the executioner broke the murderous siege. The creatures tumbled over one another in their efforts to flee, abandoning clubs, torches, and drums and uttering small, high-pitched squeals of terror. The scramble kicked up a cloud of dust that enveloped the clearing and by the time it settled, covering the huts, bushes, and Van's body in a thin blanket of gray, all of them had disappeared and everything was quiet.

Matt and Susan cautiously made their way to the door and stepped outside. Looking in all directions, they saw and heard nothing. Suddenly the bushes across the clearing stirred as if brushed by a sudden wind, then parted, and out into the moonlight stepped a figure. It was another human. He was dressed in blue pants, a torn windbreaker, and thick boots, and slung across his chest was the band of a quiver filled with arrows. He carried a bow in one hand and with the other he waved lustily, as someone might who had crossed a desert, seen hundreds of mirages, and now finally has laid eyes on water.

Kane looked around. It was bleak up here, icy cold, and the sky had a grayness that was not from clouds obstructing the sun but from an emptiness that seemed to extend for miles in every direction. It's going to snow, he thought.

The Black Hawk helicopters had flown them up to Kellicut's camp. Kane had expected it to be deserted, and it was. The rest of the men were waiting in a lower field a hundred yards downhill from the choppers. He didn't want them traipsing all over the place, ruining clues in their ham-fisted fashion.

A sharp-eyed observer could pick up a lot of information. Kane had already established, for instance, that those other three scientists, Arnot, Mattison, and that fellow Van from the Institute, had been here. He knew it from the boot prints, discarded cans, and other garbage. Sodder had remarked that the transponder had already placed them here for at least one night.

Kane walked over to the lean-to, lowered his head, and ducked inside. It looked as if it had been ransacked. What animal would do such gratuitous damage? He thought back to that creature inside Resnick's cell, bound and lying on the cot.

Sodder walked over and handed him the portable phone. Kane knew who it was.

"Kane here. . . . We're there now. . . . There's not much, a small hut, some kind of larder in a tree. . . . Yes, there's a latrine, but no, I haven't investigated it. . . . Well, I just got here. . . . We'll contact you after we've looked around. . . . Roger, out."

He handed the phone back to Sodder, who had a smug look on his face. "You didn't tell him about the hole," he said.

"What hole?"

"That one over there in the middle of the campsite. The one that was dug up and filled in again."

Kane walked over to a little mound of freshly packed dirt. The son of a bitch was right. "Okay, big shot. Call the men over and tell them to start digging."

His name was Sergei, and he offered a big hand to Matt and Susan. "I'm sorry I arrived so late," he said somberly. "Your friend was already killed, but at least I got revenge." He held up the bow and arrow. "What do you think? This puts me ahead in the arms race, no?"

Sergei was about thirty-five, handsome in a Slavic way, with an open guileless face. He spoke nearly flawless English—from his studies in Britain, he told them. All the other members of the Russian expedition had perished, and his joy at finding other humans was palpable. "We've got to stick together," he said fervently. "Solidarity of the species, yes?" Susan glanced at his arm muscles, visible through a tear in his jacket, and was gratified to see that he was strong. Judging from the look of him, he had been through a rough time but apparently had emerged intact. He was sure to be resourceful, she felt.

Sergei held his exhilaration in check out of deference to Van's murder and to Matt and Susan's obvious distress over the attack upon the village. They looked over the battlefield. The moonlight was bright enough for them to see that the damage was extensive. Bodies were scattered about. The fires had by now burned down to embers that were going out rapidly.

In the center of the clearing, Van's headless body lay in a puddle of blood. They carried it to the stream. It was a grisly procession, with the three of them holding his trunk by the arms and legs and his head resting on his belly.

Under the branches of a juniper they dug a shallow grave, using stone axes. Susan wanted to cover the body with some sort of shroud but they did not have enough clothes among them, so she settled for covering his head with a rag torn from her shirt. Matt tossed in the dirt, which pressed the cloth tightly on Van's eyes and the indentation of his mouth, and Susan recited the Twenty-third Psalm, the only one she knew by heart. Then they patted the dirt on the top of the grave and walked back to the center of the village.

There, the hominids were already cleaning up the damage by the light from the moon. A dozen bodies including Lancelot's were lying side by side next to the large hut where Longface had died weeks before. Hurt-Knee, Longtooth, and Blue-Eyes, among others, had lived, though there were many wounded and there seemed to be even fewer women than usual.

The hominids appeared to be in deep mourning. Dark-Eye walked among them with his staff and stopped from time to time to touch one or two of them on the shoulder with an outstretched palm, a gesture that neither Matt nor Susan had seen before. The children, normally boisterous, were wide-eyed and subdued and helped carry off rocks and broken branches with solemnity.

Dark-Eye grabbed Susan by the arm and led her to the center of the village, where she saw what was troubling him. The fire had been extinguished. The raiders had thrown dirt in the pit, smothered the flames, and scattered the logs. This destruction of the central hearth, so carefully tended over countless generations, was an attempt to eradicate the soul of the tribe, she thought, and the little contact that she'd had so far with Kee-wak convinced her that he was malevolent enough to have plotted it. When she told the others about it, Sergei smiled and with a flourish produced a pack of matches. "Keep them," he said. "I ran out of cigarettes long ago." When Susan returned to the hearth, struck a match, and lit a piece of dry grass, the hominids fell back in amazement. Dark-Eye was watching her closely, and she handed the matches to him as a gift. He took them carefully, holding them in his cupped hands as if they were an offering from the gods, and placed them in his pouch.

Within minutes the fire was raging again, and on this particular night virtually everyone slept outdoors on the ground, close to it and to each other, extracting what little comfort they could from a communal strength and the simple fact that others too had survived the brutal assault. Moments before she fell asleep, Susan wondered about Kellicut. She had not seen him the entire night.

In the morning, Sergei joined Matt on a walk while Susan went to the lake. They had decided to leave while the hominids conducted the burials, a ritual that was bound to consume the day. Even at a distance they could hear the wailing. The Americans asked Sergei about his background and the Russian expedition.

"I work at the Darwin Museum in Moscow," he said. "We've heard tales of these extraordinary beings for years, going back as far as our records." A critical sighting came in 1925, when a mounted regiment headed by Major-General Mikhail Stephanovitch Topilski was chasing a band of White Russians high into the Pamirs. "The bandits hid in a cave, where they were attacked by these strange beings. They shot and killed one, and after they surrendered they took Topilski to see it. But his men couldn't carry the body out, so they buried it under a cairn of stone."

For three decades it had been politically impossible to investigate reports, but in 1958 the Academy of Sciences sent out a team under a botanist named K. V. Stanyukovitch. It was equipped with snares, concealed observation posts, telescopic lenses, trained sheepdogs, and even sheep and goats as bait, but it ended in failure. "Now I know why, of course. These Yeti knew everything about the movement of the hunters before they even got close."

The current expedition was sent simply because the Russians had heard that Washington was fielding one. Sergei, an anthropologist and mountain climber, was the deputy leader. They had started out nine weeks ago with guns, nets, traps, and other equipment, but when they came to the vine bridge they had had to leave most of it behind. Mysteriously, the leader insisted that they not store it but throw it into the ravine.

"Later we put our heads together and figured out that he had been afraid the equipment would fall into the hands of the Yeti. He always kept us in the dark. The rest of us didn't really know what we were looking for. We didn't even know these savage creatures possessed a higher power. There was a zoologist on our team, Dr. A. Shakanov, and he seemed to have a great deal of information about them, but he kept it to himself."

The team got trapped in a blizzard and lost practically everything, including their guns. They were able to salvage only the food they could carry. They found refuge in a cave and lived there for weeks, making excursions for wood to keep a fire going. As the wood got scarcer, the excursions got longer. One day the leader did not return. The zoologist, whose fear was contagious, insisted that they go out only in pairs. But the very next day the two who left did not come back.

"Now Shakanov and I were alone, and he finally explained everything to me; he told me there were reports from a survivor of a previous expedition about a strange power to see through another's eyes. He said this meant that we could never surprise them and that they could track us down anywhere. Our only hope had been superior weapons, but without the guns we were at their mercy."

Sergei insisted that they leave and descend the mountain. But soon they came to a slope so steep they had to climb. Shakanov got in trouble; he lost his footing and fell down twenty feet onto a narrow ledge. He could not go up or down, and he screamed, "Don't leave me!"

"I had a rope, so I lowered it down to him. He tied it around his waist and eventually I was able to hoist him back up. It took a long time and I was exhausted and having a strange sensation in my head. When I told him about it, he said this was a sign that the beasts were close."

The rest of that day the two climbed, but they did not get far. Finally they stopped to sleep for the night, taking turns on watch. When it was Sergei's turn he fell asleep. "Suddenly I heard something, and I woke up and saw him struggling with three or four of them. He shouted for help, but there was nothing I could do. When they carried him away he was still shouting, 'Help me, Sergei!' But I could do nothing, so I ran away."

Sergei ran and climbed throughout the night. He fell down a slope and hurt his shoulder. The next morning he came across a path that wound down the mountain. At the end was a crevice that brought him into the valley. Soon he encountered the hominids, who seemed different from the creatures who had killed his comrades, but he was still scared. He made a bow and arrow to catch game and lived in the wilds for weeks.

"Yesterday I felt the earthquake and heard the drums on the mountain, and I saw the other Yeti come in their skins and attack the ones here. They eat the brains, you know; that's what Shakanov told me."

Matt was impressed by Sergei and the matter-of-fact tone in which he delivered his narrative. He thought his story emblematic of human endurance. Perhaps it's that, a kind of atavistic refusal to give up, a perseverance against all rational odds, that marks us as the survivor species, he thought. Maybe we are evolution's chosen ones because we do not give evolution the choice to do away with us. We're always scheming, anticipating, playing the angles—history's original sharpies.

"This crevice, could you find it again?" Matt asked.

"That's the strange part," replied Sergei. "I went there only yesterday and it was completely blocked. The rocks above it had collapsed and filled it in.'' He paused. ''I thought it must have been done by the earthquake. Either that or—''

''Or what?''

''Or it was somehow done by the Yeti.''

''So there's no way out of the valley?''

''That's right. No way but one—through their cave.''

Kane had been right about the snow. It seemed to come down suddenly like a curtain dropping just as the helicopters lifted off. With the rotors spinning, the flakes spun against the windshield in great swirls, so that flying through them was like passing through a mixer of whipped cream. Kane had noticed that the chopper was struggling, and he was worried.

As if to substantiate his fears, the Black Hawk tilted to one side so that Kane's shoulder was pressed against the window beneath him. He felt cold wind rushing by his right ear. The aircraft seemed to be sliding as if it had hit a patch of ice, and the motor was laboring and complaining in a high-pitched whine.

''How high can this thing go?'' Kane shouted.

The pilot looked over at him, lifted off one earphone, and shouted back, ''What?''

''How high can this go?''

''Depends. This load, this speed, hovering, I'd say about twelve thousand feet.''

Kane looked over at the altimeter. It was showing 13,600. The pilot followed his eyes and grinned. ''I know,'' was all he said.

''So what do we do?''

The pilot lifted off the earphone and tilted his eartip with a forefinger. ''Hey?''

Kane shouted out the question again. Behind him he felt the men's faces turned toward the cockpit, their looks zeroed in on the instrument panel as if all those dials and needles and flip switches could tell them something.

"Your call," said the pilot. "We could turn back and wait for the storm to clear or I could chuck you out right here."

"Where are we?"

The pilot shrugged. Kane's exasperation was rising rapidly. "Have we reached the place where the transponder was?"

"Right down below."

"Can you radio the other chopper?" The pilot tried twice, then a third time. "Come in, X-Twenty-seven. Do you read?" He replaced the radio mike and said, unnecessarily, "Can't raise 'em."

"What do you suggest?"

Again the pilot shrugged. Kane felt anger flooding to his temples, which was not ideal, he knew, for making decisions. There was always the danger at a crossroads like this that momentary pique could push him into taking the wrong path. He chose such a path and knew an instant later that it was wrong, but it was impossible to turn back without losing face.

"Okay, set her down."

"It's gonna be hard. We'd better drop some stuff first. Even then you're gonna have to jump." Kane nodded a little too vigorously.

The chopper lowered blindly. The pilot was concentrating on the panel and on holding the stick steady. The aircraft was rocking, then bucking like a horse.

"Open the door!" shouted the pilot, nodding his head toward the rear. "Tell them to throw out whatever they can!"

Kane relayed the command. The door slid open with a bang and instantly the craft was filled with frigid wind and swirling snow. The gear fell noiselessly out the door and was instantly swallowed up in the whiteness.

"I'm gonna take you as low as I can, but I can't touch down," the pilot shouted. He was less cocky than before. He turned his head over his left shoulder and peered down.

Kane didn't like that; couldn't he tell where he was from the instruments? He peered down too. Nothing but whiteness. He felt as if he were on the prow of a boat searching the waters ahead for rocks. He had done that once long ago. Where was it?

Suddenly he did see rocks: ugly black surfaces rippling through the snow directly below them. The pilot cursed. The chopper slid over onto its side. Kane saw the blade tilting and spinning awkwardly. Then there was a tremendous sound, the gnarling and smashing of metal and a grinding that he felt up and down his spinal column as the body of the aircraft struck the rocks and then settled into them, moving in fits and starts, like an animal dying.

25

Before setting out for the lake, Susan had made a small bundle of some of her belongings: the pocket mirror, a comb, soap, and a sharp sliver of flint. She was wearing her last remaining pants, a faded pair of old blue jeans, and a flannel shirt that had shrunk. Following the path through the forest across a shaded floor of green dappled with sunlight, she worried, turning her fears over and over to examine them from every angle.

The evening before, Matt had told her about his talk with Van. She was aghast at the forgery of the note at the hotel and she didn't have to ask the significance of the transponder broadcasting its stationary location for weeks. "We've been used," Matt had said. "We're the wedge of a huge operation and it's going to come down on this mountain like an ax unless we can think of some way to stop it."

"The only way to stop it," Susan had said, "is to get out ourselves and meet them. That way we can divert them to somewhere else."

"We don't have much time," he had replied. "Only a few days at most."

"I need one more day here. I want to go to Dark-Eye. It's a long shot but maybe he can help me puzzle something out—something I saw in the cave." She described the

Khodzant Enigma to Matt in detail, especially the missing panels. She sketched it for him as best as she could remember, emphasizing the portrait of the lone enraged Neanderthal at the end. She knew that the Enigma was itself a key that would unlock a larger enigma.

"How do you know?" Matt had asked.

"I just do," she had replied. "Maybe ESP."

"C'mon, Susan. We've enough problems. Don't turn psychic on me."

She carried the sketch on her now, and she pulled it out and looked at it. Not a bad rendition. She bristled at the memory of Matt's remark. He was afraid, no doubt, and she had to admit that she was too. So many things were going wrong. She worried that Van's people would decimate the tribe. And she doubted that the renegades' raid upon the village was the last that they would see of them. The shock of Sergei's attack was bound to wear off, and whatever had turned them into predators had been aroused; their blood was up.

She needed to think. At the lake she chose a secluded spot—curiously, modesty had not totally abandoned her—unbuttoned her blouse, and hung it on a branch. She unzipped her blue jeans, slipped out of them and her panties, dipped her feet into the water, felt around for secure footing, and stepped in. Though it was warm, her nipples hardened as she felt the tingle of rising bubbles. When she began to tire, she stepped out and washed her body with soap and then floated out into the lake again.

Despite her palpable fear, Susan knew she was about to leave a contentment she had never known before. It was hard to separate the strands that wove it together. Certainly there was the professional side, the fact that a lifetime of scientific curiosity had been rewarded by the discoveries here. Then there was the confidence that came from living by her wits and surviving in the wilderness. But on a deeper level she had experienced a serenity that was new to her, as if her demons, that horrible floating anxiety that used to descend out of nowhere, had at last been exorcised.

One reason was this incredible valley, which opened doors to a wider universe. She felt connected to life and death in a new way, not as an insignificant speck of bone and gristle that passed through in an eye blink but as part of an eternal unfolding evolution. Life *did* have meaning after all. It was like climbing a mountain to reach a peak from which all the slopes and hills you have scaled can be seen; as you gaze upon them you realize that your past has not gone but is there spread out before you, frozen in time and infused with meaning.

Her relationship with Matt had deepened. She was certain of this. She knew it from what she felt when she looked at him, and what she knew he was feeling when he looked at her. "Love comes in at the eye," Yeats had written.

She sat on a log and cut her hair with the flint, shagging it in layers, checking every so often in the pocket mirror. She stared at herself, a piece of wet hair hugging one cheek, a dark green eye radiating out from a black pupil. With the heavy feel of the flint in the other hand, a pleasing frisson ran through her; she felt primitive, earthy in her nakedness, strong, and sensual. She propped the mirror on the ground and followed her reflection up her body, her thighs, her ribs, her breasts. Where had she done this before? Back in that hotel room in Khodzant, so long ago, when she was a different person.

Suddenly Susan felt she was not alone. She turned; there on the crest behind her, leaning against a tree trunk, was Kellicut. He did not wave or nod; he simply stared. She grabbed her clothes, annoyed. Still, much as she didn't look forward to it, she needed to talk to him—she hadn't seen him since before the raid. But when she looked for him, he was gone, as quickly as the shadow of a cloud upon the valley floor.

She dressed slowly and carefully, deep in thought. She knew, suddenly, what she had to do. Slipping the mirror in the front pocket of her jeans, she struck out on the path to the village.

Dark-Eye was inside his hut. Whether he had known she was coming or not, she could not tell, but he watched her enter with his good eye. She sat down, reached into her pocket, pulled out the sketch of the Enigma, and set it down on the ground before him in a shaft of light from the open door. He peered at it for a long time, expressionless. Then he stood up slowly, and as she rose also he fixed his claw-like hold upon her arm and led her outside.

They took a path Susan had never seen before, through foliage that was pungent and choking. It rose steeply out of the forest, and as they approached the valley wall, it was cluttered with rocks and scree and cut by ruts from rainwater, so that the going was difficult. She was amazed at how agile Dark-Eye was; he threaded his way ahead of her effortlessly so that soon she was out of breath. He used his staff like a walking stick, and even when she lost sight of him she could hear it strike the ground as if he were summoning her.

Before long they were on a slope of scrub grass and then above the treetops. At the top of the pinnacle was a cave, where he waited for her. The jagged peaks loomed high and seemingly close. One outcropping of white stone caught her eye; it protruded from the enveloping rock like a bone and was shaped with a ridged curvature. She looked at it a long time; it seemed oddly familiar. As a cover of mist moved away so that it stood out starkly against the blue sky, she thought it resembled nothing so much as the back of a clenched fist.

Dark-Eye led the way into the tiny cave, whose narrow entrance made Susan feel claustrophobic. It smelled of musk. There were boulders for them to sit upon, facing each other. When her eyes became accustomed to the light, she could see a cracked and yellow pile of bones in one corner, ancient by the look of them. Now the old hominid before her looked shrunken, sitting on a boulder with his back against the cave wall. He removed his pouch, set it carefully on the floor, and opened it to reveal a bundle of vine leaves. He stripped them away as if he were peeling a banana and held up a leaf with a small ember, still red and glowing. From a corner he picked up a handful of brown leaves, placed them in a small pile, and ignited them with the ember. He blew upon the tiny blaze until it crackled and caught. Leaning forward on his boulder, he inhaled the smoke deeply. When she did the same, she felt a surging in her lungs and a dizzying rush to her head.

Dark-Eye crumbled a piece of the brown leaf into one palm, produced a pipe from his pouch, filled it with the leaf, lit it and took three or four deep drags, then handed it to her. The stem felt hot to her lips and the smoke burned as it went down. She held it in her lungs for as long as she could, then exhaled slowly. The cave began to spin and shrink still further. She put the pipe down and when she sat upright, she almost toppled over. The smoke burned her eyes, and as she stared into the small crevices of the cave wall, closing around her, she felt the eye of Dark-Eye on her and somehow burning inside her. Her insides unfolded, as if her body were turning inside out, and her head opened wide, expanding to take in the smoke, the cave, and the wizened creature opposite her. She realized he was singing, a strange high-pitched chant.

She swooned. The cave floor opened and swallowed her. Visions entered her: spectral thoughts, apparitions. She was traveling down a long funnel of time, which turned and twisted as she fell into it, following always the burning eye before her. The cave wall shrank until she could feel it coating her skin like a membrane, squeezing her into the funnel. Eons fell away. Suddenly she found her mind floating outside the cave, and as she looked down she could see the plain below, now empty of trees. Two tribes faced each other among the boulders. There was a musky smell of wetness and the rustling of shadows. Now flames flickered along a wall covered with stick-figure paintings in red ocher. Darkness was all around, grunts and scurrying, the feel of wet hair, the smell of sweat and fear.

In the time funnel, the two tribes of warriors are not the same. One tribe is stocky and muscular with protruding heads and bony ridges that jut above sloping brows. They come from the mountains in the north and speak in silence. The other tribe is long and lithe, built for running, with thin bones and smooth foreheads. They speak in sounds and come from the forest in the south. The two tribes have learned to distinguish which eland is weak or wounded and which saber-toothed tiger is about to pounce. Nature has taught them well in her kindergarten. Survival depends upon reckoning differences and choosing sides, and so the tribes are at war, a primal battle between the species.

As her mind floats like a bird, she looks down from above and watches the tribes in combat. They posture and bluster with clubs and spears. They run forward and fall back, shifting dots on the rocky plain. One side charges and the other side flees; then they change places. There is the pungent smell of musk and wet leaves, urine and smoke.

She sees the one good eye boring into her; she feels herself watching herself, seeing the rock behind her head and then floating again through the funnel. Once more the tribes clash. With clubs flailing, they meet like two waves crashing into one another. Weapons smash onto spines and skulls. Some fall to their knees. Blood splashes onto the rocks. A head splits open and brains spill out. The sides fall apart with much yelling and more posturing. The dead are buried in the trees without their eyes. Then, with yells and feints, the combat starts again. They run at each other and clash, the two waves smacking together with the sound of clubs striking flesh and bone. From a distance, near the mount shaped like the back of a fist, the charges look strangely unreal and the sound is muffled. The two tribes join and break apart far down below for a third time, leaving bodies motionless on the ground, like waves that ride up on shore, shunting pebbles back and forth, then leaving them suddenly motionless on the beach.

Time passes, peace descends. Now two tribes approach each other warily, but not in combat. At opposite ends of the rocky plain they walk slowly toward each other, their weapons held outstretched. They glare nervously at each other as they come closer and closer. They stop some thirty feet apart and discard their weapons. Slowly they straighten up, their eyes fixed on one another, and show empty hands, palms upward. They step over the clubs and continue to walk slowly toward each other, with nervous gestures. Suddenly there is a swirl of movement, dust kicked up. The ground opens and swallows one side whole, dozens of them disappearing into pits below. With yelps of glee, the long lithe ones charge close, pouring down a rain of rocks and dirt to bury the enemy. Caught in the traps below, those with the jutting brows shriek but the earth rains down upon them until it deadens their screams and rises up around them like an avalanche. It covers all of them, slowly and inexorably, until only one pit remains, and in it the leader rants, his fist pounding the walls, his head thrown back. As the dirt falls around him, he stands firm, looking upward. Teeth bared, he opens his throat and pours out a long guttural howl of impotent rage and anguish at the betrayal carried out on him and his tribe by the pernicious thin-skulled enemy. His howl rises up the mountain and lingers, echoing in the valley and through the forest even after the grave is covered over.

Susan stepped outside the cave and filled her lungs with cool air. She looked down at the treetops.

All had become clear, she thought, as she followed Dark-Eye down the trail. Origin and survival myths have an overarching purpose; they are history enshrined and recast as object lesson. The epic of Noah and the flood, an oral legend recounted in various forms throughout Eurasia, warns of godly retribution in reprisal for moral decadence. Adam and Eve is the story of the sin of overreaching that caused mankind's fall from grace. Cain and Abel tells of the first bloodletting and the price it extracted.

Dark-Eye was far ahead of her now, out of sight as the path curved along the serpentine turns in the rock face. So this had been the singular event in the prehistoric era of the hominids, the turning point that condemned them to a hard-scrabble existence in the cold and desolate upper reaches of the roof of the world. It was the story not of how a battle was won but of how it was lost. It was lost not by inferior weapons, lesser numbers, disorganization, or cowardice. It was lost by ignorance, by naiveté, by trust that was incapable of recognizing the depths of the enemy's treachery. Surely this was a communication worth tucking away in a time capsule for the future. Perhaps it had been emblazoned on the cave wall by a tiny band of survivors of the original battle, blessed by the presence of an extraordinary artist. It was intended for generations to come who would face the inevitable enemy, and it would have one overriding message: Beware the long lithe one, for he has a capacity we do not have.

Susan came to a fork in the trail as it drew level with the treetops. Dark-Eye was way ahead, and she didn't know which path he had taken. She chose one; around a corner the path widened as it passed a hidden crevice, and just beyond, a tangle of vines lay across it. The vines were thick and she had to step among them carefully, so her footing was precarious.

Suddenly, she felt the ground give way and the vines tighten around her ankle. It was like stepping into a nest of snakes. She plunged forward headfirst, and raised her hands instinctively to break her fall, feeling the dirt and pebbles grind into her palms. Still the vines held her feet and then tightened even more, and she heard a scuttling sound behind her from the direction of the crevice and a rock flew up and struck her thigh. Before she could turn she felt an iron grip on her arms, holding them behind her back, and then other stubby powerful fingers held her shoulders and still others clutched her legs.

Helpless, she was lifted from the rear, and as she struggled and her hands were forced into a wooden snare behind her back so tight that her shoulders ached, she felt something brush across her upper back and neck. She shuddered as she realized what it was: the hard unyielding bone of a ridge across the brow.

Matt needed to tell Susan that their escape route was blocked. When she didn't return to the village by late afternoon, he went looking for her, following the path to the lake, calling her name. On the shore he circled around until he came to the secluded spot where she had bathed. He saw traces of soap bubbles among the floating debris along the shoreline, and on the bank found the thin sliver of flint, which had bits of her black hair stuck on the sharp edge. From there, the trail went cold.

He returned to the village and found Sergei. The two of them combed half the valley by nightfall, splitting it into sectors and crisscrossing it methodically. By the time they returned empty-handed, Matt was distraught. He searched their bower and went through Susan's rucksack but could find no clue; everything seemed to be in its place.

"I just don't get it. What could have happened?" he said to Sergei, as they sat by the fire. He had one overwhelming fear, of course, but he did not want to give it a voice.

A figure approached out of the semidarkness on the other side of the fire, and at first Matt's heart leaped, but then he saw that it was Kellicut, whom he had not seen since before the attack by the renegades. Kellicut sat down wearily, not even acknowledging the presence of Sergei, whom he had never met; the Russian was too astounded to speak and only stared at him. Kellicut barely glanced at Matt; as he picked up a stick and poked it into the fire, bringing down a burning pile of embers in a splutter of sparks, he seemed weighted down. Matt was abruptly certain: *He knows something.*

"I heard you calling her," Kellicut began, clearing his throat. "I think you're looking in the wrong place."

Matt held his breath, too nervous to speak. Kellicut was talking in a cold, wooden way, and Matt didn't want to break whatever spell had taken hold of him. But then the man fell silent again. It was maddening.

"Tell me," said Matt, the tension strangling his voice so that it came out almost in a whisper.

"The shaman knows where she is."

"How do you know?"

"I saw them go up the mountain together this morning."

"She hasn't come back. Why didn't Dark-Eye come to let me know?"

"He's praying. He's trying a higher power."

Matt jumped up, dashed across the village to the shaman's hut, burst through the closed door, and almost tripped over him. The holy one was on his hands and knees, praying. Matt lifted him up as if he were a bag of twigs and leaves and carried him to the door. Then he saw Susan's sketch of the Enigma on the ground and stooped to pick it up.

He carried the old shaman in his outstretched arms like a bundle, all the way to the fire, and set him down there. Dark-Eye peered around uncertainly, his eyes reflecting back the fire glow like a cat's.

"How do we ask him?" said Matt, trying to calm himself.

"Well, there are ways to communicate, as you know," replied Kellicut, "but they take time. It means going up the mountain with him to his sacred temple."

"We don't have time for that," protested Matt.

Sergei got up abruptly and came running back a few minutes later, carrying Susan's beige cotton work shirt. "Show this to him," he said.

Matt held the shirt out to the shaman, who took a long

look. Slowly he gathered up his bony limbs, walked over to the fire, pulled out a burning stick, and blew out the flame on the end of it. Then he walked over to a flat rock and sat on his haunches before it. Holding the stick in his fingers, he moved it in a graceful arc, bearing down upon the rock. As Matt came and stood behind him, a black line appeared. Gradually the figure took shape, the outline of a hominid.

Dark-Eye went back to the fire for another stick, and with it he filled in the details. There was the hair and the protruding brow. Then with a flourish came the ghastly telltale touch; he drew animal skins across the chest and around the trunk and added a fur collar around the sloping crown. All in all, it was an excellent picture of Kee-wak.

26

Susan dug her heel into the earth to see if it was soft. It was igneous rock and dirt compressed by millennia of volcanic action, so tunneling was clearly impossible. Not to mention that there was no place to tunnel to, and also the fact that her jailers would perceive in an instant what she was doing.

As irony would have it, she was in Van's pit. She examined it. The pit had been dug deeper since then so that now anyone would be hard pressed to get out. Nor could she see over the edge into the main cavern, even by standing on tiptoe at the far end. She tried such little experiments to keep her mind off the danger.

After she had fallen into the trap, her hands were fastened behind her in the snare so tightly that she almost screamed in pain. She felt that her shoulder sockets were being pulled apart. She was carried roughly, hung upside down with her face to the ground. All she could see was the legs of her captors, squat ankles and splayed toes caked in mud. By twisting her head to the side, she could make out the lower portion of the rock face, and she could tell by the jolting movements that they were hurrying downhill.

She knew by the darkness when they entered the cave. The rock walls at her eye level were occasionally washed with the yellowish glare of unseen torches above. Three times her shoulders and knees scraped against the rock as they veered sharply around corners: With all the twists and turns of the route, she could not memorize it. The blood rushed to her head but she did not black out.

She stood up in the pit and took stock. Her feet were free but her hands were still imprisoned behind her in that damnable snare. Her shoulders ached; when she flexed them the pain shot through her joints, but she was relieved to realize that they were not dislocated. Her blouse had come undone in the ambush, and there was a cut across the top of her chest. She also had a bruise on her forehead from when they had tossed her into the pit. She looked around. There were bones scattered about, and she bent down to examine them with her expert's eye. They were animal bones, and the thin cut marks on the side were from human canines, so they were refuse from meals, not the bones of victims themselves. That was some consolation.

She wondered if Matt had any idea what had happened to her. What if no one saw her ambushed? What if Dark-Eye was too far ahead on the path? Matt and she had talked about the renegades kidnapping members of the tribe, so eventually when she didn't turn up, he would reach the right conclusion. But how long would that take and, once he did, what could he do? She knew he would try to rescue her because he would never abandon her, but what plan would stand even the remotest chance of success?

She took a mental survey of what was at hand. Not much, but there was the mirror in her front pocket. She bent at the waist to see if she could determine whether or not it was still whole. She did not feel the crunch of broken glass. She pivoted her upper torso to one side and twisted her bound hands to reach the front of her pants, like a contortionist, straining at the snare and swiveling her pelvis, but was unable to hook a finger into the nearest crease of the pocket.

She heard a sound above. Looking up, she saw a creature leering down at her, leaning casually on a spear. An overwhelming sense of revulsion seized her. The brute was so hideous that its presence could be detected by smell alone. There was a spark of cleverness in its eyes but it was the glint of low cunning, not the refined brilliance of an august being.

Who do you think you are, she wanted to say, to be looking down on me like some animal in the zoo? She stopped wiggling and stood up straight; she wanted to lift her chin and proclaim, How dare you treat me like this— I, *Homo sapiens sapiens*? Then she felt the filling up of her mind, as the sense of an alien presence moved like a huge clot of black blood into her cortex.

The sensation lasted for some minutes; then the creature picked up its spear and turned away without a backward look. She shuddered. The sensation she had just experienced was not at all warm and intimate, as it had been with Leviticus. It felt hard, cold, threatening. She realized there was something she feared more than anything else: the moment when Kee-wak stood there focusing his sinister energy on her psyche.

Matt sat in the bower, his head in his hands, thinking deeply. He took from his rucksack the fragment of Neanderthal skull that Kellicut had given him, letting the silver chain run through his fingers like sand. That was another lifetime ago, that dig in southern France—several lifetimes ago.

Matt completed an inventory of the goods they had brought with them from the outside world. There was his knife, his tape recorder, the flares they had taken from Van, the medical kit, two sleeping bags, ten feet of fishing wire, a few tins of food, a metal plate that doubled as a frying pan, and other odds and ends. In Susan's rucksack was more food, bits of chocolate, notebooks, Kellicut's diary, her tape player and tapes, vitamins, some archaeology tools, masking tape, and a small inflatable pillow. He smiled at the pillow, her one concession to luxury, which she had not yet used.

It was the image of Susan alone and frightened that drove him crazy. He had no idea even where she was being held, and he imagined the worst. Perhaps he should try to arrange for his own kidnapping; then at least they would be reunited. But what if they weren't? Perhaps he should send Sergei to look for the outside reinforcements who must be on their way. But what if that expedition was only a fiction? Maybe he and Sergei could make some bows and arrows and try to shoot their way in. No, they wouldn't get very far.

He had to come up with a strategy. He and Susan had managed to extract Van, but that time they had luck and surprise on their side. Now surprise was out of the question, for certainly the renegades would be expecting a counter-attack. And who was there to help him launch it, aside from Sergei and one or two hominids? The tribe had been decimated by the raid, and some of the best fighter-hunters, like Leviticus and Lancelot, were dead. This time it would be impossible to steal quietly through the back tunnels. The renegades were sure to post sentries; they were not naive and incapable of formulating plans like the valley hominids, and as hunters they were accomplished in offense and defense. Furthermore, if they did station sentries, the power they possessed would make them virtually infallible.

As Matt pondered, he let his eyes roam through the shadows of the forest, the treetops, the gathering darkness of the late afternoon. Off to the west he spotted the moon, a pale cream-colored disk, almost perfectly round. With a start, he remembered Van's theory about the full moon.

Susan thrust her pelvis against the protrusion of rock and hooked the rim of her pocket on it. She spun quickly along the wall, hearing a rip as the pocket opened and the mirror spilled out. Quickly she lifted her right foot to break its fall. She squatted and picked it up behind her back, then found an indentation in the rock at waist level and propped it up. Only when she was sure that the mirror was secure did she turn around. It was positioned just right.

Then she paced a bit—like Van, she realized with a shudder—and let her mind sort through her predicament. If only she had seen Matt when she had come down from the mount, if only she had been able to tell him what she had learned up there in Dark-Eye's cave. Surely the lesson enshrined in the tableau was the key to everything; it was the Rosetta Stone, providing a sudden illumination to the most critical event of prehistory. She thought of the battles between the species, *Homo sapiens sapiens* against *Homo sapiens neanderthalensis,* and she thought of the pathetic Neanderthal in the final panel, and his sense of rage that seemed to shimmer forth from the rock itself. Matt had seen her sketch but did he understand its message? If only there was a way to get through to him. She sat down, leaned her back against the wall, closed her eyes, and concentrated.

It seemed impossible. Perhaps she was too terrified to concentrate. She breathed deeply five times and told herself to relax. She tried to wipe her mind clean, like a sponge across a blackboard. First she made herself imagine Matt, summoning up an image of him from their younger days. Then she thought of him now, as he had appeared when she saw him at the Institute: the gray hair around his temples, the lines around his eyes, the new becoming familiar again. She thought of their lovemaking. Then she tried to summon him, trying to tap into portions of her brain never before used. She repeated his name over and over while she pictured his face. When she felt she had a firm hold on both, square in the center of her mind, like a diamond in its case, she talked to him silently. Over and over she repeated the same thought, trying to project it as if she were a transmitting tower sending a radio signal. Keep it simple, she told herself. One word, that's all, repeated again and again like a mantra: *Deceive, deceive, deceive.* She called him by name silently, and when she felt she must have reached him, she did it again: *Deceive, deceive, deceive.* And again and again, for hours on end.

Matt picked up Susan's sketch of the Enigma and stared at it. He let it fall from his hands, put his arms behind his head, and looked straight up at the sky. Then he had an inspiration. He had let his mind wander free, which was when it did its best work. It meandered back through the whole adventure, reliving it, except this time he rearranged the pieces of the puzzle in chronological order, not the order turned up by chance. It was a bit like rearranging the panels in the Khodzant Enigma for them to make sense, he reflected.

First, people start disappearing in the Pamirs. Somehow the U.S. government hears about it. A hominid is captured. The Institute is set up, fronting as a legitimate research center. It runs experiments on the hominid, highly classified, and calls it Operation Achilles. It discovers that the creature possesses special powers. The Institute sends Kellicut over to locate the tribe. He sends back proof they once existed, then disappears. They send over Matt and Susan to pick up where Kellicut left off. Van is sent along as a minder and a plant to call in back-up force when contact is made. So far everything fits.

Achilles was a strange name to choose, Matt thought. The great Greek warrior. He searched his memory. Achilles' mother, Thetis, was a sea nymph. She had been told by the Fates that he would die young and he was marked by destiny to disappear—like the Neanderthal. When he was a baby, Thetis dipped him in the River Styx, hoping its magical waters would protect him from all wounds. But she held him by the heel, which the water did not touch. Was that a clue? Was the government searching for a weak spot in order to control the Neanderthal? Or was the heel the hidden weakness that doomed them to extinction? When the Trojan war broke out, Achilles was a great fighter, until he argued with King Agamemnon and refused to go into battle. He lent his armor to his friend Patroclus, who was killed by Hector. Achilles slew Hector, but then the poisoned arrow, guided by Paris, found its mark, his heel.

Matt sat bolt upright. Of course! *There* was the stratagem. It was lying there all along in the past, waiting to be plucked: history's most famous battle, history's most famous deception.

The wind died down during the night, and in the morning light it was clear that the blizzard had passed. By dawn the air was so thin and clear that the men could see for miles. When the sun came up it deepened the blue of the sky and gave the snow crust on the window of the chopper, in which Kane had been trapped since the crash, a golden hue.

He felt relief; they had established radio contact with Sodder, who flew back to camp in the other chopper, and now that the storm was over they would be rescued. Only when his sickening fear lifted did he realize how profoundly it had taken hold of him, penetrating his bones like the cold.

He shifted and felt a searing pain travel up his lower back. He had shared the wrecked cabin with Sheriden, who had cut both his eyes on window glass in the crash and wore a bandage wrapped around his head. The man snored through the night while Kane froze. The rest of the men camped just outside, tunneling through the snow to sleep in a small tent.

Now he heard the men walking around outside, then a long whistle of astonishment.

"Hey, you should see this thing. You guys are really close to the edge. You're damned lucky you didn't go over."

A hand brushed away the snow on a small patch of the window, then scraped at the ice. When Kane raised himself painfully on his elbows and peered through, he saw a head blurred by a thin layer of ice. By craning his neck and looking down he could just make out the top of a snowdrift several feet away, and beyond that nothing but space. If the wind had been stronger, it could have swept the helicopter over the edge. A giddy feeling overtook him, the elation of danger past. Thank God he hadn't known just how precarious their shelter was.

On the other side of the helicopter, the men set up a Sterno can and made coffee. They handed a mug in to Kane, and he cupped it in both hands and felt the warmth radiate up to his elbows. He was worried about his feet; he was able to move them but they had no sensation at all. He could only tell he was flexing his toes by looking at his boots. Frostbite, for sure. Well, at least it would be his ticket off this mountain. He was fed up with the mission; he had read Dr. Arnot's letter left at the campsite for Kellicut, making sure no one else saw it. She referred to some kind of diary; it was obvious that the professor had found the creatures. Maybe they weren't far away at this very moment.

They passed in a ready-to-eat meal. It was barely edible, and he used what was left of the coffee to wash it down. One of the men helped Sheriden, cutting large bites and shoveling the food into his mouth as he opened wide, like a baby bird.

Sodder called on the radio and said they were getting ready to set out and were packing some last-minute supplies into the rescue chopper.

"Commander." The pilot poked his head inside the cabin. His tone was perfunctory. "Seeing as how we've got some time before they get here, we thought we'd check out where that transponder is. It's not far away."

He's telling me, not asking me, Kane thought. But why not? "Okay, but be quick about it. We've got to get Sheriden to a medic. We can't wait around."

"They'll have to take us out in shifts anyway. Can't overload our last bird at this altitude." Kane grunted. He still bore a grudge for the crash, which was the pilot's fault.

In his mind he'd been composing the complaint he was going to lodge.

He heard crisp squeaks in the snow as the men walked away. It sounded like all of them were going. He hadn't realized that. Soon it was quiet except for the sound of a slight breeze.

"Hello?" he ventured, not too loudly. "Anyone out there?"

There was no reply.

"What's wrong?" said Sheriden, a trace of panic in his voice.

"Nothing."

"Why'd you yell?"

"I didn't yell. I was just seeing if anyone was there."

Kane reached over and fiddled with the radio to make sure it was on. He called Sodder's helicopter, just to have something to do, but there was no reply. Guess they haven't started out yet, he thought.

Then he began to feel something funny, as if the cabin was slowly filling up with water. But it wasn't happening inside the cabin; it was inside his head, a strange, frightening occupation of his skull. It was familiar, and he knew where he had felt it before. His heart began racing. But it was impossible!

"What's going on?" Sheriden cried. "I feel something weird." He ripped the bandage off his eyes, revealing two blood-caked slits.

Kane felt it before he saw it: something above him, the presence of a thick dark shadow. Slowly, with dread in his heart, he raised his head. There, on the other side of the window caked with ice, staring down at him, was the overly large face, the mouth as wide and ugly as a scar, the flat nose, the murderous eyes. The features were blurred, as if encased in ice, but they were wicked, arrogant, filled with unrelenting hate. The two of them locked stares. In his mind, Kane heard an echo: *You'd do the same to us, wouldn't you?*

Then he heard others moving around. How many of them were there?

"What's happening?" shouted Sheriden hysterically.

Kane didn't answer. He was too terrified. He heard the sounds they made as they took up positions around the chopper, the grunts, the rending as the metal scraped against the rock below. He felt them lifting, a few small bounces, more scraping.

"What's happening? Shit, why don't you answer?"

The cabin tilted like a tree in a storm, rocked for a bit, then slowly turned downward in a large arc. The moment seemed frozen in time. The radio flickered on, and Sodder's voice said, "Hello, hello, do you read?" Sheriden screamed. There was a huge crash as the chopper smashed once more on the ledge and then toppled over soundlessly into space. Kane was floating, falling down, too scared to scream, waiting for it all to end with his body and brains smeared into a thousand pieces. As he floated upside down, he thought vaguely that he was pissing in his pants.

Not long after the fireball in the ravine, Sodder's helicopter landed close by. The spinning of its blades obliterated all traces of the footprints in the snow. The other men, who had heard the crash but did not see it, came running down the slope. They all agreed that it must have been some kind of freak wind gust out of nowhere.

Matt awoke early in the morning and went to the village. First he looked for Longtooth and found him fast asleep in a hut. Not far from his head were leftover bits of raw meat on a stone slab. Longtooth had continued to be a hunter and had even drawn two other young males out on expeditions. Matt woke him by rocking his shoulder gently, and together they went outside and sat near the fire pit. Longtooth rubbed his eyes, stretched, and looked around. It was a brilliantly clear morning with dew on the juniper bushes. Cotton clouds had replaced the steel-gray sky that had dropped tons of snow on the other side of the mountain.

Matt took out a notebook and pencil and tried to draw a picture of Susan, hoping that Longtooth would understand that he was asking him to communicate with her. But it was hopeless; Longtooth didn't understand, and Matt quickly gave up.

Then he gave Longtooth a task to perform, the most dangerous one in his short career as a hunter. He drew an animal he wanted Longtooth to slay, and worked carefully to portray it unmistakably: the bulk, the sheen of the fur, the powerful claws, the flat head with long teeth and small beady eyes. It was a good representation of a cave bear. Then he drew Longtooth attacking the beast. The hominid watched him closely, noting the pencil moving on the paper in fascination. Matt drew Longtooth with his spear next to a dead bear, then handed the notebook to him to examine. The hominid got the message. He appeared excited; he went to his hut and reappeared with his spear. In his heart Matt wished him luck, for Longtooth's success was essential to the plan.

Next Matt went in search of Sergei. He found him washing at the stream and explained the plan to him, watching the Russian furrow his brows as he took it in. He could tell that Sergei doubted its efficacy but was too kindhearted to say so. He had been distressed by Susan's abduction and clearly would do anything to try to rescue her.

"It is very imaginative," he said finally, offering a handshake as if to close a deal.

"Let's get started," Matt said. "The less time we lose, the better." In the far distance he heard an alien, mechanical sound, muffled but steady. His gut tightened: It sounded like a helicopter. The forces of the Institute were getting close.

First they needed lumber. It was beyond their capability to fell huge trees and carve them into boards, but they had some ready-made bits of wood that had been used in roofing the huts. They demolished three of them. For the longer pieces, they roamed the forest until they found downed trees.

Matt fashioned a large stone hammer and attached a handle, talking out loud as the hominids watched his every move.

"This is called hafting. You guys never learned how to do it, according to the textbooks." Then he shaped large pieces of flint into wedges, holding the lumps of rock carefully in one hand and with the other using a rock to strike off a series of small chips. "The Levallois technique, we call it," he said as they gave him uncomprehending looks. "Named after a Paris suburb. Your ancestors were pretty good at it back in the Middle Paleolithic. Of course, that was before you gave up France for this place."

Matt knocked the wedges into the trees already softened by decay, hammered them home with the ax, and split the trunks. It was exhausting; he and Sergei took turns. After two hours, they had a large stack of usable beams, which Blue-Eyes, Hurt-Knee, and five others helped them carry to the village.

They drafted more workers and Matt helped them make stone axes. He had spent a summer years ago with archaeology graduate students who replicated the lifestyle of prehumans in the woods of Massachusetts—and soon the group was turning out tools, a tiny prehistoric workshop. The clinks of their shaping could be heard for miles. When they had half a dozen axes, Matt and Sergei took a group back into the forest, searching for strong pines with flawless, rounded trunks. They hacked down four of them, cut them into logs ten feet long, and used stone axes to chisel the ends smooth.

Back in the village, they collected all the animal skins that remained from their earlier hunts. They stacked them in a pile near the beams and logs. By evening, when almost everything was prepared, the whole center of the village was taken up with their new equipment.

Matt was too worried about Susan to eat a proper meal.

He had lost a whole day making his preparations, but there was no other way. With a notebook and pencil, he sat down at the fire near Sergei. Earlier, the Russian and Longtooth had roasted a haunch of antelope on the fire; now the hominid had gone off to distribute the cooked meat to his coterie of hunters. Sergei had crushed bits of raspberry leaf, heated it with water for ersatz tea, and followed this with a crude cigarette made from bits of jasmine leaf wrapped in vine. He took a long drag, coughed, and offered a drag to Matt, who shook his head and began sketching. He was dissatisfied with his first attempt, crumpled the paper, and threw it in the fire.

"It doesn't have to be perfect," Sergei said.

"No, but it's got to do the job."

He tried again, beginning from the base this time. He sketched a rough platform, supported by two of the logs, which would act as wheels. The other two logs could be placed ahead, so that the whole apparatus could roll forward. From the platform, he drew four upright beams, the supports for a smaller platform ten feet in the air. On that he drew a chamber, and then, extending from one side of it and still higher, a cylinder representing a neck. Then came the skull: a huge, frightening, unmistakable bear's head. Finally, on the underside of the belly of the chamber, he added a small trap door. It looked good, a perfect representation of the renegades' godhead. A perfect Trojan horse.

So involved was Matt in examining his handiwork that he did not notice Kellicut until the older man eased up next to him and looked over his shoulder. Then Kellicut looked away, sniffed the air, looked at Sergei, and addressed him for the first time. "You've been cooking meat." It wasn't a question but a declaration of fact, and was stated as an accusation. Sergei nodded and casually took another drag on his cigarette.

Kellicut gazed into the fire for a long time, and it became clear that he was contemplating a major pronouncement.

"You know," he said finally, turning to Matt and dragging out the words for maximum impact, "you have no right to do what you're planning to do. This nasty little trick is a violation of everything we believe. It's against everything I have devoted my life to." He looked deeply into Matt's eyes.

"You cooperated with the Institute," Matt retorted. "You came here first. You're the one who opened Pandora's box."

Kellicut paused. "Yes, that's true," he said. "I was always suspicious of the Institute—but not as suspicious as I should have been." He paused. "I needed them. Without them I never would have had a chance to come here."

"They were using you."

"I knew that, but I was using them too. I was wary from the beginning. The scientists weren't world class, their studies were all recent, they had too much money to throw around. But frankly, I didn't care, not at first. They told me they had vague reports of sightings in the Pamirs. They wanted me to investigate. I jumped at the chance. Who wouldn't? A prehistoric band of hominids—the mind reels at the thought. Even if there's one chance in a million, it's worth taking."

"Did you know they were here before you?"

"Yes. I found that out from Sharafidin's father. That made me even more suspicious but also more intrigued; they acted like they really believed in these things. I began to believe it too."

He stared into the fire. "Then when I got here I found these incredible beings. I saw they had this special power. And suddenly all my suspicions took shape and I was on to their game. I knew the power could be used for darker purposes—that was what the Institute was all about. I decided to cut myself off."

"But you sent back the skull."

"Right. A final message to discourage them. It didn't work."

"Why did you bury the diary?"

"That was for you. I thought the Institute would send you looking for me. I knew only you could locate it. At that point I still cared about things like reputation—I wanted you to know what I had found. But I didn't count on them sending someone with you. I became suspicious that you had joined them. By then, I didn't care about sharing my discovery. I cared only about the power, learning it, acquiring it, a road to a higher truth."

"We were never part of the Institute, Jerry. You should have known that," Matt said.

"Maybe. But you're still part of the problem."

Matt put down his pad, but he was sure Kellicut had seen his blueprint. He considered telling him that Van had been sending back satellite messages and that there was reason to believe that the Institute's enforcers were already on the way, but decided not to.

Kellicut nodded at the notebook. "Now perhaps you see why your scheme is wrong, morally wrong. It's beyond the pale. You saw what happened when you rescued Van. You cannot bring concepts from the outside world into this one. To do so is evil. It cannot be allowed to succeed, I'm afraid"—here his voice dropped a notch, which made it sound menacing—"even if that means allowing Susan to perish."

Matt looked at him in disbelief. "You can't mean that," he said.

Kellicut didn't flinch. "I do." He paused and looked into the fire again, so that the flames lit the outline of his face and his eyes became two black holes. He sighed, as if reluctantly assuming a burden, and said, "It can't be allowed to succeed. I won't let it. If you choose to go ahead with it, then you will die as well as Susan."

Kellicut rose and within seconds disappeared into the forest, under the full moon.

27

Susan knew Kee-wak was coming before she could hear him because she detected a buzz of excitement in the cavern above the pit and also, in a way she couldn't define, she was able to intuit his approach.

Her thirst was so powerful her whole mouth felt sucked dry. She thought of feigning sleep but knew the ruse would not work; there was nothing to do but wait for him.

First came the praetorian guard, two creatures with striped yellow skins hung over their shoulders like capes. They peered down contemptuously, and she felt each of them briefly probing her mind, two clouds that passed through her consciousness and were gone. She held no interest for them, and they backed away from the edge of the pit.

She dropped her eyes to the dirt floor and saw the bulky shadow appear over her own like a gargoyle. She looked up and there Kee-wak was on the lip of the pit, his height accentuated because he was above her, a grotesque statue on a pedestal. He had red paint around his mouth so that it looked like an open wound, his eyes offset in black were sunken like a hyena's, and around his brow was the ragged black-and-white monkey skin.

He seemed to know she was thirsty, and he lowered a half skull with filthy brown water in it, but with her hands behind her she could not raise it to her lips. He made no attempt to help her. The water looked too rank to drink anyway. He jumped into the pit behind her, and clasped the snare, pulling it even tighter. The smell of him, an odor of musk and blood, made her reel. He grabbed her by the hair, pulled so that she fell to her knees, and stood towering behind her. She could feel the slap of the gun holster against her back. Then she felt what she had dreaded: He began to enter her through the mind, slowly, like a leak spreading. Then the pain began, a dull ache, at first, which grew sharper and sharper until she wanted to scream. He was right behind her; it was as if he were inside her, looking out through her cornea, receiving what she saw upon his own retina. But he was also infiltrating her pain center.

She maneuvered herself nearer to the pit wall. Inch by inch, she pulled herself closer, disregarding the pain in her shoulders and the spreading ache inside, until she saw the object she was searching for. She did not look at the mirror until she was only two feet away, and then she opened both eyes wide and stared straight ahead into the silvery reflection, seeing her own eyes staring back, widened in fear but recognizable, deeply green. She looked at her own eyes as if they were twin wells of green water and she was falling into them, until suddenly she felt a jerk behind her, a retreat, and the ache that had closed in on her mind like a tightening fist abruptly relaxed and disappeared. Kee-wak cried out—in confusion, not in pain, it seemed—and with a single bound he leaped out of the pit and was gone, like a specter disappearing with the dawn.

She stood up. There was a smidgen of grease on her lower back where he had touched her, and she rubbed her wrist in it, working it around and loosening the bind of the snare.

Kellicut felt no fear. He was like prophets of old, the Christian believers praying in the underground tunnels of the

Coliseum. He was driven by the all-encompassing conviction that what he was doing was right.

He skirted the burial ground and arrived at the mouth of the cave at first light. There was no one about, nothing to interrupt the calming music of the birds. He had one shirt left to his name and he had decided to wear it—out of a sense of occasion and also because he was an emissary and emissaries dressed for their role.

Kellicut touched the pocket and felt the piece of paper there. This was his message, his mission, but he could hardly hand it over like some courier arriving unexpectedly in Caesar's Rome from the outskirts of the empire. This would take some doing to be done right.

He looked around outside before he stepped inside the cave. He was not saying good-bye exactly, he told himself, because he might well return. He was just fortifying himself with the sight of the out-of-doors for his trip through the tunnels. He had never been inside the cave but he had often imagined how dark and oppressive it must be.

His mission was not without perils. What if he stumbled upon a thick-headed guard who decided he had come for some nefarious purpose and cut him down on the spot? What if he could not reach the one he needed to, the only one who was sufficiently intelligent to figure out the warning he was attempting to deliver?

The tunnel was huge and cut straight into the mountainside as if it had been constructed for a giant railroad. He felt dwarfed by it, listening to his footsteps echoing back. There was no point, really, in being quiet, since he had come to be discovered. The tunnel curved, then gave way to a large underground cavern, lit by torches set into the walls. He stopped and listened: nothing but the occasional drip of water from stalactites landing on the stalagmites below. He was overtaken by a wave of doubt and had to fight it down. He thought he felt them invading his mind but he couldn't be sure.

Just keep going, he told himself, and soon he lost himself

in the details: the niches cut for torches, which intrigued him, and the occasional abandoned hearth. He chose the largest passageway and followed it as it rose gradually, moving up inside the mountain. He passed more pathways on either side and was bewildered by the possibilities. The tunnel turned left, then right. He saw a narrow entrance under an arch, took it, and found himself inside a giant cavern, and a dozen faces turned toward him.

He had expected to catch them off guard but instead he was the one surprised, as powerful arms grabbed him from behind, squeezing his shoulders so tight he couldn't move. As the pain cut into his shoulder blades, the truth struck home: They had lured him to the cavern—that was why he had encountered no one in the tunnels. Now he had only one hope, that they were sufficiently endowed with curiosity to keep him alive, to wonder why he had come, and that they would take him to the highest authority.

He was not kept in suspense. Three of the creatures trundled him along a side tunnel, one on each side and the third holding the point of a spear in the small of his back, until they came to a side chamber. Inside, reclining on a rock slab, was Kee-wak, who turned his head slightly to look at him but otherwise did not move. Kellicut was thunderstruck: So majestic was the creature lying there, so powerful, so manifestly superior to those Kellicut had been living among these past months. He felt a curious flood of relief; the decision he had made, risking his life, had been correct. The renegades were clearly marked by destiny as the future of the species. His relief was quickly followed by another feeling, of Kee-wak's energy pouring inside him and unrolling to occupy his receptor field. It made him feel shaky, almost panicky, because it was so much stronger than anything he had experienced before.

Kellicut sat on a boulder and reached into his shirt pocket. The movement caused his guards to stiffen but Kee-wak did not stir. Slowly, Kellicut pulled out his own sketch of Matt's blueprint for the creation that mocked the renegades' godhead. He opened the paper, held the sketch before him, and stared at it, concentrating on the lines and trying to view it as a whole. Inside the godhead, Kellicut had given away the secret, drawing something that Matt had not drawn: figures, soldiers lying inside the belly, waiting to attack. Now he stared directly at the figures, which he had drawn as realistically as possible. He looked over at Kee-wak to see if he was taking it in, but he didn't really have to since he felt Kee-wak inside of him, looking as he looked at the paper trembling in his hands.

Thank God, Kellicut thought, the message is getting across; Matt's scheme can be neutralized. He did not see Kee-wak make a tiny motion with one hand. But something else suddenly floated into his mind, a vision. He was using the power, he realized; he had conquered it at last. The vision focused and took shape—it was the back of a head, his own head. Why his own head?

He did not have time to ward off the blow that came from behind and struck his neck like a blade, so powerfully and perfectly placed that it cut right through his spinal cord. His death was instantaneous, which was just as well, since his last thought was hopeful. The optimism was engraved on his face, slumped over, resting upside down on his chest.

Matt found a good spot to make the structure, a small, picturesque glen close to the mouth of the cave. It was separated from it by a row of pines, which would allow them to work in relative seclusion, provided they worked quickly.

He walked over to the edge of the pines and peered at the cave. The comforting scent of pine needles rose up from the soft ground, reminding him of the Vermont mountains he loved to roam in the autumn.

Mentally he charted a path for the godhead to reach the cave. There was one difficult stretch, but for the most part the ground ran slightly downhill. Once the structure was built, they should be able to roll it all the way to the cave mouth, using the rounded logs two at a time and switching the back ones to the front as they went. He hoped the hominids could grasp the concept because they would be doing most of the heavy lifting. Once the damned thing was in place, the rest would be up to the renegades.

He and Sergei had arrived early. A group led by Hurt-Knee and Tallboy was carrying the construction materials to the site. They still refused to cross the burial ground, so they had had to carry the branches and huge logs around the periphery, twice the distance and across more difficult terrain. But they arrived in good time and hadn't even worked up a sweat.

Matt stowed his rucksack in the crotch of a tree. It contained the special items, including the one he worked on late into the night, which he would install later as the finishing touch, when no one else was around.

He put his sketches in a line on the ground. He had made eight drawings, one of the overall design and others of individual parts and joints. The most difficult job would be constructing the body and the head and making them look like the godhead in the cave. That would be hard enough even with real lumber and with a proper hammer and nails, he said to himself, but this way . . . he didn't even finish the thought.

They laid their tools out and examined them, a rudimentary assortment of vines, bones, chipped stones, heavy round rocks, bits of wire, and thin slivers of flint. At least he had his pocketknife.

Sergei seemed to be reading his thoughts. "The tools may be prehistoric," he said. "But the minds behind them are twentieth century." He smiled encouragingly.

They chose two of the thickest logs for the base and laid them parallel. Two more logs were laid across them at either end, like a raft, and lashed in place with vines. They attached beams extending upright, and then built two platforms high in the air for the body, securing the joints by hammering in slivers of bone and rock. Heavy branches were set in place like ribs until the frame was strong enough to stand in. Reluctantly, Matt abandoned the idea of a trap door in the belly; instead, he left an opening between branches and covered it with animal hides.

Matt stood on the platform, inside the belly of the godhead, and stepped to the edge and wiped his brow. From where he was, he had to admit that the structure looked impressive. It was about twenty feet off the ground and it was solid.

Then he saw Longtooth emerging from the woods, striding purposefully. Behind Longtooth came two younger hominids, carrying something on their heads and staggering under the weight. It was long and dark and, as they approached, Matt could see a huge round head and black fur. Longtooth had succeeded in his mission—he had killed a cave bear. Now the godhead would be an exact replica.

Sergei leaped up and gawked, his mouth open. He ran over to examine the bear hide and hugged Longtooth, who was hard put to disguise his satisfaction. Then the two joined the others in building and quickly finished off the hollow body, filling in the sides with tightly packed branches and then draping animal hides over them to complete the illusion of a monster.

Next came the head. Matt crafted a hideous-looking lower jaw, careful to leave large holes for the mouth and nostrils. They would be needed later. Across the top half of the face he placed the bear's head, with its mean and tiny eyes. The black fur hung down the back and around the front of the neck like a collar, so that the effect was the same as that of the godhead in the main cavern: to inspire fear.

Matt jumped to the ground and inspected his handiwork. It looked to be a dead ringer for the original, even in daylight, and it seemed possessed by the same malevolent spirit. The hominids looked at it apprehensively and kept their distance.

As they had discussed, Sergei slipped away to construct

a secret hiding place. He searched the area for quite a while until he found the perfect spot, a narrow ridge that was not far from the cave mouth but that dipped down out of sight. First, he dug a wide shallow pit. He covered it over with logs that looked much the same as the logs used for the body of the godhead. Then he tossed skins on them. He squeezed inside to examine it. The darkened interior was cramped, but it had room enough for six.

"Mission accomplished," said Sergei, when he rejoined Matt. He stared up at the godhead, which loomed above like some malignant force. "So that represents an advance in terms of civilization?" he said, shaking his head. "What kind of god do you think it is?"

"I'm not sure," replied Matt. "But I'd say it's connected with the hunt and with shedding blood. The cave bear is almost a deity; he rules the mountain. There is nothing that does not fear him and nothing that he fears. So it's natural that they would look up to him as they turn to killing and eating meat. We know from prehistoric burial grounds that to them the cave bear was sacred."

Sergei shuddered. "I'm not sure you're right," he said. Matt clapped him on the back and they got going.

With the help of the hominids, they placed the rolling logs underneath the base platform. Then they all took up positions and, straining with all their might, they pushed at the giant statue until it began slowly to creak and then finally to inch forward. Others pulled on vines attached to the body. They pushed and pulled harder and harder, and it began to roll. They placed two more logs ahead of it and retrieved the two left behind. In this way, they kept the structure moving over level ground until at long last, half an hour later, it sat directly in front of the cave entrance.

They aligned the spare logs between the godhead and the cave mouth and left the vines for tugging hanging down. At last, the finished creation was in place, ready for occupancy. Matt put on his rucksack and climbed back into the structure. He entered the belly through the flap of loose skin, squeezed up through the neck into the empty head, and did what he came to do.

Then he went back into the belly, and finally he climbed out and dropped to the ground. He hammered a stake into the earth, attached something to it, and left. As he moved toward the glen, he noticed that the sun was already well past the meridian. Soon it would be late afternoon, hunting time, when the creatures would stir out of their lair. He had to pray that they would come, that they would send out sentries or perhaps another raiding party. He turned to look back at the godhead. It was evil and majestic, standing there with the sun glinting off the black fur, a giant offering, a tribute not to be refused. He understood at once the mendacious creativity behind the Trojan horse, the supreme joke of the poisoned gift that cannot be turned down.

He turned at the glen and went to the ridge, where he joined Sergei, who was dozing. He lay in the long, warm grass and felt exhaustion overcome him, but he could not risk falling asleep. He had to keep watch. The real struggle had not yet begun. He knew he would soon need all the reserves of energy he possessed.

Susan had slipped one hand out of the snare but she kept it behind her most of the time to fool them. Her caution was largely superstitious; she knew enough about their powers to believe that they could not view her from afar, that they could only see through her own eyes. But she didn't want to take any chances. She did use one hand to lift the half skull that Kee-wak had dropped. It still had a bit of brown water resting at the bottom, but it smelled too foul to drink.

She could see no way out of the pit. The wall was too sheer to climb. There was a promising ledge high up on one side. If I could grab it, I could pull myself up, she thought. But it was too high to reach, even by jumping. She'd have to stand on something.

Susan was still upset by her encounter with Kee-wak.

She knew with certainty that he would be back, and her trick was unlikely to work a second time. She pocketed the mirror anyway, just to have it handy. A sixth sense told her that something was up in the cavern above, a restlessness that suggested some activity or ceremony was about to take place. It could be preparations for my own sacrifice, she thought.

She dreaded pain. She always had. It wasn't death she feared as much as torture. And these monsters were capable of torture, not for some nefarious end but simply because they were so lacking in empathy they didn't bother to weigh the consequences of their actions.

Her thoughts were interrupted by a hubbub above. She looked up but it was hard to see, because glare from burning torches washed out everything but the stout legs standing on the rim of the pit. In the accentuated darkness there seemed to be a line of creatures holding something, a shroud perhaps—was it the gown she was to wear as a death maiden?—and now they held it directly over the wall and let it go. It fell heavily and hit the bottom of the pit with a thud and she could see, in the pool of light, an arm unbending, then a leg. It was a body, a human body. The creatures left. Slowly, cautiously, she approached it, bent over, moved her hand from behind her back, and turned it over. It was Kellicut! His face was distorted, terribly shrunken somehow, and his eyeballs were glazed and bulging. As she gasped and let the corpse fall back, it fell on its belly and she could see a thick deep wound at the top of the spine. She could see through the wound and right into the skull and she screamed and screamed again, because she could see the inner bone. The skull was empty. The brain was missing.

The creatures crept out of the cave slowly, staring up at the godhead as if it might strike them down at any moment. Some blinked, as though they were looking at the sun. They surrounded it, and the brave ones approached it and then held out their hands tentatively and touched the wooden base upon which it sat.

From the hiding place, Matt watched them nervously as he fought down a new worry: Maybe the deity was too ferocious, maybe they would not summon up the courage to move it. Everything depended on their transporting it inside the cave. He had convinced himself that that would be their instinctive response, but perhaps he had misjudged them; perhaps he was too unable to enter their mental world and predict their behavior. He still felt in his gut that one among them, Kee-wak himself, would want to make that creation his own, possess it, use it to magnify his power.

At precisely that moment, as if Matt had conjured him up, Kee-wak appeared in the mouth of the cave. There was no mistaking his tall, gaunt silhouette and the collar of monkey fur that thickened his brow. Matt saw the handle of the revolver glinting in the sunlight as the creature stood tall, taking in the godhead and then—the only one to do this—scanning the horizon.

Quickly Matt ducked inside the hideaway. His knee struck Sergei's back and together they huddled in the darkness while the mysterious, dangerous sensation crept into the cortex, starting at the center and expanding outward like ink in water. Sergei was frightened. He gripped Matt's arm and squeezed it so tight he cut off the circulation, until Matt reached over and patted him on the knee. Soon the sensation passed.

"Don't worry," said Matt. "That was just a little exploration. It's probably safe to go outside now."

From the ridge they watched as the creatures labored like Lilliputians to haul the gigantic structure into the cave. Some pushed and others pulled but it wasn't until they figured out the tow lines that they were finally able to budge it. Matt was silently urging them on, resisting the impulse to shout directions on how to use something as elementary as the wheel. Then the concept seemed to dawn on them, and slowly the construction moved forward on its rollers, awkwardly, like a schooner sailing into an uncertain breeze. It seemed to take forever but finally it arrived at the cave mouth, lingering there for a bit while the small dark figures in the distance cleared rocks away. Then at last the godhead moved forward and was gobbled up by the dark hole.

"Let's go!" shouted Matt, and he was off and running before Sergei was out of the hideaway. They ran down the ridge, across the clearing, and up to the side of the cave. Matt listened; there was a cacophony of noise, of stones smashing, logs rolling, grunts, footsteps, shuffles, and creaks, but none of it sounded close by, and he slipped inside. Sergei was right behind him. They waited some moments for their eyes to become accustomed to the darkness, flattening themselves against the cave wall to avoid daylight as a backdrop. Ahead, just where the tunnel curved, they could see the godhead moving like a ship of state and turning to show its side, its features distorted by the lights of torches and casting hideous shadows upon the rock. Out of nowhere, the pounding of the drums began, low, steady and ominous.

Matt had to consciously hold himself back. When he judged that enough time had passed, he stole along the tunnel with Sergei behind him until he reached the bend, and there he stopped to peer around the smooth rock face. The scene before him was nightmarish. The godhead occupied the center of the cavern, seeming even larger indoors and twice as hideous surrounded by the jagged edges and daggers of stalactites and stalagmites. Bats fluttered and careened around its bear's scalp. Warriors surrounded the godhead on all sides and, as Matt was quick to note, they carried their clubs and spears. To one side drummers flailed their instruments, dark wooden bowls stretched tight with skins. Others carried flaming torches. And presiding over it all, dressed in his usual regalia, sitting on a carved stool that served as a throne, was Kee-wak.

Kee-wak stood and the drummers stopped. He stared up at the godhead above him, seemingly uncertain. He ap-

peared to read it, again and again, as if to decipher its secret. They all stared at the hideous icon. Then Kee-wak
made a gesture and other creatures carried armloads of
wood, which they piled around the base of the structure.
When this was done, the drummers started up again, but
Kee-wak silenced them. He stood again and stared at the
icon, trying to ferret out its mystery, to reach every corner
of its insides with his powerful seeing eye. Something,
somewhere, was wrong. Dead wrong. At that moment, from
within the godhead, arose a cry, at first tentative but quickly
insistent, a high-pitched whine, a sound of keening. It was
the hominids' cry of alarm. The creatures dropped back in
fright, falling over one another in surprise. But Kee-wak
rushed ahead almost as if he expected such a thing. He
grabbed a torch and with feverish movements lit the wood,
rushing around the entire base until flames licked up from
all sides.

He threw the torch down and stepped back as fire consumed the godhead. It burned up the beams until it reached
the belly, scorching the wood and then igniting it. The
drummers started up again, and the smoke rose to cover
the vaulted ceiling, agitating the bats so that the roof turned
into a squiggling, chattering mass of heads and wings. Then
something unexpected, most unexpected, happened.

From somewhere within the bowels of the deity came a
roar and a steady beat and the music of Bruce Springsteen
suddenly burst out into the cave, echoing up and down with
a mad intensity. *"Born in the U.S.A. . . ."* And just then
the flames crawled up the neck and reached the head and
the beast appeared to rear back, its eyes and mouth split
open, and it spit out fireballs, colored flames that flew out
twenty feet and more. They scorched the cave wall, struck
the floor, and turned the once cool cavern into an inferno
of smoke, flame, and ash, with the bats flying above and
the music pulsating throughout, up and down the tunnels.

The creatures panicked. Driven by the vision of the
avenging deity, picking everyone up in their path, they fled

through the main cavern and kept going, deep into the cave, the music biting at their heels. With them, running flat out and pushing others out of his way, was Kee-wak. In the cavern he paused a moment and ran over to the pit. It was empty, save for Kellicut's body, which had been pushed up against one side underneath a rocky ledge so the prisoner could escape. Kee-wak screamed in fury and then ran on with the others, as fast as he could, until they came to the upper reaches of the cave and the main entrance. There they piled outside and into the safety of the deep snow, floundering in the depths of the newly fallen drifts.

Matt charged behind the fleeing creatures. When he reached the main cavern it was empty. He saw the pit and was about to go to it when a voice called to him from behind.

"Matt, don't. It's horrible. Kellicut's body."

He took Susan in his arms and held her for a long time. She was quivering. He was still holding her moments later when Sergei rushed into the cavern, along with Hurt-Knee, Longtooth, and the others who had been waiting in the hideaway. They resumed the chase, rushing through empty tunnels and past hearths abandoned only moments before, until they came to the entrance, the very place where Matt, Susan, Van, and Rudy had first caught sight of the creatures so long ago.

They drew up side by side and watched from the mouth of the cave as the renegades, still in panic, thrashed about outside in the pits of snow, flailing about like wounded animals. The creatures struck out wildly, even hitting each other and sending driblets of blood upon the churning snow. Matt and Susan saw Kee-wak rising up in the middle of the chaos, still a figure of commanding power.

Kee-wak stood tall and those around him fell away. In a moment forever frozen, he lifted up his chin and turned his vicious gaze upon Matt and Susan and Sergei. In a single instant all became clear to him. His blood raged at the treachery. He screamed, his head thrown back. Then very calculatingly, he raised up the holster over his head and took the gun in hand. He turned it this way and that, poked and pulled, until finally he hit the trigger. The explosion roared off into the distance. The bullet flew off harmlessly into the snow. But it was followed by another and then another.

And then came a different sound, a deeper, rumbling sound, almost like an earthquake. It grew and came closer and grew again until the mountainside itself was trembling. Then down from above came a thunderous rush of snow, falling like a glacier.

"Look out!" shouted Matt. "Avalanche!"

He and the others fell back inside the cave. But in the split second before they did, they looked out again and spotted Kee-wak, with the heavy snow raining down upon him. Kee-wak looked upward, and in his final comprehension, he stood tall, bared his teeth, and opened his throat. Out poured a long guttural howl of rage. It was a ghostly sound, bitter and anguished; it seemed to echo back through time, through centuries, through the millennia. Then the snow stopped falling and all was quiet.

28

Matt and Susan awoke with the sun already high in the sky and gathered up their things to prepare to leave. Everything they had fit easily into their rucksacks except for their windbreakers, which they carried. They would need them for the descent on the other side of the mountain. They looked around their bower one last time.

"In a crazy way, I'm going to miss it here," said Susan.

"Crazy is right," Matt replied.

"What do you think we should do about publishing?"

"I don't know. I've been wondering about that. Obviously, if we write anything, this place is finished. Even if we disguise it, sooner or later, people will come. Kellicut was right—at least about that."

"I agree. But I hate to think of all we've learned and all we know just going to waste. Think of science. Isn't there any way we can communicate it or hand it down to later generations?"

"Not that I can come up with," Matt said. "Not unless this society disappears sometime in the future and we have no way of knowing when that happens—*if* it happens."

Susan shook her head in frustration. "How can I ever read another paper about Neanderthal? Or write one, for that matter?"

"You may have to branch out," joked Matt. *"Australopithecus. Homo habilis."*

"Or my new favorite. *Homo erectus.*"

They laughed.

Sergei waited near the fire pit. He had even fewer belongings than they did and was anxious to get going. But they had one last important function to perform, and the hominids had been preparing for it all morning. Kellicut's body had been brought from the cave pit and was lying naked on a slab of rock, his head propped in place but still slightly sunken. Nearby a huge bonfire was blazing, crackling twenty feet into the air and sending up shivers of heat waves that made the clouds dance in the blue sky.

Matt looked around the village. "They're throwing everything into the fire. Look, they're destroying their huts, everything."

"That's because they're moving up inside the mountain," said Sergei. "They're taking over the cave vacated by the others." He shrugged. Matt and Susan exchanged looks. "I guess they like indoor living," Sergei said.

The whole village turned out for the funeral. Susan was relieved to see that the population was still large, as she had feared that the earthquake and raid had decimated it. But women and children and others who must have taken refuge in the forest turned up until the congregation gathered around Kellicut's body extended beyond the central clearing.

A place of honor was reserved for Matt, Susan, and Sergei. Behind them the young men with hollow logs perched across their legs sent up a sound of slow, mournful syncopation, and others danced in that strange, lugubrious way, turning their knees and elbows at odd angles. The fire roared ever higher until finally Dark-Eye emerged from his hut, bearing again the shell filled with oil. He trod upon a pathway of embers that was laid down for him and thrust the shell in the fire. He walked over to Kellicut's body with a long sliver of flint in one hand and placed the sharp tip next to the nose.

"You may want to look away," Matt told Sergei, but he could tell by Sergei's gasp a moment later that he had not heeded the advice.

Dark-Eye retrieved the shell from the flames and poured the scalding oil onto Kellicut's chest and legs. Then the body was wrapped in thick vine leaves and tied like a bundle, and as the drummers sped up their pounding the grave tenders materialized to carry it off. They placed it upon a newly fashioned bier that rested upon logs, crudely hewn to work as wheels.

As they left, Dark-Eye retreated into his hut with his pouch across his shoulder, ready to add Kellicut's eyes to those of the other tribal members that preceded him.

"Okay," said Sergei. "I've been patient long enough. Tell me everything. How did you pull this off?"

They had just finished a meal, their last in the valley, and were relaxing before starting the long trek out. Matt was lying down, his head resting upon his arms, looking up at the sky, and Susan was stretched out nearby, her legs extended straight and her upper body raised on both elbows.

"There's not that much to tell," she said. "Have you heard of the Khodzant Enigma?" Sergei shook his head. "It's a pictograph. It turned up not far from here sometime in the last century. Part of it was missing, so no one could decipher its meaning. They didn't have the original so they didn't even know how old it was. If they did, they wouldn't have believed it. It would have been like finding the stone tablet of the Ten Commandments.

"Our first time in the cave, running away from those creatures, we saw it painted on one of the walls. Only of course it was complete. Later I went back to study it. It depicted a battle, or rather a series of battles, between two implacable foes. On one side was *Homo sapiens,* us. On the other, *Homo neanderthalensis*. At some point, the two sides come together. There's a peace council, weapons being thrown down. But on the way, *Homo sapiens* pulls a fast one. The soldiers rig pit traps to catch the Neanderthals, and it works. They're the victors, though not through a fair fight. It's a victory of cunning. With me so far?''

''So you mean to say there was one single battle? And one single trick wiped out all the Neanderthals?''

''No, not quite. There was probably an endless round of battles. They may have extended over years, scores of years, maybe centuries. But the outcome was usually the same: *Homo sapiens* won. In other words, the Enigma is not a single narrative out of the past, it's a visual metaphor, an explanation for the destruction—or near destruction—of an entire species. It's intended as the embodiment of a historical lesson. It's teaching something. It is telling the tiny relic bands that live on through the ages, Don't forget; there is something you should know about *Homo sapiens*.''

''And that is—''

''That he is duplicitous. That he cheats. That he lies. And therefore that he always wins.''

Matt spoke up. ''And so if you yourself are to survive, you must learn from him. You must become like him.''

''The question that was always asked,'' said Susan, ''the question that intrigued archaeologists and paleontologists and everyone else from the moment that first human-looking skull was found in the Neander Valley a century and a half ago and identified as belonging to another species, was: Why me and not him? Why did we survive while he died out? He was as smart as we are. He was stronger. He was probably more numerous, over a million at least. He lived through the horrors of the Ice Age throughout Europe and Asia and was around for some two hundred thousand years. What happened to him? What critical trait did he lack?''

''And what was it?''

"Deception. The ability to deceive. Nothing more and nothing less."

"And it's a learnable trait or they wouldn't have bothered to instruct," said Matt. "But it's not an easy one to pass on. You should have seen how long it took me to teach them that it was easier to capture an animal in an ambush than to stand in its way and kill it with a spear."

"How did you come up with the plan?"

"It just came to me," said Matt. "When Susan was captured, I realized I had to come up with a strategy. The numbers and brute strength were on their side, so I needed a trick. I needed deceitfulness to even up the score. I sensed that that was what was at the heart of the Enigma, that was its secret message."

"You sensed it?" asked Susan, with a smile.

"Yes. It just came to me. A fit of inspiration."

Susan smiled again.

"Okay," said Sergei. "So you decide you can trick them to save Susan. How did you come up with the Trojan horse?"

"The oldest trick in the world. So perfect it's every kid's favorite Greek story. I knew from looking at their godhead that they couldn't turn down the impulse to possess it. If I could make the replica close enough to the original, they would take it into the cave."

"Then why didn't you put fighters inside?"

"That's the tricky part—in more ways than one. My strategy relied ultimately on Kee-wak's being able to figure it out, at least halfway. I began with the importance of the Enigma. Why was it so essential for them to preserve it? Because of the lesson it taught: deception. If the creatures are so determined to be on the lookout for deceit, they should find it, I figured. Set a trap that they can solve. Let them undermine it. And then put a trap within the trap. It's simply raising deception to the next level."

"Of course," said Sergei.

"It's the kind of thing we humans do as second nature.

That's what chess is all about. Or the arms race. Fake and counter-fake. Levels of dissembling and misrepresentation reaching up to the sky. *Tactical deception* is what the psychologists call it.''

''Like those experiments with chimps,'' added Susan. ''A chimp can learn to deceive on one level—say, to hide bananas from a stronger chimp in a box and pretend they're not there. The second chimp can learn deception on the second level—to pretend nothing's wrong and spy on the first chimp until he opens the box. But chimps have never been able to achieve a third level of deception—figuring out that they're being spied on and opening the wrong box.''

''That's right,'' said Matt. ''I assumed that Kee-wak could not reach the higher level. He had learned the lesson of human mendacity, because that's what the Enigma taught him, but he had no idea of the depths of that mendacity.''

''But how did you get him to think there were fighters inside?''

''First, because he was predisposed to. And second because he would obviously read it with the special power. That's why I asked you to build the hideaway and that's why we left the hominids inside it, for Kee-wak to enter them and see what they saw: semidarkness with slips of light filtering in between the branches.''

''What about those sounds from the godhead?''

''The finishing touch. I made a tape for Susan's tape deck with my own recorder. I left it blank for half an hour. Then I inserted noises of alarm that I recorded from the hominids weeks ago. And for good measure, I added the works of one of our most distinguished musicians.'' He smiled at Susan, who smiled back. ''The rest was easy, rigging it up to go off. I put the tape deck between two slats of wood in the belly. I turned the volume up, pressed the on button, and inserted a wooden wedge so it wouldn't release. I attached the wedge to a wire, ran it out the back, and fixed it to a stake in the ground. You move the structure and—*bang!*—half an hour later you've got hominids screaming.''

"How did you know that Kee-wak would burn it?"

"It's a natural way to destroy something once you've hauled it into a cavern lighted by flaming torches. Especially if you're suspicious of it to begin with."

"And the fire set off the flares that you put behind the eyes and mouth?"

"Exactly."

"I have to say, you Americans are even more devious than we are."

"We were raised on Uncle Remus."

"What's that?"

"Never mind. Just watch out if you hear somebody say, 'Please don't throw me in that briar patch.' "

They made their good-byes as best they could. A group of hominids walked with them up to the cave, led by Hurt-Knee, falling into his role of guide. Longtooth, now decked out in marks of red ocher and charcoal that streaked his face and chest, did not linger long. He was about to lead his group of young hunters on an expedition through the valley, where the animals, never having been hunted, were easy prey. The youths were all painted like him, and equipped with an array of spears, axes, and clubs. Longtooth himself proudly carried Sergei's bow with the quiver of arrows upon his back, a gift.

Traversing the tunnels, they saw that Sergei was right: The hominids were moving in and taking over the abandoned hearths and smaller chambers scattered along the side passageways. They usurped the animal hides that were being cured on the walls and the ones that were spread before the fires for sleeping.

"Matt," said Susan. "Have you noticed that the children are splitting up into smaller groups? Do you think this new living space is imposing its own logic on the social group-ings?"

"If you mean do I think they've just invented the family, the answer is no."

"Why not?"

"Well, for one thing, as you well know, the family was a division of labor that began when the men went off hunt-ing and the women stayed home to tend the children. Not enough of the men are hunters yet. It was in the first text-books we read."

They passed a small chamber where an adult male and an adult female were tending a small fire. "Guess they're not up on the literature," Susan remarked.

When the group came to the main chamber, Susan ducked away for a few minutes. Matt assumed that she wanted to see the pit where she had been held by Kee-wak, but instead she went to the sacred chamber for a last look at the Enigma painting. She walked over to the final panel and fixed upon the solitary figure there. No, she had not been wrong. The artist had captured the emotion of the moment brilliantly: the defiant posture stretching upward but already stooping under the weight of the earth pouring down, the ragged teeth, murderous eyes, the full-fronted rage of betrayal. She knew just how perfect the depiction was because she herself had seen it.

Like a silent stream, Susan felt the filling up again, her mind being taken by another. She turned and there in the shadow of an arch was another stooped figure, much older. He stepped forward so she could see him. Dark-Eye. He walked over to her and stood at her side, looking at the painting. Like her, he concentrated on the lone Neanderthal. He stared at his ancestor, who was railing at his betrayal, as if he realized that he was caught in something more than a trap, a cul-de-sac of disastrous, historic proportions. For an instant, Dark-Eye himself seemed to be in that moment, clutching it to him. Susan felt a three-way communion, a triangle of pain and suffering but also courage and survival, and she knew with a certainty hard to explain that they were all the same, that the two species were one and that the Neanderthal were like older brothers and sisters who died in infancy but who continue on in ourselves.

At the cave entrance the hominids approached to say fare-well—Blue-Eyes, Tallboy, Hurt-Knee, they all came. They looked flustered and uncertain, their faces turning a deep scarlet. Departures were not reckoned with in their world, thought Matt. Hurt-Knee, with his scar flaring across his bulging brow like a special mark, accompanied them down the slope. As they walked away, moving awkwardly through the snow, Matt and Susan and Sergei felt the hom-inids behind them casting their spells, gradually receding, like walking away from the surf on the shore.

It was warm and soon they left the snow line behind. Hurt-Knee appeared apprehensive about venturing so far from the cave, but he stayed with them until they came to the ravine with the bridge of vines. Here Hurt-knee stopped and waited, as one by one the three shinnied across. Some-how it was easier going in this direction, away from the mist-enshrouded summit; even so, Susan felt herself freeze up with fear halfway across. Lest she look down, she closed her eyes and rested immobile, to collect herself. Then, with her eyes still closed, she began to see the vine ahead of her, to feel the handholds, and to know that it was strong enough to carry her. She continued on until she made it to safety. Hurt-Knee stayed on his side of the ravine.

On the other side, the three humans waved. Hurt-Knee stared back but did not try to imitate the gesture. So they turned and left and started down the mountain. They had walked only about twenty paces when they heard a rumble behind them, a consuming rumble that sounded a bit like the avalanche, only sharper. They turned around to see the bridge collapsing in on itself, crunching up like a straw and then plunging into the ravine. Hurt-Knee had tripped the destruct mechanism. They could see only his back, already disappearing up the slope.

They rested near a cold mountain stream, in the same spot where they had stopped on the way up.

"Sergei," said Matt, "something I've been meaning to ask you. Did your people ever figure out why Kee-wak's guys were trading? Whatever possessed them to come down off the mountain and exchange goods?"

"It wasn't because they wanted goods. They had everything they needed—at least at this stage of development."

"Then what was it?"

"What they wanted was humans," explained Sergei. "The skins they left were bait. They wanted to lure people up onto the mountain."

"But why?"

"For sacrifice. To appease the demons causing the earthquakes. That's what Shakanov said. We've been tracking disappearances in this area since the early 1900s, and they always correspond to a resurgence of volcanic activity."

"And the godhead?"

"I'm not convinced it's a god of hunt. I think it's a god of terror, the god that makes the ground tremble. They believe that god is the cave bear. The cave bear is the one animal whose hide we've never found below. It's sacred. At least, that's the theory of our scientists. Up to now our scientists have only been guessing; they've never actually seen a Yeti."

"So your guys don't have any absolute proof?" asked Matt.

"That's true."

They were silent for a bit, listening to the water. Then Sergei spoke up. "I was thinking about what you said earlier about deception. Isn't it ironic that our worst characteristic is the one to determine survival?"

"I'm not sure it's our worst characteristic," said Susan. "In some ways it's inseparable from intelligence. Metaphorically speaking, it's our opposable thumb. It allows you to manipulate the world. If you have brains, you're smart. If you have guile, you're clever."

"Think of it as the ability to create illusion and surprise," said Matt. "And then you're in the realm of art and magic and music and storytelling. Think of it as our own inner eye, our own ability to project ourselves outward by our imagination."

Sergei was indeed thinking. Susan looked at him closely and posed the question the conversation had been inexorably moving toward. "So now that you know, are you going to go back and tell the government they're right?"

Sergei leaned over to take a sip of cold water, and when he finished, sitting up and wiping his chin, he was smiling. "When have you ever known a government to be right?"

"Son of a bitch!" shouted Matt at full voice. Susan leaned over and touched Sergei's arm. Matt fished in his rucksack and came up with his tape recorder and two tapes and Kellicut's diary. He flung them far away, into a ravine where they disappeared noiselessly. "Here's to deception!" he said.

"Long live deception!" countered Sergei.

Eagleton was waiting for them, rocking his chair back and forth nervously inside the Quonset hut, the cage he had come to hate. He had been rocking and chain smoking from the moment he had received Sodder's call from the chopper, not long after the new team commander found the three of them walking down the path several miles above Kellicut's camp.

"Three of them? You mean doctors Arnot, Mattison, and Van?"

"Not Van. Someone else. A Russian."

"A Russian? Impossible."

Eagleton couldn't interrogate him further without the others overhearing his answers. Nothing to do but wait. He felt like a drink. Damn, he hadn't had a drink in ages.

The whirring of the helicopter came a good three minutes before the sudden earth-sucking roar as it swooped to set down on a rock ledge in the compound. He peered out the window, pulling back and leaning over to look through one eye so that they wouldn't see him. There *was* a stranger: long dark hair, easy stride, Slavic features. Eagleton moved over to his desk and feigned composure.

They didn't even knock. First came Sodder, then the woman, then Mattison, finally the stranger. They looked thin, exhausted. Nobody shook hands, and Eagleton struggled to find the right voice—concerned, not commanding.

"We were so worried. You were up there so long, totally out of contact. Tell me everything. What happened?"

Matt drew a long breath. "It was a disaster. We got stuck in a blizzard. There was an avalanche. We found Kellicut's body. Van died too; he was crushed by a falling boulder. There was nothing we could do to help him. We're lucky we got out alive."

Eagleton wanted to ask about the Neanderthal, but instead he gestured at Sergei. "And who is this?"

"Sergei Ilyich Konyanov." Sergei stepped forward and offered a hand.

Eagleton reluctantly took it, recoiling. "Russian."

"You bet."

Eagleton turned to Matt. "I don't understand."

"We found him wandering around up there. Apparently the Russians sent an expedition of their own. They lost everyone but him."

"We're exhausted," said Susan. "Do you mind if we sit down?"

"We could use some food, too," Matt said.

Eagleton, flustered, told Sodder to order up some food and bring in chairs, but Sodder, his curiosity piqued, was reluctant to leave, and in the end Matt and Susan and Sergei said they were too tired for more questioning right now and needed to recuperate. Eagleton's counterfeit politeness forced him to give way, and he hid his anger.

He tried one last time, rolling his chair around the desk and grabbing Matt by the arm. "Do you really mean to say you wandered around in subzero weather in a blizzard for weeks on end, and you managed to survive without any help?"

"We were lucky. We found a cave where we waited out the storm. Then we found a more temperate valley. But it was rough."

"And you didn't see any sign of the Neanderthal?"

"I didn't say that."

Eagleton straightened in his chair.

"We brought you this," Matt said, reaching into his pocket and pulling out a small sliver of mandible. One edge was smooth where he had broken off the piece that had a drill hole for a necklace. "You might want to have it dated."

On the plane Matt ordered champagne right away. The steward, who seemed taken with Susan, gave them each an extra bottle, so that by the time they were at thirty thousand feet, they were already feeling giddy.

"Incidentally," said Susan, "I wasn't going to say this, but you seem to be driving me to it. I was right, you know."

"About what?" Matt knew about what.

"It was war, not sex, that did them in."

"Who?"

"Don't play dumb."

"Oh, those guys. I've already forgotten about them."

"I wouldn't doubt it."

"Okay. Let's say for a minute—just a minute—that perhaps just conceivably you are not totally incorrect. What are you going to do about it? Who are you going to tell?"

Susan frowned. "It's a problem, I know. I've been thinking about it too. Of all the people in the world, there's only one who knows just how right I am, and that's you. I can't stand that thought."

"And I can't say anything either. So you're stuck. Either you keep me around and you're constantly validated, or you make long-distance calls whenever you get depressed."

"That could mean a lot of calls."

"My point exactly." He took another sip. "Seriously, what are you going to do?"

"I'm not sure. I was thinking of going to East Africa, the Olduvai Gorge."

"You're kidding! That's where I was going to go. Maybe Lake Turkana in northern Kenya. I'm excited by the recent finds there. The bipedalism they reveal pushes our human ancestry back even further. But why you? What bones would you look for?"

"Actually, I was thinking of something more along the line of molecular biology."

Matt's face dropped. "Susan, no. Not DNA. You're not going to turn into one of these people who go around collecting placentas to prove we all came from a common ancestor named Eve?"

"It's the wave of the future, Matt. It's real science, quantifiable, verifiable. Not all that guesswork about how old the bone is, what geostratum it was found in, and the rest of it."

"You're nuts. You can't possibly believe that you and I and everyone else came from an African bushwoman only two hundred thousand years ago?"

"The rate calculations may be off. It could be a little longer than that."

"Susan." Matt's voice rose. "Genetic dating challenges my whole theory that we all left Africa more than a million years ago. You're going to attack everything I stand for."

"Now, Matt, take it easy. I didn't say that. I might not attack it directly. I just think you may be a little off—say, six hundred thousand years."

"Six hundred thousand years! That kills the whole thing!"

"Matt, pipe down. People are beginning to stare."

"How could you?"

"Well, I may give you a chance to talk me out of it."

"When have I ever talked you out of anything?" He sighed as he put his arm around her.

"There's always a first time," she said, snuggling in and taking another sip.

Outside through the plastic window, they saw the roof of the world receding, black-and-white jagged peaks that looked purple in the sunlight and were softened by distance.

BIBLIOGRAPHY

Blum, Howard. *Out There* (London: Simon & Schuster Ltd., 1990).

Cadogan, Lucy. *Digging* (London: Chatto & Windus Ltd., 1987).

Darwin, Charles. Struggle for Existence and Natural Selection, *Origin of Species* (London: Orion Books, 1996).

Gould, Stephen Jay. *Adam's Navel* (London: Penguin Books, 1995).

Leakey, Richard. *The Origin of Humankind* (London: Weidenfeld & Nicolson, 1994).

Schick, Kathy D. and Toth, Nicholas. *Making Silent Stones Speak* (New York: Simon & Schuster, 1993).

Shackley, Myra. *Neanderthal Man* (Hamden, Connecticut: Archon Books, The Shoe String Press, Inc., 1980).

Shackley, Myra. *Still Living?* (New York: Thames and Hudson, 1983).

Shreeve, James. *The Neandertal Enigma* (New York: William Morrow and Company Inc., 1995).

Slesser, Malcolm. *Red Peak* (London: Hodder and Stoughton, 1964).

Stringer, Christopher and Gamble, Clive. *In Search of the Neanderthals* (London: Thames and Hudson, 1993).

Toates, Frederick. *Biological Foundations of Behavior* (Milton Keynes: Open University Press, 1986).

Trinkaus, Erik and Shipman, Pat. *The Neandertals* (London: Jonathan Cape, 1993).

White, Edward and Brown, Dale. *The First Men* (New York: Time-Life Books, 1973).

White, Michael and Gribbin, John. *Darwin: A Life in Science* (New York: Dutton, 1995).

A HOSPITAL WITHOUT DOCTORS OR NURSES. JUST TERROR.

Surgeon Chad Dunston helped create The Center, a revolutionary medical facility where computers, not humans, treat patients. Its cure rate is unequaled, its medical successes unrivaled...until a child named Christine Lassiter mysteriously dies. The girl's older sister Maxine can't get Christine's records, her body, or even her death certificate. Maxine wants Chad Dunston to find out what happened. But the more questions Chad asks, the more dead-end answers he receives. He has only one option left: check into The Center as a patient...and enter a machine-made nightmare, where the only way out may be death.

Author of the bestselling medical thriller *The Unborn*, Dr. David Shobin has returned with a chilling cautionary tale about the direction of today's high-tech medicine...medical care without the caring, greed raging out of control, and deadly terror as the new specialty.

THE CENTER
DAVID SHOBIN

"A non-stop roller-coaster ride into medical terror!"
—Michael Palmer, author of *Critical Judgment*

AVAILABLE IN AUGUST
FROM ST. MARTIN'S PAPERBACKS!

Six-year-old Paul Haines watches as two older boys dive into a coastal river...and don't come up. His mother, Carolyn, a charter boat captain on the Mississippi Gulf Coast, finds herself embroiled in the tragedy to an extent she could never have imagined.

Carolyn joins with marine biologist Alan Freeman in the hunt for a creature that is terrorizing the waters along the Gulf Coast. But neither of them could have envisioned exactly what kind of danger they are facing.

Only one man knows what this creature is, and how it has come into the shallows. And his secret obsession with it will force him, as well as Paul, Carolyn and Alan, into a race against time...and a race toward death.

EXTINCT
by Charles Wilson

"Eminently plausible, chilling in its detail, and highly entertaining straight through to its finale."
—DR. DEAN A. DUNN, Professor of Oceanography and Paleontology, University of Southern Mississippi

"With his taut tales and fast words, Charles Wilson will be around for a long time. I hope so."
—JOHN GRISHAM

It is 1953. Joseph Stalin, the world's most tyrannical dictator, is teetering on the edge of insanity, and about to plunge the world into nuclear chaos. Only one man and one woman can penetrate the Iron Curtain and stop this madman, before it's too late.

But someone inside the Kremlin knows. And as the KGB's deadliest manhunter pursues these two CIA-hired assassins, another duel unfolds, between secret warriors of the West and East, with a U.S. agent caught in between. Now that agent must do the unthinkable: find his way to the heart of the Soviet Union and stop the mission he himself set in motion—before it ignites World War III.

SNOW WOLF

The International Bestseller from

Glenn Meade

"A riveting thriller in the tradition of The Day of the Jackal... A white knuckler!"—Washington Post Book World